P9-DHA-612

Praise for Suzanne Enoch

"High stakes, spirited characters, and off-the-charts chemistry keep the pages turning as Enoch balances humor, heat, and tension. This is Highland romance done right."
—*Publishers Weekly* starred review on
Scot Under the Covers

"Enoch delivers another fresh and fun Highlander/English romance with notes of scandal, secrets, cunning escapades, and off-the-charts chemistry."
—*Booklist* starred review on *Scot Under the Covers*

"[An] enticing, enchanting ride."
—*The New York Times* on *Scot Under the Covers*

Praise for Amelia Grey

"Grey's unconventional meet-cute, compelling series backbone, and authentic characters move an interesting plot forward. . . . An engaging series start."
—*Kirkus Reviews* on *The Earl Next Door*

"Grey's prose is strong and her characters are fun."
—*Publishers Weekly* on *The Earl Next Door*

Kissing Under the Mistletoe

SUZANNE ENOCH

AMELIA GREY

ANNA BENNETT

St. Martin's Paperbacks

This is a work of fiction. All of the characters, organizations, and events portrayed in this book are either products of the author's imagination or are used fictitiously.

First published in the United States by St. Martin's Paperbacks, an imprint of St. Martin's Publishing Group

KISSING UNDER THE MISTLETOE

For information, address St. Martin's Publishing Group, 120 Broadway, New York, NY 10271.

www.stmartins.com

ISBN: 978-1-250-79744-5

Our books may be purchased in bulk for promotional, educational, or business use. Please contact your local bookseller or the Macmillan Corporate and Premium Sales Department at 1-800-221-7945, ext. 5442, or by email at MacmillanSpecialMarkets@macmillan.com.

Printed in the United States of America

St. Martin's Paperbacks edition / October 2021

10 9 8 7 6 5 4 3 2 1

Contents

Great Scot!

(A Wild, Wicked Highlanders Novella)

BY

SUZANNE ENOCH

Chapter One

Jane Bansil threw the heavy blankets over her head and burrowed deeper beneath the covers. Still the sound continued, a sharp, endless wailing that made her hair stand on end and seemed to emanate from everywhere at once. Grabbing a pillow, she pulled that over her head as well. Warmth turned into suffocating heat, but still the sound went on and on and on.

Finally, gasping for air, she flung off the blankets and the pillow and sat up. "For God's sake, stop!" she yelled, then slapped both hands over her mouth, too late to hold in her very unladylike bellow. *Blasted, stupid, infuriating bagpipes.*

A knock sounded at her door. "Jane?"

Wonderful. Now she'd be caught both complaining and lying abed at seven o'clock in the morning. "Just a moment!" she called, and slid her feet onto the icy stone floor. Stifling a responding yelp, she stepped into her slippers, grabbed her robe, and flung it over her shoulders. "Good morning," she said, pasting a smile on her face as she pulled open her bedchamber door.

Amelia-Rose Hyacinth MacTaggert, her blond hair loose and a heavy robe around her own slender shoulders, blinked at her from the hallway. "Did I hear you yelling, Cousin? Is something amiss?"

"I'm so sorry," Jane returned, broadening her smile. "I was just talking to myself. With more volume than I realized, evidently. I didn't wake you, did I?" Unable to help herself, she lowered her gaze to Amy's thickening middle.

"Not at all. Niall went out hours ago to help find someone's cow. Or so he claimed. I actually think he and Aden went fishing." Jane's younger cousin grinned. "I hope they went fishing. I don't need him following me about all morning and flinging pillows beneath me. I would certainly inform him if I were uncomfortable."

"Then I'm also happy you have the morning to yourself." Jane took a half step back, not enough to be unfriendly, but she hoped enough to inform her cousin that continuing the conversation wasn't necessary.

Amy, though, followed her retreat with a step forward. "Actually, Miranda and Eloise and Persie and I are going down to the village for breakfast at The Thistle. Evidently, it's a tradition for the MacTaggert women to do so before Christmas, and we're nearly out of time. Will you join us?"

Abruptly the wailing stopped. For a bare second Jane closed her eyes, pulling the silence around her like another cozy blanket. "I'm not a MacTaggert."

"Not in name, but you live with a great many of us. Aside from that, you're *my* family, which by extension does make you a MacTaggert. And you're definitely a woman."

She was that, and probably the only virgin left in the house, but she wasn't so certain about the rest of it. The MacTaggerts, male and female and born to the family or married into it, were bold and boisterous and rather wild. None of those words came anywhere near to describing her. "Please don't feel like I need to be entertained or something," she said. "I have duties, you know."

Reaching out to take one of Jane's hands, Amy nudged her backward deeper into the bedchamber and shut the door behind them. "I need to speak plainly with you, Jane," she whispered.

The morning's annoyance at the bagpipes twisted into genuine alarm. "Are you well, Amy? If you need to return to London, I will of course accompany you. Is—"

"Jane," her cousin interrupted, a smile again lighting her face, "hush."

Clamping her mouth shut, Jane kept hold of Amy's hand. The past few months swirled about them still, chaotic and full of adventure, romance, a trio of Highlander brothers, and a quartet of weddings—and now Amy's pregnancy and arriving but five days before Christmas at a place none of the ladies had ever been before but now would be calling home for at least part of the year.

"I can never thank you enough for what you did for me— for Niall and me, Jane," Amy said, squeezing her hand. "It cost you your home and your employment. I know you've assumed the position of Lady Aldriss's companion, but . . . is that what you truly want?"

Jane winced a little. Another discussion about possibilities, when she'd exhausted them all ages ago. "I *am* a lady's companion, Amy. What should I be, a baker's apprentice?"

"Yes, but, I mean, I know my mother managed to make you feel grateful that she was willing to offer you a position as my companion. That is not all you have to be, though. Your family may not have been as wealthy as mine, but your birth is certainly equal to mine. What I mean to say is, if you wish to do something else, to find a different life, I will see to it that you—"

"I'm quite fine, Amy," Jane broke in, her heart easing as

she realized this was only about her cousin's guilt at having the happier life. "I am three-and-thirty, far too old to be dancing through London looking for a husband, of all things." She winced again at that thought. "And, as you know, I have a preference for quiet and peace."

"Yes, but—"

"Being Lady Aldriss's companion gives me all the exposure I want to life's fineries. And she's kind, if a bit intimidating, the first being very welcome, and the second being something to which I am quite accustomed." Indeed, just discussing her former employer and aunt, Victoria Baxter, left her with a twitch and a hunch to her shoulders. Good heavens, she was pleased to be away from that and from being reminded constantly how grateful she should be to have a roof over her head and someone willing to put up with her timid ways enough to keep her employed.

Now she'd fallen into a position that, while Lady Aldriss expected competence and a degree of independent thinking, at least made her feel valued, if not entirely necessary. After all, the countess had a daughter, and this summer had added three new daughters-in-law to her family. A companion seemed superfluous, even to Jane. She'd been ignoring that fact for the past few months, however, and intended to continue to do so until she managed to convince herself that this was where she was meant to be.

"I just want you to be happy," Amy pressed. "You are a good person, you know."

"Thank you for concerning yourself about me, when you have so many other things on your mind."

Amy put her free hand over her stomach. "I can hardly believe how differently this year is ending from the way it began. I was a burden, never proper enough, never saying the right thing, and never going to be able to make a beneficial marriage. Now I'm married to a Highlander, of all people,

I'm deliriously happy, and I'm going to be a mother in three months."

"And you're in Scotland. Don't forget that," Jane added as the wailing bagpipe began again.

Laughing, Amy hugged her. "I know! We'll have snow for Christmas. Can you imagine?"

"I can imagine. It nearly feels like it could snow here inside the house."

Amy only chuckled again, but then she had a very handsome, very charming husband to keep her warm at night. At that thought, Jane's cheeks warmed. It wasn't jealousy, she reminded herself. She was as happy that Amy had escaped Mrs. Baxter's household as she was that *she* had done so. It was only a realization that she was not one of the lucky people meant to have a happily-ever-after life.

"Say you'll join us for breakfast," Amy pressed, releasing her again.

"I shall try," Jane hedged. "Lady Aldriss may need me this morning."

She understood Amy's sideways look: Not only had Lady Aldriss seen her four children married within twelve weeks, she'd also found a way to bring her estranged husband down from the Highlands after seventeen years of separation, and she'd managed to see all of them together with new husbands and wives for Christmas. In Scotland.

The woman didn't *need* help. She'd offered a position out of kindness and charity, and Jane had accepted it out of necessity. It was supposed to be temporary, until something long-term where she could be more useful came along, but thus far she hadn't even had a nibble.

"You might *ask* her if she requires your presence; she's down in the morning room."

Blast it. Lady Aldriss had already risen? "Oh dear," Jane said, scowling. "Excuse me, Cousin. I must dress."

"Of course. But ask her about joining us. We leave in twenty minutes."

Once her cousin had left the room, Jane dove into her wardrobe for her warmest gown, a plain blue dress with long sleeves and a high neck. It rather resembled all of her other gowns, actually, but that had been the case for her entire adult life. A half-dozen practical gowns, two night rails, three bonnets, four shifts, two pairs of shoes, a quantity of hairpins, and some personal toiletry items both kept seeing to herself to a matter of moments and made it simple for her to prepare for a day or a week or a lifetime lived at someone else's beck and call.

Blowing out her breath at her reflection in her dressing mirror, Jane decided her present melancholy was entirely the fault of the weather. Winter in the environs of London could be chilly, and on occasion a storm brought a dusting of snow, but here . . . Well, just beyond the main buildings of Aldriss Park the snowbanks rose above her head, and down the slope where Loch an Daimh hugged the lower reaches of hills and mountains for five miles around all the edges of the water were now ice.

Even her black, straight hair felt cold as she brushed it out. She would rather have left it down to cover and protect her ears and the back of her neck, but she'd worn the same tight bun for as long as she could remember. There were times she half expected her hair to knot itself into a bun all on its own, she'd done it so many times.

That, though, was just silliness. At least now, though, she could relax enough to indulge in thinking silly things from time to time. Previously it had taken all of her wits just to keep from overly annoying her aunt. And that was why, despite the snow and the cold and the very large number of MacTaggerts running about, she was rather happy to be in

Scotland. Even with the bagpipes wheezing to life first thing in the morning.

On her way to the morning room she darted inside the large breakfast room for half a slice of toast, which she choked down as she reached the doorway at the far end of the hall. Rapping her knuckles against the frame of the half-closed door, she ran her tongue around the inside of her mouth to loosen the last of the sticky crumbs from her teeth.

"Come in."

The low, rumbling voice clearly didn't belong to any female, much less to Lady Aldriss. Even so, Jane took a breath and pushed the door open wide. "Good morning, my lord," she said, dipping in a proper curtsy.

Lady Aldriss's oldest son, Viscount Glendarril, turned away from the front window. "Jane. Ye after my mother?"

"Yes. I was told she was in here."

"She was. When I informed her that the house didnae have any gold thread for mending, she started spinning in a circle and then vanished in a puff of angry smoke."

"I—"

"I did no such thing," Countess Aldriss commented, stepping up behind Jane. "I went to ask Pogan to fetch me what sewing materials remain here."

"I should have done that, my lady," Jane said, turning to curtsy again. "I overslept; I'm so sorry. It won't happen again."

"Nonsense," Francesca Oswell-MacTaggert countered, moving past her to take the chair nearest the roaring fire. "I thought you were going down to The Thistle for breakfast with my daughters."

"I . . . You don't mind?"

"Well, I could send you up and down the stairs after needle and thread all morning, but since the house hasn't had a woman tending it for seventeen years, I'm afraid what you might find." The countess sighed. "Go have breakfast."

"But if it's tradition for the MacTaggert ladies, shouldn't you be attending?" Jane pursued.

"Aye, she should be," the viscount broke in, frowning. "That's what I've been telling her for twenty minutes."

"I am well aware just how unpopular I am here, Coll," Lady Aldriss returned. "I am not about to go stomping about the village on my first day back in Scotland. They'll throw tomatoes at me."

"Nae, they willnae. It would be potatoes. But I'd see to it they didnae throw anything at ye."

"Give them all a bit of time to become accustomed to the idea that I may be here more often, first," his mother cautioned. "I'm in no hurry. Nor am I entirely certain your father and I are ready to reconcile."

"Och. Ye're back here at Aldriss Park. That's someaught I'd nae have expected before I set eyes on ye walking up the front steps yesterday afternoon. Go find yer thread, then. I've a meeting with an architect." He tilted his head, a slight grin touching his handsome face. "Four of us lads could live here in peace, all being men and reasonable. Now we're ten, with bairns on the way. Temperance and I need our own damned house."

They all got on fabulously as far as Jane could tell, but she could see why the eldest, especially, would want to be beneath his own roof. Aldriss Park, she'd realized after only one day here, could be very noisy, indeed. And that was quite the accomplishment, after the chaos of Oswell House in London.

"Jane, dear?"

She blinked, facing the countess. "Yes, my lady?"

"Go. If you run across any gold thread suitable for embroidery, please return with it. Otherwise, I suggest you make the most of social gatherings here. There aren't many of them."

Now it was a gathering? Oh dear. A breakfast had been more than enough. "Is that an order, then?" she asked briskly, drilling her stiff fingers together and attempting not to look like she was holding her breath.

Swift disappointment crossed the countess's face and just as quickly vanished. "No, it isn't. I only want you to have friends and a social life, my dear."

"I have employment and my books. Both make me happy. And if I may be forthright, my lady, your daughter and daughters-in-law, including my cousin, are very kind and . . . confident, and they don't seem to be afraid of anything. I am afraid of a great deal, most of all the looks they will pretend not to exchange when they want to go next to the milliner's or the jeweler's or the bakery and I try to beg off."

Lady Aldriss settled her hands into her lap. Lord Glendarril muttered something under his breath and fled the room. "Considering that is the most words I've heard you speak together in six months," the countess commented, "it would be foolish of me to presume that you don't mean them. Do as you will. I won't require you until after luncheon, to assist me with boxing gifts for Christmas."

Oh, thank goodness. "Yes, my lady," Jane said, dipping again.

"Wife," came from the hallway door, and the broad-shouldered Earl Aldriss himself strolled into the morning room. "I require a word with ye."

"Husband," the countess returned, and subtly angled her head at Jane. "You've found me in a mood to listen."

Stifling a yelp, Jane took the hint and left the room. She'd heard a few brief arguments while the earl had been visiting Oswell House in London, but from what she'd gleaned from overhearing bits of conversation among the MacTaggert men, the fights between Lord and Lady Aldriss had once been legendary. She had no wish to be in the middle of one of those.

With an unexpected few hours to herself, Jane went about exploring the rooms of sprawling Aldriss Park. Because she didn't wish to hear the MacTaggert ladies' response to learning that the countess's paid companion wouldn't be joining them for their outing, either, she stayed away from the entire front of the house, in fact, but all those contrary thoughts left her head as she discovered the library.

Considering the masculine feel of Aldriss Park, the well-stocked library surprised her. Yes, she knew all three of the MacTaggert brothers enjoyed reading, but she'd also spent the last six months at Oswell House in London in the company of a stuffed deer named Rory that had previously been proudly displayed in this very room. The two full suits of armor standing ready for battle against one wall had sufficient space between them that a full-grown red deer with very large antlers would have fit there quite nicely. She walked over to take a closer look at the well-polished metal.

"The one on the right there belonged to my great-great-granddad," an unfamiliar male brogue came from the doorway behind her. "Ye can see the dent in the helmet where a mad Sassenach tried to put a club across his skull."

There was indeed a marked indentation on one side of the ornate helmet. "He survived, though?"

"Oh, aye. I cannae say the same for the Sassenach." A pause, and booted footsteps approached behind her. "Ye're English. Are ye one of the brides, then?"

"No. I'm Lady Aldriss's companion." She wanted to turn around and see to whom she was speaking, but then she would stammer and her face would flush and she'd be . . . herself again. Squaring her shoulders, Jane took a step forward and ran her fingers along the dent. "You said 'your' great-great-grandfather. You aren't one of the brothers, though."

"Nae. I'm a cousin. Angus—the earl—is my uncle, brother to my mother, Ava. I'm Brennan Andrews."

"Jane. Jane Bansil."

"Pleased to make yer acquaintance, Jane Bansil. Though I do have to wonder why ye willnae turn around and look at me. Unless ye've heard, of course."

Oh dear. "Heard what?"

"About the accident. Some years ago, I fell from a horse onto a wooden fence. Coll says it improved my appearance, but then it was his horse that threw me—the only benefit of that being him feeling obligated to hire me when he decided he had need of an architect."

The architect Lord Glendarril said he would be meeting with this morning. Well, now she really wanted to look. Reminding herself not to stare, not to make a face or appear shocked in any way, Jane squared her shoulders and turned around.

Considering what she knew of the MacTaggerts, she'd half expected to see a walking, breathing god standing before her, the tiniest of scars brushing one otherwise perfect cheek. The reality, however, was somewhat different.

Brennan Andrews *was* a very fine-looking man. There could be no argument about that. Elegantly curved brows, black hair swept back from his face but nearly long enough to brush his broad shoulders, a refined nose and strong chin—and one fine green eye with a twinkle in its depths. The left eye, or the place where it should have been, was covered by a black leather patch, which did little to conceal the end of a scar trailing crazily down along his left cheekbone almost to his mouth.

"Y . . . Oh," she stammered, then flushed furiously when she realized how completely idiotic she sounded. "I thought you were either jesting or that you'd have a wooden arm or something."

He glanced down at his arms. "Nae wooden arm. It was quite the fence, though. I dunnae frighten ye, do I, Miss Bansil?"

Jane cleared her throat. "No," she said aloud. "You did make me wonder to whom the other suit of armor belonged."

His right eyebrow lifted just a touch, and then he turned his gaze beyond her to the iron suits. "Ah, that one. Domnhall MacTaggert himself wore it on the day he told King Henry—the eighth one—that a man should be allowed to wed as many women as it took to get him a son. He was made Earl Aldriss that very day, and in that armor."

"Goodness," she said, but then realized she'd forgotten to turn around and look at it. Instead, she stood there gazing—or, rather, staring—at Brennan Andrews in his eye patch, thick gray coat, red and white and green kilt, and heavy boots. "So, you're an architect."

"Aye." He visibly shook himself. "As a matter of fact, I'm in the middle of a meeting with Coll. I came in here for a map of the estate."

"Oh. Of course. Excuse me." Bobbing awkwardly, she moved out of the way to browse a shelf that might have held books about dirt for all the attention she paid.

Inclining his head in return, he walked to a stand in one corner where a dozen rolled maps stood. "Nae," he muttered, setting one aside and opening the next one. "Nae."

Jane grimaced. "Do you . . . I mean, might I assist you?"

"Aye." Removing a map from the stack, he held one end out to her. "I'm after one that has the entire Aldriss property, with all the current buildings and topography notations."

"Won't Lord Glendarril be residing *here* eventually?" she asked, unrolling the heavy paper to see a plan for the upper floor of Aldriss Park.

"Aye. I dunnae ken if ye've noticed, though, but there are quite a few MacTaggerts. Once they have their bairns there'll be even more. So this new house Coll has in mind will be used, nae matter who ends up with it."

Plucking another roll from the stack, Jane opened it up. "Is this what you wanted?" she asked after a moment's perusal.

He moved closer, bending his head beside hers. As he did so, Jane inhaled. Snow, pine trees, and, very faintly, old leather came to her, together with an image of a warm fire and a room full of old, carefully bound books.

"Aye, that's the one," he said, favoring her with a slight, crooked grin that made her breath catch just for a second, before she remembered that she was, after all, Jane Bansil, poor relation to the blue-blooded Baxter family and paid companion to Lady Aldriss.

Brennan took the rolled paper from her, their fingers brushing as he did so. "Good," she squeaked out. "I'm glad I could help."

"If ye'll excuse me, then, I need to talk with Coll before he charges out and begins tossing logs into a pile to make himself a house."

"Of course."

Halfway to the door he turned to face her, though he continued his retreat. "The books over there on the top shelf," he said, aiming the map at the leftmost side of the library, "are true Scottish histories. They're a bit bloody, but there isnae much about Scotland that isnae bloody. There's one on architecture there ye might find to yer liking. Perhaps. *Scottish Castles and Highlands History: A Tangled Web.*"

With that he left the room, leaving the door standing open behind him. Jane watched the empty doorway for a moment, then sank into a chair. *Good heavens.* If she hadn't been three-and-thirty and *well* past looking to make any sort of match, if she still owned a young lady's fantasies of fairy tales, that magnificent one-eyed specimen of manhood smiling at her might very well have had her swooning.

At least she hadn't come across as an utterly deranged hobgoblin—or so she hoped, anyway. Lady Aldriss might claim to want her companion to make some friends of her own, but Jane more than suspected that had more to do with the countess wanting some time to herself than with a plan to fill Jane's social calendar. The countess was a formidable and much-respected member of London Society, after all.

Francesca MacTaggert had accepted a quiet, awkward, and unnecessary spinster into her employment, but an embarrassing, drooling flirt with no sense of her own . . . limitations was another beast entirely. Not even Lady Aldriss's largess would accommodate that.

Well, Jane *did* know her own limitations. And so she accepted a moment's pleasant conversation with a very well-favored man for precisely what it was—a pleasant moment. Standing, she walked over to peruse the shelf at the far left of the library. And then she selected the book about Scottish historical architecture, simply because she enjoyed reading about architecture. No other reason.

Chapter Two

"Aye, ye'd have a good view from the mountaintop," Brennan Andrews said, pulling the map around to take a better look at the indentation where Coll had shoved his thumb. "Ye'd also risk being blown off said mountain every winter by the storms."

"Nae if ye bury the foundation deep enough."

"Ye'd nae be able to go outside without getting swept into the air, ye lummox. Well, *ye* might be able to. Nae yer wife or any bairns." Narrowing his good eye, Brennan slid his own finger a half mile to the south and west, where the west edge of Loch an Daimh dug long fingers into the western foothills. "This'd suit ye better."

The viscount leaned closer. "How far is that from Aldriss?"

"Nae more than half a mile. Ye could take a boat across the loch in ten minutes. Riding, though, I'd say a mile."

"I dunnae want my brothers taking a spyglass and looking in my windows, Brennan."

"They couldnae. See the curve of the bank here? Ye've a hill and a great stand of trees hiding Aldriss from whatever ye put there." He cocked his head. "Aside from that, it's the finest spot on the loch. And ye ken that Aden and Niall will see what ye're about and want their own homes here, as well."

"Dunnae try yer clever ways on me, ye bastard," Coll rumbled. "I've an idea that Aden and Miranda mean to live here with Da, and Niall's had his eye on the old Creag Falaichte house since he was a bairn. So I'm yer only chance to build a proper manor house."

For the moment ignoring the fact that Creag Falaichte was a ruin that would definitely require at least new walls and a roof, Brennan grinned. "Aden and his bride living with just yer da, then? Was seeing Lady Aldriss walking down the stairs this morning my imagination?"

"That, I've nae comment about," Coll returned. "She came up here for the holiday. If she stays longer, well, then Da's going to have to learn to be more charming."

And less stubborn, Brennan thought, though he didn't say that aloud. "Seems to me that ye and yer brothers learned a few of those lessons, yerself. Ye are all married, after all. Ye should have heard the lasses weeping when the news came north."

"Oh, shut it." Coll sank into one of the chairs pushed up to the table. "Get out yer paper and pen, and I'll tell ye what I want for my house. Then ye sit with Temperance and she'll tell ye what she wants, and ye'll mark out all my nonsense that doesnae fit with hers."

Brennan gazed at his cousin for a moment. "I was nearly four when ye were born, Coll," he said finally. "Ye stood for me at my wedding. And until this moment, I've nae thought ye'd find a lass who could stand up to ye. But ye do love her, dunnae?"

The fond, introspective look on Coll's face nearly made him jealous. "Aye. She's the one, Brennan. And ye've the right of it. She stands up to me. Temperance is a damned independent, brilliant lass, and I'm looking forward to spending my life in her company."

"Good."

Almost immediately the viscount's expression sobered again. "I shouldnae be saying such things to ye, though. Ye had that, and what happened . . ."

Taking a breath, Brennan rolled up the map again and set it aside. "What happened, happened. I dunnae begrudge ye a moment of yer happiness, *Co-ogha*. Eithne wouldnae, either."

The name tasted strange on his lips. Foreign, almost. It wasn't that he didn't think about Eithne Andrews any longer—he did so almost daily. It was just that he rarely spoke about her to anyone any longer. It had been seven years since the fever had claimed her, and God knew no one else in his extended family wanted to see him moping about or bemoaning his fate. He'd already lost an eye; he didn't reckon there was anyone more pitiful than a one-eyed weeper.

Aside from that, Coll was just beginning what would, he hoped, be the best part of his life. Simply because he had an older cousin who'd seen his best bits taken from him didn't mean the viscount wanted to be endlessly reminded of it. No one did, including Brennan.

"Even so," Coll said aloud, his expression still dour.

"Even so, how many bairns do ye mean to have?" Brennan countered. "I reckon I cannae fit a house with more than forty rooms on the shore or it'll slide straight into the water."

"*Trioblaideach*," his cousin muttered, his grimace growing more amused again.

Brennan put a hand to his chest. "Me? I'm nae a troublemaker. I solve other people's problems. Starting with yers. So tell me what ye had in mind for a house."

As he made notes about what Coll wanted, Brennan's thoughts drifted back to the library. He hadn't expected to find anyone there at this hour of the morning, but there she'd been—a tall, black-haired lass with porcelain skin and her hair pulled back so tight it was a wonder she could shut her eyes enough to blink. But she'd had kind brown eyes, he recalled. Kind and patient, and a wee bit sad.

"Who's Jane Bansil?" he asked abruptly, interrupting something about a fireplace grand enough for a man to stand upright inside.

"What?"

"Miss Bansil. I ran across her in the library. She said she's the countess's companion."

"Oh, Jane. Aye. She's Amy's cousin. Tried to keep the lass out of trouble, and then found herself sacked by her own aunt when she decided to help Amy and Niall elope."

"No wonder she's skittish, then."

Coll nodded. "Timid as a rabbit, that one. Did ye write down the grand fireplace?"

"Aye. I even put a line under it so I'd nae forget." He drew a second line, just to be certain. If she'd been sacked by her aunt, he could understand why she'd be nervous; if her own family treated her that poorly, she wouldn't be expecting much from anyone else.

"Dunnae pretend to humor me," his cousin stated. "It's cold here in the winter, and I've a wife who's nae accustomed to it. She did grow up in Cumberland, but that's still nae comparison to the Highlands in January."

Brennan hadn't met Temperance MacTaggert yet, but he had read about her, both in the letter from his uncle and in the newspapers when they finally made their way this far from London. "Dunnae punch me, but she's an actress, aye? Do ye truly mean to let her continue onstage? She's Lady Glendarril now, after all."

"She'll do as pleases her, and that will please me." Coll rolled the map back and forth between his big hands. "I honestly thought she was nae but an actress, and I fell for her anyway. Persephone Jones, the most famous actress in London. And then after I decide I'm ready to take on all the MacTaggerts and all of clan Ross to keep her, she tells me she's a runaway heiress named Temperance Hartwood. She'd been on her own for eight years, and made a damned fine life for herself, Brennan. She can have a hundred fireplaces if she wants 'em, and she can act in every play ever written."

"Do ye want a room in yer hundred-fireplace house for performing, then? Someaught with a raised stage so she can rehearse?"

Coll leaned forward, jabbing his finger at Brennan's notes. "Aye. Ye write that down. And underline it, too."

He did so and then went on with his questions and suggestions for the next hour as Coll sorted through what he wanted. Lady Glendarril and the other lasses were still down at the village, so after he'd finished with his cousin he took the map, ruler, and some fresh sheets of paper and returned to the library to sketch.

The lass wasn't there, but he put his disappointment to not having anyone about to commiserate with him at the number of bricks that would be needed for all the damned chimneys Coll wanted. Outside, visible through the trio of windows the library boasted, a light snow fell in slow, swirling silence, just enough to remind him that Christmas was but four days away, and Hogmanay only a week after that.

A shadow crossed the empty doorway, then vanished again. Brennan noted it, but continued working, humming "Auld Lang Syne" under his breath as he drew. He'd told Coll where he'd be and assumed that when the lasses returned he would be meeting with Lady Glendarril. Until then, he wanted to at least figure out a rough layout of what he assumed would be called Glendarril House—as the original

Glendarril had burned well before the end of the Jacobites at Culloden and had never been much more than a wee hunting cottage to begin with.

Movement caught his attention again. He looked up, canting his head a little to the left to give himself a better view of the doorway. This time he caught sight of a blue skirt before it passed out of sight again.

The lass. Jane Bansil. She'd been wearing blue, a stiff, high-necked gown that looked as if it might break if she let out her breath. Still humming, he pushed to his feet and quietly crossed the room. Leaning against the wall beside the doorway, he waited for the swish of skirts, then stepped out into the hallway.

"Good afternoon, Miss Bansil," he said, inclining his head and pretending not to notice her squeak of surprise.

"Mr. Andrews. I . . . You're still here. I didn't know."

That was obviously a lie, but he only nodded. "Aye."

"Do . . . Do you require any more assistance? I'm free until two o'clock, it seems."

Women here in the Highlands as a rule didn't attempt to force themselves into conversation with him. They knew him as a widower, and they'd known Eithne as a friend, and not a one of them wanted to be accused of attempting to take her place or, worse, leading him astray. It was ridiculous, of course, but Pethiloch was a small village, and everyone knew everyone else's bloody business the moment it happened.

Perhaps she wasn't flirting, and perhaps her offer had been precisely what she claimed, but he didn't know for certain. That in itself was invigorating. "I'd welcome a female opinion," he said, moving sideways to give her access to the doorway. "I'm trying to design a house for Coll—Glendarril—and all he's told me is that he wants a great many fireplaces for keeping his lass warm in winter."

That wasn't entirely true, but he and the MacTaggert brothers had grown up together and in a very heavily masculine setting. A few insights into what a proper lass wanted, an English lass at that, *would* be helpful.

"Oh," she said, touching the back of the chair opposite him as if trying to decide whether she'd been invited to sit with him or not. "My experience with great houses is limited to ballrooms and foyers for the most part, I'm afraid."

He gestured at the chair as she continued to hesitate. "A house needs certain things, always. A kitchen, rooms for sleeping, a place to put things. For a great house, ye add a morning room, a dining room, an office, a library, mayhap a music room, a drawing room if they mean to entertain or have a large family, a room for playing cards or billiards. A nursery, places for servants to sleep and eat, and outside, a stable and a garden. It's the proportions that differ, mostly."

"The MacTaggerts practically live in each other's pockets," she said, finally sitting, "so a very, very large dining room and drawing room, for certain."

"Aye." He made a note beneath the note he'd already made to himself about that very thing. "What do ye know of Lady Glendarril? I was thinking she might want a sunroom for flowers and sunlight in the winter, but I'm nae certain."

"She's very gregarious. I don't know how much solitude she would require. But the house she was renting did burn down six months ago. She moved into Oswell House after that, and of course stayed after the wedding."

"I hadnae heard that." He sent her a sideways glance. "Ye've been surrounded by chaos, I reckon."

Her mouth curved in a brief, attractive smile. "That I have. The MacTaggerts do seem to upend things a great deal." Her grin slammed shut again. "No offense meant, of course."

"Nae a bit taken. I'm half MacTaggert, but I've eyes—an eye—to see with. 'Upending' is a gentle way of putting it."

Her shoulders lowered a little. Brennan felt a wee bit like he was trying to coax a wild foal to take grain from his hand. That smile, though . . . He wouldn't mind seeing it again. Teasing it out of her might take some effort, but it would be worth it.

"She could likely use a place where she can try on costumes and see the effect from different angles," Miss Bansil put in abruptly. "She's an actress. A very fine one."

"So I've heard. Mayhap a sitting room with an arc of mirrors on one side? Or a room with a stage and a space for seats, and the mirrors in an alcove?"

She sat forward. "Oh, that would be perfect. With a place for canvas scenes to be displayed behind the stage."

Brennan made another note, not atop one he'd already made. "Anything else?"

"Curtains? In front of the stage, I mean. And heavy ones for the windows. A miniature theater."

"Aye. I like that." Setting aside his notes, he took a larger paper and did a quick sketch of what she'd described, then turned it to show her. "Someaught like that?"

"That is exactly what I'd imagined. My goodness. You— You're very talented, Mr. Andrews."

"Och. Brennan, if ye please. I'm nae as high-and-mighty as the MacTaggerts, Miss Bansil."

Her pale cheeks flushed. "Jane, then. It's only fair."

Realizing he'd been gazing at her rather intently, Brennan cleared his throat and shifted another piece of paper. "Well, Jane, I dunnae mean to keep ye from yer duties, but if ye've a few minutes, I'd like yer help in figuring out the rest of the house."

"I doubt you require my assistance," she returned, "but if you'd like the company, I have nowhere to be until this afternoon."

He met her pretty brown-eyed gaze again. "I *would* like

the company. Generally sitting by myself while I scribble is peaceful, but more and more I find it a wee bit . . . lonely."

She visibly swallowed. "You aren't married, then?"

"Nae. I was, once. My wife, Eithne, died of a fever seven years ago now."

"My condolences, Mr. An—Brennan. She kept you company, then?"

"Aye. She always recommended an overabundance of sitting rooms, but that did remind me to put at least one or two into the plans." He started to clear his throat, realized that he'd just done that and would likely have her thinking he had a fever, himself, and then choked as he tried to stop himself.

Immediately she fled the room. Before he could do more than frown and begin cursing at himself while he pounded his own chest and hacked, Jane returned with a glass of water. "Take a drink," she instructed. "Small sips until the spasms cease."

He did as she ordered. "Ye know someaught about choking on yer own spit, then?" he managed.

"Oh, definitely. I almost constantly have to stop myself from saying something idiotic."

A laugh surged up from his chest, making him cough all over again. He managed to down half the glass without choking again and finally took a deep breath. "While I recover my wits, tell me someaught about yerself. Ye were Amy's companion? Niall's lass?"

She nodded. "My parents passed away when I was seventeen. I took work as a seamstress for a time, but I wasn't terribly efficient at it, and . . . earning enough money to keep a roof over my head began to prove difficult. My aunt, Victoria Baxter, agreed to allow me to live with her family if I would help look after her daughter, Amelia-Rose. There are fifteen years between us, so I nearly felt like an aunt rather than a cousin, but we got on well."

Despite her matter-of-fact tone, Brennan could imagine that being suddenly alone at seventeen, likely raised properly but without the funds to have a Society debut or make a good match, would have been terrifying. And then agreeing to become in essence a surrogate parent to a youngster, knowing she was turning her back on having her own children and her own life . . . This was a practical lass sitting opposite him. "But now ye're companion to Lady Aldriss."

She nodded, fiddling with one of his sketch papers. "Aunt Victoria had some very . . . strong opinions about the life Amelia-Rose should have. But she and Niall seemed so well matched, and—Well, I decided to help them elope. No one should have to live a miserable life when other options are so clearly available. Aunt Victoria rightly accused me of failing in my duties and sacked me, but Lady Aldriss was kind enough to take me in. I know it was purely out of gratitude for me helping her son find a bride, because I am certainly not an exceptional companion, but here we are."

"Aye, here we are. A man with a ruined face who tries to imagine perfect buildings, and a lass who enjoys solitude and reading trying to keep track of a busy countess's social schedule."

"Your face isn't ruined," she protested. "You look very rakish with the eye patch." Her cheeks darkened again. "In my opinion, of course. But I believe you know you're quite well favored."

Eithne had always said so, and the lasses before Eithne, but since then all the females seemed to think it some sort of sin to tell him that he looked like a man when he was a widower. And that wasn't much of a description. Aye, he had a mirror, but mostly what he saw there was an eye patch and a mouth that seemed to grimace more than it did smile. "Thank ye for saying so. Ye're a fair flower, yerself. But tell me, what room would ye want to be the largest in a house that belonged to ye?"

She put her arms around her own sides, hugging herself. "If I had a house? Oh, it would have a massive library, two stories tall with ladders for climbing to reach the books up on the highest shelves." She smiled again, the expression lighting her face. "Perhaps I'd even have two libraries, one for actual histories and science, and one for works of fiction."

"That's a great many books. I reckon the floor would have to have extra beams beneath it to carry the weight."

"You know, that's something I would never have considered." Her grin flashed. "I would have made myself a lovely library, only to have it all collapse into the cellar."

"Nae if I were yer architect," he countered, bending his head to sketch out a wide, high-ceilinged room with bookshelves reaching twenty feet up in the air, divided by tall windows and countered by long, wide tables and comfortable chairs in the middle of the room. He fiddled with a few more details, not entirely certain why he felt the need to do so, then handed it over to her. "How close did I get?"

For a long moment she gazed at it silently, and he began to wonder if he was just being an idiot, acting foolish because she was the first woman he'd met in seven years who made him want to smile. Who made him want to linger in her company.

Then a tear rolled down one pale cheek, and he reckoned he'd done even worse than insult her. "I'm sorry, lass," he said, reaching for the paper. "I was only playing."

Jane jerked the sketch out of his reach. "This is so lovely," she said, another tear sliding down the other cheek. "Don't you dare make light of it. May I keep it?"

"Aye, of course."

As she gazed at it, he had the strongest, oddest urge to

storm out and build her a library just like the one he'd
sketched for her. To give her a lifetime's worth of books and
a very comfortable chair in which to sit and read them, without having to worry about being at anyone else's beck and
call.

He looked at her all over again, or what he could see with
her sitting at the table as she was. She was fairly tall, with
that tight-pulled black hair and rich chocolate eyes. Small-
bosomed, she was, and nearly straight as a fence post, but he
imagined that if she stopped feeling like every bit of food
she ate made her more obligated to someone else, she might
have a few curves to her. In a sense she seemed like a hearth
fire at dawn, grown cold except for deep down where the em-
bers still smoldered. All she needed was for someone to give
her life a good stir and she would burst into bright flame.

"Do you live here, at Aldriss Park?" she asked, and he
wondered if that was an abrupt change of subject or if he'd
simply missed the first part of her conversation because he
was staring again.

"Nae. I've a cottage at the top of the hill above Pethiloch,
but a mile from here. My house doesnae have a name, but I
like it well enough."

"Yes, most of us don't live in houses with names, do we?
I think they—the ones who do—forget that, sometimes. But
I suppose if you own three or four or five homes, you need
to name them or no one will know to which one you're refer-
ring."

"Exactly. Though this place—Aldriss Park—is near four
hundred years old. I reckon if a house can keep itself together
for that long, mayhap it *does* deserve a name."

"I suppose you have the right of it. Did you design your
house, or purchase it?"

"I designed it. My da's family owned the land, but the wee
cottage that sat on it wouldnae keep out a light breeze."

They sat and chatted about his house, and the house Coll wanted for himself and Temperance or Persephone or whatever name she chose to go by, and about books and whatever else came to his mind to keep her there at the table. Now that she'd begun to relax a little he could clearly see that she had a quick wit and a sharp sense of humor, even if it seemed more designed to cut at herself than anything else.

"There ye are," Coll's voice boomed from the doorway.

Jumping, Brennan looked up. Beside his cousin stood a lovely lass in a deep blue gown, her honey-colored hair a jumble of curls. He stood. "Ye'd be Lady Glendarril, I presume."

Across from him, Jane Bansil stood as well. "Excuse me," she said in a hushed voice. "I need to see to Lady Aldriss."

With that she vanished through the second doorway. Brennan had to remain, making more notes about a house that would be grander than any he could ever hope to reside in, and his thoughts on a much more practical theme—where and when he would be able to find an excuse to chat with Jane Bansil again.

Chapter Three

"What do you mean, 'we aren't celebrating Christmas'?" Eloise MacTaggert-Harris demanded, jabbing a finger at her middle brother. "It's only three days away!"

Aden finished his bite of venison and washed that down with a swallow of whisky. "Just what I said, *Piuthar*. This is Scotland. We dunnae celebrate Christmas here."

"Why the devil not?"

"Eloise," her mother admonished, though from Lady Aldriss's grimace she knew precisely what Aden was talking about and had intended to ignore it until someone brought it up. At least that was what Jane had to assume, since she'd spent the last day and a half wrapping and boxing gifts brought all the way up with them from London.

"It's illegal here," Aden returned. "It's been illegal here since Cromwell."

"But Cromwell banned Christmas nearly two hundred years ago. And it only lasted for what, fifteen years?" Eloise's new husband, Matthew Harris, put in. "If I recall my tutor's droning on about it correctly, that is."

"In England, it only lasted fifteen years. Here, nae a one

of yer English kings or parliaments bothered to lift the ban. We go to church, and we go about our day, just like any other day."

"But I brought gifts," Eloise protested.

Lord Aldriss chuckled from the head of the table. "Gifts, my dear, are what Hogmanay is for. That and setting things afire."

Jane put a hand to her chest. *Good heavens.* She knew the MacTaggerts were thought of as barbarians by the rest of London, but for the most part they'd been charming and rather warmhearted. But this didn't sound at all civilized. Or safe.

"Setting what things afire?" Miranda MacTaggert, Aden's bride and Matthew Harris's sister, asked, lifting an eyebrow. "Do I need to hide my clothes?"

"Nae," Aden answered. "First, we clean the house, and the fireplaces especially, to be rid of the burdens of the year. On Hogmanay eve we *saine* the house—bless the house, I mean—by sprinkling about water from a river crossed by both the living and the dead. Then we burn juniper branches in all the fireplaces to choke out the rest of the bad spirits hiding in the corners."

"After that," Niall took up from Aden, "we throw open all the doors and windows to send the regrets and burdens away and let in the fresh air of the new year. That's followed by a dram of whisky and breakfast."

"This sounds like an excuse to clean the house," Amy said, frowning. "And it seems very smoky."

"Aye, and uncivilized, I reckon," her husband, Niall, returned with a grin. "But that's nae all of it. We have to all sing 'Auld Lang Syne' together, holding hands, and then we go visiting the houses of relatives and friends. It's good luck to be the first guest of the new year. We begin that right at midnight."

"I heard it's especially good luck if your guest is tall, dark, and handsome," Temperance, Lady Glendarril, said with a sly smile. "No doubt the three of you were very good luck."

"That depends on who ye ask, my lass," Coll rumbled with a faint grin.

Jane immediately conjured an image of tall, dark, and handsome Brennan Andrews. He'd spent a great deal of the day at Aldriss House yesterday, but today he must have been in his quiet home doing his sketches and measuring, while she'd been attempting to box a saddle. That hadn't gone at all well.

"And then we sleep the rest of the day, I hope?" Amy countered, rubbing her pregnant belly.

"Ye can if ye wish, love. But after breakfast we exchange gifts. When evening comes again, we all go down to the village and light torches. Coll's been known to swing a fireball about his head for a good mile as we parade along."

"Nae this year. I dunnae wish to fling sparks on any of the lasses," Coll said.

"Of course ye will, Coll," his father protested. "It's our tradition!"

"Anyway," Aden took up again, "then we all gather at the shore of Loch an Daimh and cast the flames into the water."

"To cast out the rest of the evil spirits, I presume?" Temperance asked.

"Aye. If ye can, ye should always begin the year with nae evil spirits in yer house. Or yer life." Aden grinned.

Jane couldn't tell if they believed all of the superstition or if they simply, as Lord Aldriss had put it, liked burning things. It seemed more wild than festive to her, but of course none of the other women in the house seemed to think it all intimidating. Lady Aldriss had put on a frown, but then as the matriarch she was the most practical of them all.

"You do know it'll be the first of January. In the Scottish

Highlands," the countess said. "We are not going to risk anyone getting fever or chills."

"We march with damned kilts on, woman," Lord Aldriss
protested. "Ye can bundle up as much as ye like. In fact, I
recall ye carrying a torch or two yerself in the first few years
ye were here."

The countess blushed. "That was a very long time ago."

"I'd like to drive away bad spirits," Amy said. "I have a
few I'd like never to see again."

"As do I," Miranda said feelingly.

"I will definitely be marching with a torch," Temperance
MacTaggert added. "Perhaps two torches."

"Before we all get carried away with torches," Eloise put
in, "I want to be certain I understand. We don't exchange gifts
at Christmas, but we do on New Year's Day, yes?"

"Aye."

"Well, that's fine, then. You should have begun with that,
Aden."

The middle MacTaggert brother shrugged, his shoulders
brushing against his longish hair. "Where's the fun in that?"

Well, at least now Jane had an additional week to finish
wrapping all the gifts. Lady Aldriss might have hired her
out of charity, but that only left Jane more determined to be
useful. And the countess wasn't the only one who'd asked
for assistance. At least wrapping and boxing gave her mind
time to wander, even if it had spent an inordinate amount of
time thinking about yesterday in the library with Brennan
Andrews. She couldn't recall a more pleasant day—or a
more interesting man.

As dinner ended, the stout, ginger-haired butler, Pogan,
approached Lord Glendarril with a note. In London it would
have been delivered on a proper silver salver, but here the butler simply handed it over.

Coll opened it, then frowned. "Brennan wants to know if

I can go see him tomorrow at ten o'clock. He has some more questions and wants to look like a proper architect with an office and drawing board, I reckon. I cannae go, though; I've a meeting in the village."

"I'll go," Temperance said.

"I can accompany Lady Glendarril," Jane blurted, no doubt startling everyone who'd forgotten she was even there.

"Aye, that'll do," Coll agreed. "Brennan likely has a few more questions about paint colors and such."

Temperance wrinkled her nose. "Then I'm definitely going. I'm half convinced you would wish everything painted in clan Ross colors, with brown curtains."

He leaned sideways to plant a kiss on his wife's temple. "As long as ye dunnae choose white lace curtains, I reckon I'll be doing naught but nodding my head, anyway. And thank ye, Jane."

"Certainly," Jane chirped, hoping she didn't look as warm as she felt.

"What happened to Cousin Brennan's eye, anyway?" Eloise asked.

"Yes," Lady Aldriss seconded. "He had two of them the last time I saw him."

"It was my fault," Coll stated, a brief scowl crossing his face. "I'd just gotten Nuckelavee, and he didnae mind as well then as he does now. Th—"

"Nuckelavee doesnae mind anyone but ye, and he nae once has," Niall countered. "That horse is a devil."

"Aye, but he's *my* devil. Anyway, Brennan came by to see him, and said he didnae look so fierce. I'd just been thrown off into a field of thistle, and I wasnae feeling very friendly, so I told him he could have the black if he could ride him."

"Coll, you shouldn't have," his sister admonished.

"I was eighteen, and Brennan was two-and-twenty, so

dunnae ye go saying that I led him astray. But I shouldnae have let him ride Nuckelavee. Nae when I couldnae do it yet." He sighed. "Anyway, he stayed aboard for about ten seconds, and then Nuckelavee jumped in the air and landed on his back through a fence. Brennan took a nail down his face and broke his leg. The leg mended; his eye didnae." He dug into his plate again. "But that was eleven years ago and he's nae once held a grudge about it, so done is done. His wife didnae look at me too kindly for a time, though."

Murmurs of "poor Eithne" went around the table at that, and Coll even crossed himself. Brennan had told Jane that he'd lost his wife seven years earlier. He'd been married for at least four years, then—not that that mattered. He'd been a husband, and he'd lost his wife. The amount of time they'd had together didn't seem to matter as much as the fact that he'd seemed genuinely to love her, and that now his house felt quiet and alone.

"I was about to take that wager," Aden said after a moment, "so I feel more than a wee bit grateful to Brennan for doing it in my stead."

"Good heavens," the countess breathed. "When I think of the peril the three of you were in after I left Scotland, it keeps me awake at night."

"Ye reckon ye could have stopped me from a damned thing I wanted to do?"

Jane looked over at Coll MacTaggert. At more than five inches above six feet and all muscle, the viscount likely had never been stopped from doing anything—except perhaps by his bride. She wished Temperance well, because being married to such an imposing man would terrify her. Just speaking to him gave her the shivers.

"That isn't the point," his mother countered. "You needed a guiding hand, and clearly your father declined to provide it."

"And yet there they are," the earl stated. "Nae a one dead

and all of them tall, fine lads wed to the best yer England has to offer."

As the two of them began to argue over which had had the greater hand in seeing their sons married, Jane went back to picking at her dinner. Men like the MacTaggerts were a large reason she remained rather thankful to have missed her debut Season and all the ones that followed. If one of them had decided to pursue her, she would likely have fainted to the floor. It would have been worse, though, to have attended all the dances and the recitals and the dinners and have no one notice her at all. That was the far more likely outcome of her imaginary trip through Society. At least now part of her role was to avoid being noticed. She excelled at that.

As dinner ended, everyone adjourned to the drawing room. The countess gestured at her as everyone began to settle in to listen to Aden read a Scottish ghost story. "A word, my dear?"

"Of course, my lady. Should I fetch you a wrap?"

"No, Jane." Lady Aldriss took Jane's arm, pulling her away from the others. "I know you don't think yourself necessary here."

Jane blushed. "My lady, I am exceedingly grate—"

"The thing is, Lord Aldriss has asked me to join him for a holiday, directly after Hogmanay. A month or more, in Italy and Spain." The countess's mouth curved in a slight smile. "Places I've been, but where I once asked him to take me, and he refused."

"Oh, that's lovely, then," Jane offered, since something seemed required.

"Yes, it is. You need to make a decision, though. You may accompany me, in which case we will assume you mean to remain in my employ, or you may remain here with the rest of the family through the winter as our . . . guest. For however long you wish to stay, really. Or I will happily write you a letter of recommendation if you wish to find another position closer to London. I know you are more comfortable there."

That was it, then. Accept that she would keep Lady Aldriss company for the remainder of that woman's life, whether she was necessary or not; be reconciled to being a useless bit of charity the MacTaggerts would feel obligated to include on all of their jaunts and holidays; or leave and find a position less auspicious, if more useful, with one of the countess's elderly friends. And then do the same thing over and over again until she was too old to be useful to anyone.

"I see," she said slowly. "When do you need my answer?"

"By Hogmanay, I would think." Lady Aldriss squeezed her hand. "You are loved and wanted here, Jane. I want you to feel that you have some stability, whatever you choose."

Jane nodded, feeling rather hollowed-out inside. "Of course. Do you require me now?"

"You don't wish to stay?"

"I'm a little tired," she returned, "but of course I'll stay if you need me."

"Jane, you . . . Of course you may go." The countess sighed. "Or remain. And since we have an additional week now to box gifts, please take tomorrow to do as you please. After you accompany Temperance to Brennan's home, that is. I may go down to the village for a bit more shopping."

"Thank you, my lady," Jane said, dipping a curtsy and leaving the room before anyone could call her back, and before she could hear the silence if they didn't.

Upstairs she walked to her window and looked outside at the silent trees and drifts of snow. Visiting Europe for weeks might have been a dream for other young ladies, including all of the ones presently downstairs. For her, well, she didn't have Italian, and her Spanish was horrible. In addition, Lord and Lady Aldriss, whatever they might say, were of course attempting a reconciliation. The last thing the countess needed was to be worrying over whether her companion had been overset at having to attend some soiree where she didn't know the language.

"Damnation," she muttered, lowering her forehead against the cold glass. Making a decision was difficult enough. Making one that would decide her entire future . . . Heavens, the last decision she'd made had seen her sacked. The employment with Lady Aldriss had simply happened, without her ever seeking it.

Blowing out her breath, she retrieved the Scottish architecture book and sat by her small fire. Dwelling on the impossible now would only keep her awake. Determinedly she opened the book and began reading.

Most of the dwellings in the Highlands seemed to have been either mud and peat huts or giant stone fortresses meant to keep the English and the other clans at bay, but the author had an amusing, light touch and a great many interesting stories to go with the facts and histories. In her opinion, Mr. B. Conchar might have had more literary success if he'd simply told the tales without the architectural details.

Every time she read the word "architecture" her mind went to Brennan Andrews and the way he'd so effortlessly sketched the library of her dreams right in front of her eyes. She meant to have the drawing framed as soon as she could manage it—not that she anticipated having a wall on which to hang it anytime soon—and presently had it pressed between other papers in her small writing desk to keep it safe.

Around her the house began to quiet, but she kept reading until her eyes would no longer stay open. Then she closed the book and wandered back over to one of the nearest of her trio of bedchamber windows. The pale moonlight turned the snow outside a silvery blue. It looked frightfully cold, but she couldn't deny that the effect was lovely and a bit magical. No wonder Highlanders still felt the need to burn juniper branches and light torches to banish dark spirits. If those things could live anywhere, it would be here.

And there she stood, indulging her imagination when she had practicalities to decide. "Nodcock," she muttered, and pulled the curtains closed. Back when she'd lived with her parents in a small cottage in Derbyshire she'd had dreams—simple ones, things she could imagine happening to her. Her, married to a solicitor or an army captain, as opposed to her being taken by pirates and ending up a princess on some foreign shore. Those imaginings were for young ladies with wealth and comfort to buoy their dreams.

But then her parents had died within six months of each other, and repaying doctors and other debts she hadn't known about until afterward had taken the house. That was when she'd stopped daydreaming. She hadn't had time for it. In fact, until yesterday she couldn't remember engaging in such fanciful imaginings. Perhaps Scotland did possess a little magic.

Regardless, as she neatly folded her gown and pulled on her simple white night rail, she allowed her mind to wander toward a one-eyed Scottish widower with a clear talent for drawing and who, she imagined, would be fond of sitting by the fire in the evenings reading aloud in his charming brogue to his beloved, who of course very closely resembled herself.

There would of course be hand-holding and kissing and other things that became rather heated, because he would of course be a splendid and virile hus—

Bagpipes screeched through her brain, and Jane sat straight up in bed. "Oh, for God's sake!" she hissed, only belatedly realizing that light shone around the edges of the curtains and that she had, in fact, been dreaming. And some very intimate dreams, at that.

According to the small clock on the mantel it was once

again six o'clock in the morning, just as it had been yesterday and the day before when the torture had begun. Given
the lack of success she'd had in ignoring the racket previously,
this morning she flung off the covers and got dressed, this
time choosing a long-sleeved brown and yellow gown. It was
still frightfully plain, but it was also her best.

As she reached the foyer the butler, Pogan, straightened
from tying a rope about the neck of BròGan, the black English spaniel Aden had adopted after she had stolen one of
his boots back in London. Four black puppies, now nearly the
same size as their dam, bounded about the butler's feet.

"Good morning, Miss Jane," he said, nodding. "The dogs
and I are about to make the rounds in the garden."

"I'll see to that," she decided. "You have a great many
other things to see to."

"That I do," he returned with a smile, handing over the
rope. "Thank ye. I reckon ye're better acquainted with them
than I am, anyway."

"That I am."

She bent down to scratch Bròsan between the ears, then
headed outside with the furry pack when Pogan opened the
door for them all. There had originally been five puppies, but
Smythe, the butler at Oswell House, had been gifted one
of them. They'd been born on his bed, after all, and he did
seem to adore them.

Brògan stayed by her side as she picked her way through
the light snow to the garden, but the pups charged out in every
direction, black dots zooming across the white ground. Cold
crept up her legs beneath her skirts, and she tugged her
heavy wrap closer around her shoulders.

The bagpipes were even louder outside, and she looked
toward the roof of Aldriss Park to see a kilt-clad man standing there silhouetted against the sky, pipes in his arms. She
wanted to throw a snowball at him, but she'd never be able

to reach that far. Instead, she trod up and down the garden, the cold slowly leaving her legs as she marched.

Walking the dogs was likely the most useful thing she'd done since she'd joined the Oswell-MacTaggert household, she reflected. Oh, she detested being someone's charitable project, even when the someone was as kind and generous as Lady Aldriss. The truth was, though, that she required that charity. Without it, she might well have been on the streets by now. That put her new trio of choices into a better perspective, but they remained choices. And she needed to decide.

"Jane, what in the world are you doing out there?" came from above and behind her. "You'll catch your death!"

She turned to look up at the house. Lady Aldriss leaned out a window, a scowl on her face. "I'm just helping with the dogs!" she called back. "I'll be in in a moment. Do you need me?"

"This is your day to do as you please, remember? Just do it indoors, where it's warm."

"Yes, my lady."

The countess retreated, and the window shut again. Yes, Lady Aldriss and all the MacTaggerts were kind and generous, and they told her she was part of the family, but if she hadn't stood up for Amy, they wouldn't even know her name.

After another ten minutes she couldn't ignore her cold fingers and toes any longer, and she herded the dogs back into the house. Thank goodness she'd volunteered to accompany Lady Glendarril to Mr. Andrews's home, because she generally had no idea what to do with herself when left to her own devices. Read, of course, but when she closed a book she always found herself back in her own skin, and that did, on occasion, grate.

Shortly before nine o'clock Lord Glendarril and his great

black and nearly murderous Friesian warhorse galloped down to the village. Thankfully, Lady Glendarril decided they should set off for Mr. Andrews's house before the rest of the clan could head out to the stables to begin making torches for Hogmanay.

"Such strange customs," the actress and viscountess said, settling back in the heavy coach.

"They all seem ancient, which I rather like," Jane offered, taking the rear-facing seat opposite.

"Yes. A torch parade on a whim might seem silly, but knowing it's been done for the past five hundred years lends it some dignity." Temperance Hartwood sent her a sideways glance. "This must not go beyond us, but do you find the bagpipes at dawn as annoying as I do?"

Jane sat forward. "Oh, yes. They're horrible!"

"Coll says it announces to everyone in the valley that the laird is well and all is calm, which I imagine is another ancient tradition, but I find it very alarming every blasted morning."

"So is there a more strident bit of music they play when all is not calm?" Jane wondered, blushing when she realized she'd spoken aloud.

Temperance, though, only laughed. "I hate even to imagine it." Stifling a yawn, she turned to look out the window. "The mornings have been lovely here, but I'm still more accustomed to *very* late nights and sleeping well into the day."

"But now you're Lady Glendarril. And eventually you'll be Lady Aldriss, and the bagpipes will be on *your* roof."

"Then the bagpipes will begin playing at noon every day, or the piper will find that the laird of the house is not at all well, because I will have murdered him." She grinned. "Although as you said, that would likely only make the tunes worse."

Of all the MacTaggerts, Jane likely understood Temperance the least. They were the closest in age of all the females, with Temperance but five years younger than she was, but this was a woman who'd had wealth and family growing up and had willingly turned her back on both to avoid being pushed into a marriage she didn't want. And of all things, she'd chosen to make a living as a stage actress. Standing in front of hordes of people every night, people just waiting for her to make a misstep, and she'd wowed them all.

"Were you ever afraid?" she asked, knowing she would be better off simply keeping her mouth shut rather than risking inserting her foot into it. "Onstage, I mean."

"No," the viscountess returned, facing Jane again. "Not onstage. Before I stepped onstage, yes. The anticipation, I suppose, the worry that I would forget all my lines or trip and fall into the audience or catch my costume on fire on the footlights. Once I stepped out, though, well, the reality I suppose was far less frightening than all of my imaginings."

Perhaps that was her difficulty, Jane decided. She spent a great deal of time anticipating trouble and never had that moment of metaphorically stepping onstage. Stifling a sigh, she turned her own gaze outside.

The village was larger than she'd expected, with two or three dozen shops, taverns, and various other buildings, and four or five times that many homes, with a large church in the center, and a curving main street with public stables at one end and a small waterfront and docks at the other.

Everything looked quaint and pretty with the layer of snow everywhere, though she imagined in the springtime the road would be nearly impassable from all the mud. The coach continued up past the stable and around the hill just beyond, winding upward as they climbed. At the top it flattened out, with three homes well spaced from one another occupying the crest.

They rocked to a stop in front of the last house, which

was bordered by a white wooden fence and a small front garden that must have been lovely in springtime but now sat bleak and icy. The front door opened and Brennan Andrews stepped outside, pulling on a coat as he approached. "Thank ye for coming here to meet me," he said, pulling open the coach's door and offering a hand to Lady Glendarril. "All my papers are here, and they dunnae suffer the cold and wet at all well."

"It's no trouble at all," the viscountess said. "Coll informed you that he has a meeting?"

"Aye. And ye've . . ." He turned, and his one-eyed gaze met Jane's. "Ye've brought someone much easier on the eye in his stead, for which I thank ye," he continued smoothly, though she had no idea what he'd originally meant to say.

He caught her gloved fingers in his. Firming his grip a little, he helped her down to the snowy ground. "Good morning," she said belatedly.

"Good morning, lass," he returned, still holding her fingers. "I've put on a pot and found some tea, as I hear ye English lasses prefer that to coffee."

"Hot tea sounds wonderful," she commented, abruptly wishing she could put this moment beneath glass and keep it forever. Just her and Brennan Andrews standing in the snow and holding hands, his fingers warm through her gloves.

"If we stay outside any longer," Temperance said, a shiver in her voice, "I'm going to have to request a dram of whisky in that tea."

Brennan released Jane's hand. "Aye. Let's go in then, shall we?"

And the moment ended. Her breath visible in the air, Jane stepped sideways to allow the two actual participants in the day's meeting to precede her. Halfway to the door, though, Brennan turned around to face her.

"Where are my manners?" he muttered, stepping back and

offering his arm. "I'm happy to show ye my house, Jane. I hope ye like it."

Why did he hope she liked his house? And why did sudden, sharp excitement dig through her chest in response? "I'm certain I will," she said aloud, putting her hand on his forearm and keeping her mouth firmly closed over her silly questions—and the very small, very quiet hope that the answers were the stuff of her daydreams.

Chapter Four

She'd come. He'd sought about for an hour last night, trying to figure a way to include Jane Bansil in his invitation, but he hadn't been able to conjure a reason that didn't make him sound like a lunatic. She wasn't precisely a servant, but she was in the countess's employ. He couldn't invite her for tea without raising every eyebrow in the household and sending attention in her direction—attention that she wouldn't want. But there she was.

As Brennan and his guests walked into his modest foyer and then turned right to enter his office, he reached around Lady Glendarril to straighten a stack of books half collapsed on his windowsill. Coll and all the locals who used his services knew he tended to surround himself with clutter; one never knew where one might find inspiration for a fireplace or a staircase.

Abruptly, though, his office seemed to be full of rubbish, disheveled when he could easily have put it into order. He lifted a stack of papers off the second chair facing his desk and set it on the floor in the corner. His sudden obsession with organization didn't have anything to do with the pretty vis-countess taking the seat he offered her, either. Hell, he'd had a duke in the house once and hadn't bothered to straighten a damned thing.

No, his unexpected nerves had everything to do with the brown-eyed lady's companion taking the second chair as he held it for her. Highborn ladies accustomed to having a myr-iad of servants cleaning up after them would be more likely to notice his disarray, he supposed, but Jane—well, it mat-tered that she not have a poor impression of his home.

"What was it you wanted to show us?" Lady Glendarril prompted, her quick smile taking any reprimand out of her words.

Because yes, he was staring again. Clearing his throat, Brennan sat at the far side of his desk from the ladies and turned his sketchbook to face the viscountess. "I made three versions of how I interpreted yours and Coll's wishes for the exterior of the house," he said, setting the three pages side by side. "I know nae a one of them will be perfect, but if ye could go over each element with me, I'll end with a much clearer view that hopefully better matches yers."

"Goodness," Lady Glendarril murmured, looking at first one sketch, then the next. "These are very grand."

"Coll claims that this will be where he spends the rest of his life," Brennan commented. "I suppose ye should be moving back to Aldriss once he takes the earldom, but the brothers are so close, he may just leave it to Aden to live there. So I'm attempting to give ye a house for now, and a house that'll still suit when he's a clan Ross chieftain."

"I'm very glad you have some knowledge of the inner workings of the MacTaggerts," Temperance said feelingly. "I've lived with them for six months, but their roles in England were very different than they are back in the Highlands." She reached out, touching the middle sketch. "I like the portico here, but the Ionic columns from the first sketch are . . . warmer, I think. More welcoming."

He drew a line from the columns out to a blank space and wrote "Ionic" upside down. "Ye could stain them brown if ye like," he commented, cocking his head to view the drawings. "Give the house that warmer feel, even with all the white stone on the exterior."

"I like that. Yes. And perhaps color the windowsills or the exterior shutters to match." She indicated the shutters he'd added to the third sketch.

He made a note to add shutters, glancing at Jane as he did so. She sat still, but her gaze roamed the bookcase just to her right. "Ye'll find most of these books in the Aldriss library, as well," he said, "except for the ones on the center shelf there. Those are a bit technical to qualify as light reading."

"I've been reading the book you recommended," she said, meeting his gaze. "It's quite enjoyable, really. A bit technical, as you say, but the tales that go with the various architectural examples are quite entertaining. Do you have anything else by B. Conchar?"

His heart thudded. "Ye liked it?" he asked, no doubt frightening her with his absurd grin.

Jane nodded. "I did. He's quite a good writer."

"I . . . Thank ye."

That made her scowl, her delicate brows drawing together. "Why are you thanking me?"

"The, um—well, ye see . . ." He grimaced. "My middle name is Conchar. Brennan Conchar Andrews. I wasnae certain how the book would be received, so I didnae use my own name entirely. It was a wee bit silly in retrospect, I suppose, but I was only twenty when I wrote it, and architects are a stuffy lot, for the most part. I—"

"Just a moment. *You* wrote *Scottish Castles and Highlands History: A Tangled Web?*"

"Aye. Coll said I should have called it *Blood and Buildings*, but I rarely take his advice seriously."

Lady Glendarril snorted. "He is rather straightforward, I've discovered."

Brennan blinked. He'd forgotten for a moment that the viscountess was even there, which would never do, since she and her husband were the ones who'd hired him. "I didnae mean to offend, I hope ye know."

"Oh, I'm not offended. I do mean to use that title suggestion against him sometime in the near future, however." Her grin deepened. "He's also mentioned that *Much Ado About Nothing* should be retitled *Nae a Soul Says What They Mean.*"

He laughed. "That's Coll, for certain." Shifting a little, he attempted to refocus his attention on the task at hand. "Let's have a look at the windows, since we're talking about shutters."

For the next hour he managed to avoid looking at Jane Bansil for the most part, even if she didn't leave his thoughts for more than a second at a time. She hadn't responded aloud to his admission that he was, in fact, B. Conchar, but he was absurdly pleased that's she'd admitted to enjoying the book before she'd known the identity of its author.

When he couldn't think of a single additional question to ask about three rather simple drawings, he stacked them up and asked the ladies if they wished another cup of tea. Both refused, of course, and so he ushered them toward the front door.

As Jane passed him her fingers brushed his, and he abruptly felt electrified. Whether it had been by accident or on purpose, she'd touched him, and he felt it all the way to his bones. "Ah, I forgot something," he muttered. "Jane, will ye assist me? We'll be but a moment, my lady."

"I'm in no hurry to return to the snow," the viscountess commented, continuing on into the foyer.

Wordlessly he took Jane's arm and led her back around the corner to his office. As soon as they were inside, he faced her, cupped her face in his hands, and leaned down to kiss her. She would no doubt be shocked and dismayed, as gentle a soul as she seemed, but—

Her hands winding around his, she lifted on her toes to kiss him back. Silently, he backed her against the wall, taking her mouth hungrily and forcing himself not to paw at her clothes. She kissed like a woman who hadn't been kissed back nearly often enough, but he couldn't fault her a whit for heat or enthusiasm. She shifted her hands to his lapels, wrapping her fingers into them fiercely, and that aroused him further. Jane Bansil wanted him.

His cock jumped, reminding him forcefully that he might have lost an eye, but the rest of his parts worked just fine. It had been forever since he'd been interested in a lass, but thank God he remembered how to kiss, and how to hold on to his lust hard enough that he wouldn't embarrass himself.

Finally, he broke the kiss, pulling in a quick breath. With the viscountess just around the corner he didn't dare say anything that might compromise Jane's reputation, but he ran his thumb along her lower lip, then straightened a few stray locks of her hair with his fingers before he gave in and kissed her once more. When he couldn't find another excuse to keep them in the room, he grabbed a book without even noting the title, shook out his coat, and nodded at her.

When she nodded back, he stepped past her, and she followed him out the door. The viscountess stood looking out the front window beside the doorway, and he handed her the book. "Coll wanted this," he said, hoping Lady Glendarril wouldn't ask why he'd needed Jane's assistance in pulling a book off a shelf.

She took the book, though, tucking it under her arm. "Thank you, Brennan."

"I'll do a new sketch for ye with all the bits ye liked," he continued. "Give me a day or two, and I'll bring it by for ye and Coll to see. Once that's approved, I'll start on the technical drawings."

He wanted to go do it immediately and bring it by before dinner, but that was only because he wanted to see Jane again. Brennan lowered his gaze to Miss Bansil's backside as they left the house for the coach. Doing haphazard work would only have Coll asking him what the devil was wrong with him, and that would never do.

"Are ye still having a Christmas Eve dinner?" he asked.

The viscountess stepped up into the coach, then leaned out again. "Of course. I hear it's tradition."

"Aye, it has been, but things at Aldriss are more than a wee bit different, now."

"They aren't so different that we wouldn't have MacTaggert family and friends over—even if we're not to celebrate anything." She smiled. "Aside from that, you'll provide someone else for us to ply for information about Hogmanay."

"I'm happy to do that, my lady."

"Good. And you must call me Temperance. Or Persie, if you prefer."

"I'll work myself up to it eventually, my lady." Helping Jane into the coach as an excuse to take her hand again, he grinned. "I reckon ye'll see me tomorrow evening, then."

"That will be pleasant, I'm certain," Jane returned, taking the rear-facing seat in the coach, her color high and her gaze darting anywhere but his face.

Aye, it would be pleasant, if he could keep his hands off her.

Jane kept her hands in her lap and her gaze out the coach window. *Good heavens.* So *that* was the kissing that Amy and Eloise and Miranda and even Temperance made such a ruckus about. She felt devoured and set ablaze all at the same time. And even more glorious than the kissing was the fact that *he'd* kissed *her.*

She hadn't imagined a connection between them, nor was the interest one-sided. What it all meant she had no idea, but in all her thirty-three years she'd never felt so close to . . . bursting. She wanted to sing, and dance, and spin about in a circle with her arms outflung. Touching him, being touched by him, made all her worries simply fizzle into smoke, unimportant and unnoticed—for the moment, anyway.

"I don't know why Coll would be interested in the topic of flooring," Lady Glendarril said, turning the book with which Brennan had gifted her in her hands, "but Coll does have more dimensions than I ever would have expected on first meeting him."

"No doubt," Jane returned, feeling some response was needed.

"Are you feeling well, Jane?" the viscountess pursued, setting the book aside. "Your color is high."

"It's just the cold, I think." *And the fact that a man, a delicious man, kissed me.* "I don't feel at all feverish."

"Good. I think we all will need to be fit enough come Hogmanay to run away from the house if the men should accidentally set it ablaze."

Putting a smile on her face, Jane nodded. "They do seem very enthusiastic about the bits with fire. Not to change the subject, but I think your home is going to be lovely. And with a view that London could never match."

"I hope so. I grew up overlooking a lake in Cumberland, but this . . ." She gestured at the land outside the coach. "It's magnificent here. I don't think I could ever tire of it."

"Would you give up the stage for it?" Jane asked, then mentally clamped a hand over her mouth when that earned her a rather piercing look. "Someday, I mean," she added belatedly.

"Between you and me," Temperance said slowly, her voice more thoughtful than Jane expected, "I have a contract for the coming Season with the Saint Genesius Theater. I will honor it. After that, well, I don't wish to be some entitled woman putting on plays to elevate her own sense of self-worth. I mean, Charlie Huddle—he's the manager at the Saint Genesius—would feel obligated to allow me to perform now. I'm a viscountess. I'd no longer be earning parts on my own merits." Scowling, she fiddled with her gloves. "Does that make sense?"

"It does, but being married doesn't diminish your talent. Or your enjoyment of the career you chose. There must be a balance somewhere." *Balance.* That was what she needed, as well. A balance between something she wanted to do and someone who needed her. The more she considered that, the less sense it made that she could remain, however, with Lady Aldriss.

"I do enjoy it," Lady Glendarril returned feelingly. "Very much. And I daresay I'm fairly good at it; I did earn all those roles before I married Coll." She sighed. "I don't know, Jane. I suppose I'll figure it out when I have to. I do know that I couldn't very well expect to play Juliet any longer. She's too young for me now, and I have this awful dream where I take the stage and begin the balcony soliloquy and everyone laughs and I look down and realize I'm eight months pregnant." She put a hand over her eyes. "Good God."

"You could do it, I'd wager," Jane stated. "You'd simply convince them that you're a plump Juliet, or something."

Temperance laughed. "Thank you for that. With a plump Romeo it might suffice. We could call it *Romeo and Juliet: Or, the Overfed Italians.*"

That made Jane chuckle, as well. She liked Temperance Hartwood—or MacTaggert, now—even if she couldn't imagine standing onstage like the viscountess had done for the previous seven years. Temperance had stood up for herself and had made her own way in the world. Jane had been pushed into doing the same thing and had failed at it.

Except that now her calm, quiet, well-ordered life felt more than a bit off-kilter, and not merely because of the countess's ultimatum. That would have filled her with dread, but this morning she could feel the just-submerged excitement of a new, unexpected thing tugging at her. This feeling *was* new, and that made it terrifying but at the same time . . . hopeful. Was that what it was? Hope? Last night she'd been full of the doldrums. Until she'd begun reading Brennan's book, that was.

"May I . . . May I ask you a question?" she squeaked, then immediately wished she hadn't said anything at all.

"Of course."

"Oh, never mind. It—I—Never mind."

"Very well." Temperance tilted her head a little, blue eyes speculative. "Do you think Coll and the others know that Brennan Andrews is also B. Conchar, the author?"

"I don't know. I certainly had no idea."

"But he writes well, you said."

"Yes. I enjoyed his stories about the grand houses more than I liked the actual descriptions of how the houses were built, but if a book about architecture can make me smile, as this one did, then I have to say he has some skill."

She wanted to say more, but gushing about Brennan wouldn't do anything but make her look silly and desperate. Perhaps she was those things, and perhaps he'd only kissed her out of curiosity or gratitude or something, but she hoped she was the only one who would know that.

She needed to remember that she was not some silly debutante receiving her first kiss; she was a well-on-the-shelf spinster receiving her first kiss. She needed to take it for what it had been—a new experience—and move on. Because she'd more than likely stared at Brennan Andrews so much that he thought her some forward lightskirt and had acted accordingly.

No matter the tingle she'd felt, that made more sense than anything else. He'd seen her desperation and misinterpreted it. If he mentioned it again, she would simply have to set him straight. What was the alternative, after all? That the first stranger on whom she'd set eyes in Scotland . . . fancied her? And he just happened to be handsome and clever and well-read?

If she read it in a book, she wouldn't have believed it. In actuality, it made even less sense, and that was that. Another silly daydream, where she'd managed to make a man believe her to be forward because she had no idea how to converse with anyone. She had actual troubles to decipher. She didn't need to add imaginary ones into the mix.

"Do you mean to stay on as Lady Aldriss's companion?" Temperance asked on the tail of that thought.

Jane shook herself out of her foggy thoughts. "Why? Have you heard something?"

"I heard that the countess has offered you a permanent position."

Oh. All the MacTaggerts likely knew about it, then. That she had to decide which road her life would take. For them, of course, it was a momentary, idle curiosity. Her presence or absence wouldn't affect them, with the possible exception of Amy, for more than a moment. "Lady Aldriss is very kind," Jane answered carefully. "And I do adore the family. I just . . . She has a great many friends and social engagements, and I'm hopeless at that sort of thing. Aside from that, if Lord Aldriss and she do reconcile as they seem to be doing, she won't have much need of me."

"But do you wish to remain in her employ?"

"I didn't precisely answer that, did I?" Jane grimaced. "I will never find better employment anywhere, but . . ." Sighing, she shrugged. "I don't know. It's like you and Juliet, I suppose. Do I leave before I become ridiculous?"

"You are not ridiculous. And my future has also taken some turns lately that I never expected." The toast of London smiled at her. "I suppose we follow where the road leads."

Jane rather liked that; taking things as they came was much less stressful than attempting to figure out catastrophes and exultations in advance. "And wear sturdy shoes," she seconded.

Lord Glendarril rode into the Aldriss Park stable yard just as they stepped down from the coach, and Temperance greeted him with a warm smile and the book Brennan had given her. "He said you'd asked for it," she explained.

"Why the devil would I want a book about marble floors?" Coll asked, opening the book and glaring at it. "Sometimes I reckon my cousin's spent too much time alone."

"You can ask him tomorrow," Lady Glendarril returned, wrapping her hand around his muscular forearm. "You should see the exterior drawings he showed me. Coll, it's . . . more than I ever dreamed of."

"Good. More than ye ever dreamed of is precisely what I want to give ye, Temperance." Twining his fingers with hers, he leaned down and kissed his bride.

Abruptly feeling distinctly unwanted, Jane backed away and went into the house. Everywhere she turned, first at Oswell House and now at Aldriss Park, people were kissing and blushing and flirting, deep in the rapture of true love. Even the earl and countess, who'd been apart and feuding for seventeen years, had spent the last six months more together than apart. This holiday to the Continent was the logical next step in their reconciliation, as inconvenient as the timing was for her.

All that aside, perhaps that was why she'd had such romantic thoughts where Brennan Andrews was concerned; she was surrounded by the bloom of new love. It made sense that such nonsense should be on her mind.

Returning to her room, she retrieved Brennan's book and opened it to the first page again. Now that she knew he'd written it, she could hear his voice telling the tales of how various castles and forts had come to be and of the people who had inhabited them.

An entire afternoon to herself, and all she wanted to do was sit and read. Someone more adventurous would no doubt be sledding down the hill behind the house or attempting to skate on the ice along the shore of the loch where the water had frozen. To her, though, a warm fire and a good book was practically perfection. A few weeks ago, she would have called it precisely perfection. Now, though, she felt a bit . . . upended. As if she had gone sledding and had ended up with her head buried in a snowbank.

A knock sounded at her door, and she jumped. "Come in!" she called, starting to sit on her book before she remembered that she'd been given permission to do as she pleased.

Her cousin pushed open the door and walked into the room. "I'm going down to the village to visit the jeweler's," Amy said, shutting the door behind her. "I wanted to find something Niall might like for Hogmanay. I thought you might want to get some fresh air."

"I'm fine, really," Jane answered, "though if you want the company, of course I'll join you."

"I don't wish you to do me a favor or feel obligated, Jane. I just . . . Do you want to go?"

Jane put a smile on her face. "I really am quite happy sitting here, Amy. I'm employed, I have access to a fine library, and no one sneers at me. They may feel some pity or something, but I can't do anything about that."

"No one pities you, dear. We only want you to be happy."

Carefully she set aside her book. "It seems to me that your idea of me being happy is for me to be someone else."

"No, that's not—"

"Isn't it? I'm not someone who likes crowds or going shopping, or traveling to faraway places in the company of people who would rather be alone. You know that."

Her cousin sighed, sitting on the edge of the bed with a swish of her green skirts. "Yes, I know. And I know you consider kindness to be charity. You're leaving us then, aren't you?"

It was certainly beginning to seem that way. "I haven't decided anything yet," she said aloud. "But please don't worry about me. I am fine. Truly. And you have a baby to prepare for, not to mention the fawning over you're already receiving from your husband."

That made Amy grin. "He is very good at spoiling me." She stood again. "Very well. Eloise has already agreed to accompany me, so your presence isn't required. It was only desired." Amy reached down to squeeze Jane's hand before she waltzed back out the door.

Jane had barely found the page on which she'd ended when another knock sounded. "Come in."

This time a footman stood in the doorway. "I'm to tell ye that Brennan Andrews is in the foyer and asks if ye'd come have a word with him."

Jane stood up so quickly from her chair that she nearly sent it over backward. "Certainly," she managed, setting aside the book and just barely resisting the urge to look at her reflection in her dressing mirror. He'd seen her this morning, for heaven's sake, and she wasn't some jewel that needed to be constantly polished.

With the footman leading the way, she kept to a civilized walk down the hallway and descended the stairs. Her heart thumped like a racketing drum, but she did her best to ignore that. Then she spied Brennan, his gaze on a note in his hands, and her heart stopped beating altogether for what felt like a solid minute. In his dark brown coat, a plaid scarf that matched his kilt around his neck and down one shoulder, and heavy boots on his feet, he looked simply delectable.

There were no two ways about it. Whatever he thought of her staring and stammering, she liked him. Very much. And she wanted more kisses, more private conversations, more . . . everything. Oh, this was all going to be such a disaster, and even knowing that she still walked up to him with a smile on her face. "Good afternoon, Brennan."

Chapter Five

Brennan faced her and then forgot what he'd been about to say, which was idiotic, because he'd been rehearsing for an hour. "Jane."

"Did I leave something behind when Lady Glendarril and I called on you?"

Well, that was a better excuse than the one he'd made up. "Aye." Trying to stifle a scowl, he dug into his pockets, finding only some coins and some folded notes. He pulled out one of the papers. "The notes ye took for the viscountess," he decided, handing the page to her.

Jane looked down at it, her attractive mouth twitching. "Ah, yes. Thank you."

While Pogan stood to one side looking increasingly curious, Brennan shifted. "Would ye care to come see the village with me? Unless ye've been down there already. Or ye have someaught to see to."

Saint Andrew and the heavenly choir. He'd known how to be bold and flirtatious and romantic once; he'd found a wife, after all, and a lovely, lively one, at that. But he hadn't felt this . . . tightness in his chest for seven years, and he hadn't had to be charming for better than eleven. If he'd described himself today, "bold" wasn't a word he would use, any longer. "Cautious" fit him better. Or "wary." And perhaps a wee bit broken.

"It was just a thought," he went on, reaching behind him for the front door. "I'll be back here for dinner tomorrow, so ye dunnae—"

"Will you give me a moment to fetch a wrap?" she interrupted, already turning up the stairs.

"Aye. Of course."

Well. She hadn't laughed at him, anyway. Brennan took a quick breath. For God's sake, he was a bloody Highlander. He saw something he wanted, and he took it. That would likely send her fleeing in terror, though, so mayhap patience and a light touch would serve him better. It suited him better, these days.

"Temperance said she liked yer drawings," Coll drawled from down the hallway.

"Aye? Nae one perfect one, but I think with all three I may have found enough of what she wants to go forward."

"When will ye have the final drawing?"

"I'll have it to ye by Hogmanay. We cannae begin building until spring, so dunnae be in such a damned hurry, giant." Aside from that, he hadn't done a thing but half tear apart his own library and sketch Jane for the third time since she and the viscountess had left his house.

"If we're nae in a damned hurry, what are ye doing here already?"

"I thought Miss Bansil would like a walk through the village without having to worry over having everyone buzzing about like bees at seeing the MacTaggert brides."

His cousin nodded. "She's a shy one, Jane is. But I dunnae expect ye'll have any more luck than the lasses in convincing her to leave the house, so—"

"I'm ready," Jane said, trotting down the stairs again.

She'd donned a heavy blue coat that looked too big for her, but at least it would keep her warm. These ladies from England didn't seem to like the Scottish winter very much. Uncle Angus had said on at least a thousand occasions that Sassenach lasses were more delicate than hothouse flowers, but the ones the MacTaggert brothers had found seemed fairly capable.

"Do ye fancy a walk, or should I have Gavin bring the coach around?"

"I think a walk would be splendid," she returned, pulling on her bonnet and tying the blue ribbon beneath her chin with swift, confident fingers.

Ignoring Coll's skeptical look, Brennan pulled his own gloves back on and offered Jane his arm. When she gripped his coat sleeve, he was certain he could feel her warmth running all the way from his wrist and down his spine.

They set out from the house, descending the hill and keeping to one side of the hard, icy road. She'd worn her walking shoes, but he kept her arm pinned against his side in case she lost her footing. "Is there a particular place ye wish to see, or will ye let me give ye a tour?"

"Give me your tour, if you please," she returned promptly. "I wouldn't know where to begin."

"Actually," he said, turning his head to view her with his good eye, "I was wondering if I needed to apologize to ye."

The cold-touch pink of her cheeks deepened to red. "For kissing me, you mean? Heavens, no. I should apologize to you. I . . . You're a handsome man, and I'm afraid I kept staring at you. I'm just . . . I'm not very polished, and so—"

"I'm nae so polished, myself," he cut in, the meaning of her words just beginning to sink in. She liked him, and she thought she'd been what, too forward? "I should have asked yer permission before I kissed ye. If ye dunnae want me doing it again, tell me so and I'll do my utmost, though I cannae guarantee that I'll keep from staring right back at ye."

She stumbled a little, and he gripped her tighter until she found her feet again. "I don't understand," she muttered.

"What dunnae ye understand, lass? Ye've a wit to ye, and the prettiest brown eyes, and I wanted to kiss ye. I should've asked ye first, but I didnae want Lady Glendarril thinking either of us was being improper, so I risked it."

"You didn't think I was acting like a hoyden?"

He'd seen nuns who acted less reserved than she did. "Nae. Jane, ye're a fine, fair lass. When I saw ye in the library at Aldriss, ye caught my attention in a way nae other lass has caught it in . . . years. I'd like to know if that doesnae sit well with ye."

They walked at least half a mile in silence. Coll had called her shy, and Brennan had certainly seen evidence of that, himself, but he hoped she could muster something to say. He couldn't—and he wouldn't—continue his pursuit if it was one-sided.

"Lady Glendarril has asked me to travel with her and Lord Glendarril to the Continent right after Hogmanay," she said abruptly, her words fogging the air. "If I don't wish to go, then she's offered to find me employment elsewhere."

For a moment he felt like he'd been punched in the chest. "Ye're nae even to stay the winter, then?" For God's sake, how could he figure this—her—out if she was to leave in less than a fortnight?

"I suppose not. It . . . I could remain in the countess's employ, of course, but everyone, including me, knows she doesn't need me here. I detest not being necessary." She shook herself. "But that's not why we're here, is it? You're showing me the village."

"Aye." If she left the MacTaggerts, he'd never see her

again. He knew that for a certainty. And that didn't sit well
with him. At all. "Aye," he repeated. "Most visitors, nae
that we have that many," he forced himself to continue, as
they crossed a short bridge into the village proper, "come
into Pethiloch this way, over the bridge. An old Laird Aldriss had it built because in the spring the water's just deep
enough to wet a lass's skirts when she's sitting in a wagon
to drive across the stream and his lady didnae like walking
about with wet hems."

"Does the stream have a name?"

She didn't want to speak about her employment, clearly,
but neither had she responded to his declaration that he liked
her. A fairly weak declaration it was, he supposed, but then
he'd only known her for three days. "Aye. The *Duilich Sruth*.
It means 'annoying stream.'"

Her mouth quirked. "You're bamming me."

"I amnae. That's what the lady called it, and the name
stuck. But as I said, most visitors come this way, which is why
the stable's on one side of the street, and the Round Cow tavern is on the other. A place to put yer animal, and a place for
a cheap mug and some warmth."

"It's pretty. Pithiloch is, I mean."

"Aye. It's been well kept-up, mostly thanks to Laird Aldriss and his generous funds." When she lifted an eyebrow,
he nodded. "And aye, everyone about kens where the money
truly comes from, though the idea of being beholden to an
Englishwoman doesnae sit well with most of 'em. We all pretend we dunnae know that Lady Aldriss funds everything."

"Is that why she claims to be disliked here?"

"Partly. Mostly it's because she left the Highlands."

"She's said she found it lonely."

Brennan nodded, still somewhat surprised at how very
easy it was to chat with Jane Bansil, even if she seldom spoke
about what she might truly be thinking. "Uncle Angus's idea

of entertaining is to go down to the Round Cow and buy a round of drinks. He's nae one for proper soirees or dinners."

"And for Lady Aldriss, proper soirees and dinners are some of her favorite things in the world."

She shuddered as she spoke. "Ye're nae fond of such things, I take it?" he asked.

"I never know what to say, and standing about alone while everyone else is chatting is . . . humiliating."

"Ye just need to find someone who'll stand there with ye," he returned. "This is the bakery. Mrs. Wass makes a fine Tain cheddar bread that'll make yer peepers roll back in yer head, and Mr. Wass makes shortbread biscuits that ye'll dream about after but one taste."

Pushing open the door, he stepped aside to let her enter the bakery. She stopped in the middle of the entry, one hand on the door. "It sits well with me," she said in a rush, and walked forward again.

Heat stirred deep in his chest. "What sits well with ye?" he asked slowly, moving around in front of her to keep her from retreating farther. "Ye tell me. I want to hear the words."

Her bosom rose and fell with her quick succession of breaths, but he wasn't going to relent. This was important. Damned important. He'd moved beyond the age of fooling about, but if this was simply her first taste of flirtation and she had no intention of allowing anything more than that, he needed to know.

"Oh dear," she muttered almost soundlessly. "You liking me sits well with me. And I enjoyed the kisses. I don't know what it all means, but I liked it. I like it."

"I'm nae certain what it all means, either," he returned in the same tone, "but I like it, as well."

Perhaps that wasn't entirely true, because while he did have an idea what he wanted, at the same time he'd become . . . not quite comfortable with his life, but accustomed to it.

Before he risked that and risked himself, he wanted to know her better.

"What do we do, then?" she asked, her mind clearly traveling along the same road as his.

"First," he said, pulling out a chair from one of the quartet of small tables at the front of the bakery and motioning her to sit, "we have a bit of Tain cheddar bread and a hot cider. And then we chat."

Whether it was the comfortable, quiet setting or the dash of whisky Mr. Wass always added to the cider "for flavor," over the next hour Brennan and Jane ate nearly an entire loaf of bread and he learned all about her life before she'd come to be in the employ of Lady Aldriss. For God's sake, the lass had never had an easy moment. And while her cousin Amy had been kind enough to her, the new Mrs. Niall MacTaggert had also been too young for most of their acquaintance to do anything about improving Jane's situation.

"Ye stood up to Niall and made him alter his plans," he said aloud, taking another swallow of cider. "That's nae an easy thing, Jane."

"I don't want to sound overly romantic or sentimental," she returned, "but he and Amy were so perfect for each other that the way he kept trying to take such careful steps not to upset her began to annoy me, honestly. I mean, if you're going to be in love, then *be in love*."

Brennan sliced off another piece of bread and handed it to her. "Aye. There comes a time when everyone around ye can see what's afoot, and if ye cannae, then it's up to someone else to set ye straight. Or at least give ye a kick in the arse."

Her quick grin flashed. "I knew as soon as I opened my mouth that my aunt would sack me, but even if Lady Aldriss hadn't offered me a roof and a bed beneath it, telling Amy to make a blasted decision still would have been worth it."

Deliberately he brushed her fingers as she reached for the butter. "Have ye nae been in love yerself, then, Jane?"

Color tinged her cheeks again. "No. I mean I've seen a man or two I thought handsome, but by now I'm practically an antique."

"I dunnae know about that. Yer mouth is soft and sweet enough."

"Brennan, please." She ducked her head as if trying to hide.

"Should I stop? Does that embarrass ye?"

"I'm not embarrassed," she retorted, lifting her chin again. "I don't like to be teased."

He leaned closer across the table, pushing aside the remains of the bread. "I am nae teasing ye, Jane Bansil. Ye heat me up inside, in a way I've nae felt for some time. I also ken that I'm a novelty to ye. I cannae begin to guess how many of the Sassenach lads must be blind nae to have seen ye, but I'm here now, and *I* see ye." Slowly he took her fingers in his. "I like what I see. I dunnae want ye going back to London to sit with some other wealthy lass."

Keeping his gaze, she picked up her cider and drained it. "I'm sorry," she rasped, "but that doesn't make any sense. I'm . . . dull."

How many people had told her that during her life? he wondered. Enough to make her believe it, clearly. "We cannae all be the sort who kidnaps a lass and sweeps her off to Gretna Green, I reckon. That's a sweet fairy tale, but nae all gestures need to be so grand." He took her hand again, ignoring the faint cluck of interest from Mrs. Wass at the back of the shop. "Ye're nae dull. Ye're cautious. As am I."

"Can a person be so cautious she misses her chance to be in a fairy tale?" she asked after a moment, the sadness that made him want to wrap her in his arms touching her eyes again.

"Nae. I've nae ever heard of such a thing." Brennan smiled. "I'll tell ye what. Ye've seen the MacTaggert dinners. Every soul sits wherever they choose. I'll plant myself somewhere in the middle tomorrow night. Ye come sit beside me, Jane. That's precisely how bold ye need to be."

Perhaps it was his own pride talking, but he wanted her to approach him. He wanted to know that he hadn't simply found a woman who didn't know about his past and therefore looked at him with more interest than pity, and that he was in the process of falling for her for no other damned reason than that. And he needed to know soon, because unlike his cousins, he couldn't afford to hie down to London for weeks and weeks in order to woo a lass who was aiming for nothing but a quiet, uncomplicated life.

Now, though, she would likely fret for the next day and a half over whether she had enough courage to sit beside him or not. Brennan pushed back his chair. He didn't mean to torture her, for God's sake. "I've still a good half the village to show ye. Do ye feel fortified enough to venture out in the cold with me again?"

"Yes. I actually feel quite warm." Standing, she took his proffered arm, and they stepped back outside into the cold Highlands winter.

Things like this simply didn't happen to women like her. That sentence kept beating about in her skull, bashing against the secret thoughts that perhaps Brennan Andrews truly did like her enough to wish to . . . court her, and that "Jane Andrews" had a rather nice ring to it.

That was indulging in daydreams again, though, and she certainly knew better than to do that. Especially when she had a decision about her employment to make, and very soon. At the same time, there they were, the two of them, currently walking past a small dress shop with frost on the windows and snow plopped artistically atop the sign reading: MILLY'S FINERY FOR LASSES.

"Is this cold for the Highlands?" she asked, mainly because she felt like she'd been silent for hours.

"It's a bit balmy today, actually," Brennan returned. "In late January the true cold comes. Some of us even put aside our kilts for trousers then."

"So, it gets too cold for even a Scotsman's knees," she quipped, waiting for him to grin and then unable to keep her own mouth from curving in response. He appreciated her humor, and that all by itself was rather intoxicating.

"That it does. I meant to ask ye, are ye going to join the rest of the family at church on Christmas Day?"

"I expect I will. It still seems odd, to not have the family opening gifts or singing carols."

"Just wait another week. We make up for it then." He pointed out yet another tavern, then continued up the road toward the small dock where a handful of fishing boats had been tied. "Well, that's near the end of Pethiloch. What do ye think of our village?"

"It's pretty. And everyone has seemed very friendly," she offered, doubly grateful that it had been him showing her about alone rather than with one of the MacTaggert brides. They'd bypassed going into the jewelry store simply because of the crowd standing about there, all of them talking about how fine it was to see young Eloise back where she belonged, and how lovely Amy was and whether she'd give Niall a strong Highlands son.

"We have a lending library as well, or that's what my house has become, anyway."

"That's good. I had you figured for the village scholar."

Turning away, his profile folded into a brief grimace before he faced her again. *Oh dear.* She'd missed something important—or, worse, insulted him—and now he was probably wondering how in the world he could escape her company without offending her.

"I have a few books I've brought with me that I could give for your collection," she added. "I'd be happy to share them with other readers."

"That's very generous of ye. Thank ye."

They continued along the wooden dock, toward the open loch beyond. A handful of children scrambled about on the ice near the shore, their excited shrieking both at odds with and complementary to the picturesque scene around them.

"What I mean to say is, do ye like it here?" Brennan burst out. "Is it a place ye'd nae mind seeing fairly often, or will these few weeks be enough to give ye yer fill of the Highlands? Could ye leave and nae look back and be satisfied?"

Good heavens. He wanted to know if she would mind *living* there. If she would be willing to tolerate weather cold enough to drive a Scotsman to wear trousers. Most important, he wanted to know if she wished to live there *with him*. A fourth choice. One she'd never expected and had no idea how to react to.

Her knees felt abruptly wobbly, and she grabbed onto a post with her free hand. It wasn't a request for her hand in marriage, but she didn't think she was too far off in believing it to be the lead-up to one. *Her.*

"Whoa. Steady, lass," he said, shifting to cup a hand beneath her elbow. "I've kept ye out in this weather for too long. Let me see ye home." He waved a hand at a passing cart, and the hay-laden wagon rolled to a stop. "Sòlas! Give us a ride up to Aldriss, will ye?"

"Aye, Brennan," the driver replied, tipping his cap as they reached the near wheel. "It's warmer behind the hay than up here."

"Thank ye." They moved around to the rear of the cart,

and then Brennan slid his hands around her waist and lifted her onto the back end.

It made her breathless and he released her far too quickly, but she preferred that he think her chilled rather than cowardly. Aside from that, when he hopped up beside her Brennan put an arm around her shoulders and tucked her up against his side. Oh, this—*this*—was something to which she could become accustomed. The fact that they had a logical reason for her to be in his arms didn't hurt, either.

"I'm sorry, lass," he murmured as they bumped along the road. "I wanted to spend the afternoon with ye. I didnae think how cold it must be for ye. Och, I'm an idiot."

"No, you're not. Don't even think such a thing." That came out more forcefully than she meant, so Jane shivered a little for good measure. "I had fun today. And I enjoyed the company."

"As did I." He paused. "If I've overset ye, then I apologize. If . . . Well, perhaps we'd best keep to a walk. Nae sense rushing into anything. I dunnae like the idea of ye leaving my life, is all. That's for me to manage, I suppose. Ye dunnae need another burden."

That last bit stopped her heart. She knew perfectly well what he meant—that he'd begun to realize she was far too timid and reserved, and that he might have made a mistake with his initial attraction.

She *was* timid. She *was* reserved. As they reached the front drive of Aldriss Park, she allowed him to help her down from the wagon and walk her to the door, and then she fled inside, up the stairs, and into her bedchamber. Slamming the door felt a bit satisfying, but it didn't solve the true problem—which seemed to be her.

Brennan Andrews liked her. She hadn't gone out of her way to dress provocatively or flirt outrageously. In fact, she'd done nothing but be herself, and he liked her for it. Taken by itself, that didn't sound so terrible.

She liked him, as well. She liked that he was thoughtful and had an understated sense of humor, that his office had stacks of books and papers strewn across every surface, that he spoke to her like someone his equal. He wasn't some idle, rich aristocrat, and he wasn't some larger-than-life heroic, brawny Highlander who flung villains into the loch or rescued kittens from burning buildings. He was a man. A man who'd been hurt, physically and emotionally, and who stood tall despite that.

Jane crossed the room, put her hands on her hips, and glared at her reflection in the dressing mirror. Rail straight, black hair pulled tight with not a strand out of place, a simple, high-necked gown with long sleeves, and not a bit of makeup on her face. That was indeed her. But at the same time, it wasn't entirely accurate, any longer. She felt warmer inside, and perhaps an inch bolder. And more than anything else, she felt like she was getting in her own way.

Did she want to remain Lady Aldriss's unneeded companion? Did she wish to sit and knit or embroider and chat about nothing in particular with some woman who paid her, go to dress fittings and evenings at the theater and soirees and dinners because a lady shouldn't attend such things alone? Be a . . . a warm body who could help someone else fulfill her obligations to Society?

It would be easier, certainly. All she had to do was nothing more than she already did on a daily basis. She'd already demonstrated to the one man who'd ever shown an interest in her that she was cow-hearted, and as a result he'd already begun to back away. She could decline to sit beside him at Christmas Eve dinner and finish this without having to utter a word. Nothing would change. Ever. Only the setting. Not the circumstances.

Jane turned her back on herself. She wasn't very good company, after all. As she caught sight of her small writing desk, though, she walked over to it and opened the lid. Inside lay the sketch Brennan had made for her of her perfect library. Picking it up, she examined it again. Shelves and shelves of books, sliding ladders to enable her to reach the higher stacks, comfortable chairs beneath the window . . . and there to one side, half hidden by a globe and a flower vase, a man's legs.

She looked closer. The legs had boots on and were crossed at the ankles. Someone else sitting in her perfect library. Bare knees, and the edge of a kilt. *Him.* Brennan had put himself in her library, presumably sitting in another comfortable chair and reading.

Jane took a quick breath. This vision wasn't so very different from her perfect future. He'd only added one thing. An important thing. And she liked seeing it that way. The only hitch was that it would take courage on her part to make it happen. To leave behind everything she knew and step into the unknown. Did she have that much courage?

Chapter Six

Amy and Eloise hadn't yet returned from the village. That left Lady Aldriss, Lady Glendarril, and Miranda MacTaggert at Aldriss Park this afternoon. Three brilliant, vibrant women with whom Jane had almost nothing in common except for her sex.

Taking a breath, not quite certain which of them she least wanted to encounter first, Jane left her bedchamber and went wandering down the hallways, peeking into open doorways and still half trying to convince herself that if she didn't run across anyone that would be a sign that nothing was meant to change, after all.

"—not saying you're being cowardly," Miranda's voice came from the upstairs sitting room. "I'm only asking why the MacTaggerts were willing to defy the kilt ban and the bagpipe ban on more than one occasion—and that's according to your own tales—but declined to celebrate Christmas."

Jane leaned into the doorway. Miranda and Aden stood close by the fireplace, their attention on a painting of a very formidable and very long-bearded man who wore a kilt and had a deer carcass slung over one shoulder, a musket in his free hand.

"I cannae answer that," Aden returned. "I reckon we stopped celebrating it during Cromwell's initial ban, and then when the laws changed for everyone but Scotland we'd already gotten out of the habit of it."

"Christmas is too civilized, anyway," Lord Glendarril's voice took up, and Jane spied him sitting beside Temperance at the other end of the room. "Praying and cooing over a bairn. Hogmanay has whisky and fire to it. Now *that's* a celebration."

"The number of times you three have discussed fire and Hogmanay is beginning to concern me," Miranda stated, amusement in her voice. "The . . . Jane? Come in, my dear."

Blast it. Squaring her shoulders, Jane walked into the room. "Good afternoon," she said, giving a curtsy.

"Did you need something?" Miranda pursued with her easy smile. "Not that you have to need something. I—Lady Aldriss said you had the day to yourself, is all. And now I sound like a lunatic. May I offer you a cup of tea?"

She could say yes. Or she could claim to be looking for the countess. It wasn't too late to change her mind. Jane put her hands behind her back, clenching them hard together. "I was wondering if someone might have a gown I could borrow for Christmas Eve dinner. Something pretty. Prettier than what I generally wear, I mean."

The four of them stared at her, while she wished she could sink into the floor. It was just a request for a gown, for heaven's sake, but even she couldn't remember the last time she'd voiced the urge to wear something pretty.

"Of course we can assist you," Temperance put in belatedly. "Is there any reason in particular you . . . No, never mind. I am in no position to question anyone's motives."

"I'd like to know," Coll said over that, and his new wife punched him in the chest. "Damn it, woman."

"Aden and Coll need to go play billiards or axe throwing right now, as it happens," Miranda took up, squeezing her husband's hand and then shoving him toward the door.

"Well, I vote for axe throwing." Aden cocked his head at his older brother, and the two men skirted past Jane and out to the hallway beyond.

Moving swiftly, Temperance shut the door behind them and locked it. "Now. Tell us how you wish to appear," she said, wrapping her hands around Jane's left arm and pulling her toward the couch.

"Just . . . pretty. Less plain," Jane stumbled, her cheeks heating. Both of these ladies were younger than she was, but it was at moments like this, when she realized how much experience she lacked in certain areas, that she felt like a very silly child.

"Does this have anything to do with Mr. Andrews?" Lady Glendarril asked, sitting and pulling Jane down beside her.

Oh, heavens. They knew? "I—Who?"

"Oh, please. I was there this morning, you know."

Miranda sat on Jane's other side. "Brennan Andrews? Aden's cousin? Oh, tell me, Persie. What happened this morning?"

"Nothing, except the two of them kept gazing at each other and forgetting to speak. There were a few moments I thought I should excuse myself so they could stare uninterrupted."

"That is not true!" Jane burst out. "I was sitting behind you, anyway, so you couldn't have seen me staring at him."

"Ha! You *were* staring, then. I thought so, and he certainly wasn't spending his time looking at me. It was actually rather disconcerting; I'm accustomed to men staring at me, you know."

Yes, that sort of thing did happen to famous actresses, Jane imagined, and Temperance, back when she'd been Persephone Jones, had been among the most famous in England. "He wasn't staring, either," she said anyway.

"If you say so. But it is about him, yes?"

"It's Christmas Eve. I'd like to look nice for it."

Beside her, Miranda sighed. "Of course. And there needn't be anything more to it than that."

If she'd answered any other way, Jane wouldn't have said anything more. But these MacTaggerts, born or married to Highlanders, were kind people, and not one of them had ever given her the impression that her presence was less than welcome among them.

"Thank you," she said aloud. "And Brennan Andrews is a very fine-looking man."

"I knew it!" Temperance whispered gleefully, squeezing Jane's arm. "With everyone to whom we've tried to introduce you over the past months, you mean to say it's a Highlander who's caught your attention?"

"I don't . . . Yes, he has caught my attention. I don't know whether I've caught his—though he says I have—or whether he simply feels sympathy for a bookish woman past her prime."

"You are not past anything," Miranda stated.

"Come with us," Temperance took up. "I have some fabulous gowns, and my Flora had me looking splendid for years. We'll have you looking like a queen, Jane. It won't be sympathy he's feeling toward you."

A flutter of nerves ran down Jane's hands. "A duchess would be acceptable," she said, allowing the unsettled smile she felt to appear on her face. "I don't wish to kill him, after all."

Miranda laughed. "Well. Nothing less than a duchess, then. Come, come!"

Brennan shed his coat as he entered Aldriss Park, shaking the light fall of snow off his shoulders and stomping the white stuff off his shoes. During the years when there had been no lasses at the manor house, Christmas Eve had been like any other winter night. This was the first time in years that he could recall the day, the evening, feeling special. And looking special.

It might have been the holly bows draped over the mantels, or the artistic stacks of pomegranates on the tables scattered amid sugared cakes and biscuits, and the clove-addled oranges that had the house smelling, well, festive. Of course, it was the influence of the Sassenach lasses, and while strictly speaking it could see them all jailed, he rather approved.

Pogan, though, looked dour as he finished shaking out Brennan's coat and hung it over a peg in the foyer. "Look at all this daintiness," the butler muttered. "Lace and sentiment, and bound to make trouble for us all."

"If the law should come by, ye tell 'em that this is the Sassenachs celebrating a Sassenach holiday and the rest of us have nae part in it," Brennan suggested.

The butler brightened a little. "Aye, that'll do, I reckon. I dunnae mind it, truly, as long as they dunnae think we mean to bypass Hogmanay now."

"They wouldnae dare."

"I hope ye've the right of it, Mr. Andrews. The family's mostly gathered in the drawing room. I'll be opening the dining room doors in but a minute."

Grinning, Brennan nodded and made his way down the hall to the drawing room. However much things had changed over the past few months, he was glad to see his cousins back home. The estate needed their care and attention, and as well-liked as Laird Aldriss was, it was the three brothers who kept the land and its inhabitants—both human and animal—as well-maintained as they were.

Niall greeted him with a slap to the back as soon as he entered the room, and almost immediately he found himself in the middle of an argument over whether there was a difference between acknowledging a holiday and celebrating it. Father Gormal Taggert and old Mrs. Gilanders and her daughter Maeve had been invited as well, as was the Mac-Taggerts' habit for villagers who had no other family in the area. Aye, he was one of those as well, even if he hadn't been their nearest relative.

As he looked about, taking the glass of whisky someone offered him, he couldn't help noticing one absence in particular. He'd half thought Jane might decline to sit beside him tonight, that she might have taken the ensuing day to decide either that she didn't like him as much as he'd hoped or that going on as she had been with her life was simply easier.

Since he'd first spoken to her, he'd wondered if she was more relieved or more resigned that life had passed her by, and he might have just gotten his answer. It wasn't the one he'd wanted, but he hadn't asked much of her tonight. If she couldn't even screw up her courage enough to make an appearance, then he needed to know.

"What's amiss, Brennan?" his uncle Angus, Laird Aldriss, asked, putting a hand on his shoulder.

Brennan mentally shook himself. "Nae a thing. I'm just trying to get accustomed to seeing a bit of sparkle and elegance in the house."

The earl laughed. "Aye, it's odd, isnae? Ye should've seen Francesca's house in London—fresh flowers and lace on every tabletop. It was enough to make a lad shiver. But I have to say, it's nae unpleasant here."

"It isnae," Brennan agreed.

"I wanted to thank ye again for keeping an old man company while my boys were dragged down to London." Glancing past Brennan, Lord Aldriss cleared his throat. "If nae for yer attention, I'd nae have recovered from my deathbed, I'm certain."

Brennan turned around to see Lady Aldriss eyeing the two of them, one eyebrow lifted. "My lady," he said, bowing. "We've missed yer refined touch here."

"You were only sixteen years old when I last was here, yes?" she returned with a cool smile. "I doubt you appreciated my fine touch back then."

Snorting, he inclined his head. "Mayhap I didnae. But I did miss it after ye left. The house, as ye nae doubt saw when ye arrived, has gone a wee bit rough."

"I did see that." Tilting her head, she put a hand on his arm. "I'm sorry about your wife. I hope my sons and my husband gave you the support you needed, and I regret that I wasn't here to do so. Or even to meet her."

"That's kind of ye to say. Eithne did from time to time attempt to bring a bit of softness up here, outnumbered though she was."

"I'm glad to hear that. I shall see that her efforts weren't in vain."

"Thank ye, my lady."

"Aunt Francesca," she corrected.

"Aunt Francesca, then."

The double doors dividing the drawing room from the dining room swung open. "Dinner is served," Pogan announced, his chest puffed out, before he stepped to one side.

They'd put the two additional leaves into the long dining room table, extending it to its greatest length, and the size by which his family had grown over the past six months truly hit him. With the addition of cousin Eloise, even the number of MacTaggerts-by-blood had increased by one. The dining room felt full to bursting, even if he might have privately wished there had been one more person there.

Miranda MacTaggert sat beside him on one side and Lady Glendarril on the other. Brennan nodded, putting a smile on his face. Behind that, though, he felt as if he'd nearly touched the sun only to go outside, arm outstretched, and find it raining. He'd missed that damned feeling of breathlessness, of anticipation at the mere sight of someone, and now he'd lost it again.

Pogan made an odd sound from the doorway, and Brennan looked up. And his heart stopped beating.

She'd dressed in scarlet. A gown of deep red, silver beading about the bodice and the skirt, and silver lace at the half sleeves and the low-cut neckline, a black ribbon about her waist and emphasizing her slender figure. Jane's hair was upswept, not in a tight bun as usual, but with a cascade of soft waves interwoven with scarlet and silver ribbon flowing about her shoulders.

"Good . . . bloody God," Coll muttered from beyond Temperance.

Brennan stood. That was what one did when a lady entered the room, and Jane Bansil looked every inch a lady. A seductive, lovely, regal lady. With an almost comical abruptness, the rest of the men present followed his lead.

Her color high, her chin lifted a little, Jane swished gracefully around the table and came to a stop behind Miranda. "Might I trouble you to trade seats?" she asked, her voice not entirely steady.

"Certainly," Miranda said easily, rising and moving over to sit at the empty place on the far side of Aden. Her husband lifted an eyebrow at her, but she only gave him a level glance.

None of the lasses seemed to be surprised, Brennan re-alized. Even Lady Aldriss ignored the goings-on, simply gesturing for Pogan to bring out the first course from the kitchen. That meant several things, but when he turned his head to gaze at Jane he forgot what most of them were.

"Ye look like fire, lass," he said in a low voice, noting off-handedly that the conversation in the room hadn't quite re-turned to its previous cacophony.

"It's a bit much, I think," she returned in the same tone, "but I wanted to make a statement."

"That ye've done. I . . . I thought mayhap ye'd decided nae to join us tonight." A black strand of her hair strayed below one ear, and his fingers twitched as he imagined brushing it back into place.

"Half of me still doesn't quite trust that you could actu-ally be interested in me," Jane whispered, fiddling with one of the trio of forks in front of her. "And then I asked myself which would hurt more: not knowing if I might have missed finding something important, or finding something and then being wrong about it. I decided not knowing would be worse. So here I am."

He looked at her for a long moment. "Then we should figure out what we've found," he murmured. As far as he was concerned he already knew, but she'd taken a huge step toward him, and he had nothing against giving her a bit of time to come to the same realization. While he did everything in his power to convince her, of course, before her deadline came to leave the Highlands.

"I would like that, Brennan."

Lady Aldriss stood, a glass of wine in one hand. "I know it is illegal, but I should nevertheless like to wish everyone a happy Christmas," she said, lifting the glass.

"Happy Christmas," everyone echoed, lifting their own glasses.

He didn't even remember what he ate. It had been satisfying and tasted well enough, but every bit of sinew and bone in his body felt attuned to the woman seated beside him. She was no simpering debutante, no bairn of a lass without an idea about what tragedies life could bring with it; whether she'd ever been in love or not, she'd certainly experienced hardship and pain and loneliness. And he wanted to see to it that none of those things ever dared touch her again.

"Ye're staying in the green room, aye?" he asked as they finished what seemed like the meal's fiftieth course.

"I am. It has a lovely view of the loch."

"I recall." He leaned a breath closer, scenting the lavender in her hair. "I dunnae wish to frighten ye, lass, but I've a mind to visit ye in the green room tonight. What do ye say to that?"

Her fork clattered onto her plate. "I'm sorry," she said, retrieving it, her cheeks pinking again. "Too much wine, I think."

Eloise across the table chuckled. "I'm going to fall asleep sitting right here."

Jane took another bite, chewed, and swallowed. "Evidently I'm not as composed as I pretend," she muttered.

"Neither am I, Jane."

"Come call on me, then. I . . . Just promise me you're not playing about. I am too old to face what would follow being ruined."

"Ye and I are the same age, Jane, and I dunnae think it's so old. But I'm nae playing about. I am past wasting time. And I do mean to call on ye tonight."

He meant to call on her. In her bedchamber. The words batted around in Jane's mind for the rest of the evening. She was certain her generally reserved conversation was completely incomprehensible, though everyone made certain to at least walk by and compliment her appearance, because all she could think about was the man seated halfway across the drawing room.

She could admit to herself that she'd entertained carnal thoughts about him since they'd first met, and that she hadn't really done that before. Yes, in passing she'd thought so-and-so handsome or wondered what it would be like to be in a different so-and-so's arms for a night, but nothing as intense as this. And certainly nothing as likely to be realized as this.

"Jane, did it work?" Amy asked, sitting close beside her and capturing one of Jane's hands in both of hers. "Did you catch his attention?"

"It wasn't about that as much as it was about deciding, I suppose, who I want to be for the rest of my life," Jane returned. "And I would like to be someone who, on occasion, wears red."

"You look splendid in it," her cousin commented, glancing over at Brennan. "He likes you, then, does he?"

"Yes, I think he does. At any rate, he noticed me—which is something unusual in itself."

"Jane, you shouldn't say such things."

Jane smiled. "My dear cousin, I have spent much of my life trying to be noticed as little as possible. Surely you haven't noticed me well before now."

Amy chuckled at that. "There were times when I wished I had your talent for it. Especially where Mother was concerned." She lifted Jane's hand and kissed her palm. "You are to tell me if something goes amiss, or if you have any doubts or fears at all. I perhaps didn't appreciate you as much as I should have, but I do love you, Jane."

She couldn't remember the last time anyone had told her that. "Thank you, Amy. Brennan doesn't frighten me. He makes me . . ." Jane thought about it for a moment. "He makes me feel happy." Happy and extremely nervous about later that night, but happy nonetheless. Unless she did something stupid and put him off her completely.

"Happy is a very good thing."

Amy might be her junior by some fifteen years, but her cousin did have some knowledge that Jane simply didn't possess. Asking advice might be helpful, but she couldn't do it. If something went awry, if she ended up alone again, she didn't want *anyone* knowing just how far she'd gone in abandoning propriety. How far she'd gone in following her heart, of all things.

"Am I to assume you won't be joining Angus and me on the Continent?" Lady Aldriss murmured from behind her as Niall pulled Amy away.

"I—I am so grateful for the opportunity, my lady," Jane said, turning to face her employer. "You've been so very kind, and I—"

"When you first knocked on the door of Oswell House to inform me that Niall and Amy had eloped and that he'd offered you a roof over your head, I had some misgivings," the countess broke in. "A companion needs to be loyal above all else, after all."

"I understand. Th—"

"Then I realized that you were being loyal—to Amy. You did something that allowed her the greatest happiness, and you suffered for it without complaint. Beyond that, Jane, I enjoy your company. When you bother to speak, you are quite clever." The countess reached out and took her hand. "I did and do wish you to be happy. And I will still provide you a letter of recommendation, should you ever require one."

Jane took a deep breath. "I think—I hope—I have found a position where I am both welcome and necessary," she whispered. "Of course, I may also have completely misread the situation, and I will be knocking on your door come next week."

Francesca Oswell-MacTaggert smiled. "I watched Mac-Taggert men fall for their lasses all Season, my dear. I do recognize the look."

Well, that was heartening. Exceedingly so. Jane sent her soon-to-be-former employer a small smile in return. "If I may say so, my lady, I hope that your successful efforts on the be-half of your family also signify a hope for you, personally."

The countess's cheeks darkened just a little. "Just when I thought I was beyond being touched by fancy again, it appears I'm being delivered the lesson that one is never too old or too dignified for Cupid's arrows. And such things cannot and should not be ignored, Jane. By anyone."

With all of her heart, Jane hoped the countess was correct about that. She didn't make a habit of upending her life, and tonight would be the second time this year that she'd done so. She glanced in Brennan's direction, to find his one-eyed gaze on her. Just one fairy tale come true wasn't too much to ask, was it? Just this one.

Chapter Seven

The evening seemed to drag on for at least a month, until finally friends left the house and family began separating for the night. When Jane looked over at Brennan's chair again he was gone, though she had no idea when he'd left the room or whether he'd left the house entirely and meant to climb in through her window as Niall had done while pursuing Amy. Oh dear, they hadn't planned this very well. Perhaps she should leave her window unlatched, just in case.

As she bade Lady Aldriss good evening and offered to make certain the countess was awake by eight o'clock so she could attend the Christmas morning church service with her husband and the rest of the family, Jane scurried up the stairs to her bedchamber.

She closed her door, leaning back against it for a moment. So she was unemployed, now. Or she would be, when the countess and the earl left the Highlands without her. Even that, though, didn't unsettle her as much as the idea that Brennan would be calling on her. Since she had no idea from where he meant to make his appearance, she decided she'd best leave both the door and all the windows unlocked. After

she'd unlatched all three windows and made certain twice
that the door could still be opened from the hallway, she sat
in the chair by the fire.

"What do I do now?" she muttered. Presently she wore the
finest things she'd ever donned. Did she keep them on? Did
she put on her plain night rail and climb into bed? Did she
simply remove all her clothes and wait to be ravished? Oh,
perhaps she should have asked Amy some questions, after all.

Growling under her breath, she fidgeted for a moment
and then rose to check the windows again. Outside snow fell
silent and cold on the hillsides, with no sign of footprints below her window—or anywhere in her view.

"What are ye doing there?" Brennan asked quietly from
the doorway.

She whipped around as he slipped inside and shut the
door behind himself, turning the key in the lock. Her heart
skipped several beats and then began racing like she'd run
for miles.

"I thought . . . I thought you might be climbing in through
the window. Several of your cousins have been known to do
that."

He grinned. "I dunnae doubt it. *I*, however, prefer nae to
cling to stone walls out in the snow in the middle of the
night."

"That's very sensible of you."

Nodding, he strolled toward her. "I'm glad ye're still wearing that gown. I've been imagining peeling it off ye since I
saw ye in it."

Oh my. "I borrowed it from Temperance."

"I reckoned the other lasses knew someaught was afoot.
There was far too much smiling going on for any man to be
easy."

"I'm sorry. I shouldn't have said anything, but I didn't

want to wear the same gray dress I've worn for the past seven Christmases."

"Tell whoever ye wish to, Jane. I've nae a thing to hide." Reaching out, he took both her hands in his. Unlike hers, his fingers were warm and steady. "I cannae believe I've known ye for but a few days. I've had a lass or two cross my path in the last seven years, and nae a one of them gave me goose bumps. Ye do."

"I give you goose bumps?" It was likely a silly question, but what he said sounded so wonderful that she couldn't quite believe he was talking about her.

"Ye do." Tugging her a breath closer, he leaned his head down and kissed her.

Jane closed her eyes, the warmth of his mouth, his breath against her cheek, the faint taste of whisky, all mingling and stirring in her senses, thick enough she could almost touch them. But she *could* touch them, because she could touch *him*.

Slowly she ran her fingers up his forearms, then higher, until she could slide her arms around the back of his neck. With a low sound that made her shiver all the way down her spine, he deepened the kiss, teasing at her mouth until she opened to him, and their tongues tangled.

"I should tell you something," she managed, her voice ragged.

"Aye?"

"I've sacked myself from Lady Aldriss's employ."

His muscles tightened around her. "Ye mean to leave for London, then?"

Jane shook her head. "No. At the moment I seem to have no plans, whatsoever."

"Well now. That's a bonny thing, I reckon, lass." With a slow smile he put his hands around her waist and then slid them upward, brushing the outsides of her breasts, and she shivered again. If she'd ever dared dream about a man who might want her, the image of him would have been Brennan Andrews. Quiet, thoughtful, funny, kind, compassionate, handsome—and quite spectacular at kissing. She even liked that he wasn't quite perfect, because Lord knew she was far from perfection, herself. And there he stood, gazing at her with his one green eye, his arms close around her.

"I don't know what to do," she admitted, running her fingers along the scar below his eye patch. "And I don't want to do something wrong."

"I know what to do," he returned, "though it's been a while. And as long as ye dunnae laugh at me, I'll have nae complaints."

"So you say now. Just please tell me again that you're serious about this. About me."

"Jane," he murmured, his gaze holding hers, "I am serious about ye. Good God, lass, I've been thinking about nae but ye since I first saw ye. I like ye, a great deal. I want ye. If ye dunnae believe that, then just look at me."

With that he took a step back, gesturing at himself. Unable to stop herself, Jane looked down. The unmistakable jut at the front of his kilt—she knew what that was, what it meant. And it was because of her. A man couldn't pretend that.

"Turn around, Jane."

She did so, her breath catching as Brennan opened the buttons running partway down her back. "Please don't ruin it," she said, abruptly remembering what she was wearing. "I need to return it."

"It should be yers. Scarlet suits ye, lass."

When he'd unbuttoned the dress, she untied the ribbon beneath her breasts and pulled the gown off her shoulders. As a warm mouth kissed the nape of her neck and trailed slowly down her spine, her breath caught. This was not some imagining. He was real. He wanted her. And for heaven's sake, she wanted him.

Turning around again, Jane caught his mouth with hers, wrapping her hands into his coat to hold herself closer against him. Desire, need, arousal, flooded through her, unaccustomed but intoxicating.

Brennan tugged down the front of the gown, holding her away from him a little as he lowered his gaze to her exposed breasts. She was by no means voluptuous, but if that disappointed him she couldn't detect it. When he sent her a brief, wicked grin and then lowered his head to lick one of them, she gasped.

Then he closed his mouth over it, his tongue flicking across her nipple, and lightning shot down her spine. The warm damp between her legs, the delighted shivers running beneath her skin . . . *Good heavens.*

With him dividing his attention between her breasts and her mouth, he shrugged out of his coat, dropping it onto the floor beside them. Brennan pulled his shirt off over his head and let it fall from his fingers. "Touch me, Jane," he murmured, taking one of her hands and placing it on his chest. "I want to feel yer touch."

While he unbuckled his kilt, she sent her hands exploring him. He was lean and fit, hard muscles beneath soft, warm skin. Muscles that jumped as her fingers and her palm caressed him. A man—this man—reacting to her touch. It was a powerful, heady sensation.

Why he'd chosen her she didn't know, but it occurred to her that she'd never felt shy or awkward in his presence, either. It was as if they fit, somehow. As if they belonged together. "Brennan," she whispered, kissing him again, kissing his mouth and his jaw where a stubble of rough beard had begun.

His kilt landed atop the rest of his clothes. Jane couldn't

not look, so she lowered her gaze. Jutting, large, and unmistakable—a shiver of nervousness went through her again,
tangled as it was with a very large measure of unseemly
lust. "You do want me."

"As I've said, Jane." He cupped her face in his hands, holding her gaze with his. "And I mean for this to be the first
night. Nae the only night."

She nodded, dropping her own hands to the top of her gown
so she could wriggle out of it, being as careful as she could
with every nerve jangling. For a moment she felt very unco-
ordinated, until she caught Brennan gazing at her breasts,
his expression avid. *Well then.* Exaggerating the shift of her
hips and the roll of her shoulders, she shed the gorgeous
gown and left it in a scarlet puddle around her feet.

"Ye're stunning, lass," he muttered, and bent to sweep her
up in his arms.

Gasping again, she flung her arms around his neck. Just
having her hair not tied back in her proper bun this evening
had left her feeling a bit wanton. This, though—she couldn't
even put words to this feeling.

"I want you," she said unevenly as he laid her down on her
bed and moved over her.

By way of answer he shifted down her body, kissing, lick-
ing, caressing her as he went. So much attention he paid her,
almost worshipful. Could it be true that she was someone
for whom he'd searched? It made her seem, and feel, special.
Important.

But then his hands traveled up the insides of her thighs,
and she couldn't think of anything but how very naughty
she felt, and how very much she wanted more of this sensation. When he touched her . . . there, sliding a finger inside
her, she jumped, grabbing onto his shoulders and biting her
lip to keep from shrieking.

"Ye're wet for me, Jane," he muttered huskily.

"Is that a good thing?" she asked when she could speak again.

"Aye. Ye excite me, and I mean to have ye. If ye've changed yer mind, then, ye need to tell me. Now."

That "now" sounded very urgent, and very significant. But it didn't alarm her as much as it might have previously, because as far as she was concerned, she'd already made this decision, and any that went with it later on. "I was more worried that you would change *your* mind. I am feeling rather brave right now. But I am trusting you, as well." And she did trust him, in a way she hadn't ever trusted anyone. Ever. With but a few days of acquaintance between them, trust felt mad, but it also felt right.

"I've nae followed my heart for a good long time, either," he returned, making his way back up her body, pausing at her breasts and making her squirm with delight again. "Dunnae break it, Jane."

That hadn't quite occurred to her before, that he was giving her a great deal of his trust, as well. He'd lost his wife, and in seven years he hadn't found anyone else to share his life. Until her. "I won't," she whispered.

Kissing her deeply, he parted her legs with his knees, set his hands on either side of her shoulders, and canted his hips forward. The tight, hot slide of him entering her felt indescribable and so, so satisfying. "Ye've nae done this before, ye said," Brennan whispered, "so this next bit may hurt. I willnae hurt ye again. Ever. Ye have my word, Jane Bansil."

Digging her fingers into his shoulders, she nodded. He kissed her again, openmouthed, tongues tangling, as he slowly pushed deeper inside her. Sharp pain bit at her and she winced, squeezing her eyes closed but refusing to try to shut her legs. She wanted him there. She wanted all of this.

After a moment she realized he was staying very still, and she opened her eyes again. His right green eye met her gaze and held it, his expression the most intimate, intense one she'd ever seen. So much attention he paid, and all of it focused on her.

"I'm fine," she panted. "Don't stop now."

His quick grin pierced her heart. "As ye wish."

Slowly he pushed deeper, burying himself in her as she moaned beneath him at the sensation, and the weight of him across her hips. *Good God.* When he withdrew and then entered her again, she shivered from her spine to her toes.

His pace began to increase, and a delicious tightness spread through her. Everywhere he touched her felt alive and warm and aroused. When he groaned, everything let loose at once, sending her into shuddering, moaning ecstasy.

Brennan grunted something in Gaelic, moving into her hard and fast until he froze, shuddering. Panting, he lowered himself onto his elbows and rested his forehead against her shoulder. "Damnation, lass."

Jane couldn't speak. Instead, she swept her arms around him, torn between delighted laughter and tears. Her entire world had shifted in one evening, and it had happened in a rather magnificent way.

He turned them sideways, so they were lying face-to-face. "I meant to wait until Hogmanay to do this," he said, brushing a strand of hair from her eyes, "because I reckoned it would be spectacular with the bonfires and celebrating. But I have realized that ye and I, Jane, we arenae about bonfires and crowds. We're quiet folk, favoring books and a crackling fire in the hearth and mayhap a stroll through the village."

She didn't know quite what he was talking about, but the things he said sounded dreamily wonderful, especially on a Christmas Eve with silent snow falling outside. "That sounds perfect," she breathed, and he kissed her again.

"Aye, it does. I love that ye like to read, Jane. I love that ye're clever and funny. I love that ye shiver when I kiss ye.

I love the way ye look me in the eye when ye speak to me. I love nae that ye've had a hard life, but that it's made ye . . . strong."

"You're saying very nice things," she murmured.

"I'm nae finished. I love that when ye see a problem ye dunnae blurt out any nonsense, but ye look at it from all the sides and then figure out exactly what's needed. And I love that ye trust me."

Had she done all those things? Or was it that he simply liked—loved—who she naturally was? That was amazing. "Thank you, Brennan."

"I suppose," he went on, studying her face, "that if I love all the facets of ye, then the natural conclusion is that I love ye. I'm in love with ye. I ken it's only been a few days, but as I said, I'm nae fooling about. Having ye here has been like seeing spring's first sun."

"Brennan, I don't know how long a person is supposed to wait before they've decided they know someone else well enough, but I feel the same way. I love you. I never believed in love at first sight, but I love you."

"God's sake, Jane," he said quietly, running a finger down her cheek. "I'm nae a youngster looking to begin a life. I ken what I want, and who I want, and that is ye. Will ye marry me, Jane Bansil?"

The Jane of a few weeks ago might have closed her eyes, preferring to weigh such an important decision logically, without the temptation of a very handsome man lying well within arm's reach. She would have hesitated, weighing the advantages and disadvantages of such a union, and what it would mean to her future employment possibilities and the convenience of all the people around her.

This Jane didn't want to close her eyes, because she very much liked the man at whom she was looking. This Jane had learned a great deal about herself over the past few days.

And she liked this version of herself. And she liked where her life was leading her now. Very much. If it had taken an arrow or two from Cupid to send her in this direction, to send Brennan to her, then so be it.

"You've made me excited about my life again, you know. And hopeful, and happy. Yes, Brennan Andrews, I will marry you. I would marry you twice, if I could."

He chuckled, kissing her slow and deep. "I do love ye, lass. And I've changed my mind about Christmas. I reckon we'll be celebrating it from now on."

That made her laugh. "Don't let on that I've converted you; your cousins will begin calling you a Sassenach."

"They can try." Placing a kiss on her forehead, he rolled them again, so she lay atop him. The position made her feel breathless and powerful all at the same time. "I should tell ye, the minute ye left my house yesterday, I started pulling down the wall between my parlor and the wee library. I'm making ye a grand library, Jane, with space for every book ye'd ever want."

"You started it yesterday?" she asked, wiping at an unexpected tear.

"I couldnae imagine a life without ye in it. Happy Christmas, Jane, my heart."

Taking a breath, she lowered her head to kiss him softly on the mouth. "Happy Christmas, Brennan, my love."

Christmas at Dewberry Hollow

BY

AMELIA GREY

Chapter One

Who wanted a curmudgeon staying at their inn during Christmastide? Not Isabelle Reed. It was her favorite time of year. She preferred to celebrate with family, friends, and good cheer. Not guests. However, she agreed with her mother they couldn't deny the old duke's request when he'd written to say he was coming to spend a few days. The extra money would boost their rapidly dwindling finances.

The December day was bone-chilling cold and so were Isabelle's hands. Her fur-lined gloves had ceased to keep her fingers warm during her walk home. It was near sundown, but not a speck of sun had pierced the hazy gray sky. Nor had it for days. It wasn't usually so frigid or dreary this early in winter.

Shortly after she'd left the village and entered the woods, she'd seen deer tracks in the snow and followed them until, in the distance, she saw the buck leap into an evergreen thicket on the other side of the clearing. She had inched closer to the grove and for a moment thought she'd lost sight of it, but now watched the lower limbs of a cluster of spruce rustling.

Isabelle kept her heavy weapon by her side, ready to lift

it against her shoulder, steady it, and shoot. For now, she couldn't see clearly because of the dense growth of saplings and gnarled spindly underbrush beneath the larger trees. She didn't want to miss the one shot she'd have to bring down the animal.

So she waited.

Though her mother had never approved of Isabelle learning how to use the rifle, she would delightfully be happy to have the extra venison to serve while the duke and his men were lodging there. The duke had boarded with them when Isabelle was a little girl, but she didn't recall him, being only four years old. Too many guests had passed nights at The Inn at Dewberry Hollow for her to recall them all. Her mother remembered him as a most thoroughly commanding, obstinate, and difficult-to-please grump.

From what Isabelle had been told, the last time the eccentric peer stayed with them, the fusspot had come with an army of people to attend his every whim, including his own cook to oversee the kitchen. If he brought that many this time, it would be a lot of extra people to feed properly, and their reserves were already decidedly low.

"No matter," she whispered to herself, keeping her gaze solidly on the thicket.

Isabelle would see to it they managed until she could figure out what to do now that her mother's uncle had passed away and the new viscount had cut their allowance to a pittance. Her mother had written him a letter asking for it to be restored. Assuming that would do little good because the viscount was miffed at Isabelle for not having already come to London and snared a husband to take care of her, she went in a different direction.

Two afternoons a week she was teaching the Petersons' daughter how to read and write in exchange for eggs and milk every morning. Last week, Mrs. Miller asked if her three daughters could attend the classes, promising each would bring a fresh-baked pie to the inn every week. That would certainly help feed the duke and his staff. After Christmas, Isabelle could add more girls.

Right now her mother wouldn't consider the idea of raising the lodging price at the inn for their two boarders or even overnight travelers, but Isabelle would revisit that with her in the new year. They weren't squandering their money. It was just difficult maintaining her mother's high standards for how the inn should operate.

Neither would Isabelle allow a cranky duke to ruin the Season for her. Just the thought of Christmas, now a week away, lightened her heart. She had cut holly berries, mistletoe, and pinecones. With the help of their footman, she'd snipped bundles of every variety of greenery that grew in the hollow to decorate the inn. The fresh wintergreen fragrance of the drying limbs of pine, fir, and baskets of leaves would perfume the rooms with the crisp smell of the holidays for days to come. The cook kept the delicious scents of orange, cinnamon, and pastry bread wafting from the kitchen each day.

Isabelle and Mrs. Boothe had been spending time in the evenings making bows out of colorful satin ribbon and hanging them from mirrors, paintings, and doorways. Even Mr. Thimwinkle helped string red and green berries together to weave into the trim for her hair and some of her clothing. It was a joy to watch the two elderly boarders' excitement when she'd started filling the rooms with nature's bounty of winter gifts. After Isabelle had finished with all the decorations, there wasn't a more festive place in all of England.

Movement caught her eye. Isabelle tensed. Was the deer leaving? She still couldn't see more of the animal but was certain the thatch of grayish-brown fur was the large buck she'd seen earlier. There was no time to second-guess herself. She couldn't let him get any farther away. Even at this range, her accuracy was uncertain. Taking the chance, she quickly positioned her gun, sighted down the barrel, and gauged the animal's height by what little she could see of him. She followed the movement and pulled the trigger. The kick of the stock slammed against her shoulder with a jerk. She grunted as the loud crack of sound reverberated in her ears, chest, and around the hollow.

A second later she heard a man yell, "Take cover! I've been shot! Take cover!"

Isabelle felt as if her heart jumped to her throat. *No—impossible! Who would be in the woods so far off the road?*

Panic spiraling, and without thinking, she started running in the direction she'd fired. Her boots crunched hard on the frozen ground and skidded on icy patches of snow, but she'd never made it so fast across the wide clearing. Bitter wind swept her hood to the back of her shoulders. Needlelike leaves of the small pines and firs scratched her cheeks and tore at the back of her long braid. She entered the grove racing, refusing to allow fear to overtake her.

Sucking in one deep rapid breath after another, she spotted an older man sitting on the ground near a cluster of leafless bramble bushes holding one arm close to his chest. "Sweet Clementine," she whispered as she dropped down to the thin, bearded fellow and laid her carbine aside. Thick gray brows rose high above small brown eyes that blazed with shock and caution. She could see the bullet hole on his coat near the upper arm and shoulder. That he wasn't screaming in pain was a good sign she'd missed the bone. "Let me see how severely you're injured."

"Don't worry about me, miss," he said, looking all around and motioning for her to stay low. "Someone's shooting at us."

All she could think was she could have killed this man

as she reassured him with a, "No. We're safe. Don't worry about that."

Her hands were shaking and her fingers felt brittle, but she knew what needed to be done. Forcing herself to remain calm, she carefully started unbuttoning his greatcoat, wanting to see if the bullet had traveled somewhere into his chest, hip, or elsewhere.

"Can you lift your arm?" she asked.

Seeming disconcerted by her help, he moved it a little, and offered, "I'll be fine."

Fine? He wasn't fine. She'd shot him. Why hadn't she taken the time to be certain the movement was the deer she'd seen and not a person? Because it never crossed her mind anyone might be in the evergreen grove.

Paying the man's protests no mind, Isabelle gently opened the lapels of his greatcoat. That's when she heard the rumble of boots hitting the ground hard and fast.

More than one pair. An icy chill of dread quaked through her.

And then the shout, "Hornbolt! Where are you?"

This couldn't be good. Panic clutched her chest again. What could she possibly say to explain? She scolded herself for not making sure it was an animal in her sight.

"Over here, sir!" the man on the ground called, trying to brush her hands away. "It's all right now, miss. Mr. Gatestone's coming. He'll take care of everything."

Isabelle winced and her trembling fingers stilled for a moment. She knew that surname. Gatestone was the Duke of Notsgrove's family name. May the saints have mercy on her. The duke probably wouldn't. If he didn't have her arrested and sent to the nearest prison, her mother would most definitely insist she be more ladylike and never carry a weapon when she walked in the woods.

There was no time to worry about that. "He's not here yet,"

she told Mr. Hornbolt, ignoring his efforts to stop her from attending to him. "I'm not waiting. Be still and let me see how badly you're hurt."

Moments later a tall young man slid to his knees beside her. Their eyes met for a second or two with equal amounts of shock and dismay at the wounded man before them, and then for another, longer glance that she was certain neither of them had intended but couldn't avoid.

A tingle of something pleasurable raced through her. He was breathtakingly handsome. Without benefit of hat, and his cloak swept to the back of his broad shoulders, she could see he was powerfully built through the chest. His waist narrowed to flatteringly slim hips. Strength was evident in every part of his body. His windswept dark honey-blond hair fell attractively tossed across his forehead. The back length of his mane brushed the collar of his cloak as the ends fluttered in the piercing December wind.

"I'm sure it was a clean shot, Mr. Gatestone," Mr. Hornbolt said. "Only a little pain. I can see to it later."

"I'll have a look just the same," he assured the older man in a voice that meant he wasn't going to take no for an answer. He immediately started helping Isabelle take off the man's winter coat.

Mr. Gatestone's breathing was as deep and fast as her own. Familiar scents of campfire smoke and old saddle leather clung to the fine wool of his black riding cloak and swirled around her. An unexpected heat suddenly warmed her. Seeking its source and glancing down, she saw that the man's muscled thigh had come to rest firmly against hers.

A tremor shook her while a shiver of something wonderful spread throughout her chest and soared up her neck as she became overwhelmingly aware of him. How could she have felt his heat through the thick fabric of her worn cape and layers of clothing beneath it? She should scoot away. It was the proper thing to do, but she couldn't deny herself the unanticipated comfort of his touch. It didn't matter he seemed to have no awareness of their contact. Perhaps that was the reason she didn't move but shamelessly indulged and savored the warmth of feelings enveloping her.

Mr. Gatestone shoved the coat down Mr. Hornbolt's arm, but not with the gentleness Isabelle would have taken. Two other men suddenly arrived and quickly surrounded them, scanning the woods and keeping their muskets poised to shoot—a nonexistent threat.

The young man glanced their way. "Did you see anyone?"

"No, sir," one of the men answered.

Isabelle gave a final tug on the cuff of Mr. Hornbolt's coat and it fell away from his arm. Staring at the sleeve of his white shirt, she had to fight off a wave of dizziness. She thought to flee from the damage she'd inflicted. If she couldn't see it, perhaps it hadn't happened. Quickly quelling that irrational feeling, she leaned away from him, realizing she'd held out hope the bullet hadn't actually hit him until she saw the deep red stain of blood.

"You're right," Mr. Gatestone said to Mr. Hornbolt after examining his arm. "You're lucky it's only a flesh wound." He turned to Isabelle, met her gaze with his own, and asked, "Who's shooting at us?"

He had the most beautiful golden-brown eyes she'd ever seen. All she wanted to do was stare into them, lose herself in their depths, and be perfectly happy doing so, except she needed to say something. But what? Her breath seemed to freeze in her throat, choking out all sound. It was never easy to tell on oneself. And certainly not to such a handsome man for such a terrible offense.

An awkwardness she was unaccustomed to settled around her. Mr. Gatestone's brow creased as he waited for the answer.

"No one," she managed to whisper on a broken gulp as a gust of frosty wind stung across her cheeks and eyes. "You can tell your men to put down their weapons. I'm the one who shot Mr. Hornbolt."

"You?" A frown of suspicion pinched hard at the corners of his wide, attractive mouth. He shifted his wide shoulders and glanced at the short-barreled carbine lying beside her before his gaze focused on hers again.

"Not intentionally, of course," she hastened to say, a little more defensively than she'd intended as more guilt peppered her. "I thought he was a—Never mind about that right now." She caused this and *she* needed to fix it.

Isabelle shifted from her knees and settled on her rump. Taking a short knife from a sheath attached to the narrow leather belt she wore, she gathered her skirts to the tops of her boots and proceeded to proficiently cut a long, narrow strip from the hem of her white linen underdress.

"Here," she said, handing it over to Mr. Gatestone. "Tie up his arm with this and get him to the inn so his wound can be properly cleaned and sewed."

Mr. Gatestone's expression of disbelief hadn't changed. That's when she looked around and realized all the men had been watching her in stunned silence as she'd pulled her skirts above her ankles. A small portion of her wool stockings still showed as well as the bottom of her fine-flannel petticoat.

But for a good purpose, she reasoned. *Surely.*

He took the cloth without comment. Isabelle pushed her dress over her boots and returned the knife to its casing. She then rose and stepped away from them while Mr. Gatestone tied the bandage above the wound and helped Mr. Hornbolt to stand.

"Get him back to the others and take care of him," the young man said to his men as he helped Mr. Hornbolt shrug back into his heavy coat. "Explain to the duke this was a hunting accident and no cause for alarm. He'll assume it was a stray bullet. Let him. This isn't to be spoken of in any other way or again after this day. If I hear it has, you'll answer to me. Head on to the inn. I'll join you there."

"Wait," Isabelle said, stepping forward, regret accumulating more fully inside her. Taking a deep breath and holding her chin high, she attempted to keep her voice calm and offered, "Before you go, Mr. Hornbolt, I want you to know I shouldn't have been in a rush to get off the shot. I'm sorry."

"Don't worry, missy." He gave her a twitch of a smile and a slow, tight blink of his small dark eyes. "You have gentle hands." He turned and walked away with the other two men.

Isabelle felt her shoulders sag and her chin dip slightly before she realized Mr. Gatestone wasn't leaving with them. From the corner of her eye she noticed him watching her. Intently. Instinctively she straightened, and looked at him—all of him for the first time. What she saw made the muscles in her stomach curl tight in response. Isabelle prided herself on staying calm, but when she looked at Mr. Gatestone it was as if some pulsating vibration had control of her body.

Before her was a powerfully built man who appeared as rugged as the land he was standing on, and she felt immensely drawn to him. He couldn't be more than half a dozen years older than her twenty-two, if that many. The tilt of his head and carriage of his back and shoulders spoke of a refinement that was largely absent in the men of Dewberry Hollow. Not surprising since he was from the house of an historic dukedom.

His warm gaze seemed to be patiently measuring her with the same concentration of awareness she had of him. It was more than a casual, fleeting interest building between them. There was solid attraction that hadn't gone away from their first glance at each other. No doubt about it. If anything, it was growing. She knew what the sensation was no matter she'd never fully been awakened by it before. It never crossed her mind a total stranger would be the first to do so.

Forcing her eyes to look away from him, she whispered, "You should go with your men. I don't know what else I can say."

In one long stride he closed the short distance between them and said, "I can't believe you shot my guard."

There was no condemnation in his tone. To her surprise, his voice held a bit of admiration. So did his expression. That made her feel a little better about the horrible accident. Isabelle thought back to Mr. Hornbolt. He was rather frail-appearing and didn't look as if he could protect anyone. He had to be fifty, if he was a day, and a good head shorter than the strong, magnificent-looking man standing intimately close to her.

It was her turn to be perplexed. "I can't believe he is your guard, sir," she answered.

As if knowing what she was thinking, and with a bit of a smile, he said, "It's more of an honor and a long-held tradition in the Gatestone family."

"It must be," she murmured more under her breath than aloud. This man needed no one protecting him.

"What are you doing in the woods shooting?"

Isabelle had always hated explaining her actions but felt compelled to say, "I thought he was a deer, of course. I had followed fresh tracks but was too far away and couldn't see well through the thicket . . . but . . . his hat, coat, and even his trousers were the same grayish-brown color and texture as a deer's winter coat. He should have been wearing black as we are, or perhaps the red coat of a foxhunter."

He eyed her with curiosity as wind fluttered his hair. "Perhaps he would have if he were hunting game. He was merely looking for a certain kind of pine needle to make his evening tea. He swears the winter leaves have health benefits."

Her mother felt the same way about the evergreens, but the tea was far too bitter for Isabelle to enjoy. "I wasn't trying to insinuate he was in any way at fault for what I alone—" Mr. Gatestone started nodding before she finished. Her words faltered to a stop.

"I know," he said without a hint of reproach. "I didn't think you were."

She took in a cold, steadying breath and wished he wouldn't look so closely at her and speak with such gentleness. He should be angry with her. Too, she was still trying to make sense of the way he made her stomach quiver and chest tighten. The sensations she was feeling were so unexpected it kept her off-balance. This extremely appealing man would be staying with them for the next few days. Reminding her of not only what she'd done to poor Mr. Hornbolt but also how he had made her feel when his leg had been pressed so innocently against hers.

"By your name, I assume you're related to the Duke of Notsgrove?"

"He's my grandfather."

By all the saints in Heaven, Isabelle thought, and inhaled unevenly with a silent huff of annoyance at herself once more. Why couldn't the fine-looking gentleman have been an out-of-favor nephew or a wastrel second or third cousin? Why did he have to be the duke's grandson? Her mother would be livid when she found out what her daughter had done.

There would be no getting out of it. Isabelle would receive more of her mother's outraged glances and lectures on how a proper lady should behave. But that wouldn't be the worst of what she would say. Shooting a man was really bad. And on top of that, what would they do if the duke now refused to stay at the inn? The money he would pay was needed for the rest of the winter.

"Did you mean what you said earlier?" she asked, wondering if Mr. Gatestone would hear the hope mingled in her voice. "That you won't tell anyone and your men will stay silent about what happened here today?"

He lifted his head ever so slightly, as if trying to figure her out. "I keep my word, and I know my guards. They won't speak of this. No man wants others telling how he was mistaken for a deer and shot by a woman. I did it out of respect for Hornbolt."

As he should have. "I hope you don't mind that I feel lucky it benefits me as well."

He gave her a twitch of a smile and it was ridiculous how quickly and thoroughly it warmed her chilled body from head to toe.

"Are you from The Inn at Dewberry Hollow?" he asked.

"Yes." It was all she could manage to say at the moment.

"And is that yours?" He motioned with his head toward the rifle.

She nodded.

He reached down, picked it up by the stock, and propped the barrel comfortably against his shoulder. "I'll leave it for you at the inn."

"What do you mean?" She regarded him intently and reached for the gun. He swung his shoulder away from her so she couldn't grasp it. Isabelle felt as if lightning had struck between them. Blood rushed to her ears. "How dare you, sir. That is my weapon."

He nodded nonchalantly, seeming not the least concerned by her affront. "I'm taking this with me to make sure you don't shoot any more of my men."

"I'm not likely to. They're leaving," she reminded him,

feeling the beating of her heart slamming against her chest at his show of authority. "What nerve you have, sir. Even for a duke's grandson."

His eyes narrowed attractively as he gave her another quirk of a smile. "I'm not taking any chances."

"You can't do that," she protested spiritedly, the tension between them rising. "It's stealing."

In a gesture of impatience, she reached again for her rifle, but before she realized what he intended, and with unbelievable speed, he moved the carbine around to his back. With his other arm he caught her around the waist and pulled her close.

Inhaling a sharp, startled breath, she instinctively struggled for a moment but then felt his consuming warmth dissipating the damp cold of the day. It calmed her racing heart. Somehow, she knew she wasn't in imminent physical peril, but something far more dangerous.

Their breaths mingled in the freezing air. Their eyes searched. The strength with which he held her was tight and forward to be sure, but not reprehensible. She was at a distinct disadvantage against his power, but the inexplicable thing was she didn't feel threatened. Instead, that astonishing and wonderful tingle of pleasure she'd felt when he first arrived and knelt beside her swept through her once more.

It was heavenly. Against better judgment, and relying only on what she was feeling, she chose to stay still in his embrace.

Being so close to him, she couldn't help but notice his narrow, high-bridged nose, well-shaped lips, and beautiful eyes that now seemed filled with a tender charm. He hadn't shaved recently and the scruff of beard seemed to add to the rugged way he held her—as if she belonged to him and he didn't intend to let go. Rather than that observation making her angry he'd treat her so unacceptably, it made her feel soft, pliant, and fiercely protected. That rare feeling made her want to press her cheek against his chest and cling to his strength and heat.

Just as she was ready to lean into his rock-hard chest, settle against him, and take more comfort, he spoke.

"I'm not going to keep it," he said huskily, his gaze keeping an unyielding hold on hers. "You'll find it waiting for you in the kitchen."

The kitchen?

When the meaning of his words penetrated the joy of her swirling emotions, Isabelle drew in a long, wintry, and uneven breath. So that was it. She should have known he thought her a servant at the inn. A scullery maid he'd expected to accept his orders without complaint and not the owner's daughter who was also the great-granddaughter of a viscount. No wonder he hadn't bothered to ask her name and felt comfortable not just restraining her but also taking possession of her rifle.

She almost huffed a laugh. Apparently, the duke's grandson wasn't very observant. While she had donned her old and worn cape for her afternoon stroll, her boots, which there was no doubt he'd seen, and the belt around her waist were made from the finest of leathers. But then, she thought curiously, maybe he hadn't looked at her boots. It was quite extraordinary, not to mention scandalous, for a lady to show the hem of her underdress or petticoats—no matter the reason.

"My horse isn't far away," he said, adjusting the gun more securely on his shoulder. "It's best you come and ride with me to the inn. It will be dark soon and you're half-frozen. I assume you'll have to walk through those trees. I'm not sure how far it is, but it doesn't look like a safe place for a woman to be on her own after dark."

Isabelle felt a stab of anger. "It would be if you hadn't taken my gun. I was born in this hollow, sir, and need no recommendations from you." She shoved against his chest and he let her go. "I know these woods. I'll make it to the inn before you and before dark."

His eyes narrowed as if trying to ascertain if she'd be willing to put a wager on that pronouncement and prove it. But before he could, she gave him a confident smile, turned, and rushed toward the clearing.

He was an arrogant man—but she had to admit he was a refreshing change from all the boys she'd watched grow into men in the village, not that it mattered. Isabelle had one hard and fast rule: Never pay attention to the men who came to stay at the inn. They were only guests and would be leaving. Their lives and destinies were elsewhere. Not in the hollow. She couldn't afford to get involved with them. A lady certainly couldn't trust one of them with her heart. Isabelle had learned the hard way they weren't looking to make a home in a small village in the wilderness.

So had her mother.

They had both fallen for a good-looking, smooth-talking guest who'd wintered at the inn to paint the frozen landscapes. With his easy charm and smooth talk, he had her widowed mother thinking she'd be a wife again and Isabelle thinking she'd finally have a father. It had been over ten years, but Isabelle hadn't forgotten. Whenever Mr. Moore, by chance, crossed her mind—like now—she always sent up a silent wish that it would be the last time.

It never was.

If there was anything good about the experience it was that his abandonment made her strong and taught her there was no need to depend on a man and that included the new viscount. She could take care of her mother and the inn.

The problem was that in all the years she'd known the young men in Dewberry Hollow and the ones she'd met and danced with in London, not one of them had ever made her feel the immediate, intense, and sensuous sensations that wove, dove, and spun so easily through her the way they had when she looked at Mr. Gatestone.

And when he looked at her. There was something about him that made her feel as if she'd been waiting to experience all those things with this man.

"Which is ridiculous," she muttered to herself as she stomped back across the clearing, still a little breathless from her encounter. "That isn't going to happen."

Feeling such things about a man who would be leaving the hollow after only a few days was disturbing, pointless, and dangerous to her future well-being.

She wasn't about to break her own rule because of an immensely appealing grandson of a duke.

Chapter Two

His grandfather hadn't told him there were so many damned trees. Thousands. And Gate was supposed to find just one with a heart carved on it. In a week! He'd promised his father and uncle he'd have the duke back home in London in time for Christmas Day dinner.

"No way in hell," John Cabot Gatestone mumbled to himself as he rode into the village. This was no little hollow in the middle of the woods as his grandfather had described it. It was a full-blown forest.

The air was frigid and still. Dry, earthy scents of woodlands were all around. Twilight had caught up with him as he'd expected it would, but The Inn at Dewberry Hollow wasn't difficult to find in what appeared to be a thriving little town. It loomed straight ahead at the end of the road.

The center of the tall, wide-stone manor house was flanked by smaller wings on each side with mighty-looking turrets standing like sentinels at each corner. It was a welcoming beacon to a man who'd spent most of a long day in the saddle. Lamplight glowed from some of the windows on the lower floors. Gray smoke puffed into the dusky sky from two of the several chimneys poking out of the roof. The inn was grand and a complete contrast to the rows of much smaller thatch-roofed houses and shops making up the main thoroughfare.

Snuggled away in northeastern Berkshire, the inn was known all over England as a place where kings, queens, and dukes were once received for public visits and private affairs. Duels had been fought on the grounds behind the garden walls for a variety of reasons: card games that ended badly, a man's family honor, and women. It was rumored that over the years several military generals had gathered at the house to plan and study their strategies for implementing battles and winning wars.

On their journey to the hollow, the duke had told Gate the history of the house and how it became a successful and prestigious inn. A young viscount inherited the massive structure close to half a century ago and soon discovered he didn't have the income to keep it in a flourishing state. Since it was only a day's carriage ride from London and already a favorite meeting place for noblemen and gentry, the viscount decided to open it as an inn and make guests pay for the privilege of staying at the highly regarded place.

And they did. Gate's grandfather had been one of them. Before and after he married.

The quaint village of Dewberry Hollow was situated on the southern edge of a wide valley floor between two tree-covered hillsides that were dark with woods. Ash, oak, maple, and more birch and evergreens than he'd ever seen anywhere. The dense forest was probably rich with small and large game and most likely the reason the young miss had been hunting there.

Trekking through such coppices looking for wild animals or birds was usually something a man would do, but Gate knew of women who were quite skilled with guns as well as bow and arrows. Though he was sure the miss he'd met hadn't been hunting all day. He'd caught the invitingly fragrant scent of her skin and the fresh-washed smell of her lush, dusky-summer blond hair that she'd fashioned into a long attractive braid.

Gate admired a woman who knew how to shoot, wasn't afraid to get on her knees to tend to a wounded man, and had the courage to offer a strip of her petticoat without embarrassment when it was needed. She hadn't shivered at the sight of blood or been intimidated by him. Her countenance had remained calm and controlled in spite of what she'd done, proving she was confident, and strong.

Looking at her delicate beauty, he wouldn't have known she was a hearty woman of the land, natural as a spring day, and cool as a thawing brook kind of belle. Her skin was unblemished, with rosy cheeks, full pink lips, and sparkling green eyes that had challenged him more than once with boldness and determination. Her speech was no different from that of the ladies in some of London's most famous drawing rooms. If not for the short carbine and worn cape and gloves she wore, he would have sworn to anyone she was a highborn lady of the ton.

Gate remembered the appealing show of defiance in her expression, and how the span and narrow curve of her waist was just the right size to fit into his embrace. She was tall but not towering, lean but not bony, firm but not hard, and so temptingly feminine. It had been a few heady moments when he held her close. Desire had surged strong within him to do more than just hold her. He wanted to wrap her securely in his embrace with both arms and feel her lips yielding in passion beneath his. He sensed she had the same desirous impulses about him—if only for a few seconds.

Most of all, he remembered the first things seen in her expression when he was kneeling beside her were compassion and concern for Hornbolt.

The miss was enticing to be sure. But not available for him to pursue, he groused silently. The Duke of Notsgrove had a strict code of conduct for everyone in his family when it came to the staff of his household, or anyone else's.

They were to be left alone.

No arguments. No excuses. No forgiveness if evidence of such bending the rules was ever presented. According to the patriarch of the family, a man's natural, primal urges should be attended to by his wife or a paid mistress. The duke highly approved and encouraged such services.

Gate had always agreed.

He didn't want to be the first male Gatestone to test the duke's commitment on that no-forgiveness rule. And certainly not with his grandfather at the point he could hardly walk ten paces without stopping for a rest. No matter how tempted by the young miss. That's why he hadn't even asked for her name. It was best he forget about her and the thoughts of passion she'd so easily aroused in him. He needed only to concentrate on the reason for his stay at the inn. To keep his word to his family that his grandfather would be safe in Gate's care, to find the tree where his grandparents had carved the lovers' heart, and return the duke home by Christmas dinner.

That was Gate's only goal. Then he could return to festivities planned in London where there would be plenty of women to woo.

His grandfather hadn't been well since the beginning of autumn—really since Gate's grandmother had died more than a year ago. After recently hearing the physician say his days on earth might be coming to an end in a matter of months, he decided there was one thing he needed to do before he passed from this world to join his beloved wife. He wanted to return to Dewberry Hollow and find the tree with the carving of a heart and their initials. It was something the duke promised her they would do one day. A promise often restated to satisfy his wife's yearning, but he was always too busy with more important things.

Now the duke felt it was a task left undone and he was going to do it—no matter it was the dead of winter and on the brink of Christmastide, too. He wouldn't be dissuaded from finding the tree, reliving the sweet memories of that time with his wife, and tying one of her favorite hair ribbons on the tree over the initialed heart.

Gate's father, uncle, and a couple of his older cousins had all balked at the duke's idea. It was too dangerous. He was too weak. He'd never make the journey back alive. All to no avail. The duke showed them he might be sick but he wasn't dead. He was still head of the family. Seeing how determined his grandfather was and knowing no one could change his mind, Gate spoke up and said he'd take him.

And he'd bring him back alive.

In time for Christmas dinner.

But that was before he'd seen all the damned trees surrounding the hollow.

Gate had no problem indulging the duke's wishes. He was the only unmarried grandson with no responsibility. Because of who his grandfather was, Gate had lived the privileged, indolent life of a wealthy young man who had no dreams or goals of his own other than the next card game, house party, or horse race.

When he was younger, Gate had resented the fact he wasn't the heir. Not that he wanted the title. He didn't give a damn about that. He wanted something to do—to learn about the estates, the companies, and the holdings of the entailed properties. But he couldn't be privy to that information. No. It was only for the heir's son, Gate's oldest cousin who would one day be the duke. All Gate was given was plenty of money to pursue his pleasures. And he had.

Recently, though, he was once more seeking something more worthwhile to do. His carefree life of a gentleman of means had become stale. Doing this for his grandfather was important to him and gave him responsibility for a change. And he hoped it would help settle his yearnings and disquiet of wanting something more in his life.

All the duke's other children and grandchildren had fallen dutifully in line and married long before Gate's age—twenty-seven. Some in the family reminded him he was becoming an old bachelor. He cared not for their bluster.

Gate enjoyed dancing and conversing with the young ladies making their debuts at the beginning of each Season. Each one had charm, intelligence, and beauty. That was the problem. None of them stood out as special or different from the others. For him, it was more important to find the right lady to marry than take a wife out of obligation and ritual. He had enough traditions to follow—such as traveling with unnecessary guards.

Gate had never minded spending time with the duke. Nor did he have a problem with his arrogant, no argument allowed ways. Neither had his grandmother. She had been as sweet as the duke was querulous, but there was no doubt they'd loved each other. He'd seen it in the way they'd smiled at each other when they thought no one was looking. Gate had grown up watching the love and friendship between them and knew he hadn't come close to finding that kind of love.

Whenever Gate married, the wanted the kind of feeling that made you want to carve a heart on a tree and put initials in it. Gate's father and uncle hadn't understood why his grandfather wanted to do that, or why he now wanted to go back and find it.

But Gate had.

That's why he was helping his grandfather risk his life to fulfill his final wish. And he was going to find that carved heart for the duke even if he had to look at every blasted tree in the hollow. And there was certainly a lot more than his grandfather had led him to believe.

With an inward sigh, Gate guided his horse around to the back of the inn where the servants' entrance was generally located and suddenly there was a leap in his pulse, a pounding in his chest, and a catch in his breath. The miss was casually leaning against the door framing, arms folded across her chest, and softly drumming her fingers as if she'd been impatient for him to return. That sent a thump of wanting straight to his loins.

He wasn't surprised she had the gumption to be so daring. He liked that spark of self-assurance her actions seemed to show. It heightened her allure. Whenever he looked at her, his lower body paid no mind to how the duke expected a family member to behave with servants or staff.

Warm, tender, and exciting attraction flowed between him and the miss. He'd felt it when their eyes first met and moments later when he'd realized that in his haste to see to Hornbolt he'd accidentally pressed his leg against hers. That same heat shuddered slowly and invitingly through him now, causing the same desirous response. It was heady and gratifying.

His gaze met hers as he reined in the horse. Holding her rifle in one hand, he threw his leathers across the pommel with the other and dismounted.

"Here before you, and before dark," she said confidently as she straightened and confronted him with the attitude of a woman who knew her worth.

When she spoke, her shoulders moved just enough to entice him with languid thoughts of long, deep kisses and slow, gentle caresses before a flaming fire. She radiated a wholesomeness that drew him to the point of being fascinated with her. The natural ease with which she interacted with him was stimulating. He liked that she wasn't awed by the fact he was a duke's grandson. She wasn't trying to entice him with the way she approached him. But she did. Everything about her was as natural and elating as the air around him.

"Here before me? Yes." He took in another cold breath and deliberately looked around their surroundings. The skies were dark. Lamps had been lit over all the doorways at the back of the house. His gaze found hers again and he challenged her by narrowing his eyes in concentration. "Before dark? Questionable."

She gave him a frown of exasperation, which was almost as beckoning as her self-assured smile. "Really, sir. It may be now, but I will have you know I've been waiting fifteen minutes for you."

"That long? *For me?*" he quizzed with a raise of his brow and a slight quirk of his head. A teasing grin formed on his lips. "That's nice to hear."

Her eyes widened slightly, and her windburned cheeks turned rosier after she realized what she'd said. "So I could retrieve my gun," she insisted immediately. "I wanted to make certain you didn't intend to keep it from me for retribution for the accident."

He knew she didn't believe for a moment he wanted to keep the carbine. She was at the door because she wanted to see him again. *Good.* There was something much more important between them than that weapon. She was downright fetching with a bit of annoyance in her tone and looked as if she wanted to freeze him solid on the spot. It made him want to invite her to try to take the weapon again and give him another reason to touch her one more time before he entered the inn.

To tease her further, he lifted the gun in both hands and looked it over carefully. "It is well made; perhaps I *would* like to have—"

"Give me that," she said with more annoyance, grasping the carbine between his two hands and giving a determined tug. "It was made especially for me. You are probably a menace to everyone who knows you. The only reason I allowed you to bring it home is because it gets heavy. I decided it would serve you right to bear that burden. So, thank you, and I'll take it now."

He chuckled and let go. She whirled and placed it in the corner between the door and the jamb. She was breathing unevenly when she turned back to him. He did that to her, he thought, and only then realized that his own breaths were choppy, too.

"How were you planning on getting a deer to the inn if you had shot one?"

"I would have marked the spot and sent one of the grooms to get it."

"So, have you shot a deer before?"

"No. Not yet." She paused. "I've never actually shot anything other than birds. Except for Mr. Hornbolt, and I'm extremely sorry about that." She looked away for a moment and cleared her throat. "You'll be glad to know as soon as I arrived I checked on him. His arm has been tended to. It will be swollen and sore for several days, but as long as he keeps it still and there's no infection he should heal fine."

There was no doubt in her tone. Gate nodded. He'd believed that to be the case when he'd looked at the wound and was glad to have it confirmed. Hornbolt was a gentle old soul who had been with Gate for as long as he could remember.

"That's good to know. Just the same, I'll check on him as well and take him a pint of ale."

"I took the liberty of sending over a bottle of port. I thought he might want to add a splash to his pine needle tea. I hope you don't mind. I felt it was in order."

"Not at all. I'm sure he will enjoy it."

"Your *guards* will be staying in the carriage house while you're here. Should you need them during the night." She paused and added a hint of a smile. "It's the building directly behind you. All the others traveling with you will reside in the servants' quarters, which is the building to your left."

Gate shifted his stance. "I should explain about the guards," he answered.

Her lips quivered into an engaging smile, causing a slow roll in his stomach that carried all the way to his shaft and heated him like a blazing fire.

"No need, sir. A duke and his family are important people and need protecting in a place as wild and dangerous as Dewberry Hollow."

He met her amused gaze with one of his own. She was enjoying bedeviling him about the guards. If she thought it would deter the way they were feeling about each other she was wrong. His interest in her had settled deep in his loins when he first saw her and he didn't think it was going to fade away anytime soon.

He sensed a seductiveness in every move she made, and he'd swear to anyone she was unaware of it and how it caused shivers of desire to shoot through him. He stepped in closer. The door was to her back, and though he could easily keep her from moving past him, he sensed she had no desire to bolt. It was the way she looked at him that had him believing she was as interested as he was. She left no detail in his face untouched by her gaze.

Light from the lantern hanging above them on the post shimmered attractively in her hair. He wanted to untie the ribbon that bound her tresses into a loose braid and let them fall softly around her shoulders. With great difficulty, he kept himself from bending down to claim her mouth. Now wasn't the time, but he felt in his gut the time would come when he would have to defy his grandfather's directive.

"I like you," he said softly.

Her eyes narrowed with suspicion. "You don't know me," she answered with conviction that held solidly in her features.

It was an understandable assumption, but he took exception to it. "I do. From what happened with Mr. Hornbolt and how you handled the incident, I know enough to understand there's much more to you than your delicate beauty suggests. You have an uncommon inner strength, obvious good character, and fairness."

"And you are a man who's standing too close to me, Mr. Gatestone. I never get familiar with guests who stay at the inn."

"That is wise, but it's too late for us," he said with conviction he knew she couldn't deny.

Her admission had him assuming she'd been *too close* to a guest in the past and it hadn't ended well for her. He could understand that causing her to be wary, causing her to deny the sensations that were like thousands of fireworks shooting between them. He had his own reasons to be careful about the desires he was harboring for her, too.

But he was a man, and some things were just so instinctive they shouldn't be denied. She tempted him greatly. When had he ever had one cause a catch in his breath and leap of his heart by just looking at her?

He hadn't, and now with her lips mere inches from his he

was fighting the urge to give into his growing ardor and kiss her.

He stood his ground and didn't step back, but out of honor, held up his hands, as if giving her proof he wasn't forcing her to do anything. "Push me away if you feel I'm too close." His words were more of a whisper than a demand. "Unless . . ."

"Unless what?" she whispered softly, seeming caught under the same spell that held him.

He moved his gaze to her full lips, making his meaning clear before he offered huskily, "Unless you want me to kiss you."

Her eyes searched his in the dim glow, but she didn't make a move. She was being cautious, he decided, thinking about the offer he put before her and the ramifications of how she might react. That gave him hope she would, at least, admit to how he was making her feel. He waited and gave her all the time she wanted to decide as night continued to fall softly around them.

Finally, she inhaled a deep, steady breath. "Your grandfather is getting settled into his rooms as should you. Guests gather in the drawing room at eight. Dinner is served at half past the hour. Now, I have things to do." She turned to open the door.

"Wait," he said. "I want to see you again."

She hesitated before turning back to face him. "You will soon enough. Not that it will change anything between us," she answered, picked up her rifle, and then slipped through the doorway and out of sight.

Gate cursed under his breath.

"Such a tempting forbidden miss," he ground out in a frustrated whisper, followed by another curse.

Was that what made her so unbearably exciting no matter

what his grandfather preached? He'd never met a young woman so strong and confident. Everything about her was drawing him toward her.

Yet . . .

He couldn't forget the way he was brought up.

Chapter Three

Oh, he was a naughty one.

Seductive. Shameless about it. And almost irresistible.

Isabelle couldn't ignore thoughts of the man or the faint trace of anticipation about the evening ahead while dressing for dinner. Perhaps it was more than faint.

Her breath quickened.

Again.

"Yes, much more than faint," she whispered to herself.

It was as if she couldn't wait to get downstairs to see Mr. Gatestone. That was utterly maddening. And not something she wanted to think about. Much less enjoy! What was wrong with her? She'd met charming men before. There were actually several in Dewberry Hollow of varying ages, including Mr. Bloom, who was fifteen years her senior, prosperous, and hadn't yet accepted she would never be his wife.

She'd met plenty of gentlemen since she'd turned eighteen four years ago. Every spring she and her mother made their month-long visit to London to have new dresses, gowns, and other clothing made. Viscount Pailsworth, her mother's uncle, recently deceased, had always held a dinner party for

them as the Season was usually in full swing. Eligible gentlemen were invited. Some had made overtures of interest.
Perhaps she should have encouraged at least one or two of
them to visit her when they'd asked for an invitation to pay
a call. According to the new viscount, she should have a
husband taking care of her. Not him. She probably would
be married by now if any of the gentlemen had aroused the
same extraordinary feelings in her that Mr. Gatestone had.

This sudden desire to be held and kissed was new to her.

Isabelle didn't know why Mr. Gatestone had given her
these wondrous sensations and none of the other handsome men she'd met ever had? When the duke's grandson
moved in so close to her at the door, she was certain he was
going to catch her up in his arms, hold her as if he'd never
let go, and kiss her with all the passion she sensed harnessed
inside him.

And *she* was going to let him.

But then *he* had to ruin it by stopping himself and letting
her be the one to decide about the kiss. He should have never
done that.

Of course she had to evade the issue.

Why couldn't he have just gone ahead and done the un-
gentlemanly offense and kissed her without permission? He
could have then asked forgiveness for being so boorish as
other gentlemen had when they'd kissed her without first
seeking permission.

But no, Mr. Gatestone left the decision totally in her hands.

Drat the man's honorable intentions!

Isabelle picked up her pale green gown that wasn't much
more substantial than a velvet underdress and tossed it over
her head. She then slipped her arms into the matching deco-
rative long-sleeved spencer that fit snugly under her breasts
and fastened it up the front. When she made it to the top satin-
covered button that would close the garment over the swell

of her breasts, she hesitated and, as uncommon as it was for her to do so, she left it open.

She didn't want to think about the reason why. Or why she wondered if Mr. Gatestone would find the shade of green flattering to her.

"Oh, good, you are finally back," her mother said, sweeping into the room with her deep-rose-colored gown fluttering around her legs like a butterfly in summer. "And getting dressed, I see. You shouldn't have missed the duke's arrival. You were supposed to be standing with me to greet him. It's not your day to teach the girls. Where were you?"

Alma Helen Pailsworth Reed was still a beauty even though she was a few springs past forty years of age. As tall as her daughter, she'd kept the slender figure of her youth. Her light brown hair showed only a few strands of gray, and except for the occasional forlorn expression of past deep hurts, her dark hazel eyes sparkled with life.

"Walking," Isabelle answered, and turned away from her dressing mirror to face her mother.

"Just out enjoying the frigid cold, I suppose," Alma said with a slight reprimand in her tone.

"I'm sorry, Mama. I know you don't like for me to be late when we have guests staying at the inn, but I saw a deer and was tracking him in hopes of adding to our Christmas Day dinner, but he got away."

"Oh," her mother huffed loudly. "We have men from the village who hunt for us, Isabelle." Alma sighed again and walked over to stand in front of her.

"And they charge us dearly for it because of who we are," Isabelle answered, barely holding in her vexation at her mother's continued lack of concern for how serious their financial problems were. "Besides, I wasn't actually hunting." Well, not until she saw the tracks in the snow.

Alma lifted her hands and slowly shook her head. "How

many times do I have to tell you that even though we live away from Polite Society, you are still a lady and must conduct yourself as one at all times?"

"At least a thousand more times, Mama," she retorted with a weary smile, paying no mind to her mother's repeated admonishment. "I shall never get tired of hearing it."

"You're an impossible daughter to reason with," Alma said with a huff of indignation. "But it's my fault. I should have never allowed Mr. Canon to teach you how to shoot. You've been a nuisance about it ever since. I never dreamed you'd take it so seriously. After your father died I should have moved back to London so you could grow up as a proper lady."

"You would have hated every moment of it," Isabelle reminded her.

"That's not true," she argued without conviction as she looked in the mirror and straightened the band of rose-colored silk in her hair. "However, you know I could never leave this place because your father loved it so. I only wish you hadn't become such a country miss in wanting to do so many things for yourself—including hunting."

It would do no good arguing about a lady and guns and how the two should never meet. Best Isabelle move to a more practical matter.

"The fact remains, Mama, that it worries me our larders are almost bare and our coffers all but empty. Our supply of chickens and geese dwindles because you want to feed every guest four and five courses as if we're entertaining the king. We simply can't continue to do so now that our allowance has been cut in half."

"What nonsense, dearest!" Alma exclaimed, turning away from her reflection in the mirror and facing Isabelle again. "Of course we will. I will not feed our guests rabbit stew or fish broth be he duke or gentry. We will dine as all Polite

Society dines. We may have lost most of our allowance for a time, but we haven't lost our manners." Alma inhaled a deep breath, seeming to calm herself. "I know the situation appears dire right now. Especially with Christmas so near. But remember, the duke's visit will give us extra money we don't usually have at Christmastide."

"Perhaps we should consider turning off some of the staff in the new year," Isabelle said without thinking.

"That's a horrible idea." Alma looked at her daughter as if she'd lost her mind. "What would we do without them? Where would they go? Now, we have a duke to entertain, so let's think about dire things later, shall we?"

Isabelle reached over and kissed her mother's soft cheek and then smiled. "Of course, Mama. It was just a suggestion. And we don't have to decide anything tonight."

Most people stayed with relatives this time of year. Not at an inn with strangers. Isabelle wondered, and not for the first time, why the duke wasn't spending the Season at home with his own family—other than his grandson.

Christmas Day traditions were important to Isabelle. Church in the morning. A feast early in the evening and chess, cards, or charades by the fire after dinner.

Alma cupped Isabelle's cheek briefly. "No one must know we have money concerns. If word got out, we'd never have another guest of such quality or distinction. I so wish we didn't have to think about money at all. It's a man's responsibility to take care of such things, but since the only man we have in our lives is my cousin, what can we do?"

"We will manage," Isabelle assured her mother with a confident smile, knowing she'd planned to add more students to teach. And she would push her mother to raise their lodging rates—but not until after Christmas.

Right now they didn't have enough funds to give a shilling to all the staff on Boxing Day. Most of it had gone to buy food for the duke and his men. But they would have extra money when the duke and Mr. Gatestone left. At that thought Isabelle's stomach tightened. He'd only just arrived but already she didn't want to think about him leaving.

Isabelle swallowed her troubling thoughts. "Now tell me, is the duke as brusque as you remember him?"

"Cranky as the old rooster that pecks around the herb garden. I didn't spend much time with him. He wanted to go directly to his rooms."

Isabelle tensed, immediately thinking he might have been told about the accident with Mr. Hornbolt after all. "Did he seem upset?"

"No. Feeble. Out of breath. It took him a long time to climb the stairs. His valet asked that a bottle of brandy and a pot of tea be sent up. I suppose the ride from London was a tiring one."

Isabelle picked up her hairbrush. There was certainly nothing weak about his grandson. Strength showed in his features and in his embrace. He was a self-confident man who had just the right amount of arrogance to make him enchanting.

"I should check to see how many bottles of brandy we have left. Not many, I'm sure, and men enjoy their drinks in the evenings."

"Why do you worry about such things? Leave it to Mr. Danvers. If we're running low, he'll take care of it, dearest. Not you."

"It gives me something to do, Mama." Isabelle enjoyed being a part of everything concerning the inn. Her mother knew this but most of the time chose not to recognize it because she'd grown up the perfect young lady who would never do anything that might be considered work. The kind of young lady she was always trying to get her daughter to be. Isabelle grabbed half of her hair, pulled it to the top of her head, and fastened it with a comb. "Did the duke bring as many people as he did last time?"

"You know I don't ask Mr. Danvers questions like that. However many there are, we will take care of them appropriately. Our responsibility is to entertain our guests. It may be an inn, but it is our home first." She paused, reached up and fastened the top button on Isabelle's spencer. "He did mention that the other set of rooms reserved are for the duke's grandson, but he was delayed. He didn't say why. Nothing serious, I hope."

Isabelle felt a nip of guilt and twinge of relief. It didn't sound as if the duke knew of her involvement in the incident with Mr. Hornbolt. Surely he would have mentioned it to her mother. She twisted up the other half of her hair and added another comb, but more tendrils fell than stayed in the bun. She would give it another try. After the way she'd looked this afternoon clothed in her worn cape and pieces of twigs in her hair, she wanted to look more than just presentable to Mr. Gatestone tonight.

"Ah, well, there's the clock chiming eight. I'm off to greet our guests and you must hurry."

It took Isabelle several more tries, but she managed to get enough pins and combs into her hair to hold it up. She added a strip of dark green and red-berry-trimmed ribbon across the crown of her head and tied it at her nape. After finishing, she looked at herself in the mirror and realized she was stunned by how much she wanted to look pretty.

That was so unlike her. She unfastened the top button of her spencer, added a sprig of mistletoe to her hair, grabbed her gloves, and headed belowstairs.

By the time Isabelle rounded the corner of the drawing room her stomach was jumping with anticipation. Much to her chagrin, her eyes immediately sought and found Mr. Gatestone. Her chest expanded at the sight of him. He stood before the low-burning fireplace holding a glass of claret and conversing with her mother. He must have sensed her walk through the doorway because he immediately turned toward her. Even from across the room, she saw surprise in his expression.

Just as she'd hoped. And it felt wonderful.

Beside him stood a man who had to be his grandfather. He was almost as tall as his grandson but much thinner through the chest. Except for the gray thatch of thinning hair and a bit of a stoop to his shoulders they could be father and son.

Also in the room were the inn's two permanent boarders, who were not considered guests because the inn was their home. Like Isabelle and her mother, Mrs. Boothe's and Mr. Thimwinkle's heritage was steeped in the birthright of Polite Society. Mrs. Boothe had been with them the longest. She was a small-framed, soft-spoken widow who had visited the hollow more than six years ago and decided not to leave. She said she'd grown up in a house much like the inn and it reminded her of childhood.

Each spring she watched the groundskeeper plant every flower and often made suggestions as to what section of the garden to place them. Most evenings she delighted everyone within earshot by playing beautiful scores on the pianoforte. The large rooms and cavernous corridors allowed the sounds to drift throughout the manor and in summer when the windows and doors were open the music carried to the servants' buildings as well.

Only recently had Isabelle noticed that all wasn't well with the gentle lady who kept herself busy reading or with embroidery as a proper lady should. She was more than a little forgetful. Just last week Isabelle had witnessed Mrs. Boothe dipping cream from the pitcher into her tea and pouring an abundance of the sugar. She never seemed to notice the mistake, but the concoction must have tasted dreadfully sweet.

Mr. Thimwinkle was a short, rotund older man with hair and beard as white as snow. He kept a pair of spectacles perched on the bridge of his nose. No matter the color of his coat and trousers, he always wore a bright red waistcoat. She'd never seen him wearing any other color. He was a jolly fellow with ruddy cheeks and a deep, jovial laugh. Isabelle was certain he couldn't be as old as he looked. He could bound up the stairs faster than she could. He'd joined them three years ago.

After visiting the hollow, he wanted to stay because of the woods surrounding it. She would often see him sitting on the back steps whittling animals, soldiers, ships, horses, and other things not much bigger than the palm of his hand. On Christmas Eve he'd leave a small bag of wooden toys by the door of every household in the hollow that had a child.

It took great effort not to glance at Mr. Gatestone as Isabelle walked over to where he stood, but somehow she managed.

"Ah, there you are," her mother said. "Your Grace, may I present my daughter, Miss Isabelle Reed?"

Isabelle curtsied and the duke took her hand in his. Even though she wore gloves, she could tell his hand was cold, his fingers weak and trembly. Now that she was close to him she could see his cheeks were thin and pale. He didn't have the look of a well man. There was a noticeable unnatural rise and fall to his chest with every breath. His strain to remain poised was evident in his features.

"Yes, we've met before, Miss Reed. Not properly. You were far too young for an introduction, but I remember you just the same. You ran into me at the bottom of the stairs and almost knocked me down the last time I was here."

The brash and unexpected greeting startled her momentarily. Her first thought was that he'd taken an instant dislike to her. He really was a curmudgeon. But Isabelle recovered quickly when she realized there was no malice in his tone or expression. He was simply curt and deliberately honest.

"Apologies, Your Grace. I'll be sure to refrain from racing down the stairs while you are here."

"See that you do," he said sternly, but then smiled charmingly and kissed the back of her palm. "I'm not as strong or agile as I used to be and I might fall down."

Isabelle smiled, too. "I will be extra careful."

"Not too careful, I hope. You had an abundance of spirit as I recall. By the look in your eyes, I suspect you've not settled down much since then."

"I don't believe I have," she answered, seeing no reason she shouldn't be truthful.

"Good. It's a terrible thing when one loses their spirit. Let me introduce you to my grandson."

Isabelle turned to Mr. Gatestone. His attention had settled on her and he was looking at her as if there were no one else in the room. That made her happy she'd taken the extra time to get dressed. The duke continued talking. She answered at all the appropriate times, but she really couldn't hear a word he said or remember what she responded.

She was captivated by his grandson. Gone was the rugged-looking man with tousled hair and more than a day's growth of beard. He was freshly shaven with his hair combed attractively away from his face. His collar points were just the right height to settle under his strong-looking jaw and his starched neckcloth was elegantly tied, adding to his astonishing good looks. When he kissed the back of her hand, she felt as if the fire in the hearth behind them had suddenly flamed out of control.

Mr. Thimwinkle walked up and asked if he might join them. The duke nodded consent and said to him, "I've never seen anyone with a beard so white. Usually they are gray, as is my hair. Has anyone ever said you look like Father Winter?"

The old man gave a deep, hearty laugh. "Not recently, Your Grace," he responded in a buoyant manner. "It heartens me to hear you say it. You would have no reason to remember me, but we were classmates at Eton."

"You're right," the duke said disagreeably. "I don't remember. I suppose you have the same opinion of me as others who say I was a stiff piece of wood back then. I haven't changed. More's the pity."

The jolly Mr. Thimwinkle chuckled again and Mr. Gatestone turned from his rather blunt grandfather and moved closer to Isabelle, making her aware of the breadth of his shoulders beneath his well-tailored evening coat. Somehow, his physical presence so near felt wonderfully right.

He bent his head toward her and in a low, husky tone said, "You could have told me you were Miss Isabelle Reed and great-granddaughter of a viscount."

"If I had done that," she answered softly, inhaling the clean scent of his fresh-washed face, "I would have missed the look of surprise when I entered the drawing room."

"I can see that pleased you." For a moment he seemed to stare at her as if he wanted to know more about her than he did. "I like seeing mischief sparkling in your eyes, Miss Reed. It becomes you."

She liked the twinkle of amusement in his, but wanting to needle him a little more, she said, "Really? You sound a little miffed to me."

"Only a little?" he quipped.

She gave him a knowing smile, enjoying their lighthearted banter. "You could have asked my name at any time."

"And you could have offered it with a stern dressing down when you knew I assumed you were with the staff of the inn."

Isabelle glanced over at her mother to make sure she wasn't listening to their conversation before adding, "Being the grandson of a duke, I suppose it's rare you are fooled by anyone."

"Not often for sure. There were things about you that gave me reason to suspect you weren't as your clothing suggested, but . . ."

"What? Go on. I'm interested."

"Mainly that you had a rifle instead of a chaperone."

A soft laugh fell from her lips. It was easy to feel perfectly comfortable with him.

He chuckled attractively, too.

"Ah, yes. Every miss in Polite Society must have a chaperone if she's going to step a foot outside her door in London. Thankfully, here in the hollow a gun is a good substitute. What else made you think I might not be who you assumed?"

"Your speech. The way you carried yourself. The way you weren't intimidated by me."

Her gaze stayed solidly on his. No. She hadn't been intimidated by him. Only enchanted. It was the first time she'd been interested enough in a gentleman to want to flirt with him.

"I can see why some young ladies would be daunted by you. Not only are you handsome, but you'll have a title one day, too."

"You flatter me, Miss Reed." He shook his head. "I'm not the heir. That duty falls to my cousin."

"Of course, you're right. Hence you are called Mr. and not Lord . . ." She paused. "What is your Christian name, sir?"

He seemed pleased she'd asked. "John, but I'm called Gate. Since my uncle's son will have the title, my father decided I should bear the family name."

"Fitting that both be honored." She glanced at her mother

again. "Knowing I'm a lady, aren't you a little upset with yourself for the unacceptable way you handled me in the woods today?"

"Not in the least," he spoke without hesitation. His golden-eyed gaze swept down her face to the swell of her breasts showing from beneath the open button and then back to her eyes. "I'd do it again to feel my arms around you."

A chill of excitement washed over Isabelle. She believed him and wanted to experience that again, too. It made her feel as if she were precious to him. He looked at her as if she was the only lady he ever wanted to see again. It would be so easy to give in to his charms.

But that was a dangerous thing to consider.

Isabelle knew the kind of heartache that thinking could bring. It would be foolish and she couldn't have any part of it. In a few days, he would be going back to his life in London. She would still be at the inn where she belonged. She couldn't let him take her heart with him when he left.

After being a widow for ten years, her mother thought she'd found true love again with a man who would live in the hollow with her. It was only a foolish dream built on false promises. Isabelle wouldn't go through the same kind of heartache.

She allowed her gaze to drift sweetly over his face just as his had over hers before saying, "My being a lady and thinking you are as handsome as an early-morning sky in summer doesn't make me any more available to you, Mr. Gatestone. Now, if you'll excuse me, I'm going to see to having dinner served early. Your grandfather looks tired and in need of rest."

Chapter Four

Something roused Isabelle from deep sleep. She rolled over and listened. Music. Was Mrs. Boothe playing the pianoforte again? In the middle of night?

Isabelle came wide awake.

The sound would be echoing up the stairwells and into the guest wing of the house.

"Sweet Clementine," she whispered, tumbling off the bed. Not bothering to don her slippers, she grabbed her dark gray woolen bed coat, putting it on as she raced from her chamber. The wood floor was like stepping on ice to her bare feet.

She met her mother in the corridor, looking as surprised as Isabelle that one of Beethoven's rousing scores was filling the rooms.

"It's too cold in the house for you to be up, Mama. Go back to bed. It has to be Mrs. Boothe. I'll take care of her."

"Are you sure, dear?" she asked, holding a candle in one hand and doing her best to tighten her robe about her chest with the other.

"Yes, of course. I'll see to her."

"All right, but take my light with you. I don't want you stumbling about in the dark."

Isabelle waved her mother aside and didn't slow down. "I don't need it, Mama, but be sure to put it out before you fall back to sleep," Isabelle said, tying the sash of her garment as she hurried past.

"I am not in my dotage yet, young lady," she heard her mother grumble behind her.

Isabelle's and her mother's bedchambers were on the ground floor in the south wing of the inn. All the guest rooms were abovestairs on the first and second floors. Not wanting to invade anyone's privacy, Isabelle and her mother never went to that section of the large house, but she was quite sure the pianoforte could be heard up there.

She quickly padded past the dining room, drawing room, and cut across the vestibule and down another corridor to round the doorway of the music room. Mrs. Boothe was sitting at the pianoforte wearing a lavender house robe and lace-trimmed nightcap. Somehow, she'd managed to light a five-pronged candlestick and place it on top of the pianoforte. She looked so peaceful sitting in the golden glow, gently swaying as she played.

Not wanting to frighten her, Isabelle called her name softly as she walked closer.

Mrs. Boothe instantly stopped playing and turned to Isabelle, her small bright blue eyes filled with delight. "Oh, yes, dear. How lovely you've come to my recital, but—" She stopped and suddenly looked at Isabelle with concern. "What are you doing dressed as you are? This is a formal affair, Miss Reed. I'm told there's a duke in attendance to-night. You must change into something more appropriate for the occasion."

"It's not time for your recital," Isabelle said in a comforting tone, hoping her words wouldn't confuse the lady even more. It was heartbreaking and concerning to see her addled to such a degree. "It's much too late in the evening and everyone has gone to sleep."

"But I'm sure I was told they were ready for me to begin playing." She looked around the room as her expression morphed into a questioning stare. "The candles are lit, the chairs are lined up correctly, but the room's empty. Where is everyone? Oh, I must have arrived too early."

She looked down at her lap and touched the fabric of her robe. Reaching up to her head, she fingered her nightcap. "I'm not dressed, either." She turned her troubled face to Isabelle. "I'm not at a recital. Only practicing for one. How did I become so confused?"

Isabelle gave her a smile of affection. "That doesn't matter now. You can rehearse again tomorrow. It's not a good time to play."

"Quite right." Her gaze took in the room again. "It isn't. I don't know what I was thinking to disturb everyone at this hour."

Isabelle knew some people became forgetful and disoriented at times as they aged. She hated to see that happening in Mrs. Boothe. Isabelle made a mental note to visit the apothecary tomorrow after she finished her lessons with the girls. He might have a concoction or elixir to add to tea that would help Mrs. Boothe.

She touched the back of the woman's shoulder compassionately and continued to keep her voice low and calm. "No harm done. But you do need to get back under your covers."

"It is quite cold down here without the fires burning, isn't it?"

Isabelle nodded. "Why don't I walk you back to your room? Will that be all right?"

"Yes, of course." She rose from the seat, smiled, and then

laughed lightly. Her eyes twinkled with happiness as she reached for the candelabra.

"No, not that one," Isabelle said quickly. "Let's leave it here in the music room so it will light the way for me when I return. We'll take the candlestick you brought down with you back to your room. I'll return and put out the others."

"You're such a dear to help me. I don't know how I became so discombobulated."

"It's nothing to worry about tonight," Isabelle assured her, though in truth, she wasn't sure at all. But if there was any way she could help Mrs. Boothe, she would.

"I am feeling a little weary now and do need to rest before playing again. I didn't used to be so forgetful."

Isabelle cautiously slipped her hand around Mrs. Boothe's elbow. She didn't seem unsteady on her feet, but there was no use in taking chances at this time of night.

"Now, tell me," Isabelle said as they walked out of the music room. "What color of gown are you going to wear tomorrow evening?"

"The midnight-blue velvet. With my pearls."

"I think that will be perfect."

Within minutes, Mrs. Boothe was safely in her bedchamber and Isabelle was heading back to extinguish the candles before she turned into a block of ice. She rounded the doorway into the music room and stopped. Mr. Gatestone leaned his tall frame against the pianoforte with his elbow resting on top of it. His broad shoulders and lean, yet muscular body showed beautifully in black close-fitting trousers and a white shirt that had undoubtedly been hastily thrown over his head and loosely tucked.

It was unbelievable how he intrigued her. Even in such a casual state he looked proud, commanding, and magnificent. For reasons she didn't want to explore, the sight of him stole her breath. Much as she hated to, she had to admit he wasn't a guest of the inn she could ignore.

She tried to calm her racing heartbeat by folding her arms over her chest and gripping her upper arms. With the sensual way he was looking at her there wasn't much chance of that happening. Even her bare feet were suddenly feeling warm on the frigid floor.

Gaining control of her senses, she walked closer to him. "Obviously, the pianoforte awakened some. I was hoping it hadn't."

He gave her a cordial smile that made her suddenly feel as if she'd been lost for years and he'd just found her. What kind of emotion brought forth such an unusual feeling in her?

"I'm a light sleeper," he offered.

Isabelle stopped near him. Too near him but she couldn't help herself. Such was her great desire to be close to him, she far exceeded what would have been considered a proper distance from a gentleman, but she was eager to feel his heat again.

Preferring to keep the conversation light, she asked, "When you found this room empty did you think we might have a friendly ghost living with us in the inn?"

He remained where he was, looking solid, permanent, and strangely as if he belonged exactly where he was. Here with her. Shaking his head, he patted the top of the pianoforte lightly. "I've never known a ghost to light candles."

She smiled mischievously. "Have you known many ghosts?"

With a soft, almost romantic chuckle, he brushed his hair away from his forehead while his gaze continued to caress her face. "I've never had the pleasure. Do you have one in the inn?"

She inhaled deeply, thinking how much she enjoyed being

with him. "If we have a ghost, I haven't had the pleasure either."

"By the time I made myself somewhat presentable and got down here, I heard how gently you were speaking to Mrs. Boothe. I didn't want to intrude and possibly frighten her, so I stepped into the shadows outside the room."

"That was considerate. Mrs. Boothe has been doing things that seem out of character for her of late. But this is the first time she's come belowstairs in the middle of the night."

"That you know about?"

"True," she admitted. "I assumed she woke and became disoriented. Perhaps she is drinking too much wine in the evenings. I should watch and take better care of her."

He straightened, inching closer to her as he did. "She hardly touched the claret in her glass at the dinner table. My grandfather's mind seems as young as mine, but his body is failing him. Mrs. Boothe sits, rises, and seems to take the stairs with no effort. She appears to be in strong and robust health, but her mind is suffering as surely as my grandfather's body. Such is life and we must learn to accept it."

"Yes, I agree," she answered softly. "It's heartbreaking though, and doesn't come easy. I'm sorry she disturbed you."

"I'm not. I could have gone back to my room when I heard you with her and knew all was well, but I waited. For you. For the chance to be alone with you. To see you with your hair gracing your shoulders as it is now. How beautiful you are."

Her senses started swirling as they had when she first entered the room and saw him. Anticipation gathered in her chest. "I have no desire for your flattery, Mr. Gatestone."

"None given," he whispered in a low tone, his gaze caressing her face as an appealing smile lingered on his lips. "Just stating the truth. I've never understood why ladies wear their hair up most of the time when it's so glorious draping their shoulders."

"It was probably a man who decided we should keep it bound." She smiled at her boldness in making such a comment. "They seem to have been responsible for most of Society's rules concerning women and men."

He chuckled ruefully. "You are probably right. Damn their souls."

She liked his teasing and believed he didn't want their time together to end. There was a subdued gleam in his seductive eyes. Isabelle didn't want to be caught under his spell, but she had no choice and knew what their exchanged glances meant.

"Did the music wake your grandfather, too?"

"If it did, he ignored it, rolled over, and went back to sleep. I didn't hear grumbling coming from his room when I passed by."

"Good."

She felt a shift in Mr. Gatestone. His head dipped lower and all of a sudden she felt vulnerable. She didn't think she'd ever felt that way about a man before. It had always been so easy to walk away from them. Now she was finding it not only difficult but near impossible. While she still had a shred of strength left, she said, "I'll put out the candles and say good night so you can retire again."

Isabelle reached up to cup her hand around the flame of a candle, and he caught her wrist.

"Not yet," he whispered huskily. "Stay."

His hand was warm, firm, but gentle. She remained still, barely breathing, and allowed him to seduce her with his touch, his words, and anticipation of something more. She'd finally met a man who made her want kisses. Lots and lots of kisses. But could she enjoy them without engaging her heart and being left with a broken one when he went away?

Trying to keep her sensible nature from completely collapsing, she pulled back on her arm and he let go. In a light tone, she asked, "Are you asking me to do something a proper young miss in London would never be allowed to do—continue to be alone with a man without benefit of a chaperone?"

"London, Paris, or the Americas, young misses always find a way to be alone with someone they want to be with. I believe you want to be right here, right now with me."

Oh, he was a charming devil. She scoffed in a dismissive manner, "Even if that were true it wouldn't make it proper."

"I have no intentions to harm your reputation," he added. "Aren't you at all curious about a man you have such strong feelings for?"

That made her cough out a soft laugh. "Strong feelings? I just met you today, sir. You think highly of yourself."

He shrugged. "I know there is something more than casual interest happening between us. I felt it the moment our eyes first connected this afternoon."

Isabelle wasn't ready to admit that to him. Needing something to distract from the tension building between them, she quickly thought to say, "I am curious about one thing."

He looked at her with a peculiar mix of questioning and challenge before his lips gave her a slow grin. "Only one?"

"One is enough," she replied coolly. "My mother would be horrified if she knew I asked any. We are never to be so impertinent as to query our guests about their lives. If they offer anything about themselves we're to be polite and listen but never pry or repeat."

"I like that you are curious about me." His voice was gentle, his expression encouraging. "Ask whatever you want."

"Why are you and your grandfather in the hollow and not planning to spend Christmastide with your family?"

A flicker of concern showed in his eyes. "It's my plan to have him back in time for Christmas dinner," Mr. Gatestone said calmly. "My grandfather is a very private person. For obvious reasons, as the duke, he's had to be. It's not widely known yet, but he hasn't been well for some time and it appears the end is near. I'll tell you why we're here but I'd rather this not be spoken about with the others."

"That would be disconcerting news for any family. I assure you no word will come from me about the duke's condition."

"Thank you." He gave her a quick smile. "Long before my grandmother passed away more than a year ago, he'd promised her that he'd bring her back here to Dewberry Hollow to see the tree where they'd carved a heart and their initials in the middle of it. Unfortunately, he was always too busy to return and kept putting off that promise until it was too late."

Isabelle's chest constricted. Losing a loved one was never easy. "I find that sad, Mr. Gatestone. I'm sorry to hear it."

His eyes shifted away from her for a moment. She could tell it saddened him, too.

"It's a regret—an unfinished task he's lived with these months—and now he aims to make it right before he leaves this earth to join her. A couple of weeks ago he decided he was going to return here, find the tree, and tie her favorite hair ribbon around it."

The thought of how lovely that was thickened her throat. Even though his wife was gone, he was going to fulfill his promise to her. "That's a sweet thing for him to want to do."

Gate's eyes narrowed and he gave her an odd grin. "Not according to my family. It caused quite the trouble between the duke and my father and uncle, who were both against this journey. All their arguments were good. It's dangerous to travel in winter. His health is poor and he's too feeble to be tramping in the cold woods looking for a tree that he can't even remember where it is. But my grandfather isn't a reasonable man. Far from it. He refuses to be told he can't do something and he wouldn't be persuaded to wait for spring. Since he was bent on making the trip, I told them I would bring him here, find the tree, and have him back in time for Christmas dinner."

Isabelle's heart softened. "It's very kind of you to do that."

His gaze caressed her face again. A tingle of something exciting swept across her breasts.

"This is more pressing than a few holiday dinner parties in London."

Isabelle pursed her lips for a second or two before saying, "I don't think you know how many trees are in the hollow, Mr. Gatestone."

"I couldn't help but notice when I rode into the village."

"The tree could even be downed by now or the bark completely peeled away so it's not easy to see."

He nodded. "But if not, I'll find it and help him tie that ribbon around it. I have three men . . ." He paused and his eyes turned thoughtful—"make that two men to help. I think Mr. Hornbolt should stay inside."

Isabelle cleared her throat as her muscles tensed and her nerves hummed. His words reminded her of her rushed decision to shoot. She'd been too eager. It was her fault Mr. Hornbolt couldn't do his job, and the poor man had been kind not to rail at her for the reckless action.

As if sensing where her thoughts had turned, Mr. Gatestone said, "The duke knows the tree was in a crop of birch, and he believes they were on the east side of the main house. He has no idea how far north or south they might have been."

"That hardly narrows your search."

He gave her a rueful grin. "But doesn't deter me, Miss Reed. Since this could be his last Christmas with family, I intend to find the tree and have him home in no time. Now, will you answer a question for me?"

She shouldn't. Already, she was feeling too involved with him. Why invest emotion into getting to know him? She would never see him again once he left the hollow. But she had never been so drawn to a man before and it was delighting her.

He lifted his hand and slowly ran the backs of his fingers across her cheek while giving her a slow, sensuous smile. His gaze remained steady on hers.

He touched her with such infinite care she wanted to lean into his chest and be surrounded by his arms. The gentleness of his caress was soothing, yet excitement tightened her lower abdomen and danced across her breasts. Her heart beat fast at the invitation she was sure he was issuing.

"It may be unwillingly on your part, Miss Reed, but I am not the only one feeling what's happening between us."

Not wanting to sound foolish denying what was so obvious, she answered, "You are the only one pursuing it."

Amusement twitched the corner of his mouth. "How can I not? It's nature's course."

She wanted to accept that. Just nature, but said, "It's a course I don't choose to go down."

His gaze lingered on her lips for a few seconds before capturing her eyes again with an intensity he hadn't shown before. "Who was the scoundrel who left you with a broken heart that hasn't mended, Isabelle?"

Startled, by his daring, as well as by his using her Christian name, she sucked in a deep audible gasp. His question was earnest. Her chest rose and fell with sudden choppy breaths. "What?" she managed to whisper while trying to ignore the acceleration of her pulse.

Leaning his hard, muscular body closer, he offered, "Someone hurt you."

It was an astute observation. She huffed a shaky laugh and shook her head. The one man she'd never forgotten. Mr. Gatestone was a scoundrel for reminding her of him at a time like this.

And even more unbelievable, she answered truthfully, "Yes, as a matter of fact, someone did." She paused and eagerly drank in the sight of the man before her. Chiseled features, strong neck, and powerful body. "He was probably a little older than you. Maybe a little less handsome and certainly not as debonair, but so charming and beguiling he was everything I wanted at the time."

Mr. Gatestone frowned deeply. "He was a rake to have loved you and left you."

"Yes, he was," she whispered. "A rake of the highest order."

He bent his head toward hers. His gaze was so penetrating it was as if he was taking in every breath she took, feeling everything she felt.

"Are you saying you don't want to explore what's happening with us because of him?"

Yes, that was exactly what she was saying. Trusting that a man would return your love and take care of you was foolish. Her mother's lover and the viscount had taught her that.

Isabelle nodded. She had to. There was no reason not to be honest with the duke's grandson.

"That's no way to live," he scoffed with an unmistakable air of exasperation. "One man shouldn't make you turn away from all men. You should move on with your life. Forgive the brute and forget about him, Isabelle."

Old hurts tore through her chest. Without hesitating, she offered with disdain, "Oh, I forgave him for breaking my heart many years ago. But I'll never forgive him for breaking my mother's and making her cry. He made promises to her. He promised he'd come back to her and to me. To us. That we would be a family. Spring turned to summer, to autumn, and to winter. He never returned and never sent one word of why."

"So, he wasn't—"

"My lover?" She blew out a soft breath of contempt and shivered at the thought of Mr. Moore. "No. He was my mother's. I was twelve and thought I was going to have a father again. So you see, I'm not interested in a man who will be here for a few days and promise me anything I want to hear for a few passionate kisses, strong embraces—a tumble in the bed as some say—and then leave to never return."

Mr. Gatestone nodded slowly as if he fully understood everything she was saying and feeling. "I'm not that man, Isabelle. He obviously made promises to your mother he didn't intend to keep. I'm not going to do that. I'm not saying I won't leave in a few days or that I have forever on my mind. I'm only asking for the time I'm at the inn."

Isabelle silently winced and sucked in a hard breath. His honesty was brutal and unexpected, but somehow she managed to appreciate it. She didn't know how it could be that she'd wanted him to want her for more than just an evening or a few days. It was ridiculous considering this was only their fourth conversation. But for some reason, she felt as if she'd known him much longer.

After all this time of waiting for a man to make her feel the way he made her feel, shouldn't she consider his offer?

She truly didn't know. She was twenty-two years old. If she was ever going to experience the passion shared between a man and woman, wasn't it time? Wasn't this the man to show her the secrets? What if these feelings and sensations he caused in her never came along again? Didn't she deserve this? Shouldn't she take this chance and indulge herself? Despite every ounce of her sanity, that was exactly what she wanted to do.

Even if in the end she would wind up bereft and grieving over his departure.

Yet there were risks. Not only of a broken heart but the possibility of a babe to care for. Could she do that to herself? To her mother?

Isabelle felt her eyes grow moist as she pondered. Her desire for him was strong but so were her memories of standing on the front lawn with her mother watching Mr. Moore ride away in his coach. Not wanting Mr. Gatestone to see how conflicted she was, she turned and hurried from the room.

Chapter Five

It was a madness Gate had innocently given in to at the time. An easy decision to make when his grandfather, uncle, and father were shouting at one another. Now he knew. There was no way in hell he was going to find that damned tree he had been so cocky with his promises to his family. He thought he'd arrive at Dewberry Hollow on one day, find the tree the next, and be on his way back to London by the third day. The fourth at the latest. Plenty of time to have his grandfather home, rested and ready for Christmas festivities.

Hell no. That hadn't happened.

Gate's nose, toes, and fingers felt frozen to the bone as he walked into the inn shedding his hat, cloak and wool-lined leather gloves. With no small amount of frustration, he threw them onto a chair in the entryway.

After three entire days spent searching the snowy woods from dawn to dark, his attitude was temperamental. He had nothing to show for his hunt except too many pheasants to count and five turkeys he and his guards had shot when the opportunity presented itself. The birds had made the cook happy, and she'd done an excellent job preparing them for their dinners. But that had done nothing to further his reason for being in the hollow.

He huffed a loud sigh and grunted with ire. What had made him think he could find a needle in a haystack? *Damnation.* He'd never really done anything worthwhile in his life. He'd never had a reason to. Everything was done for him. He didn't do for others. But now his grandfather needed him to find that blasted tree.

So far, he had failed.

And this had to be the coldest place on earth. The wind had blown like a northern gale off the coast of Scotland all day. The only thing that could have been worse was if it had been sleeting, too, but no. Instead, Mother Nature had dusted them with a light, powdery snow that had been the only bright spot in the dreary, uncompromisingly frustrating day.

What the hell was he doing here? He should be at White's sipping brandy by the fire and laughing with his friends or attending a dinner party and dancing until the wee hours. That was his life. Not this. Maybe tonight he would do what he'd planned before meeting Miss Reed in the evergreen thicket. It was odd for him, but after being with her and holding her close that first afternoon, all thoughts of a visit to the village tavern to play a few games of cards, drink a glass or two of port, and find a willing woman had faded from his thoughts. Odd as it was for him, he'd been content to spend the evenings listening to Mrs. Boothe entertain on the pianoforte in the music room and then playing cards or other parlor games with Isabelle and the other guests in the drawing room.

Suddenly remembering how empty his life had felt in London and how beautiful the snowy landscape—

"Mr. Gatestone."

Gate looked up. Isabelle was coming down the corridor toward him carrying a large basket of wood.

"What's this?" he asked, taking long strides to meet her. "Give me that." Frowning, he took the basket from her. "Do you often do the servants' work for them?"

She gave him a surprised glance and continued to walk. "As a matter of fact, I do," she said pleasantly. "I was coming this way, so why not bring a load of wood with me rather than walk empty-handed and force the footman to bring it later?"

"Because you are a lady," he said irritably.

"Oh, I see you believe the same nonsense my mother does." She huffed a laugh as they entered the drawing room. "I am perfectly capable of doing everything in this inn that others can do whether it be to help Mr. Danvers balance the account books at the end of every week or carry the wood."

He was quite sure she was no frail weakling and was as intelligent as she was beautiful. "Just because you *can* do everything doesn't mean you should," he grumbled, and placed the basket beside the hearth where she pointed.

Isabelle reached down and picked up a dark brown bottle from the wood. "Dare I say you sound a bit miffed today, sir?"

Frustration caused him to grit his teeth. It was true his attitude was irritable, but when he straightened from positioning the wood and looked at Isabelle all his irritation seemed to drain from him. Wearing a simple cocoa-brown high-waisted velvet dress that flattered her slim but womanly figure, she captivated him. The neckline was just low enough he could see the gentle billow of her breasts. Her smile was soft and welcoming as a ray of sunshine.

Looking at her now, he felt as if he didn't want to *ever* be without her in his life. It was as if he not only wanted her with a desire that wouldn't abate but also needed her to talk to and confide in.

As absurd as that thought seemed, considering he'd only known her a few days, it didn't stop the unexpected feeling from sweeping over him at the prospect that it might be true. "What's in the bottle?" he asked.

Isabelle held it up and looked at it. "I'm not sure exactly. I stopped by the apothecary this afternoon after teaching the girls and explained Mrs. Boothe's problem. He gave me this and said to put a spoon of it in her tea every morning and evening. Perhaps it will improve her memory." She gave Gate a confident smile that seemed to be inviting him to come closer. "So you see, I can also take care of errands for our guests."

He chuckled as his gaze feathered down her face. He wanted to take her in his arms to kiss her and wondered what she would do if he did. Would he scare her away as he had the other night? Or was she feeling as comfortable with him now as he felt with her?

"I have a feeling you can do anything you set your mind to, Isabelle."

As soon as he said the words an idea he should have thought about days ago flashed through his mind and he studied on it.

"I know a fire's been lit in your chambers, but do you need to warm by the big fire here before you go up? It's been a bitter day."

"No. I'm not chilled," he said, and knew it now to be true. It was impossible to feel the leftover effects from the arctic wind when she was near.

Her eyes sparkled and the corners of her luscious mouth twitched ever so lightly. For a moment he thought she was going to contest his statement. Instead, she offered, "Very well. I asked Mama if we could move up dinner while the duke is staying with us. He seems tired by the end of the day. She spoke to the duke about changing the time and he agreed.

We'll be gathering in the drawing room at six-thirty and dine at seven. I hope that's acceptable for you as well."

"Yes," he answered, thinking as long as he could see her he didn't care what time they dined. Or if they dined.

Isabelle looked at the bottle in her hand and sighed softly. "I best get this to the kitchen and explain how it's to be used. Thank you for your help with the wood. Now you haven't much time. I'll leave you to go up and prepare for dinner."

"Before I do, Isabelle, I have a request."

"No, Mr. Gatestone," she said with a surprised laugh. "You must stop using my name. It simply isn't permissible. You presume on a relationship we don't have when you do so."

He tilted his head and smiled warmly at her. "We do whether or not you acknowledge it exists. I want you to come into the woods with me tomorrow."

She remained perfectly still but blinked rapidly. "What?"

Gate drew in a ragged breath. "I meant I would like for you to join me in my search for the carved tree. You know these woods, and I feel the hunt would go much faster if you were helping. It seems as if we've been looking at the same blasted trees two and three times a day."

Her brow furrowed. "I'm sure you weren't. It's just that most birch look alike as do ash, oak, elm, and all the others."

How well he knew.

Giving her head a little tilt, she asked, "Didn't you take a dye with you to mark the areas you'd examined?"

He shifted his stance uneasily. "I'm reluctant to say that while I've had all good intentions for this venture, I didn't fully realize the size of this undertaking before arriving or since. My grandfather's memory of this place had it much smaller than it actually is."

"I'm sure our inn and the forest surrounding it are woefully insignificant when it comes to his estates and lands, which must be tremendous."

"The duke's lands can't hold a candle to the trees on the wings of this hollow," he murmured with all truthfulness.

Her expression softened. "You sound exasperated, Mr. Gatestone."

"With good reason," he muttered, thinking it was much more than exasperation. "The time I can remain here is short. Which brings me back to my question to you. Will you help me find the tree? Not for me but for the duke. I confided in you how ill he is and how important tying that ribbon around the tree is to him."

"I do know these woods," she answered noncommittally. "Aside from the fact I don't get involved with the lives of guests who stay here, what you are attempting is almost impossible since your grandfather remembers so little about where he was when he made the heart. It's going to take a miracle for you to find that tree—and quite frankly, I'm fresh out of them."

Gate never had a reason to need a miracle, but he was looking for one now. And he knew finding that miracle had something to do with Isabelle.

He suppressed the sudden desire to pull her close and simply hold her in his arms and feel her slim body next to his. Instead, he said, "I need you."

A flash of emotion skittered across her face and he knew she wavered.

"And you will be helping an old man who is a guest in your lodge the same as you are helping Mrs. Boothe with the tonic."

Isabelle seemed to study over his words. "I do try to help everyone who stays here. But I have more important things to do during the day than walk the forest with you. I have another teaching lesson for several of the girls in the village tomorrow. Besides . . ." She paused and gave him a half-playful smile. "Your guards are helping you, are they not?"

He felt the unmistakable rise of desire in his lower body. Her teasing showed him no mercy and he was drawn to it. But he really was going to have to explain about the guards one day.

Once again squelching the urge to pull her into his arms and kiss her tempting lips, he said, "Day after tomorrow is Christmas Eve. I am running out of time, Isabelle. I will make it worth your while and pay extra for your time."

Her eyebrows rose more than a mere fraction. Gate didn't know if she was offended or interested by what he said but it certainly was the right thing to say to get her attention.

Betting on the former, he said, "You wouldn't have to keep the money if you didn't want to. You could spread the Christmas cheer around and give extra to your staff on Boxing Day. My grandfather is a demanding grumbler, and they'll deserve it by the time we leave. Or maybe there are some villagers who might need a few things to make their Christmas or Twelfth Night dinner a little merrier. Perhaps even something for the girls you tutor."

She remained quiet. Thinking. He definitely had her curious with the possibility of increasing payment for their time at the inn. But she wasn't committed. Yet. A little more persuasion was obviously in order.

"In addition to that, there's the other little matter."

Her head tilted and her gaze searched his face trying to determine what he meant. Gate enjoyed being looked at by her in such finite detail. It made him want to hold his arms out to his sides and tell her to come close and search every inch of him carefully for anything she wanted.

"What are you talking about?" she asked with a small amount of suspicion lacing her tone.

"You owing me."

Her chin lifted higher and her shoulders rose precipitously. She cautiously leaned in toward him. "What on earth are you trying to say, sir?"

She was absolutely gorgeous and he loved it when she was annoyed with him. "That I should receive some consideration from you for keeping the whole truth about Mr. Hornbolt's arm injury from the duke and your mother."

Her lovely fan-shaped brows drew together in a determined frown. "You said you wouldn't tell."

He shook his head innocently. "No, no. Not me. I wouldn't, but maybe someone might—I am desperate, Isabelle and need your help."

She harrumphed. "You want to have your grandfather back safely in London for Christmas dinner and the day after tomorrow is Christmas Eve. All right. Believe me, the sooner I can get you out of here, the better it will be for me, too."

Her words surprised him. He knew she was as attracted to him as he was to her. That tempted him to ask, "Why is that?"

Isabelle stared at him and he watched the rigidity leave her body as she softened. "You know I'm fascinated by you. You know I am fighting the way you make me feel when you look at me. Much to my regret, I am not immune to your charm."

Gate's body tightened. His skin prickled with pleasure and possibilities. "I'm glad to hear you finally admit that."

"I also acknowledge I want to help the duke. He's old, sick, and came all this way to fulfill his dying wish. I don't want him disappointed." She placed the bottle of tonic on top of a table. "I'll give this to the kitchen later. Right now I want to do what I must to get you out of here before I do something stupid. Follow me."

Whipping around, and without waiting for him, she started marching down the corridor. Gate smiled and followed.

He assumed they were headed for the sitting room, but she passed it without the bother of a glance. They made a left turn and proceeded down a different, darker corridor where no lamps had been lit. They continued and passed an area he hadn't seen before with rooms on each side of the corridor until they came to what appeared to be the back of the house, where they entered a tall-ceilinged, spacious library.

The air was cold, drafty, and held the scent of leather and stale, brittle parchment. The room didn't appear to be used often. There were no comfortable reading chairs placed about, no tray with decanter of brandy and glasses, and no type of correspondence on top of the large oak desk. Shelves filled with books of varying sizes lined both sides of the room. A lone window bracketed by pale blue velvet draperies centered the back wall. Isabelle went immediately to one of the bookshelves and started searching for something.

"Should I light the lamp for you?" he asked, thinking she seemed very determined.

"Yes, thank you," she said without turning from her hunt. "The one on the desk should be enough."

After taking care of the light, he walked over to her. He enjoyed watching the way her softly rounded shoulders moved as she pushed, pulled, and shifted books, looking at first one and then another. Wispy strands of her blond hair had fallen out of her chignon to grace the nape. He wanted to move them to the side and kiss the back of her neck, pull her close to him, and breathe in her womanly scent. At the thought of kissing her, a warmth of slowly rising passion settled low in his loins. It was heavenly and he wanted to explore it with her.

He sucked in a deep, soundless breath to calm his desire and asked, "What are you looking for?"

"This," she said, swinging to face him with a satisfied smile and a rolled sheet of parchment. "I think it will help us. Come over to the desk and I'll show you. It's a map that shows the design of the inn and how it's situated at the mouth of the hollow."

Gate bent over her shoulder as she unrolled the delicate paper. With the palms of his hands, he helped her secure the corners of the map to hold it flat. It felt good to be so close to her. She was inviting and tempting him to deny her wishes that he keep his distance, let go of his control, and kiss her until he had his fill.

"The inn was built east to west as it shows here." She pointed to the outline of the drawing. "You see sunrise from the front of the building and sunset from the back garden and lawn. This shows the basic layout of the clusters of trees that rise from the valley and surround the inn. Along here is the main road leading in and out of the hollow. This is the evergreen thicket where we met."

She stopped and lifted her gaze to him. Gate's heart started thundering. Her lashes were thick, long and with a velvety sheen. Her eyes sparkled with lamplight and excitement from what she was sharing with him. The natural healthy color of her flushed cheeks and pink lips stirred his desire to make her his.

All too quickly she lowered her gaze back to the map and continued. "There are large clusters of birch in most of these areas. Here and here."

Gate looked at the map as she pointed out each section, but there was no doubt his attention and all his senses were on Isabelle. Not on what she was showing him. Being so near he could reach over and kiss the soft warm area behind her ear made concentration on anything other than her almost impossible.

"My mother would be horrified if she knew I was going to spend the day helping you. Despite my best efforts she is still trying to make me a proper lady. Consequently, I'll not tell her what I am going to do and I'll send notes to the girls' parents that I'll make arrangements to see them on a different day. Mama would never approve of me going into the woods with one man—let alone with three."

"You will be safe with us," he whispered near her ear.

She turned to look at him, which put their lips so close together he felt as if his heart stopped beating. He wanted to let go of the map, pull her into his arms, press his lips to hers and feel the shape of her body beneath his hands. Their gazes held for a long moment before she gave him that teasing smile he was coming to love and in a lighthearted tone said, "Yes, of course, I will. Your men are guards, are they not?"

Gate smiled, too. The way she temped him was beyond anything he could remember. He couldn't believe how caught up he was by her. In truth, he hadn't thought himself capable of feeling such rich desire for anyone. Yet, he was utterly enraptured by Isabelle.

He gripped the parchment tighter and reluctantly leaned away from her. "I can explain about the guards if you would allow me."

"No need. I told you I understand how important dukes are and their families. Now, I can't show this to your grandfather, but you can." She slipped the map from his grip and started rolling it. "Perhaps it will help him remember if they were more north or south of the inn when they carved the tree. Were they five minutes away or half an hour? Have him think back to that time and help us find the area the tree is located."

"I'll show it to him after dinner," he said, taking the map from her grasp.

"All right. I'll meet you by the carriage house tomorrow morning around nine. And remember, after this we will be even. You helped me, and I will have helped you."

"Even?" He laid the map back on the desk. "That will never do, Isabelle. What kind of man would I be if I allowed you to be even? I must always be one step ahead of you."

Her beautiful lips curved into a smile. "You are a mischievous soul, Mr. Gatestone."

He chuckled softly. "I am just a man and you are a very desirable woman. No apologies offered for that."

"None asked for," she answered, and flattened her hands upon his chest, rose on her toes, and kissed him.

Her lips were soft and only briefly brushed against his, but long enough for him to know the touch was different from that of any other woman. She stirred something inside him that had never been awakened before. It was as if she'd touched him with some kind of magic.

She settled back on her feet and lowered her hands. "I think that puts me ahead of you again and you will have to find a way to catch up, because now you are two steps behind."

"I'll take that as permission to do this," he said huskily, catching her up in his arms as his lips came down on hers.

He kept the kiss gentle but generously exploring, aching for it to last as long as possible without overplaying his hand. He understood her reluctance to be with him, but his body didn't. He wanted her with a hunger that defied common reasoning.

When Gate finally lifted his head and looked into her eyes, he whispered, "That was worth waiting for."

"You are very strong, Mr. Gatestone."

He made no move to release her. "Am I holding you too tightly?"

"No," she answered on a shivery gasp, and wound her arms

around his neck. "Your arms feel just right, but you knew I'd never be able to settle for just one kiss."

"I was hoping."

Controlling his eagerness and hunger for her was almost impossible. He kissed her again. This time he held back none of his desire. He wanted her to know he desired her with his whole being. Her lips parted and she leaned sensually into him. It was heady. Her lips were warm despite the chill in the room and, on what had to be the coldest, dreariest day of the year, she tasted like sunshine.

The velvet fabric of her dress teased his hands as he ran them over her shoulders, her back, down to the curve of her slim waist and flare of her rounded hips. She was beautifully shaped. Their kisses were seeking and savoring. Their tongues swirled, their breaths blended, and their bodies pressed together with soft urgent movements that created more hunger inside him.

His lips left hers and her head fell back as she clung to his shoulders, skimming her hands along the width and breadth of his back. He kissed his way down the long sweep of her neck and chest. With gentleness, he slid one hand up her midriff to fondle her firmly soft breast while he molded the other hand over her hip, drawing her snugly to him. A tremor shook her body, and she gave a quick moan of delight, proving she had wanted this as much as he had. The response from her shot heat like he'd never known spiraling through him.

Gate moved to slip the sleeve of her dress off her shoulder, but her hand closed around his wrist and she shied away from him and the kiss. She let go and stepped back.

Her breaths were shallow, and her eyes glazed. She seemed to swallow hard. He sensed breaking away from him hadn't been easy for her and it sure as hell wasn't for him.

"I think we forgot why we came in here." She picked up the map and handed it to him.

No. He hadn't forgotten one thing about her.

"I'll see you at dinner," she said softly.

"Meet me later," he said earnestly.

She studied on his question, considered it, and then smiled. "Of course. I'll meet you."

His lower stomach tightened with keen expectation.

"Exactly where we've been the last three nights. In the drawing room with Mama, Mr. Thimwinkle, and Mrs. Boothe enjoying a game of whist, cribbage, or loo and a spot of brandy by the fire."

With a husky laugh, Gate had to acknowledge she once again had the upper hand. "You forgot Mrs. Boothe's serenade on the pianoforte."

"So I did," she acquiesced.

He gave her a half smile. "Tonight I was thinking along the lines of something more intimate for just the two of us."

"No, Mr. Gatestone," she said with confidence.

After rolling the parchment into the palm of his hand, he turned to leave but stopped and looked back at her. "We'll have our muskets tomorrow in case we happen upon any game. You won't need to bring a weapon."

Her lovely mouth formed an O before it dissolved into an attractive grin that eased into a soft beautiful laugh. "You are a shameful man. You still think I'm going to shoot someone else, don't you?"

He shrugged casually, teasing her. "Not intentionally."

Gate felt a fluttering in his chest. That's when he knew he was in trouble.

He felt as if she, and she alone, belonged in his arms. Somehow, he knew she wasn't a woman to possess but one to cherish. That realization gave him pause. Should he be thinking about her that way? A way that he hadn't ever thought about a lady before.

"Miss Reed?"

Gate swung around to the open doorway. Mrs. Boothe stood there with a confused expression on her face. He glanced back to Isabelle. She was as startled as he by the elderly woman's presence.

"Yes, Mrs. Boothe," Isabelle said walking toward her. "What can I do for you?"

"I don't want to be a bother. You seemed to be in deep conversation but I've lost my way. Do you mind helping me find my room?"

Gate watched Isabelle's shoulders relax and she smiled as she took hold of Mrs. Boothe's arm. "No, not at all. I'll be glad to do that for you. Come with me. I want to show you something. I stopped by the apothecary for you today."

Isabelle gave Gate a parting glance and his lower stomach tightened again.

What the devil was he feeling? He hadn't come here looking for love. He hadn't even come looking for a woman to pass the time with. He wanted to find a tree. And as important as that was, he was beginning to think he had found something far more precious.

That gave him pause. He didn't know if he was ready for all the things Isabelle was making him feel. He didn't know if he was ready for her in his life.

Chapter Six

Isabelle had awakened early and with so much anticipation it irritated her. She was not winning the war with Gate. That she was thinking of him as Gate and not Mr. Gatestone was proof. Not that she needed anything more than the way he made her feel when he looked at her, touched her, and kissed her.

They'd had a wonderful time together last night playing cards, laughing, and talking with her mother, Mrs. Boothe, and Mr. Thimwinkle. Even the duke had stayed for Mrs. Boothe's recital. It was quite clear after their first evening of parlor games that Gate was a skilled cardplayer, but he was kind enough to let all of them win once or twice a night. He never minded Mr. Thimwinkle's funny *ho-ho-ho* laugh or Mrs. Boothe asking him the same question several times. He always answered as calmly as the first time. Even Isabelle's perfectly mannered mother had squealed with delight more than once during their relaxed evenings.

While decks were shuffled and decisions were made on which card to play, they talked of London, the Prince Regent's lavish lifestyle, balls during the Season, and the beautifully wooded parks. Isabelle never wanted the evenings to end. Last night when it came time for everyone to retire, she had been deliriously tempted to whisper for Gate to meet her in the library after everyone settled into their rooms.

Her yearning was deep, but knowing he wanted nothing more than a mere tryst for a night kept her from delivering the invitation, regardless of his repeated questioning glances. Maybe if she didn't give in to the temptation, her heart wouldn't be broken when he left.

For a time after she'd gone to bed, she found herself wondering if that's how her mother's affair with Mr. Moore had started. Lingering glances, soft touches, and amazing kisses that seemingly had no end. Finally, she decided that it was so long ago it didn't matter. The damage was done. Isabelle couldn't trust her heart to any man who was a guest in the inn. Not even for a single night.

So what she must do today was find that tree and send the handsome man on his way. The sooner the better for her. The hollow would always be her home. While she felt Gate fit very nicely into it, the carefree London bachelor would never feel that way even if he should want more than one night with her.

"Where are you off to all bundled up for a north wind?" her mother asked as Isabelle walked into the drawing room.

"I have several things to get done today, Mama," she replied cheerfully.

Her mother placed the quill in its stand and rose from the chair in front of the secretary. "What is there for you to do?"

"As if you didn't know," Isabelle answered, hoping Alma wasn't going to question her too thoroughly. She didn't want to fib but couldn't tell her mother the truth. "I wanted to make sure the carriage wheels are in good shape for our ride to Christmas Day church and that the blankets and everything else are onboard."

Alma threw up her hands in frustration. "And you can't trust the staff to do something as simple as that? Really, Isabelle," her mother admonished. "And you really shouldn't go visit Mr. Gatestone's guard as you did yesterday. It simply isn't proper for you to be looking in on a man."

Isabelle lifted her chin and gave her mother a questioning look. "He is hurt. It's perfectly fine for me to check on him. Besides, I wanted to take him a piece of that delicious mincemeat pie Mrs. Miller delivered. He was delighted to see me and to get the pie. It was the right thing to do whether or not it was proper."

Alma snorted. "I'll never understand you and I'll never take credit for you being so forward in your thinking."

Isabelle walked over and kissed her mother's cheek affectionately. Alma never grew tired of complaining about how much work Isabelle did around the inn or about how improper she was. It had long since caused Isabelle worry. She accepted that she and her mother were different and never had ill or hurt feelings. She adored her mother too much for that.

"Since we have only two grooms, a gardener and a groundskeeper, a footman, Mr. Danvers, and the kitchen staff, I suppose there's no one but you who can handle these important details concerning the carriage."

"You know I want to take care of them, Mama," Isabelle added with a smile. "I'm not good at sitting around all day with a book or embroidery hoops in my hands." She looked down at the secretary. "Or writing long letters about daily life here in the hollow to family members as you do. I need to be doing something more active."

"I know. Sometimes I wish we had sold this place when your father died and I had allowed you to grow up in London as a proper young lady should."

"Are you saying I'm not proper?" Isabelle asked with a smile, ignoring her mother's well-worn complaint.

"No, of course not. You know better." Her mother looked away for a moment as if she was searching for the right words. "I've seen the way you look at Mr. Gatestone and he looks at you. You must know I'm worried about you."

Isabelle had wondered if her mother had seen the exchanges between them and if she'd suspected anything. Now she knew. "Don't worry, Mama," she offered softly.

Alma gave her an almost pained expression. "Surely you know I do. I haven't forgotten how your heart was once broken."

"Our hearts were broken, Mama. I am your daughter, and like you, I am strong and will be all right. I know what I'm doing." And feeling. She just didn't know what she was going to do about those feelings.

"Oh, there you are, Mrs. Reed, Miss Reed," the duke said, walking into the room.

Isabelle and her mother greeted the duke as he stopped and rested both hands on the back of the settee and leaned over. It was easy to see how restricted his breathing was and that he was allowing the small sofa to help hold him up. A pang of compassion for the man settled over her.

"I was looking for the latest copy of newsprint," he said in a clipped tone. "Where will I find it?"

"I'm sorry, Your Grace," Alma offered concernedly. "It's usually laid out for our guests in the east sunroom."

He took in a deep breath. "Would you have someone get it for me?"

"Yes, of course. Right away."

"That would be appreciated." Holding on to the settee, the duke walked around it and made himself comfortable. "It's quite warm in this section of the inn. I'll read it in here."

"Yes, please do," Alma agreed, sending a look of help toward Isabelle. "I'll get it at once."

"No, Mama, you stay with the duke. I'll have it sent in and then be on my way. And don't worry. I'll be back and dressed for dinner on time."

"I should hope so. It's hardly past nine o'clock. You can't have that much to do."

Isabelle said good-bye to the duke, found a maid to take care of the newsprint, and then headed for the back door. After fitting her wool bonnet low over her ears and tying the ribbon tightly under her chin, she buckled her leather hunting belt around her cape at her waist. She then grabbed one of the four bags she'd had the cook prepare and draped it across her shoulder. Picking up the other three, she opened the door and stepped out.

A blast of arctic air hit her. It was going to be a miserable day with the gray sky showing little hope of the sun shining. She kept thinking surely the excessive cold would abate and give them a reprieve soon.

As she neared the carriage house, Isabelle saw Gate and his two guards standing outside looking at the map she'd given him yesterday afternoon. Just the sight of him invigorated her, and she knew she wouldn't be daunted by the biting temperatures.

Gate rolled the parchment in his hands and headed toward her. "Good morning," he said, smiling.

She responded in kind and thought any morning she could see him would be a fine day. "You thought to bring the map. That should help."

"What did you bring?" he asked, looking at the bags in her hands.

"A jar of red dye to mark where we've been, food, and four drams of port for each of us."

He chuckled. "Well done."

Isabelle knew he'd be pleased. She turned and spoke to each of the guards as she handed them one of the sacks before giving the last one to Gate.

He moved closer to her and opened the map.

"What did the duke have to say when you showed him the map?" she asked. Feeling his warmth, she had to force herself not to touch him.

"The most important thing he remembered was making the carving on the middle tree of a cluster of three."

"That is helpful. As long as all three trees are still standing. At this point, I think we can safely pass on all stand-alone trees, don't you?"

Gate nodded. There was an air of eagerness and excitement about him and what they were about to do.

"I took the duke onto the east portico a few minutes ago. He's certain that's where they started their walk. They didn't go very far before finding a tree Grandmother said was perfect. He believes they went straight out from the lawn this way and into the forest, but admitted they could have wandered north or south before stopping."

"What area did you and your men cover yesterday?" she asked, taking hold of one side of the map.

"Here," he said, pointing to the lower southern portion.

"All right," she said with a confident smile. "We'll start on the opposite side. Let's head over to the east portico to get started."

Hours passed. The frigid wind never stopped. Their pace was fast, thorough, and fruitless. Most of the time Isabelle couldn't see the two guards who were working down a slope from them but heard them talking and knew they were nearby. Gate, on the other hand, was seldom out of her sight. When they first started, she tried to remain aloof, not glancing his way, though it was soon clear that was impossible to achieve. Looking over at him after every tree she marked seemed as natural as breathing. She knew he watched her, too. They exchanged many smiles and lingering glances. Occasionally they would talk, but always continued to search. She tried to fight down the effects he had on her, but each time their eyes met, her pulse raced and her breath caught fleetingly in her throat.

Sometime after midday, Gate called out to Isabelle and the guards, "Let's hold up and take a fifteen-minute rest!"

She untied the ribbon of her bonnet as he tromped over the hard-packed snow to where she stood and started unfastening his cloak at the neck.

"What are you doing?" she asked.

"You've been working a long time. I'm going to make a warm, dry place for you to sit."

"Don't be ridiculous," she chided with real concern for his welfare. "I'll be fine, but you'll freeze to death in ten minutes. Put that back on. My cape is old and thick. It won't hurt me to sit on the cold ground for a few minutes. However . . ." She paused and tilted her head. "You can help me sit down if you like."

"With pleasure."

He took hold of her hand and gently squeezed her fingers as he lifted it to his lips and kissed. Unable to stop herself, she took a firm hold of his palm. After sitting down, he settled beside her. Close enough their sleeves brushed as they took off their gloves and then looked inside their sacks.

"Will your guards be joining us?" Isabelle asked, pulling out a napkin and carefully unfolding it to reveal bread, cheese, and dried apricots.

He blew out a laugh and shook his head. "They'll have their break where they are."

Isabelle noticed Gate took out the flask first. He pulled

out the stopper and started to take a drink but stopped and then offered it to her. She took it and handed him the slice of apricot she held. He popped it into his mouth and she sipped the strong, sweet port before returning the flask back to him.

"A good, strong drink does make you feel warmer on a day like today, doesn't it?" she said.

His gaze feathered down her face and back up to her eyes. "So does sitting beside a beautiful lady."

It was amazing how fast he could make her think of springtime and feel as if butterflies filled her chest. The cold didn't seem to seep into her bones when she was with him. But she'd keep that to herself. Perhaps the less he knew about her true reactions to him, the less it would hurt when he left.

"How is Mr. Hornbolt doing this morning?" she asked after they'd eaten in silence for a time.

"He was up and dressed, intending to come with us today."

"Oh," she whispered, suddenly feeling that now familiar pang of regret stabbing through her. "I suppose he didn't want to come when he heard I would be along. I don't blame him for not trusting me, of course."

"What?" Gate grimaced. "That's not it at all. He wanted to see you today. For you to know he's doing fine. He told me how well you've taken care of him."

Swallowing a lump in her throat, she looked intently into his eyes. "Are you sure? He's kind when I go see him, but he doesn't say much."

There was warmth and tenderness in his eyes and expression. "He never does, but I insisted it was too cold for him to be out."

"This is no time for him to catch a chill. Nor for your grandfather, either. He came into the drawing room as I was saying good-bye to Mama. His breathing seems more labored."

Gate let his gaze scan the snowy landscape. "It's true. He can barely walk from one room to the other without giving out of breath. He tries to hide it from everyone, including me. He doesn't like to show weakness and he's tough enough to endure the struggle. His physician says there is nothing to be done about his condition. The duke will continue to get weaker."

"Is it consumption?" she asked with sincere interest.

Gate shook his head and took a sip of the port. "His heart. The doctor has no way of knowing how long he has. Months, we hope." He gave her the flask again. "You love it here, don't you?"

She knew he was signaling he wanted to change the subject. He picked up bread to eat and so did she. "It's my home. Of course I do."

"There's a wild beauty to the hollow. Especially today, with the wind howling and bare limbs blowing so gracefully. The white bark of the trees and untouched snow makes everything feel so peaceful."

His words cheered her as she took a sip of the port. "I feel that way, but I'm surprised you do."

"Really?" His eyes questioned her. "I can't say I'm missing the congested streets and smoke-filled air from all the chimneys in London. I'm not even missing the crowded clubs."

"But as we have discussed," she reminded him, "the city has its pleasures."

Gate reached over and brushed the backs of his fingers down her cheek. "I'm not remembering any of them right now. I'm only enjoying this moment with you."

His words caused a fluttering to fill her chest. Her stomach quickened. Was he only saying the things he thought she wanted to hear or did he really mean them? Mr. Moore had told her mother he loved the wildness of the hollow, too.

Isabelle had to be cautious and not be taken in by Gate any more than she already was.

"What's it like here in the summer?" he asked.

"Hot as Hades."

They laughed.

"But only for about two weeks. It's also beautiful," she added. "The valley becomes a lush garden of green fields and colorful wild flowers. Sometimes it gets so hot that Mama and I complain we are roasting like a goose in the oven on Christmas Day. But the heat never lasts long and when it is too hot to sleep, it's a time to lie awake and listen to night birds chirp and frogs croak."

His expression turned serious. "I'd like to see it in summer," he said huskily.

The words *please come back* almost fell from her lips, but instead she held them back and only a loud sigh passed her lips. She couldn't make herself that vulnerable to him. She couldn't be like her mother was for so long, hoping the man she loved would return.

Loved?

No, it couldn't be, Isabelle admonished herself. She would not allow that word to enter her thoughts again. She was attracted to him. Yes. That's all it was. With jerky movements, she started quickly wrapping the leftover food and stuffing it back into her bag. She refused to allow herself to feel these emotions. Not for a man who would be out of her life in a day or two.

"Have you ever thought about living in London?"

Isabelle's breaths grew shallow, but she refused to look at him. She didn't want to think about why he might be asking such a question, but she had to answer with all honesty. "Not for long." She then did what she didn't want to do and allowed her feelings to show in her face. "My life is here, taking care of Mama, the inn, and its guests. It has always been my life and will be."

His eyes softened. "I believe that," he said earnestly.

Laughter from one of his men sounded in the distance, and not waiting for his help, she rose and said, "I think it's time, Mr. Gatestone."

He stood up. "For what? For me to kiss you again?"

She hesitated before shaking her head. She would love it. "No. Time to tell me why you have guards."

Gate folded his arms across his chest and slowly nodded. "I was hoping you would let me tell you. When my grandfather was nine, he and his family were in a coach robbed by highwaymen. It was a harrowing experience for him. One of the drivers was shot. His father was beaten and kicked by one of the thugs and left with a permanent limp. His mother fainted and spared herself the worst of it. The duke never forgot the incident."

The thought of such meanness chilled her. "How could he? That must have been terrifying. For everyone."

"After that, his father insisted on armed guards whenever any of his family traveled. My grandfather has carried on the tradition with his children and grandchildren. Hence, Mr. Hornbolt has been with me since I was a small lad."

Shooting dear Mr. Hornbolt would stay with her the rest of her life. As if sensing what she was thinking, Gate placed his fingertips under her chin and gently turned her face toward his. For a long moment their gazes held.

"He's fine, Isabelle," Gate whispered, his voice low and persuasive. "Now, it's time for that kiss. I can't wait any longer."

She made a small shivery sound of consent as his warm hands cupped each side of her neck and his thumbs gently caressed her cheeks. Their eyes closed and lips softly pressed together. The rush of warm spiraling sensations that erupted inside her were fast, tumultuous, and powerful. What he'd made her feel in the library wasn't just a chance occurrence of passion. It was real.

The kiss lingered deliciously as his arms moved to circle her waist and pull her tightly into his embrace. She leaned into his chest and was consumed by his heat. His strength seemed to nourish and bring to life all her senses.

It felt right and so natural when his kisses moved quickly down her chin, over her jawline, and around behind her ear. He breathed in deeply, longingly, before desperately seeking her mouth once more. She felt treasured and loved.

Love?

That word again.

No. Not this man. He would be leaving, and he wasn't promising her anything.

It took every bit of her willpower to draw away from the kiss. Stepping away was also difficult. She inhaled a deep, shaky breath that was almost painful, but she managed to whisper, "We've still a lot of ground to cover before darkness falls. We'd best get started."

Chapter Seven

During the afternoon, they'd had a false alarm. One of Gate's men thought he'd found the carved heart, but it turned out to be a scar from a broken branch. The search continued in vain until darkness had covered the landscape.

Reluctantly, Gate finally agreed they had to leave the woods. His mood was somber. Isabelle and the guards followed his lead on the trek back to the inn. She'd hoped her help would make a difference.

The northern wind had picked up during dinner and continued to howl like a rabid animal as Isabelle, her mother, Gate, his grandfather, and Mr. Thimwinkle walked into the music room. Mrs. Boothe had excused herself early saying there was something she needed to check before her usual evening serenade. The chairs had been lined up and the candelabras had been lit.

Mrs. Boothe wasn't in sight.

That was disconcerting to Isabelle. It was unlike Mrs. Boothe to be late and she had never missed the opportunity to entertain guests. The duke immediately took a seat and Isabelle watched Gate go make sure he was all right.

Sensing something was wrong, Isabelle hid her concern by discussing with her mother and Mr. Thimwinkle how rapidly the weather had turned into a storm that was now pelting the windowpanes.

"I'm going to send someone to check on Mrs. Boothe," Isabelle announced after several minutes had passed. "If she's not coming, we can go into the drawing room and enjoy a game of cards."

"Or perhaps we could all retire for the evening," the duke said gruffly, clearly annoyed about the delay.

Isabelle didn't like that idea. And by the quick glance Gate gave her, he didn't, either. Even though they'd spent most of the day together, and she would help him with the search tomorrow, she still wanted more time with him tonight. Whether or not the tree was found, come Christmas morning Gate and his grandfather would be heading back to London.

"Please be seated," Alma encouraged. "It won't take long for me to find out what's keeping her."

Isabelle's mother left the room, Mr. Thimwinkle engaged the duke, and Gate turned his attention to Isabelle.

"You're worried about her, aren't you?"

"Yes. You know, she's not been herself lately. She may have gone down the wrong corridor again and is in another part of the inn."

He smiled sweetly at Isabelle. "If it will make you feel better, we can go look for her."

Gate's words touched Isabelle's heart. It was easy for him to be compassionate to his grandfather, she could see he truly loved the old man. But she also saw real concern in his eyes for Mrs. Boothe.

"I'm sure Mama will find her. I think we've done enough searching for one day, don't you?"

"Don't remind me how futile my effort has been." Gate shook his head. "I still have tomorrow, Isabelle. I'm not giving up on finding that tree. This is the first time my family has allowed me to do anything for them. I'm determined to find it even if I have to—" He cut his words off quickly and glanced away for a moment before staring softly into her eyes.

Isabelle's heart started pounding. He was so intense she felt his burden. She didn't want to imagine what he was going to say. She wanted to know for sure. "If what?" she asked.

He seemed to be studying her before he answered, "Even if I have to return after Christmas and continue my search." His voice hardened. "This is my responsibility and I'm going to find that tree if it's the last thing I do."

"We'll find it tomorrow," she said quickly, knowing she couldn't allow herself the possibility of thinking he might be back no matter the reason. It would simply be too hard for her to bear.

"What are you two whispering about?" the duke asked as he stood and turned toward Gate.

"Mrs. Boothe," his grandson answered.

The duke's brows lifted and his expression morphed into a frown of displeasure. "Is that all?"

Gate chuckled softly. "Sorry it's not something more nefarious. I know you said that many years ago more than a few sinister plots were hatched between the walls in this inn, but nothing like that is going on tonight."

"I wasn't thinking about those conspiracies tonight. I was implying that you might be whispering about something more romantic."

Isabelle could see Gate was caught off guard by the duke's unexpected comment. She felt her cheeks flush but hoped the sudden guilt wasn't written all over her face.

"Don't look so surprised," the duke continued in his usual brusque manner. "With the two of you being completely suitable in looks, station, and birth I would expect there to be interest between you. My eyesight still works very well."

"It's not something we want to discuss now, Your Grace," Gate said diplomatically. "Isabelle is worried about Mrs. Boothe."

"Ah, yes. I'm sure you'll hear she's fine while I am not. I'm going to my room."

"Are you all right?" Gate asked, concern lacing his voice. "Perhaps I should go up with you."

"No need. Stay and give my apologies to her."

"I was thinking to do the same, Your Grace, and retire," Mr. Thimwinkle said. "Would you allow me to walk the stairs with you?"

The duke looked at Mr. Thimwinkle and for a moment Isabelle thought the grumpy old man was going to refuse the kind offer. But he surprised her by saying, "I suppose so."

After good nights were exchanged and the two men left, Isabelle let out a silent breath of relief. She had no problem talking with her mother about Gate, but she didn't want to be admitting anything to the duke.

"For a moment, I was afraid that was going to turn into an uncomfortable conversation," she offered.

Gate shook his head. "Not for my grandfather. He enjoyed watching us squirm like worms in hot ashes. He only wanted to confirm what he suspected."

Isabelle's breaths turned choppy. She swallowed hard, thankful the duke decided to leave. "Do you think he knows we've kissed?"

"He's a man. I'm his grandson." Gate smiled sweetly. "He's seen the way we can't stop looking at each other, so he assumes we have."

Isabelle huffed, "Then everyone probably does, including the staff. I had hoped it wasn't too obvious."

He nodded. "Much as you would rather it not be so, it is."

"She's not in her room," Alma said, rubbing her hands together in a troubled manner as she reentered the room with haste. "Nor in any of the other sitting areas in the guest wing, but . . ."

A shiver of apprehension shuddered through Isabelle. "What, Mama?" she asked.

"I was just told the door to the east portico was found standing wide open, and that concerns me."

"Maybe the wind blew it open," Gate suggested calmly, walking to stand by her mother.

"No," Isabelle replied, a knot of alarm growing in her chest as icy rain pelted the glass. "All outside doors are locked when the wind whips down the valley just so that won't happen."

Alma stared at the windows. "No one in their right mind would go out in this weather. Certainly not Mrs. Boothe."

Gate glanced back to Isabelle, his features filled with concern. She knew he was thinking the same thing she was. Mrs. Boothe might not be in her right mind.

"I'm going out to search for her," Isabelle stated quickly, and headed for the doorway.

"You're not going out there," Gate said, stepping in front of her, a deep frown on his face. "I'll go."

"I beg your pardon, sir," she argued defiantly. "You will not tell me what to do."

"But I will," Alma said flatly, folding her arms across her chest. "I'm sure she's in the house somewhere, but just in case she isn't, I'll have Mr. Danvers get the staff out to look for her."

"My men and I will aid them in the search," Gate said emphatically.

"Wait!" Isabelle exclaimed, holding up her hands for silence as her heart drummed loudly in her ears. "None of you," she said, looking pointedly at Gate, "know where she likes to go when she wants to be by herself. I do. It's possible she went there, and it's not that far away. I can get there quickly."

"I know she's forgetful and has been getting things mixed up recently," Alma remarked in an exasperated tone, "but to go to her favorite spot in the middle of a winter storm—well, she should know better."

"We don't know what she might be thinking," Isabelle added. "I'm not wasting time arguing with either one of you. Just in case she's out there, have the fire in her room blazing and warmers in her bed, Mama. Have someone light a lantern and bring it to the portico for me while I get my coat and gloves."

"Wait, Isabelle," Gate said.

But Isabelle didn't. She turned and rushed out the door. She heard footsteps right behind her. Before she knew what was happening, Gate grabbed the crook of her arm and gently swung her around to face him.

"Listen to me," he ground out intensely, his eyes set with determination. "I'm going with you. If you find her, you'll need help. I'll get my cloak and meet you at the portico. What I want from you is a promise you won't leave without me."

Isabelle hesitated. She just wanted to find Mrs. Boothe.

His hand tightened on her arm. "Promise me or I swear I will not let go of you."

He wouldn't let go of her. Those words were calming, comforting. She didn't want him to ever let go of her. Her heartbeat slowed and she nodded. "Hurry."

Minutes later she and Gate opened the door to a blast of wet, chilling rain and stepped out. "Give me your hand," he said against the wind, holding up the lantern so he could see her. "I don't want to lose you."

Those words warmed her like sunshine on a cool spring morning. *He didn't want to lose her.* If only he meant that he didn't want to ever lose her. Blinking those feelings away, she grabbed his hand, and they took off.

Sharp crystals of ice mixed with rain splattered across Isabelle's face and stung her eyes. It was impossible to turn away from the pelting and see where she was going at the same time. Within moments her cape felt plastered against her body, but where Gate held her was warm. Her satin evening slippers quickly became soaked. She felt every twig beneath the soft leather soles of the shoes. Ignoring the wet cold and pain, she pushed forward at a fast pace.

She'd never thought of the quiet little nook in the forest as far away from the inn, but as they were trudging in the storm and darkness it seemed to be taking a long time to reach it. The uneven ground was slippery and suddenly her foot went out from under her. Gate caught her around the waist with his free hand and pulled her up to his chest to keep her from falling.

"Are you all right?" he asked, lifting the lantern up so he could see her.

Rain drizzled down his face, drops fell from his hat, but he'd never looked more handsome. His arm was secure and his chest warm. She had a great urgency to hide herself from the fear of not finding Mrs. Boothe in his embrace. Instead, she wiped the wetness from her face, and answered, "I'm fine, let's keep going."

"Wait," he said, lowering the lantern but keeping his other arm around her. "Is that a bright spot in the distance, or am I seeing things?"

Isabelle followed Gate's line of vision. Through the rain she could see a dim yellowy glow flickering. Her pulse raced. "You're right. It is a light and it has to be hers. But it's not in the clearing with the stone bench where Mrs. Booth always sits." Fear clutched at Isabelle's chest. "She must have gotten lost. We must hurry before we lose sight of her."

Half running and half stumbling they raced toward the shining object and found Mrs. Boothe huddled on the cold ground, leaning against the trunk of a tree, and trembling.

Isabelle's heart thudded as she knelt to one side of the lady and Gate the other. Her bonnet and cape were drenched, but she didn't appear frightened.

"Everything's going to be fine now, Mrs. Boothe," Isabelle said softly. "We've found you." She looked at Gate and they smiled at each other. Isabelle suddenly felt like crying. She wouldn't have seen Mrs. Boothe's light if Gate hadn't been with her. Isabelle would have kept charging straight toward the clearing and she would have been wrong.

"I don't know why I'm so cold," Mrs. Boothe said in a shivering voice. "It's usually so pleasant when I come here in the evenings."

Gate gently laid his hand on her arm. "You're soaked. We're going to get you back to the inn." He turned to Isabelle. "You take the lanterns and I'll carry her."

"No, no, that's not proper, Mr. Gatestone. I can walk," she insisted, pushing his hands away.

"The ground is slippery," he said softly. "I don't want you to fall."

"Oh, I'll be careful," she said, brushing off his concern.

He shook his head. "We need to get you back as soon as possible. We've been worried about you. Trust me to do this for you."

Isabelle's chest tightened and her breath slowed as she watched Gate give the aging woman a sweet, comforting smile. He placed his hand back on her arm. Mrs. Boothe looked over at Isabelle and she nodded for her to accept Gate's offer.

"I suppose I could allow you to do this since I'm feeling quite weary."

Gate made a move to slip his arms under her knees but

she suddenly pushed his arms and said, "Wait, wait. I almost forgot why I was here. I found it, and maybe you can help me remember who wanted it."

"We'll help you with whatever you need tomorrow," Gate said, keeping his tone gentle. "Right now, we must hurry."

"No, you must listen to me." Her eyes moved frantically from Isabelle to Gate as she blinked against the drizzle. "Someone was talking about it in the library. A tree with a heart on it. I'd seen it before but couldn't remember where. Tonight I remembered and knew I had to find it."

A chill shook Isabelle. Her gaze connected with Gate's. His expression seemed to be asking her if the woman knew what she was saying.

Mrs. Boothe reached over and picked up her lantern and shined it on the tree above her head. There, in the prickling icy rain, etched into the white bark of the birch about four feet above her was the most beautifully carved heart Isabelle had ever seen. It was the size of an embroidery hoop and had the correct initials inscribed inside it.

"Your Christmas miracle," Isabelle whispered.

Gate slowly stood up and placed his hand over the heart. In the dim light Isabelle saw him swallow hard. An almost painful sigh fell from his lips. She felt relief ebbing through his body. Until now, she hadn't fully realized how important accomplishing this had been to him.

"I don't believe it," he whispered, his gaze holding steady on the tree. "I'd all but given up hope of finding it."

Isabelle stared at Gate. She wasn't sure how she felt about finding the tree. She'd wanted to help the duke fulfill his wish. It was her responsibility to do whatever she could to aid guests of the inn. But locating the tree also meant Gate wouldn't be returning after Christmas.

And that was heart-wrenching.

Chapter Eight

Gate carried Mrs. Boothe straight up the stairs to her chambers with Alma and a couple of maids following anxiously behind. Isabelle stopped in the entryway to quickly shed her dripping bonnet and cape before following them, only to have Alma immediately shoo her and Gate out the door the second she arrived, insisting their work on this matter was finished.

They walked down the corridor to the top of the stairs and paused, looking intently at each other. Isabelle remembered how gentle and caring he'd been with Mrs. Boothe. He'd known what to say to comfort and appease her so she would allow him to help. It took a special kind of man to know how to do that. It also took a strong man to defy such a powerful family as his and take on the responsibility of seeing that his ill grandfather fulfilled his dying wish when everyone else thought it was a foolish thing to attempt.

Isabelle was still trying to recover from the labored trek back to the inn. From the faint glow of light, she could see the shoulders of Gate's evening coat were saturated. Trickles of water had collected on the ends of his hair and ran down the sides of his face.

"You carried Mrs. Boothe all the way here and you're not even winded," she offered.

His eyes seemed to sparkle at her. "You're the only one who makes me breathless, Isabelle."

Her heart felt as if it tripped. Did he mean that? Had he said those exact words many times to many different women? She didn't know, but for tonight she wanted to believe him because that was the way he made her feel. Breathless. Suddenly, it didn't matter that he didn't love her. That he didn't want forever. It only mattered that she loved him.

And this was what *she* wanted.

Reaching up, she dried his cheek with her palm and then lovingly let the backs of her fingers trail under his cold chin before lowering her hand. "There are still a few ice crystals sprinkled in your hair."

"Your bonnet kept yours dry," he noted, brushing his mane away from his forehead and behind his ears with a couple of swipes.

Isabelle nodded and smiled. "But my feet are freezing. Yours must be, too."

He shook his head. "I don't feel the cold when I'm with you."

Such heartwarming words that she needed to hear. She must have known she would give her innocence to Gate when she first glanced into his eyes. What she'd felt at that moment had quickly grown and blossomed into a love that she wouldn't have dreamed possible before meeting him.

They had found the heart for his grandfather. And Isabelle had lost hers.

To Gate. There was no reason for him to stay and no reason for him to return. She had no need to fear that anymore. Only accept it.

Isabelle knew what she wanted. She stepped forward, rose to her toes, and pressed her lips to Gate's as she had in the library. They were damp. Cool. Fresh and enticing. His startled intake of breath pleased her. Leaning in closer until her breasts were against his drenched chest, she sighed contentedly and opened her mouth.

Gate answered by cupping her neck in his hands, letting his fingers slide around to tenderly grasp her nape. His thumbs softly caressed the lobes of her ears.

Isabelle's heart fluttered. Her stomach quickened and tightened with that wonderful, aching, and all-consuming feeling of desire. Quietly their lips clung together. Their tongues tasted, stroked, and explored with leisure. The longer they kissed the more intense it became. Isabelle wound her arms around his neck and tangled her fingers into his cold hair. He slid his arms around her waist and brought her possessively into his embrace.

Voices from inside Mrs. Boothe's room penetrated her thoughts and Isabelle reluctantly broke the kiss, looked into Gate's eyes, and asked, "Should we go to your room?"

His dark lashes fluttered as surprise lit in his eyes. "I don't think you mean that."

He kept his face so close to hers, she tingled all over. It was a risk, but there was no uncertainty in her. It seemed like the most natural thing in the world to say, "I do."

She felt his chest expand. His hands slipped around her neck again and his thumbs caressed her bottom lip. "You're sure?"

Her love for him was real, without pretense or doubts, and expecting nothing in return. It had taken her a while to realize she'd rather have one night with a man she loved than thousands with a man she didn't. She reached up and took hold of his hand. "I am. Are you?"

"I have been trying to keep my hands off you since the

moment I first saw you," he whispered huskily. "I have no doubt many men have wanted you, Isabelle, but I am certain none of them have ever wanted you as much as I do."

Chills of pleasure prickled across her skin. "I felt it every time you looked at me."

"That's what I wanted to hear."

Gate glanced down the stairs and then down both ends of the corridor before gripping her hand tightly in his. They rushed around the corner to the end of the long passageway where he opened a door and shut them inside.

After turning the key in the lock, he turned to her.

A single lamp burned on the dressing table. In the shadowy light, she saw desire burning brightly in his eyes. He shrugged out of his coat and dropped it to the floor before sliding his arms around her waist. With twirling and dancing moves he ushered her over to the bed and then carefully toppled her down onto the covers, and nestled beside her.

She laughed softly as she kicked off her saturated shoes and his upper body leaned over her.

"Your shirt is soaked, too," she said softly.

"So it is." Without care and with no small amount of tugging, he yanked it from his waistband and over his head, then threw it aside.

Isabelle smiled with pleasure. Gate was a stunningly masculine man. His wide shoulders and strong arms were rippled with muscles firmly outlined against his skin. With the tips of her fingers she traced the swell of his chest and skimmed down his firm midriff to the top of his trousers. She enjoyed the way her touch made his body tremble.

He rose over her, flooding her with warmth. It was meaningfully intimate and wonderfully sensuous to have him so close. In an unhurried manner, his mouth settled over hers in a lingering kiss. The same glorious sensations she felt every time their lips met rushed through her again. Exciting sensations tingled across her breasts like a warm shiver, spiraled through her stomach, and tumbled down into the lower depths of her abdomen to rest at the heart of her womanhood.

His lips moved back and forth over hers, brushing, nipping, and sometimes hovering above hers just enough to tease her with tantalizing little breaths of passion, making her want his eager, demanding kisses all the more. At other times, his lips left hers and he pressed kisses across her cheeks, behind her ears, down her neck, but always leaving pleasure wherever they touched.

With slow movements, his hands caressed her breasts, waist, and the flare of her hips beneath her dress and undergarments, sending tantalizing thrills throughout her body. She felt the shudder of wanting in his touch while she explored the feel of his still damp skin, the breadth of his shoulders and back, and every breath they shared.

They weren't hurried in their kisses or caresses but lingered and took intimate, reverent detail of each other.

With a deep breath, Gate kissed her temple and then rested his cheek against her temple. He inhaled a deep but soft breath before whispering, "I want this to be good for you, Isabelle."

She smiled. "It already is."

He kissed her so tenderly she wanted it to last forever. But then she remembered he'd only promised as long as he was at the inn.

All that mattered was he was here *now*.

Isabelle forced any thoughts of tomorrow out of her mind and lost herself in the bliss of his tender passion. She would touch him, feel him, and *have* him this night.

And she would never regret it.

With eager, respectful movements they worked together to remove the rest of their clothing and came together. Their kisses were deep, sensuous. Their delighted sighs and eager moans of pleasure were passionate and happy. The sensations were exquisite and intoxicating as each one built on another and another. For a few seconds she enjoyed a glorious, indefinable ecstasy that could never be explained, only experienced.

Isabelle hardly dared to breathe, wanting only to prolong the utmost joy singing through her body. Her arms were around him and she held him tightly as the feelings slowly ebbed. She smiled. It felt right that she was with the man she loved.

Moments later Gate's rough breathing slowed and he whispered her name as he settled himself on top of her. He moaned softly, breathlessly, and tenderly kissed that soft area between her neck and shoulders. He slipped his arms beneath her back and hugged her tightly to his chest.

Leaning on one elbow, Gate marveled at the gorgeous woman before him. Isabelle was perfect. Watching her in the golden glow of pale lamplight made him wonder how any other woman had tempted him.

Her dewy cheeks were flushed. Her lips, pinkened from his kisses, were parted slightly, seductively. Long, luscious locks of her hair lay tousled around her face and shoulders. The intensity of making love to her was so natural and satisfying his heart had lurched. It was the first time he'd ever felt that particular tightness in his chest. Something deep within him had changed.

He had to leave tomorrow. Now that the heart had been found there was no reason to stay. It was best to get his grandfather home. The duke hated to show weakness, but Gate knew the journey to the hollow had been hard on him. Still, the thought of leaving Isabelle, leaving the hollow caused something strong and vital to rise inside him. It was as if he didn't want to go. There had been too little time with her. How could his feelings for her have grown so profoundly in just a few days? He couldn't remember a time it bothered him to leave a woman.

Yet his life was in London as surely as hers was in the hollow. She belonged here. There was no doubt of that. She was as strong, wholesome, and beautiful as the land around her.

"Why are you looking at me so closely?" she asked, a twitch of humor lifting the corners of her tempting mouth.

A tremor of sensation shuddered through him. He had wanted this time with her and it was so much more intimate and blissful than he'd expected. "I enjoy looking at you with your hair down. It's more alluring than I'd imagined."

Her eyes and lips narrowed into a pretend frown. "Have you spent much time imagining my hair?" she teased.

"I have," he admitted willingly, lifting a dusky blond curl and letting it slip through his fingers as easily as fine silk. "You'd be surprised to know how often I imagined being here with you like this."

She moistened her lips and smiled. "What else have you imagined, Mr. Gatestone?"

The question sent a jolt of heat searing to his manhood. His fingers traced softly between her breasts and he sucked in a husky breath. "I believe I can show you better than I can tell you. Would you like that?"

Her eyes were bright with passion. "I believe I would."

So bold. So confident.

"Answer this first," he murmured. "Tell me what you want me to do."

She reached up and feathered kisses along his cheeks, throat, and chest. "Touch me, kiss me. Let me lie here with you the rest of the night."

Gate lifted her chin so he could look deeper into her eyes. He wanted her to know what he was feeling for her. "I had planned to do that, Isabelle. The only way I am letting you leave my bed is if your mother comes in carrying your rifle."

Isabelle laughed and hugged him briefly. "My mother has never touched a gun in her life and considers it most unlady-like that I do."

Gate huffed a breathy rumble of amusement. "Then let's hope tonight won't be the first time she grabs hold of one. But rest assured . . ." He paused and kissed her lips softly. "Even if she does, I won't give you up easily or willingly."

He lowered his head to capture her sweet mouth again. Then trailed light kisses down her neck. He caressed the smooth skin of her shoulders, arms, and breasts, reveling in how she responded to his every touch and move. He took his time, evoking and savoring every inch of her until their bodies flowed into one again. It was no less wild or tender as they stroked, touched, and pressed.

After a time, he whispered, "I've never felt—"

"Shh," she silenced him. "Don't say anything more."

"Why?" he asked curiously, letting his gaze sweep up and down her face, wanting her to know that what he felt for her was overwhelming. That making love to her had been different from the other times he'd been with a woman. It was more than he'd expected.

"It's not necessary for there to be words between us to-night."

He didn't answer immediately but remembered how he'd been immensely drawn to her from the moment he'd looked into her eyes in the evergreen stand. Even then he knew it wasn't just because of her natural beauty. He'd sensed some-thing far deeper in her at that first glance. She'd shown him his instinct was right when she'd courageously helped with Hornbolt, braved the bitter cold to aid his grandfather's quest, and gone in search of Mrs. Boothe without hesitation or fear for her own safety.

Gate had no doubt Isabelle would rise to whatever challenges came into her life. She knew how to take him to task, tease and delight him with her innocent charms and deep-feeling passions. With that understanding came the renewed need to touch and please her again.

He lifted himself onto his elbow and brushed her hair away from her shoulders. "What if I think it is necessary to talk? To say what I'm feeling?"

A catch sounded in her breath as she answered, "We both know how this is going to end. Be a gentleman and bow to the lady's wishes and let there be no more words between us tonight."

"It hardly seems fair when I want you to know how beautiful you are, how your eyes sparkle, how—"

"Thank you," she interrupted with a smile, and placed her palm against his cheek. "Then let words between us stop with those and hold me close."

It wasn't an appeal Gate had ever received before, and as much as he wished it could be otherwise between them tonight, he would give in to her request and hold her so close she could feel how hard his heart beat for her.

Chapter Nine

The rattle of harness and snort of horses woke Isabelle from sound sleep. She usually couldn't hear sounds of the workers from her rooms. Remaining still for a moment, she let her eyes and senses adjust to the dark gray light of early morning filtering in from an open slice in the drapery panels.

It wasn't her room.

Memory of last night splashed into her mind, startling her fully awake. She sat up in the bed.

She was in Gate's room. His bed. Alone. They had—

Distant male voices drifted up from below. His chambers overlooked the front of the inn and circular drive.

Sweet Clementine!

She tumbled the covers aside and rushed to the window. In the vaporous light she saw Gate standing beside his grandfather's shiny black coach with its fancy red crest. Her heart felt as if it crashed to her feet. He was leaving.

Yes, she knew he was leaving today. But without saying good-bye?

Isabelle's chest felt as if it were caving in on her and she shivered. There was no time to tarry and think about how she felt. That could be done another time. They were preparing to depart.

She turned and saw her gown and underclothing from last night lying neatly folded on the foot of the bed. How had Gate moved around the room so quietly he hadn't disturbed her? That didn't matter, either. Fear that they would leave before she made it below did. She donned the clothes as quickly as possible and then searched the bed for her haircombs while stepping into her still damp slippers.

Pulling her hair up as best she could, she raced down the corridors, the stairs, and then more corridors before making it to the front of the inn. She grabbed a thick wooden shawl she kept near the front door and wrapped it around her arms as she rushed outside, calling, "Gate!"

Smiling, he strode to meet her as if nothing were wrong. "Isabelle," he said tenderly, stopping in front of her.

She could tell by the way his eyes caressed her face he was happy to see her. That made her angry and want to cry. Something she never did. "You were going to go without saying good-bye? How unfair of you!"

Concern etched his features. "No," he admonished as his jaw clenched, clearly taken aback by her words and tone. "How can you think so little of me after last night?"

"You were leaving," she forced out on a broken breath.

"I was coming back to—"

"Don't you dare say that to me." Her words were quick, sharp, and heavy with resentment and scorn as her eyes pierced him with accusations. "Don't tell me you are going to come back."

His eyes softened so suddenly it took her breath. She could see her words had wounded him as deeply as she'd been hurt. Her head was spinning and humming with feelings she didn't recognize. It was unlike her to be so angry. So emotional.

"I was coming back to say good-bye to you after I took my grandfather to tie the ribbon around the tree, Isabelle."

She felt as if all the air left her lungs. "What?"

"You were sleeping so peacefully I didn't want to awaken you. I thought to take the coach as close to the tree as we can. From there, I'll put the duke on my horse for the rest of the way. After he stayed as long as he wanted, I was going to come back here to see you before we start the journey home."

He was coming back only to say good-bye. When she raced down the stairs, she was prepared to hate him for treating her so shabbily as to leave without a word, but now that she realized he hadn't planned to do that, she didn't know what to feel.

Sweet Clementine! It hurt even though she knew this was going to happen.

"Yes, of course," she whispered, raking a wayward strand of hair behind her ear, trying to keep the crushing disappointment out of her voice. She had told herself she didn't expect anything from him. Last night she'd believed that—but now knew she'd been lying to herself.

Taking deep breaths, Isabelle searched for an inner strength to get her through this parting. "You don't have to return to the inn. It will be better for the duke if you can get an earlier start by leaving from the main road."

Isabelle shivered. Was that anguish in his face? Concern?

"If you'd rather it that way."

"Yes," she answered, pushing past the aching sadness in her chest. In truth, she'd always expected he'd treat her as Mr. Moore had her mother.

Movement caught her eyes and she saw Mr. Hornbolt walking up. He twisted a worn felt hat between his hands. "Pardon my interruption, missy."

"Yes, of course, Mr. Hornbolt." She gave him a generous

smile. "I'm so glad to see you looking so fit and moving your arm so well."

He gave her a closed-mouth smile and nod. In an unassuming manner he said, "I appreciate all you did while I was here. It was more attention than I deserved."

"Oh, no, Mr. Hornbolt, please don't say that. It is I who appreciate you for not holding a grudge. It was not only my duty but my honor to see that you had more than you needed. You could have been filled with rancor over what I did."

He shook his head. "No, missy. I wouldn't have done that."

Isabelle's heart swelled with affection for the old man. "Thank you, Mr. Hornbolt."

The guard turned and walked back to where his horse was tethered and started cinching his saddle leathers. Isabelle looked at Gate, feeling calmer. Resigned. Determined to handle his leaving with composure. All she had to do was make it through the next few minutes and the worst would be over.

Her shoulders and chin lifted as she tightened the shawl around her. Swallowing down the anguish choking her, she somehow found the courage to say, "You'll be home for Christmas dinner tomorrow as you promised your family."

Gate's gaze stayed tightly on hers as he nodded. "I hope Mrs. Boothe will be all right."

"She will," Isabelle said confidently. "I'll write to her sister and see if she can come. Mama and I will talk about precautions we can take. We will move her to a room belowstairs and have someone look in on her more often."

"That should help."

His soft expression and the soothing sound of his voice made her want to rush into his arms. As much as she hated to see him go, she needed him to before she fell apart.

"Miss Reed?"

At the sound of her name, Isabelle looked to see the duke hanging his head out the coach window.

"What are you doing up at this hour?" he asked crustily as ever as she approached.

Isabelle had gotten used to the duke's bluntness and paid no attention to his manner when she responded with as much lightness as she could muster, "Good morning, Your Grace. I heard preparations for the coach and wanted to wish you a good Christmas Eve and safe travels before you left."

"That's the spirit I like to see," he said in a cheerful voice. "I expect you treat all your guests as kindly."

She glanced at Gate and offered a gentle smile. "We try," she said past a thick throat.

"At times, you remind me of my late wife. Sweet and delicate as summer's first strawberry she was, but strong and intelligent enough to know how to handle a bad-tempered man like me. I wish I could say I'll be back to see you, but I won't."

The heavy feeling returned to her chest. This was all her fault. She knew better than to get caught up in the lives of their guests at the inn. She was going to miss them all. The duke, Mr. Hornbolt, and Gate. "You will be welcomed if that changes."

"You come visit me should you find yourself in London." He paused and glanced briefly at Gate, before adding, "If I'm still around."

"I will," she answered, and realized she foolishly hoped she would see him again someday.

The duke then disappeared back into the darkness of the coach.

Isabelle returned her attention to Gate. It was as if she wanted to impress his face on her mind to make sure she never forgot him. A strange feeling suddenly came over her and she sensed he was hesitating.

His eyes lingered on hers. "I want you to know, it's not as easy as I thought it would be to leave you."

Yet he was going. He had to go. She had always known that. But she hadn't known how hard it was going to be to accept that graciously.

Weighted with sorrow, she managed a slight nod. "It wasn't necessary, but thank you for saying that."

He stepped closer to her. "I meant it, Isabelle. I'm not just trying to make you feel better about what happened between us last night."

"I believe you," she answered honestly. "I'm glad neither of us has regrets. You'd best get on your way so you can get your grandfather home and surprise your family that you made it on Christmas Eve instead of Christmas Day. I know your family will be pleased you were successful."

He bent as if to kiss her, but she pulled back. Her mother had been given a parting kiss. Isabelle had been standing right beside her when Mr. Moore had given it to her. Isabelle couldn't bear one.

"I hope you have a good Christmas with your family," she whispered softly.

He hesitated before stepping back. "You as well."

Isabelle didn't know how she did it without breaking down into a puddle of tears, but she watched Gate get on his horse and ride away until the procession was out of sight. Still she stayed in front of the inn, looking down the long, empty drive that led to the main road.

The fact was, it had been too late to do anything about her feelings for him the minute he'd skidded up beside her and Mr. Hornbolt that afternoon. Her heart was engaged with his at that moment. The wondrous feelings Gate had given her last night were beyond anything she could have imagined.

True to his word, he'd never promised her anything—not even in leaving. Perhaps it would have been better if he had.

At least then she could be angry with him. The heat of anger would work well to burn away tears. As it was, she was left with only sweet, beautiful memories. She thought back on his gentle touch and passionate kisses. The way he took his time and didn't rush one moment they were together. Yes, memories would be much better to live with than anger, and she would relish every one of them.

Too, sad though it was, she would get her Christmas wish. No guests in the inn for Christmas dinner. Still, she wanted to weep.

Heavenly bright sunlight had broken above the horizon and filled a blue sky for the first time in well over a week. On his journey home, Gate could see how beautiful the hollow was when sunlight glistened off the snow. Even though the winters were sometimes fierce, the sun would always return.

Eventually.

Gate wouldn't.

"I'm told you've been out here for quite some time," her mother said, coming to stand beside her.

"Really?" Isabelle asked absently, keeping her gaze on the empty road.

"Mr. Danvers said since he'd been in the house and that had been well over an hour."

"That long?" she asked with no explanation, and no move to look at her mother. She couldn't. The loneliness and feeling of terrible loss was too great. She had shared her mother's loss ten years ago and she hated the fact of her mother was now sharing hers.

"He also said the duke paid an exceedingly handsome sum for his stay. Well over the amount we charged him. Saying it was for the extra work we did for him. Do you know anything about that?"

Alma asked the question in a tone that told Isabelle she really didn't want to know the answer. Isabelle had forgotten Gate promised to do that if she helped him look for the heart. "We work hard to please all our guests at the inn, Mama."

"Yes, we do," Alma remarked in a satisfied tone. "You'll also be happy to know because of that openhandedness we now have enough funds to get us through spring and well into summer, keeping our guests at the standard they expect at such a fine inn. If our good fortune continues, it won't matter if the viscount decides not to reinstate all our allowance because you refuse to marry. However, since I feel it is due us, as soon as the worst of winter has passed I'll go see him in London and plead our case in person."

Isabelle looked at her mother and without wavering said, "I will go with you."

Alma smiled. "Good. I was hoping you'd say that. Now, tell me about Mr. Gatestone, Isabelle?"

"I'm not sure what you mean?"

Her mother gave her a disbelieving look that quickly turned to one of sweet compassion. "I know you stayed with him last night, dearest. In spite of what you think to the contrary, I know everything that goes on in this inn."

A sense of relief washed through Isabelle. It made her feel better knowing she didn't have to hide what happened. She gave her mother a tender smile. "Thank you for not judging me."

Alma shook her head and laughed softly. She reached up and caressed Isabelle's cheek as only a mother can. "I love you too much to do that."

A smile lifted the corners of her lips. "And I love you, Mama."

Her mother pursed her lips and tilted her head as she hugged her shawl to her chest. "There is something I want to know. Did he tell you he'd come back to you?"

For an instant Isabelle felt as sad as she'd ever been in her life, but then she turned and stared up at the bright blue sky again and remembered Gate's tender caresses, kisses, and the heat of his breath once more. How could she be sad about having felt desired with such passion and cherished beyond reasoning? Even for so short a time?

She couldn't.

"No, Mama. He never promised me tomorrow. I never asked for it. Only for the time he was in Dewberry Hollow."

Chapter Ten

Twelfth Night was almost as special as Christmas Day for most households in the hollow and it was no different at the inn. Keeping with tradition, mistletoe, holly berries, and colorful bows and ribbons had been taken down from the mantels, tables, and doorways and thrown away. In place of the more festive garlands, on this sixth day of January, Isabelle had seen to it that enough fresh greenery had been positioned around the house in baskets to keep the clean smell of evergreen in all the rooms throughout the rest of the month.

The kitchen staff was buzzing with last-minute preparations for the culinary feast Alma had planned to mark the end of the twelve days of Christmas. Delicate aromas of pastry, bread, cooked fruit, and roast goose had been teasing everyone's senses all afternoon.

No attention to detail had been spared when it came to setting the dining room table. The white linen had their finest china, crystal, and silver perfectly in place. Matching three-pronged sliver candlesticks had been placed at each end and adorned with sprigs of spruce. In the center of the elaborate table was a large cake decorated with preserved strawberries, apricots, and lemons.

The inn had reason to celebrate—other than the traditional coming of the Magi holiday. Isabelle had heard from more villagers wanting her to teach their daughters how to read and write and they were all willing to pay. She'd decided to start holding the afternoon lessons in the inn two days a week. They now had three more well-paying guests staying for an extended length of time—Mrs. Boothe's sister had arrived and so had Mr. and Mrs. Emmitt Perris. A young and hand-some couple to be sure.

The gentleman's family had ties to one of the wealthiest merchants in London as well as landed gentry all over the southern half of England. His father had sent him to the hol-low to establish The London Bank of Accounting. Some of the villagers complained and were slow in adapting to the idea of such a successful London business venture opening in their cozy midst. To others it was a sure sign of progress the village was growing and prospering, and a fine way to begin the new year. Mr. Perris had plans to begin building a home in the spring. While that happened, they would re-main boarders at the inn.

Isabelle and her mother had gathered in the drawing room with all their guests to enjoy a sip of punch that Isabelle was quite certain had far too little fruit and way too much brandy.

Just the way Gate and his grandfather had liked it when they were at the inn. It was distressing at times how even the smallest of things reminded her of Gate. She should tell the cook to go back to the old way of making the expensive bev-erage so she wouldn't be reminded of him every time she took a taste in the evenings. But she wouldn't do that today.

Perhaps tomorrow.

Or the day after.

Well, maybe she wouldn't mention it to the cook at all. Some memories were too precious to forget.

Isabelle still enjoyed remembering everything about the duke's grandson. She wasn't ready to give up one treasured memory of him or anything that brought him to mind.

"I was just telling Mr. Thimwinkle I think it's time the hollow had a private gentleman's club," Mr. Perris said to Isabelle. "He agreed and wants to be the first to join. What do you think of that idea, Miss Reed?"

"Since I wouldn't be joining such an organization, Mr. Perris, I'm not sure my opinion is necessary."

"Quite right, but it would be appreciated. You are well respected by everyone in the village. And I like to hear all sentiments."

Isabelle liked his answer. "That's very forward-thinking of you."

"I suppose it is," he offered. "If I get enough participation to start one, I was hoping you and your mother might allow us to lease a couple of rooms from you. In that section of the inn you seldom use, of course. I've noticed it has a private entrance and I'm told dignitaries from all over England used to come for private meetings there."

Isabelle smiled. "Yes, they did." It was clear Mr. Perris had been looking into this possibility.

"And it would only be until we could find more permanent accommodations," he hastened to add.

Perhaps there was value to his idea. Leasing more rooms meant more income to keep managing the inn to the standard her mother expected. With the extra boarders, the lessons she would teach, and a group of gentlemen paying to play cards a few nights a week, she and her mother would do fine at the inn without reliance on the viscount's meager generosity after all. As a matter of fact, they could do quite well without him.

That made her feel good.

"Yes, of course, Mr. Perris," Isabelle said. "I'll look forward to talking with you more about this next week."

In the distance, she heard the sounds of horses' hooves charging on the hard-packed lane leading up to the inn. The vibrations along with the rattles and creaks of carriage wheels drew closer. She excused herself and walked over to the window. Late afternoon sunlight sparkled on the snowy road. No wonder the noise was so loud. It wasn't one coach but three racing toward the inn. Unexpected travelers often stopped by to stay for a night—but not usually on a day that was reserved for family and close friends to celebrate together.

They had prepared the dining room for seven. She could easily make room for two more without completely dismantling the table, but more than that would take a complete remake.

"What's that I hear?" her mother asked, coming to stand beside her.

"Coaches, Mama. Three of them."

Alma stepped in front of Isabelle to look out. "Who could it be? And how many people are they bringing? Heavens! We aren't prepared. We'll have to send them away."

"Turn away a stranger? We couldn't possibly do that. Especially on Twelfth Night. Do you want us to have bad luck the rest of the year? You stay with our guests and I'll go see who it is and what they're expecting."

Isabelle picked up her shawl and walked out the front door as the lead coach pulled up. The door opened almost before the wheels stopped turning and Mr. John Gatestone jumped down. He stared at her with a tentative smile.

Her breath caught cold in her throat. She stiffened against him and the chilling wind. Her first thought was that he was more handsome than she remembered. The second was he must have returned for something he'd forgotten. And the third was how dare he come back to the hollow to torture her again! Especially looking so splendidly male, so powerful, and so at home it felt as if he'd only left a few minutes ago and not almost two weeks.

"Miss Reed," he said softly, striding over and stopping in front of her, sweeping her face with a glance that had her feeling as if she was the most beautiful person he'd ever seen. His gaze held tightly on hers. "It's good to see you."

Her breaths were so rapid she hardly managed a curt, "This is a surprise, sir."

"As intended." Gate's expression turned almost wistful. "Though not an unpleasant one, I hope." He glanced toward the door. "I know it's getting late. Am I interrupting your dinner?"

No. He was disrupting her life! She was just beginning to settle down from the heart-wrenching effects of his leaving. "We haven't gone in to dine, yet," she answered tightly.

Feeling wary, she took a step away and looked behind him, expecting someone else to emerge from the carriage. When no one did, she glanced over at the horses and saw Mr. Hornbolt dismounting. He doffed his hat in greeting, and she gave him a welcoming smile and nod.

"Is the duke with you?" she asked, cutting her gaze back to Gate, conscious of how disconcerted and on edge she felt.

"No. He's contented grumbling at home. How is Mrs. Boothe?"

Gate was much too comfortable. Didn't he know he had her feeling as if her heart might beat out of her chest at any moment? "Much the same," Isabelle answered more calmly than she felt. "Her sister is here with her now. That's quite helpful."

"I'm glad to hear that."

Isabelle's attention was diverted to one of the carriages

when she saw a footman unload a chair from the roof of one of the coaches. And was that a desk on top of another? She turned to Gate, utterly confused. "Is someone with you?"

"No one other than my valet and guards."

Her fingers had begun to tremble and not from the cold air that whistled around her shoulders. Pulling her shawl higher on her neck, she said, "There are three coaches loaded down with furniture and baggage."

"I've come to stay, Isabelle."

Startled, she lifted her chin and declared, "I'm not sure what you mean. Here?"

His expression felt like a tender caress. A white heat flushed all the way through her while at the same time a gust of winter blew across her face.

Gate closed the distance between them again. "I tried to return to my life in London, but couldn't find contentment. I missed being here with you and found no joy in my clubs or with my friends. I only thought of you and couldn't get you off my mind because you are in my heart, Isabelle. I love you."

It took her a couple of heartbeats before she gasped, before she comprehended what he was saying. His words were so unexpected she really didn't know how to respond except with, "You, sir, don't know what you're saying, and furthermore, you are out of line doing so."

His brow wrinkled and his mouth narrowed. "Why am I out of line in declaring my love for you?"

Because it was too unbelievable that he loved her, that he'd come back to her. "Many reasons," she answered quickly, but then had to search her mind to name one. "We haven't known each other that long. Your life is in London."

"My life is with you, Isabelle." His voice was husky, tender, and more heartfelt than she wanted to hear. "I returned because I love you and want to marry you."

Marry?

Isabelle's heart pounded in her ears, her chest, and hummed all through her body. Cold breath clogged in her throat. "What?" she whispered.

"It's true. Though it was a short time for us to be together, I believe you love me too. Whether or not you're ready to admit it." He smiled softly. "I always knew I'd know when I found the right lady for me. It's you."

Isabelle felt light-headed. Resolved not to get caught up with him again and reopen the heartbreak he'd caused when he left surged within her. "No," she said firmly, driven by her own uncertainty and fear to trust him. "You were wrong to come back. My life is here at the inn helping my mother, Mrs. Boothe, and other people in the village. We have new boarders, I have more girls to teach. I have responsibilities. You do not. You have a life of leisure and belong in your gentleman's world with your friends attending parties, going to clubs, shooting matches, card games, and whatever else is at your disposal to keep yourself busy."

He nodded as the wind scattered his dark honey-colored hair across his forehead and the fading sunlight shimmered in his golden brown eyes. "I do. But that's not what I want. I want to help you with your responsibilities here at the inn. I want to share your life and help Mr. Danvers with the account books, carry in the firewood, or entertain the guests."

She sucked in deep breaths. "We need no help." He was saying all the right things but the fear of him leaving again wouldn't leave her.

"It's true," he agreed, letting his gaze stay softly on hers. "You and I have led different lives, but there's no reason we can't merge the two, is there? I want to be here in the hollow with you, but it doesn't mean we can't go to London and enjoy the Season. I've never had responsibilities until I took on the duty of bringing my grandfather here. I saw how happy you are with all you have to do. I want to be a part of that with you. Bringing in the firewood when needed, walking the woods looking for deer, dining like a king, cards and charades by the fire in the evenings." His gaze dropped to her lips. "Kisses. Caresses. You made this wild beautiful land feel like my home." He stepped closer, his lashes lowered. "I love you, Isabelle. Say you'll marry me."

Her pulse raced. Yet, the pain of loss was too great to bear again. "You are frightening me with your talk of love and marriage and I want no part of it."

"Only because you didn't believe I'd return for you."

An intense tremor shook her. "You never suggested you would. I never asked you to because I didn't want to—"

"End up pining for a man who made empty promises."

Isabelle's throat was suddenly so closed she couldn't speak. He'd never know what it was like being a young girl and standing with her mother, where she and Gate stood now, watching the lane for a man who was never going to come down it. He'd never know how hard it was to watch him leave with his grandfather. It didn't matter that she'd known all along it would happen.

"I think I loved you since the moment I saw you," she admitted cautiously, feeling her defenses weakening. "But I had this dread of you leaving. And then you did."

He tenderly took hold of her shoulders and lowered his face closer to hers. "I had to go."

"I understood, but it didn't make the pain any less," she whispered as tears gathered in her eyes. "I can't go through that again."

"You'll never have to," he answered just as softly. "There is room for no one but you in my heart. I believe you wanted me to come back, Isabelle." He put one hand over his heart. "I feel it here. I couldn't promise when I'd return. I wouldn't do that to you, but my life is with you. I couldn't get thoughts of you, the taste of you, or the fresh scent of you out of my mind." He smiled and picked up her hands and held them in his. "I believe your love for me is as true as mine is for you. We will have the kind of lasting love my grandparents had."

A leap of faith quivered in her chest. The wind dried her eyes. Would it be foolish to trust and accept a love she never thought to have?

"The coaches are loaded because I'm staying. Whether it's as a guest or your husband is up to you. I am making you this promise. I will love you today. Tomorrow. Forever. Do you love me, Isabelle?"

A sudden feeling of peace about her life swept over her and she smiled. "Yes. I love you. With all my heart, but—" Tears gathered in her eyes again.

"But what?" he asked earnestly, squeezing her upper arms tighter.

"It is a wife's duty to go with her husband. What if you decide the hollow is too isolated for you? I can't live the rest of my life in London doing nothing but strolls in the park and afternoon tea and card parties. I am needed here."

Gate smiled. "I'm needed here, too. To take care of you and your mother. You will be my responsibility." He paused and she could see he was trying not to smile as he said, "I can take you hunting—for a real deer."

Isabelle felt her lips twitch with amusement. "Will you ever let me forget I thought poor Mr. Hornbolt a buck?"

He shook his head. "Never. Your mother won't have to worry about The Inn at Dewberry Hollow again," he added. "I'll always have my town house in London when we want to visit. But my life will be here with you. Accept my proposal, Isabelle."

"Yes," she whispered almost desperately as she threw her arms around his neck. "Yes, I'll marry you."

He caught her up to his chest and kissed her long, hard and

deliciously before lifting his head. "I have one more question to ask you."

She moistened her lips and cautiously asked, "What's that?"

"Do you want me to carve our initials in the tree under my grandparents' before or after we have dinner?"

Her chest swelled again. She believed he did love her with the lasting kind of love his grandparents had. "Do you have a knife with you, sir?"

He reached down and patted the top of his boot. "Since I saw how practical yours was that first day we met, I'd never come to the hollow without one."

Isabelle took off laughing and running. Seconds later Gate came up beside her and took hold of her hand. They raced toward the birch forest to carve their own heart and begin their own happily ever after.

My
Mistletoe
Beau

BY

ANNA BENNETT

Chapter One

Miss Eva Tiding's hands were surprisingly steady, considering she was on the doorstep of London's most disreputable rogue.

And on the brink of committing a felony.

Her heart hammered as she crouched in the dimly lit corridor of the Albany, jiggling a silver hairpin in the door lock of the Earl of Frostbough's bachelor apartment. She glanced over her shoulder, tucked an errant curl into her fur-trimmed hood, and inserted the pin at a different angle.

The earl's lock was only the second she'd attempted to pick. The first had been her own, for practice, a few hours ago. *That* had gone swimmingly. But this lock was newer, the keyhole was smaller, and—

Click.

Thank heaven.

The brass handle turned, the door swung open, and Eva almost tumbled into the apartment. Or the dragon's lair, as she preferred to think of it. She'd never met the earl, who also happened to be the heir to a dukedom, but on the few occasions she'd seen him from afar, his face was a thundercloud. A knee-meltingly handsome thundercloud, to be sure—but a thundercloud, nonetheless.

The gossip rags said he could freeze the Thames with a sideways glance. Eva's maid claimed he'd once sacked a footman for merely spilling a cup of coffee. Even the most ambitious of matchmaking mamas deemed the earl too cold-hearted, too jaded, for their precious daughters.

All of which made Eva shudder to think what he might do if he happened to discover her skulking around his apartment. Indeed, she refused to dwell on the possibility. She was on a mission not only to right a grave wrong but also to save Papa's Christmas—and she simply *had* to succeed.

She quickly shut the door behind her and, as her eyes adjusted to the dark, breathed in the mingled scents of cheroots, brandy, and pine. A small table in the entryway held a candle, which she lit, bracing herself for décor resembling anything from a brothel to an opium den.

But a swift survey of the room revealed no risqué paintings, no lewd sculptures, nor any other obvious signs of debauchery. A bit disappointing, that, for she'd hoped her first foray into a bachelor's apartment might prove at least a *little* enlightening.

Between the earl's dubious reputation and the whispers of his sexual prowess, Eva supposed her curiosity was only natural, but she refused to let it deter her from her goal. She had it on good authority that he dined at his club every Thursday evening and—after enjoying a few drinks, no doubt—generally returned home at about half past ten.

Which left her less than thirty minutes to locate the watch.

Now, *where* would he keep the gold-plated timepiece that he'd heartlessly swindled from her dear papa? Did dark-tempered, titled gentlemen have trophy cases for such things?

The sitting room she walked through had a wall full of open shelves, but few drawers or cabinets suitable for hiding contraband.

No, the best hiding spots were undoubtedly located in the dark depths of Lord Frostbough's bedchamber.

An open door at the back of the parlor revealed a massive bedpost and a glimpse of rumpled sheets. Eva hesitated but reasoned that the sooner she located Papa's watch, the sooner she'd be able to depart the devil's den. So she crossed the threshold, stole a quick glance at the decadently huge bed, and went directly to the bureau sitting against the far wall. The surface was bare, save for a small portrait of an older gentleman—his father, the duke, perhaps—and a pair of gloves. Very large gloves.

Feeling rather warm, she set down the candle, grasped the handles of the top drawer, and nibbled her lip. Part of her balked at rifling through a stranger's personal effects, but the watch was the one thing that would bring Papa a smidgen of happiness this Christmas. The only present capable of bringing a smile to his dear, wizened face.

To retrieve Mama's precious gift to Papa, Eva would have done worse.

Firmly tamping down her guilt, she slid open the drawer and sifted through mounds of white and buff linen searching for the gold engraved case. Stashed amid the neckcloths, handkerchiefs, and gloves she found an assortment of calling cards, cuff links, and coins. *Goodness.* Given the state of disarray, one would think Lord Frostbough couldn't afford a valet.

Then, in the back corner of the drawer, something glinted in the flickering light. Eva grabbed a fistful of linen with one hand and, with the other, reached—

A hand clamped her upper arm and spun her around. *Dear God.* No.

"Who are you?" The earl's voice was dangerously low, his fury barely contained, as he pulled her close, searching her face. "And what the hell are you doing in my bedchamber?"

Eva's knees wobbled like a cranberry curd, and her pulse echoed in her ears. She briefly considered kicking the brute in the shin and attempting to run for the door, but his broad shoulders, long legs, and stormy countenance told her escape was nigh impossible. So, mustering every bit of boldness she possessed, she tossed off her hood and raised her chin.

"Miss Eva Tiding," she said proudly.

The earl narrowed cold, dark eyes. "Why does that sound familiar?"

Anger sparked inside her, incinerating her fear. "I cannot imagine . . . ," she answered wryly. "Oh, wait. Perhaps you recall my name from the two letters I recently sent you"— she leaned forward till their chests were a mere inch apart— "letters which you *ignored*."

"I don't correspond with people I don't know," he said evenly, but his grip on her arm loosened slightly, and his mouth curled into the hint of a smug smile.

She clenched her teeth. "Well then, now that introductions are out of the way, I have a question for you. Why did you steal my father's watch?"

"I didn't," he said with a snort. "He wagered it. I won."

Eva shrugged. "Steal, swindle, scam—it's all the same to me. I want the watch back. And I'm willing to purchase it."

"Are you?" Amusement flickered across his face.

His patronizing tone stretched her patience to a frayed thread. "As I mentioned in my letters, the piece has considerable sentimental value. Name your price."

His large, warm hand slid down the length of her arm. Beneath the sleeve of her soft wool cloak, her skin tingled with a disconcerting mix of apprehension and awareness. Slowly, deliberately, he circled her wrist and lifted her gloved hand, in which she still clutched a wad of linens.

"Well, Miss Tiding," he drawled, "you might start by giving me back my drawers."

Heavens. She dropped the earl's underclothes like they'd scorched her fingers, provoking a chuckle from deep within his belly. The rich sound vibrated through her as though he'd plucked a string at the base of her spine.

"I'm not the least bit intrigued by your wrinkled undergarments, rakish reputation, or perverse habits," she lied.

He arched a thick, dark brow. "If you say so."

"I just want my father's watch," she choked out. "So I can bring him a little joy this Christmas."

"How touching," he said, his voice as hard as a chestnut shell. "But the watch is not for sale. It's mine now."

Eva squeezed her fists in frustration. "I'm willing to pay you twice its worth. You could purchase a new one, engrave it with your own initials. Or those of all your conquests. It matters not to me."

He smirked at that. "Let's repair to the parlor," he suggested, "where we can sit and discuss the matter civilly. Unless you'd prefer to stay here and lounge on my bed?"

She blinked at the thick mattress, littered with luxurious pillows and linens. "The parlor it is," Eva snapped, striding through the doorway.

Jack Hardwick, Earl of Frostbough, followed Miss Tiding into his sitting room, lit a lamp, and poured himself a glass of brandy. Raising the decanter, he turned to her and asked, "Drink?"

Predictably, she wrinkled her pretty, portrait-perfect nose. "I think not."

Jack shot her a suit-yourself grin and sank into the leather chair opposite her. She wore an emerald velvet cloak that matched the brilliant green of her eyes, and she perched on the edge of his sofa like it was a park bench soiled with bird droppings.

He reminded himself that *she* was not the enemy. She wasn't the monster who'd turned his father into a mere shell of a man over two decades ago. Perhaps she was ignorant of the strife between their fathers, but Jack wasn't. He might have been too young to fully comprehend their feud at the time, but he understood it all too well now. He was still living with the damage that Miss Tiding's father had inflicted.

Six-year-old Jack had witnessed his own powerful, vibrant father—Duke of Northcott—shrivel into a shadow of himself, almost overnight. His father withdrew from society, cloistered himself behind the stone walls of his country estate, and distanced himself from his only son. All because Lord Gladwood had eloped with the woman Jack's father had loved beyond all reason. The woman who was supposed to have become stepmother to a lonely and heartbroken boy.

Admittedly, Miss Tiding wasn't to blame for her father's sins; she hadn't even been born when the scandal took place. But since she *had* just unabashedly broken into Jack's apartment with the intent of committing burglary, it seemed to him that the apple didn't fall too far from the tree.

"Now then," he began, reaching into the pocket of his waistcoat and producing the watch. "I believe *this* is what you were looking for." He casually laid it on the table between them, leaned back in his chair, and stretched out his legs.

Miss Tiding's heart-shaped face remained impassive—except for the unmistakable flare of her nostrils. The evidence that he'd managed to wriggle under her skin gave Jack more pleasure than it probably should have, and yet he couldn't resist twisting the knife.

"I generally keep the watch with me. So, your robbery attempt was destined for failure."

She sniffed. "I haven't failed yet. I still plan to leave with the watch in my possession."

He barked a laugh. "And how will you manage it?"

"I'm hoping that you'll listen to reason. That once you understand the watch's sentimental value to my father, you'll allow me to purchase it—for a fair price."

"I'm already aware of the watch's significance." Her eyes widened, and he added, "I read the letters you sent. I know the timepiece was a gift from your father's wife."

"Yes. My late mother," Miss Tiding said, with a wistfulness that caused a vexing tightness in Jack's chest. He'd known that Lady Gladwood had died some years ago, but he'd always thought of her as the woman who betrayed his father. Not as someone's mother.

"She had it made especially for my father. It was the token of a private joke they shared, and now that Mama's gone . . . well, he values it above all things."

"Then it was exceedingly foolish of him to wager it in a game of cards," Jack replied bluntly.

"Agreed." Miss Tiding crossed her arms in exasperation. "But, as you were undoubtedly aware, he was deep in his cups that night. By all accounts, he was enjoying quite the winning streak until that final hand—almost as though my poor papa was being conned."

Jack snorted at that. Couldn't summon an ounce of sympathy for the old viscount. After all, *he* was the villain—the blackguard who'd destroyed Jack's father.

"I don't cheat at cards," Jack intoned. "You can't blame me for your father's error in judgment."

"No," she said, narrowing her shrewd eyes. "But I *do* wonder why you're so intent on keeping the watch."

"I have my reasons."

She tilted her head and leaned forward, her curious gaze issuing a silent challenge. "Would you care to share them?"

He hesitated a moment, inexplicably lost in the deep, verdant green of her eyes. "No," he said, quickly coming to his senses. He stood and raked a hand through his hair. "Let's just say that it's an important reminder to me."

"I see," she said slowly, as though she suspected he was addled in the head. "You've become attached to the timepiece. But it's more than an interesting trinket, my lord. It's exceedingly valuable to my father, and I'm prepared to fairly compensate you. Just tell me what it will take."

Jack sauntered across the room to his desk and frowned at an opened letter from his dear grandmother. She'd written to inform him she was coming to London for Christmastide—and that she couldn't wait to meet the young lady who had captured his heart. The young lady he'd made up out of thin air in the hopes of making his grandmother happy, damn it all. He never dreamed she'd come to visit. Not after all these years.

He shoved the letter aside and leaned against the desktop. "I'm a wealthy man, Miss Tiding. I don't need or want your money."

"It's almost Christmas," she whispered. "Surely you can find a glimmer of compassion in that cold heart of yours."

He rapped a fist on his chest. "It's frozen solid, I'm afraid. You're wasting your time. In fact, I think you should go." He strode toward the door, preparing to escort her out.

"No," she said firmly.

Jack stopped in his tracks and cocked his head. "I beg your pardon?"

"No," she repeated. "I'm not leaving until you name your price for the watch."

He blinked at her, disbelieving. "You intend to remain on my sofa?"

She nodded. "For as long as it takes."

"Suit yourself," he said with a shrug. "I won't physically remove you. But I should warn you that I intend to go about my normal evening routine." He shot her an irreverent grin, un-knotted his cravat, and whipped it off. Then he started shrugging off his jacket with obvious relish. "I hope you don't mind."

Her cheeks flushed, but she lifted her chin, the picture of determination. "Not at all. I hope *you* don't mind if I sing Christmas carols while I wait. I've been told I have the voice of an angel."

"Please. By all means," he said dryly, "do go on."

She cleared her throat and belted out, "*God rest ye merry gentlemen, let nothing you dismay . . .*"

Jack winced. Miss Tiding's song was loud and impassioned—and anything but angelic. Still, he was certain he could tolerate a few verses of off-key singing longer than she could stand to watch him undress. So he ignored the assault on his ears and proceeded to throw his jacket over the arm of his chair. He arched a pointed brow at her before methodically attacking the buttons of his waistcoat.

"*To save us all from Satan's power when we were gone astray . . .*"

Miss Tiding appeared to be torn between averting her eyes and looking on in horror, which Jack took as an excellent sign. He didn't even mind her dreadful singing. With perverse satisfaction, he tossed his waistcoat onto the potted palm in the corner, tugged his shirttails out of his trousers, and yanked his shirt over his head.

"*Comfort and joy,*" she choked out. "*Comfort and joy, oh tidings of . . .*"

Jack had to give her credit. Even in the face of his shocking behavior, she launched into the chorus with renewed gusto and a complete disregard for musicality.

Which left him no choice, really.

He threw his shirt to the floor near her feet, raised his chin in a silent challenge . . .

And reached for the buttons at the front of his trousers.

Chapter Two

Gads. Eva had known that breaking into Lord Frostbough's apartment was risky. She'd contemplated a myriad of possible outcomes ranging from complete success to abject failure. But she'd never, *ever* dreamed she'd end up sitting on a sofa in the earl's parlor, singing Christmas carols at the top of her lungs while he deliberately, gleefully, stripped off his garments, one by one.

And she'd certainly never imagined her body's traitorous response. Heat crept up her cheeks even as delicious shivers shot through her limbs. Each time an article of clothing hit the floor, her belly flipped. Every time his lips curled into an insolent grin, her core throbbed. When she pressed her knees together in an attempt to stop the pulsing, she only succeeded in making matters worse. Indeed, her whole body shimmered with a potent combination of desire and longing that could only be described as disastrous.

But Eva had not forgotten why she was there. The watch still sat on the table in front of her—so close she could make out the engraved letters of Papa's name. The problem was that it was difficult to think clearly while an exceedingly virile earl stood an arm's length away, his bare, muscled torso level with her head.

The warm glow of the lamp illuminated the smooth contours of his chest and danced over the wide expanses of his skin. Impossibly broad shoulders tapered to a trim waist, and springy fuzz covered the ridges of his abdomen. Every subtle movement caused a mesmerizing rippling of those muscles, giving her the highly improper urge to run her fingertips over the earl's body.

Her corset grew tight; her nipples puckered and tingled. The sweet pulsing between her legs grew more insistent. Indeed, the night was proving much more edifying than she'd originally thought.

But she had no intention of backing down from her odd sparring match with the earl. The pocket watch was at stake. Nay, *Christmas* was at stake. Lord Frostbough could continue stripping until he was stark naked, for all Eva cared. She wasn't leaving his apartment until he named his price for the watch.

And in the meantime, she kept singing. Badly. When the words escaped her, she simply repeated the first verse, even louder—as if the sheer volume could drown out her scandalous thoughts and inconvenient desires.

Alas, so far, it had not.

"God rest ye merry gentlemen, let nothing you dismay . . ."

The earl reached for his trousers, letting his large hands linger near the waistband.

Eva's mouth went dry, which made it exceedingly difficult to keep singing.

He slipped his thumbs inside his waistband near his hips, then slowly slid them forward. She couldn't help but notice—out of a strictly scientific interest—that the obvious bulge at the front of the earl's trousers seemed to be growing larger by the second.

With deft fingers, he undid one button of the fall flap, revealing a small but tantalizing patch of skin below his navel. He arched a dark brow at her as he reached for the second button and popped it free, exposing a darker trail of fuzz down the center of his abdomen and intriguing indents on either side.

"Was born on Christmas Day . . ." Eva cursed herself for not averting her gaze. It seemed impossible that a man she despised could create such strange stirrings in her.

As if he knew, he shot her a smug smile, reached for his brandy, and swirled it in his glass before raising it to his full lips. As he moved, his trousers slid lower, showing a swath of skin too pale to have ever seen the sun. *Dear heavens.* Those trousers were perilously close to falling off his hips. Just a fraction of an inch more . . .

"To save us all from Satan's power—" She inhaled sharply and prepared to belt out the next words but choked.

Oh, no. Her lungs spasmed, sending her into an ill-timed coughing fit. She covered her mouth with one hand and pressed the other to her chest in an attempt to suppress the tickle at the back of her throat but couldn't stop the body-wracking coughs.

The earl's brow wrinkled in concern, and he dropped to one knee beside her—and his proximity didn't help matters in the slightest. "Are you all right?" he asked, his voice tinged with alarm.

She nodded, certain the coughing would subside in due time—as long as she didn't perish from sheer humiliation before then.

Each time she hacked, Lord Frostbough frowned more deeply. Growling, he leaped to his feet, poured another glass of brandy, and unceremoniously thrust it at her. "Drink this."

She took it and swallowed two large gulps that burned

as they went down. Thankfully, however, the brandy succeeded in quieting her cough.

The half-dressed earl sat on the sofa beside her, his massive, Yule log–sized thigh mere inches from the skirt of her gown. He blew out a long breath and dragged a hand down his face. "You frightened me."

"Was it my singing or the coughing?" she quipped.

"Both."

He scooped his shirt off the floor, and when he put it back on Eva barely resisted the urge to gloat. Coughing fit or no, she'd won that round. She celebrated with another sip of brandy.

He leaned back against the sofa's cushions, his expression weary. "I had no idea you'd go to such lengths for a watch."

"I'm not doing it for the watch," she said. "I'm doing it for my father."

"Admirable," he conceded. "And I understand the desire to make the people you love happy."

She blinked, dumbfounded at his confession. "You do?"

"Despite rumors to the contrary, I'm not a monster." He stood, sauntered to his desk, and picked up a sheet of paper lying on top. He stared at the letter for several seconds, then returned the full force of his gaze to Eva. "It's from my grandmother. I'd do anything for her."

Eva set down her glass and rose to her feet, determined to seize upon this brief glimpse into the earl's human—dare she say *tender*?—side. She approached his desk, stopping an arm's length from him. "You do understand."

"Certainly more than you give me credit for."

"Then I'm begging you to reconsider. Just tell me your price for the watch."

"As I've said, I don't want your money, Miss Tiding."

"What, then?"

The earl braced his arms on the desktop and stared at the letter. "I can think of only one form of payment, one favor, that would induce me to part with the watch."

At last. "I'm listening."

"You're not going to like it."

The back of her neck prickled, but she kept her face impassive. "Go on."

"I'll give you the watch if you'll pretend that you are . . . that is, that *we* are . . ." His voice trailed off.

"That we are *what*?" she asked, wary.

"Courting."

Eva cocked an ear toward him. "Forgive me. It sounded like you said you wanted me to pretend that we were *courting*."

"I did."

"As in, willingly spending time together in an overtly friendly and flirtatious manner with the intention of becoming better acquainted?"

He cleared his throat. "As in, making my grandmother believe that we are so fond of each other that our courtship may result in an engagement . . . perhaps before Christmas."

A nervous giggle bubbled up and escaped her. "Surely you're jesting."

He glared at her with a face made of stone. "It's not a joke."

"Lord Frostbough," she said slowly, "you must realize that such a request is quite impossible. We barely know each other. And we *definitely* do not like each other. How on earth would we convince your grandmother that we were falling in . . . er, that we were fond of each other? At the risk of insulting you, I fear I am not nearly that accomplished an actress." She shook her head, emphatic. "No. I won't do it."

"Let me see if I have this correct," he drawled. "In order to procure the watch, you were willing to break into my apartment. You were willing to sit on my couch while I stripped off my clothes. But you're not willing to pretend that you like me?"

"Everyone has their limits, my lord."

"I've made my offer, Miss Tiding. Now the decision is yours."

Miss Tiding's bow-shaped lips parted slightly, and her evergreen eyes flashed with incredulity. "You're serious?"

Jack nodded. "Quite."

Her gaze flicked to the watch, still sitting on the table near the sofa. He took the opportunity to study her profile. A smooth brow, straight nose, and elfish chin—all softened by the long blond curls that framed her face. Her beauty didn't matter a whit to him, of course, but it would make the ruse more believable. And though he barely knew Miss Tiding, he suspected his grandmother would approve of her feistiness.

Miss Tiding turned to him, her expression skeptical. "How would this diabolical plan of yours work?"

Good question—the offer had left his mouth before his brain could stop it. But the more he thought about the idea, the more he liked it. "We'll keep it simple. Attend a few of the same social events. You'll pretend you're enamored of me." He gave her his best, tried-and-tested rakish smolder. "Shouldn't be too difficult."

She scrunched her nose like she'd caught a whiff of dirty laundry. "I'll need specifics, my lord. How many events? Beginning when? And, most importantly, *when* will the watch be mine?"

"My grandmother is coming to Town for the Christmas Season. She arrives two days from now and will staying at my father's house in Mayfair." Jack rubbed the back of his neck. "I haven't seen her in three years, but we correspond at least once a month. She's been so eager for me settle down and marry. To make her happy, I wrote that I was courting. I didn't provide any names, of course—just mentioned that we were quite taken with each other. Somehow, she inferred that an engagement was in the works."

"What a dutiful grandson you are," Miss Tiding snapped.

Jack picked up his glass, stalked to the decanter, and poured himself another brandy. "I'm not proud of my behavior, but it was meant to be a harmless little lie. I never imagined she'd hop in a coach and come to London."

"Then write to her immediately and tell her the truth."

He shook his head. "Even if I did, the letter wouldn't reach her in time. I can't stand the thought of disappointing her. She's traveling all this way to meet someone . . ."

"Someone who doesn't exist." Miss Tiding strolled to the armchair and sank into it, her lips pursed thoughtfully. "She's going to be hurt when she learns the truth."

"Eventually. But there's no need to spoil her visit." Jack picked up the watch by its chain and let it spin a few times before catching it in his palm. "Between now and Christmas Eve, you and I will attend three of the same parties. I'll pretend to be smitten with you. You'll pretend to be besotted with me."

Miss Tiding groaned and shivered as though a spider had crept up her leg. But Jack continued, encouraged by the fact that she hadn't yet stormed out of his apartment and slammed the door behind her.

"We'll quietly announce our betrothal on Christmas Eve," he said, "and my grandmother will be utterly delighted. Shortly after she returns home, I'll write to let her know that we've had an unfortunate falling-out—and that, through no one's fault, the engagement has been called off." Feeling more than a little pleased with himself, he placed a hand on his hip. "What do you think?"

"I think you're mad," she retorted.

"But you'll do it anyway?"

She hesitated. "When would the watch be mine?"

"On Christmas Eve, after our engagement is announced."

Miss Tiding stood and paced the length of the parlor, her long velvet cloak swirling around her lithe legs. "Three public social gatherings?"

He nodded.

"And the announcement of our engagement," she choked out, "which will be called off shortly thereafter?"

"Exactly," he confirmed. "You can be the one to cry off, if you like. I'm sure I'll be the sort of fiancé to give you all manner of reasons to flee for the hills."

She fluttered her thick eyelashes mockingly. "Undoubtedly."

"What do you say?" He approached her slowly, holding the watch in his outstretched palm. Maybe it was the palpable antipathy between them, or maybe it was pure lust. Either way, the air seemed to crackle. Her gaze lingered on the gold casing before drifting up his chest, over the exposed skin where his shirt collar hung open, and along the edge of his jaw. The flush creeping up the graceful column of her neck and the way her perfect white teeth tugged at her lower lip made him hard.

"I don't know," she said, her raspy voice arousing him even more.

"I have an idea," he said, slipping the watch in his pocket. "Something to make the decision easier. Why don't we kiss? Just to prove to ourselves that we're capable of doing it. That it won't be nearly as dreadful as we imagine it will be."

"Kiss?" Her eyes turned a deeper shade of green.

"Yes." Jack's heart pounded in his chest.

"Very well then," she said. "One kiss."

Chapter Three

Eva braced herself. The kiss would be nothing more than an experiment, a test of sorts. She'd quickly formulated a hypothesis that went something like this: A determined young woman could willingly subject herself to displays of affection from an infuriating, if handsome, man without engaging her feelings. All she had to do was keep her wits about her and remember what was at stake. Namely, her pride. Oh, and a very special watch.

As the earl leaned forward, Eva's eyes fluttered shut and her fingers curled into her palms. She felt the tickle of his hair near her temple, then the whisper-light brush of his lips across hers. He cupped her face gently, the rough pads of his thumbs cruising over her cheeks.

So far, everything was going rather well—if one discounted the fact that she had the very appalling urge to part her lips, grasp his shoulders, and pull him closer.

Indeed, it seemed as though the apartment had melted away. There was only the half-dressed earl and her, tentatively tasting and touching each other. The pressure of his mouth and the teasing tip of his tongue. His fingers caressing her nape and sliding into her hair.

Her whole body shimmered and pulsed with desire.

But then, Lord Frostbough pulled back slowly, his eyes dark and wary.

It seemed the kiss was over. And if Eva was feeling the slightest bit disappointed, well, that was only because she hadn't managed to gather all the data she required to make a fully informed decision.

She swallowed and touched a fingertip to her swollen lips. Wondered at the tingling sensation deep in her core. *Gads.* Perhaps she *did* have all the data she needed.

The earl stood close, searching her face, awaiting an answer—and she knew what she had to tell him.

"As much as I want the watch, I can't pretend to . . ." She searched for the words.

"Care about someone like me?" he offered dryly.

"I can't do it." Before she could change her mind, she pulled on her hood and headed for the door.

"Wait," he said gruffly. "Allow me to take you home. Or at least arrange for a hackney."

She shook her head. "You needn't worry. My maid is downstairs, waiting for me in the coach."

He followed her to the door and, as she prepared to leave, propped a muscular arm on the wall beside her. "The kiss was that bad?"

Good heavens. She'd rather die than admit the kiss had been good. *Too* good, in fact. Divine. So she simply said, "I regret we weren't able to come to a mutually acceptable agreement."

He frowned. "You mean you regret that you aren't walking out of here with the watch."

"That too." She stepped into the hallway and left him standing there without looking back.

But long after she'd snuck back into her house, changed into her night rail, and crawled beneath her sheets, she was still thinking about the wounded look on the earl's face.

And still suffering the lingering, tortuous effects of his kiss.

Eva hurried into the breakfast room the next morning, pleased to find Papa already seated at the table, looking unusually bright-eyed and full of vigor. She, on the other hand, had given herself a fright when she'd looked in the mirror moments ago.

And she knew just who to blame for her sorry state. Her tangled hair, pale complexion, and bloodshot eyes were all the handiwork of one extremely vexing, infuriatingly stubborn earl.

She painted on a bright smile, kissed Papa on the cheek, and handed him his newspaper, as she did every morning. "Here you are," she said smoothly. Spying his half-empty cup, she added, "Let me refill your tea."

"Good morning, to you, too," he teased. "Fussing over me, as usual, I see."

"It's not fussing," Eva corrected. "It's looking after you, and it happens to be what I do best." She helped herself to a plate at the sideboard, took a seat across from Papa, and poured her own tea.

He peered at her through his spectacles, a mild frown marring his beloved face. "Are you feeling well, my dear?"

Eva silently cursed Lord Frostbough as she stared at her egg. How dare the earl use Papa's watch to try to coax her into a fake engagement? The very idea was absurd, and she'd been mad to consider it for one single second. She'd been even madder to agree to that kiss—that knee-weakening, devastating kiss.

"I'm very well, Papa," she said before sawing a slice of ham with perhaps a bit more force than necessary. When her father arched a brow and narrowed his eyes at her plate, Eva set down her knife and deftly steered the conversation elsewhere. "I've already spoken to Mrs. Kent about the dinner menu, and Cook will be making you a surprise for dessert."

Papa's fork froze halfway to his mouth, and his blue eyes gleamed hopefully. "Suet pudding?"

Eva shot him a mysterious smile. "Perhaps."

"As it turns out, I have a surprise for you, too." He rubbed his palms together, and his boyish enthusiasm made him look closer to thirty years than his fifty.

"What have you done, Papa?" she playfully scolded. "I hope this surprise wasn't expensive."

"Not at all." He smoothed his thick salt-and-pepper hair away from his widow's peak and straightened his cravat as though he was about to make a momentous announcement.

"You're making me nervous," she said warily. "What is it?"

"I met a very nice gentleman at my club several weeks ago and have been in discussions with him ever since."

"Please don't say he's looking for an investor, Papa," she said, spreading blackberry jam on her toast. "I know how much you enjoy the prospect of a business venture, but I reviewed our accounts yesterday. We simply cannot afford any additional expenses at the moment."

Her father leaned across the table, reached for her hand, and gave it a reassuring squeeze. "Lord Goulding isn't looking for an investor."

"No?"

Papa grinned. "He's looking for a *wife*."

Eva nearly choked on her toast. "A wife?"

"He's young, fit, and good-natured." Papa ticked the traits

off on his fingers—as if he were describing a horse. "Excellent sense of humor. And he's a wealthy marquess, to boot."

Oh, no. Eva had long dreaded this day, but she'd always assumed she'd have a little warning it was coming. "I don't want to marry the marquess," she said earnestly, begging him to understand. Willing him to respect her wishes—and the secret promise that she'd made to her mother, many years ago. "I'm happy here. With you."

"You *think* you're happy, but that's only because you haven't really lived."

"Please, Papa. This is all so sudden. We've been fine— just the two of us. It feels as though you're trying to send me out to pasture."

"My dear, dear Eva. For over a decade now, you've been doting on me. Selfishly, I've allowed it when what I *should* have been doing was seeing to your future. But I won't neglect my duties any longer. Lord Goulding is a fine man and will make an excellent husband."

Dear God. It felt as though the air had been sucked out of the breakfast room and the walls were collapsing around her. She leaned back in her chair and vigorously fanned herself with her napkin.

"Just think," he continued, oblivious to her discomfort. "You'll be a *marchioness*."

She had to do something, say something, to change his mind. "That's impossible, Papa."

He blinked, clearly puzzled. "Why?"

She couldn't bear to tell him that she'd sworn to look after him, for that would only make him sadder. So she blurted the only other logical excuse that popped into her head. "My heart belongs to someone else."

His mouth fell open and, for the space of several heartbeats, he appeared to be frozen. "Well, that is . . . absolutely *wonderful*. Who is the lucky gentleman?"

A lump the size of a quail egg lodged in Eva's throat. "Lord Frostbough."

"Really?" Papa looked both shocked and impressed. "The heir to a dukedom," he mused, rubbing his chin. "I don't know him well, but he happens to be the man who won my watch at the gaming tables."

"Yes." Eva stared at a spot on the tablecloth, avoiding his gaze. "I know."

"I would have thought Frostbough a bit too . . . ornery for you," Papa said. "But perhaps you've come to know another side of him."

"I most definitely have." The earl was ornery *and* unscrupulous.

"And he has developed feelings for you as well?" Papa asked.

"I believe so," she improvised. "Although we're in the very early stages of our courtship."

"Still, this news changes everything," Papa said, puffing out his chest. "I'll want to meet with Frostbough. Make sure he's well intentioned."

"In due time," Eva said quickly. "This is all quite new. But if our relationship continues to progress, you can arrange a meeting with him after Christmas." Of course, she planned to end her little farce with the earl long before such a meeting could take place. And then she'd convince Papa she needed at least a few more months to nurse her broken heart. With any luck, the marquess he'd wanted her to marry would have grown impatient and selected another bride by then.

Papa beamed. "The important thing is that you've finally realized you deserve your own home, your own family, your own future."

"You *are* all those things to me, Papa," she said solemnly. "That will never change."

"Oh, but it will. That's just the way of things . . . and it's no reason to be sad." He waved a hand around the room, gesturing at the fragrant pine garlands she'd hung over the gold-framed mirror and laid atop the sideboard. "You're so much like her, you know."

Eva's chest squeezed. "Mama?"

He nodded, wistful. "She loved this time of year. Couldn't wait to deck the house in greenery. She put so much time and effort into finding the perfect gifts for us. Do you remember?"

Eva sniffled. "I do." And that was precisely why she couldn't marry and leave Papa all alone.

"Well then," he said gruffly, "that's enough reminiscing for today. I apologize for leaving you here, my dear, but I've an appointment at noon." He stood and instinctively reached into his pocket before realizing the watch wasn't there. Patting his chest to cover the slip, he inclined his head politely. "Right. I'll see you at dinner—and perhaps then you'll tell me more about your budding affection for Lord Frostbough."

Budding affection? Eww. She surreptitiously pressed a hand to her belly, willing her breakfast to stay put. But if she was going to pretend to have tender feelings for the earl, she supposed there was no time like the present to begin the charade. "I'd be delighted to," she said, pleased she could utter the words despite her clenched teeth.

Papa pressed a kiss to her forehead and left her alone to contemplate what she'd just done. And, worse, what she must do.

She dragged herself up to her bedchamber, sat at her desk, and yanked a sheet of paper from the drawer. With all the enthusiasm of a prisoner walking to the gallows, she picked up her pen and scratched out a note to Lord Frostbough. She didn't even bother to let the ink dry properly before she folded and sealed it with an excessive amount of wax.

She strode downstairs and handed the letter to a footman with directions to deliver it immediately. As if nature realized the import of what she'd just done, the clouds thickened, the wind howled, and frozen pellets fell from the sky.

Lord Frostbough was officially her pretend beau.

Chapter Four

"I question the wisdom of meeting in Hyde Park in the midst of an ice storm," Jack grumbled as he walked alongside Miss Tiding, holding an umbrella above her head. Frozen rain stung his cheeks and soaked the shoulders of his greatcoat.

"Forgive me," Eva said with mock sweetness. "When I picked this location, I hadn't realized you were too delicate to endure a bit of light rain. Besides, where would *you* have suggested we meet?"

"Somewhere with a roof," he quipped. "Like my apartment. Apparently, you know how to let yourself in."

Beneath the wide brim of her hat, her cheeks flushed. "I've no plans to return, I assure you."

"That's too bad," he purred. "There's a crackling fire, comfortable furnishings, and fine brandy—which I happen to know you like."

She rolled her eyes, which were even a more vivid green in the light of day. "This won't take long," she said, stepping carefully to avoid icy spots on the pebbled path. "As I said in my letter, I have reconsidered. I'm willing to go along with your diabolical scheme—as long as you give me back the watch before Christmas."

"Excellent. Speaking of that letter," Jack said casually, "I feel obliged to inform you that your handwriting is atrocious."

"Of all the—" Miss Tiding bristled. "No one appointed you my governess."

He arched a brow, couldn't help goading her a bit more. "Thank God. Your note couldn't have been sloppier if you'd penned it on a raft being tossed by the sea."

"And yet you were somehow able to decipher my crude scribblings, as evidenced by your presence here today," she said dryly. "My goal was to meet with you and work out the particulars of this little farce—not to earn first honors in penmanship, my lord."

"Fair enough," he said. "I just always imagined that my future duchess would have dainty, even feminine handwriting."

Miss Tiding stopped dead in her tracks and whirled to face him, her breath forming small, puffy clouds in the frigid air between them. "I shall pretend to like you," she ground out. "In spite of the obvious challenges. Conversely, you must pretend to like me—sloppy handwriting and all. I'll not change to suit you."

She glared at him with those soul-piercing eyes, and he knew she was talking about much more than penmanship. Deep down, he couldn't have been more pleased.

He gave a noncommittal shrug. "Then I suppose I'll have to make do."

She growled under her breath as she began walking again, following a path parallel to the half-frozen Serpentine. "I presume you could have enlisted any number of women to pose as the object of your affection. Some of them, for entirely incomprehensible reasons, might have even enjoyed the ruse. Why me?"

Jack had asked himself the same question. He'd been prepared to confess the truth to his grandmother before Eva broke into his apartment. Hadn't even seriously considered enlisting a fake almost fiancée. All of which led him to arrive at the disturbing conclusion that he found sparring with Miss Tiding rather . . . enjoyable. In a twisted, sadistic way. But he'd take a kick to the groin before he'd admit it.

"I asked you to play the part because I knew there'd be no danger of you forgetting that we're merely acting. There'd be no chance you'd develop real feelings for me and long for something that could never be."

A giggle-like sound erupted from her lips.

"Are you laughing?" he asked, incredulous.

She dabbed her eyes with the fingertip of a glove. "Forgive me. I just . . ." She took a moment to compose herself. "The idea that I might forget and fall in—Well, it's absurd. Unfathomable." She glanced at him, her expression half amusement, half apology. "Have I bruised your male pride, my lord?"

"Not at all," he lied. "Now then. I suppose we should discuss business before icicles form on our noses."

"Of course," she said briskly. "I thought it would be best if we agreed upon the important milestones of our courtship prior to publicly presenting ourselves as a couple."

He scratched the back of his head. "What milestones?"

"How we were introduced, for one," she said. "We can't very well tell your grandmother that we met in the bedchamber of your apartment."

"While you were attempting a burglary," he added.

She gave him a look that would have shriveled the ballocks off most men. "Oddly enough, I now find myself contemplating other crimes," she said smoothly. "Murder could be rather satisfying."

He grinned at that. As long as she was shooting barbs, he held the upper hand. "Do you know Lady Rufflebum?"

"Doesn't everyone?" she replied.

"If anyone inquires how we met, we'll say she introduced us."

Miss Tiding nodded her agreement. "When and where?"

"Why don't we keep the details vague?" he suggested. "It'll add a bit of mystery."

"Fine," she said, not bothering to hide her exasperation.

He stole a glance at her lips, plump and pink. Remembered what it had felt like to taste them. Contemplated all the other parts of her he longed to kiss.

"When did you first realize you were attracted to me?" she asked.

Jesus. "What the devil are you talking about?"

"It's another milestone." She spoke slowly, as though he were a toddler in leading strings. "People are going to inquire. You need to be prepared to say which of my qualities made you like me."

"Definitely not your singing," he quipped.

"My sweet nature, perhaps?" she teased. "You'll have to think of something, you know."

"So will you," he countered. "What made you fall head over heels for me?"

She made a face like she'd caught a whiff of three-day-old fish. "I'll need time to come up with a plausible answer."

"Very well," he said, "we'll both ponder the question. Any other milestones?"

"There's one more thing," she said tentatively. "Something that, while rather distasteful, should lend an air of credibility to our charade."

"What's that?" he asked, wary.

"Endearing names for each other." She grimaced. "Most couples have them. For example, I could refer to you as darling or dear when others are within earshot. And you could have an affectionate name for me as well."

"You're quite right," he said soberly. "I hadn't considered it, and I appreciate the serious thought you've devoted to making the particulars of our fake relationship believable. Which is why I think I shall call you . . ."

She shot him a warning glare.

". . . my little plum pudding."

"Don't. You. Dare."

"My saucy snapdragon?"

"Absolutely not."

"My cheeky chestnut."

Her color rose and she seethed as she turned toward him. "You are the most arrogant, insufferable—"

Before she could finish the insult, she slipped on a patch of ice and lurched backward—until Jack caught her around the waist. He pulled her close to his body. Felt her heart beating as fast as his.

She clutched his shoulders and looked into his eyes with a mixture of surprise and gratitude and . . . something else. Something soft, sultry, and dangerous.

Slowly, he straightened but didn't let go of her; she didn't release him. Frozen droplets hit the umbrella he still held aloft, tapping out a soothing beat above their heads. While a storm swirled around them, they were sheltered in their private cocoon, generating more heat than a Yule log on Christmas Day.

He wanted to kiss her again—and not as a dare or a test or a ruse. He wanted to make her sigh and fist her fingers in his hair. Wanted her to melt into him and beg him for more.

Their lips were a mere breath apart. "Are you all right?" he asked.

She blinked and, as if a winter fairy's spell had been broken, let go of him. "Yes. But I should go."

He released her and set her on her feet. "Of course. I'll escort you safely to your carriage."

"Thank you," she said curtly. They reversed direction on the path, but when he offered her his arm she declined. "I'm steady now."

He snorted at that. Why should he care if she'd rather break her neck than surrender her pride and hold his arm for the ten-minute walk back to her carriage? Her stubborn nature and extreme dislike of him combined to make her the perfect candidate for the role of his pretend love interest. He suspected his grandmother would adore her.

They walked in silence for several yards, then she said, "Perhaps it will help you avoid the temptation to tease me with ridiculous terms of endearment if I simply permit you to call me by my given name . . . Eva."

Eva. He could imagine whispering it in her ear as he caressed her bare shoulder. Could picture her eyes fluttering shut as he softly sucked the skin in the crook of her neck. "Eva," he repeated gruffly. "It's pretty. But you must admit, it lacks the romantic flair of 'plum pudding.'"

"You're incorrigible," she huffed.

"You see, we really *are* getting to know each other." He kept one eye on her as they strolled along, just in case she slipped again.

"But," he continued casually, "*if* you wanted to call me something other than incorrigible, insufferable, or ridiculous, you could try calling me . . . Jack."

She glanced at his face, then looked to the heavens like she was praying for patience. "All I want is to fulfill my part of this bargain, get my father's watch back, and put this whole affair behind me," she said.

Jack ignored the mild sting in his chest. After all, he'd be glad when it was over, too. "Then I propose we begin tomorrow afternoon," he said. "My grandmother is scheduled to arrive at Northcott House in the morning. I'll suggest she invite you for tea."

"Tomorrow afternoon?" Eva repeated, her voice tinged with alarm.

"It will be an easy way to dip your toes into the waters of deception," he said. "A small, intimate meeting. I'll be there, and you may bring your maid or a friend, of course."

She swallowed. "Will your father, the duke, attend as well?"

"No," Jack said curtly. "He prefers the country and avoids Town."

"I see." Eva blew out a long breath, clearly relieved. "I suppose tea is as good a way as any to begin. And it will serve as the first of my three obligations?" she asked.

He nodded. "The whole visit shouldn't last more than an hour. What could be simpler?"

As they approached her carriage, Eva faced him, her expression sober. "Lying is never simple."

"I have faith in you," he said earnestly.

"You do?" She looked up at him from beneath the thick fringe of her lashes, her expression so full of hope that it felt like the ice encasing his heart was in danger of cracking. Which was probably the reason he proceeded to behave like a first-rate arse.

"You'll have to be convincing," he said with a devil-may-care shrug. "And you can't tell a soul about our deal. Because if you fail to pull off the charade, I'm keeping the watch."

She lifted her chin and gave him a look that should have

instantly turned him to stone. "Don't worry, Lord Frost-bough. I intend to fulfill my part of the bargain. When this is all over, I'll give my father his watch, and I'll bask in the satisfaction of seeing him happy and content. You, on the other hand, will still be mean, empty, and alone."

With that she turned on her heel and hurried toward the protection of her carriage, leaving him standing there, holding the umbrella, and feeling like an ogre.

"Eva!" he called out.

She halted and hesitantly looked over her shoulder.

In his best approximation of an apology, he said, "You'll do fine tomorrow. I'll be there to help."

"I know." She clucked her tongue like a headmistress scolding a naughty pupil. "Heaven help us both."

Chapter Five

Eva had formed a vague image of Lord Frostbough's—
that is, Jack's—grandmother in her head. She'd pictured a
sweet, frail woman dressed in muted shades of lavender or
gray who sat in a chair with a heavy quilt draped across her
lap.

And she couldn't have been more wrong about the dowa-
ger duchess.

The moment Eva and her aunt Laurel were ushered into the
exquisitely decorated drawing room at Northcott House, the
duchess sprang out of her chair and greeted them warmly.
Half a head taller than Eva and just as slender, she wore a
fashionable sapphire gown that matched her sparkling blue
eyes. Eva's demure white dress, which had been the safe
choice, now felt drab in comparison to the duchess's stunning
silk.

"Miss Tiding, what a pleasure. My grandson has told me
so much about you—all of it good," she added with a wink.

Eva spotted Jack standing far behind the duchess, his back
to the roaring fire. *Coward.*

"The pleasure is mine, Your Grace," she said, executing

a graceful curtsy in spite of her wobbly knees. "May I present my aunt and dear friend, Miss Laurel Bailey." Though Laurel was a decade older than Eva and wonderfully clever and kind, she'd never fallen in love or married. Eva waved a hand at the golden-haired woman whom she'd always considered a sister. Laurel made a polite curtsy and smiled at the duchess.

"How lovely to meet you as well, Miss Bailey," said the duchess. "I'm delighted you were able to join us. Indeed, I'm eager to meet all of Miss Tiding's friends and learn more about the mysterious young woman who has managed to melt my grandson's heart."

Gads. Eva hadn't told Laurel anything about Jack or the charade, figuring today's tea was the official opening act of their ruse. She'd assumed that their visit would consist of a bit of small talk, a smidgen of uncomfortable silence, and a tray of dry scones. *Wrong again.*

Laurel, who had assumed the duchess was an old acquaintance of Eva's father, said, "I confess I am equally curious, Your Grace." And her tone suggested she intended to wring the information out of Eva as though she were a sopping wet towel at the first opportunity.

"There will be no inquisitions, please, Grandmama," Jack said, deigning to join them at last. "You'll scare Miss Tiding off before she's had her first sip of tea."

He shot Eva a conspiratorial grin, bowed over her hand, and pressed a lingering kiss to the back of it. It was a fine bit of acting. So convincing, in fact, that the touch of his lips sparked a frisson that traveled up her arm and through her body before settling somewhere in the vicinity of her nether regions.

The earl's appearance was to blame, dash it all. His stark white cravat, midnight-blue jacket, and snug buckskin trousers gave him a vexingly dashing air. And with his neatly combed hair and freshly shaven face, he bore little resemblance to the man who had stripped down to his trousers on the night they'd met—thank heaven.

While the remaining introductions were made, Eva did her best to compose herself. All she had to do was survive the next hour. She'd answer the duchess's questions, feign an interest in Jack's formative years, and giggle at his inane jokes. With a little luck, she'd be back in her room, cuddled in bed with her book, by half past five.

The duchess and Laurel each perched on chairs flanking the fireplace, while Eva sat opposite them on the settee. Jack took up residence beside her, oblivious to the fact that his hulking frame filled three-fourths of the seat. She did her best to refrain from growling at him as the duchess poured and served everyone.

"Forgive me for saying so," the duchess said, beaming, "but the two of you make a most striking pair."

"Oh!" Eva exclaimed. "We're not exactly a pair."

Jack snaked an arm around her shoulders. "Thank you, Grandmama," he interjected. "It's almost unfair, isn't it, having so much attractiveness wrapped up in one couple?"

The duchess rolled her eyes, which earned her points in Eva's book. To Eva she said, "You must tell me how you and my grandson met, and what it was that drew you to him. Clearly, it was not his humility."

Eva resisted the urge to jab Jack with her elbow and say, *I told you so*. Thank heaven they'd discussed these questions in the park and prepared answers—after a fashion.

"There was nothing remarkable about our first meeting, I'm afraid." Eva set her saucer on the table and nervously smoothed her skirt. "Lady Rufflebum introduced us."

"Ah," the duchess said, "Lady Rufflebum is a close friend. I shall have to thank her for bringing the two of you together."

Laurel placed a biscuit on her plate and blinked innocently. "Do tell us more. Was it love at first sight?"

"Not at all," Eva said firmly.

At the very same time that Jack replied, "Most definitely."

Eva hurried to cover their conflicting answers. "That is, I was curious about Lord Frostbough from the start, but it took some time for my feelings to, er . . ."

"Blossom into a love for the ages?" he offered glibly.

"Develop into a certain fondness," she clarified. Good heavens, at this rate, Jack would have them married before the end of tea.

She shot him a warning look before returning her attention to his grandmother. "As for what drew me to him, I must confess it was the way he talked about you."

"Really?" The duchess tilted her head, intrigued.

Eva nodded. "I'm afraid he has a reputation among the ton for being cold and unyielding, but he's different when he talks about you. His scowl softens; his eyes crinkle at the corners. And I thought that any man who adores his grandmother as he clearly adores you . . . well, he *must* have a kind heart."

The duchess set down her teacup and dabbed her eyes with her napkin. "How utterly lovely," she said with a sniffle. "Now I want to hear from my grandson. What unique and endearing quality drew you to Miss Tiding?"

"I was going to say her eyes, but I suppose that sounds trite after her answer," he griped.

The duchess smiled. "Miss Tiding has lovely eyes, to be sure. But I'm sure you can do better than that."

"Fine." Jack dragged a hand down the side of his face. "I like her courage."

"Go on," urged the duchess.

"Miss Tiding stands up for what she believes in. She'll

do anything for the people she loves. And she's not afraid of anyone—least of all me."

A warm glow shimmered inside Eva's chest. So he *had* noticed something besides her eyes.

"That makes sense," the duchess said, thoughtful. "It would take a fearless sort of young woman to breach your defenses."

"No one's been breaching any defenses, Grandmama," he scoffed, as if suddenly embarrassed.

"Of course not, dear," she said while simultaneously raising her teacup toward Eva in a congratulatory toast.

The duchess spent much of the next hour regaling Eva and Laurel with tales of Jack's youth. Apparently, when he was six he spent a whole night at the dining room table staring down a plate of brussels sprouts—and still refused to eat them. At the age of nine, he'd snuck into the stables and rode off on a wild-tempered untamed horse—only to return five hours later, miraculously, unscathed. And, when he was twelve, he'd boldly sacked a burly footman who had made unwanted advances toward his governess—before punching him squarely in the nose.

The duchess's face shone with pride each time she spoke about Jack, but she also made it a point to ask Laurel and Eva about their families, friends, and interests. Jack, meanwhile, ate an obscene number of sandwiches and moved about the room—too restless to stay put, apparently—but Eva sensed that he listened intently. Probably just to make certain that she played her part well.

As it turned out, having Jack as a pretend beau was not nearly as onerous as she'd anticipated. Indeed, his grandmother was such a kind, gracious hostess that Eva found the visit—the first of her three obligatory social events—thoroughly enjoyable.

The duchess was just about to relate an incident from

Jack's days at Eton involving a summons from the headmaster when Jack strolled over and gave her shoulder an affectionate squeeze.

"Forgive me for interrupting, Grandmama," he said smoothly, "but I'm sure Miss Tiding and Miss Bailey have heard enough stories from my misspent youth." He reached into his pocket, checked his watch—*Papa's* watch—and added, "Besides, they must be expected at home soon."

Eva tamped down an unexpected twinge of hurt. She shouldn't have been surprised that Jack was eager to send her on her way—the briefer the visit, the less risk of them making a blunder and exposing their ruse. Better to leave now, while everything was still going according to plan.

"Never fear, my dears," the duchess said to Eva and Laurel. "I shall finish telling you the sordid Eton tale another time."

"We shouldn't have monopolized so much of your afternoon, Your Grace, especially since you've only arrived in Town this morning. But I've enjoyed the visit immensely," Eva said sincerely.

"As have I." The duchess stood, reached for Eva's hand, and gave it a squeeze. "Which is why we simply must see each other again soon. My grandson and I are hosting a party three days from now. I do hope you and Miss Bailey will be able to join us."

Jack fumbled the sandwich he'd been eating—his sixth, by Eva's count. "What party?"

"Just a small affair. A chance to reconvene with friends whom I haven't seen in years." Eva looked over the duchess's shoulder at Jack, who was brushing bread crumbs off his jacket. He met her questioning gaze and gave a surreptitious nod.

And with that it was decided. The duchess's party would serve as the second of her three social obligations.

"I'd be delighted to attend," Eva said.

Laurel's shrewd gaze flicked from Eva to Jack and back again. "*I* wouldn't miss it for the world."

"Excellent," said the duchess. "I'll look forward to seeing you then. We'll have a proper toast to celebrate the wonder of Christmastime *and* the thrill of young love."

Jack groaned out loud, and Eva felt herself blush from the neckline of her dress to the roots of her hair.

Laurel cleared her throat. "Before we go," she said to the duchess, "I wonder if you would be so kind as to tell me a bit about the lovely portrait above the mantel?"

"But of course, my dear," said the older woman, delighted to conspire with Laurel in her obvious ploy to give Eva and Jack a few moments alone.

The moment the duchess and Laurel were out of earshot, Jack grinned at her. "That went better than I expected. My grandmother likes you."

Eva bristled. "Did you doubt she would?"

He shrugged. "She has high standards. Wants nothing but the best for me."

"Right." She sighed and adjusted the reticule that hung from her wrist. "I'll not be goaded into sparring with you while your lovely grandmother is standing on the other side of the room."

"She's looking at us. You might try not to scowl."

She flashed a toothy smile. "Better?"

"Much." He leaned closer, his breath hot on her ear, and, to her everlasting shame, her belly fluttered. "The good news is you only have to wait three days to see me again," he drawled.

"Aren't I the lucky one?" she quipped, hoping he couldn't hear the wild beating of her heart. Why did his face have to be such chiseled perfection?

His heavy-lidded eyes crinkled at the corners. "You look pretty today."

"You don't have to pretend, Jack," she scoffed. "No one can hear you."

"I know." His deep voice and wicked grin melted her insides like chocolate. "That compliment was just for you . . . my shapely sugarplum."

Chapter Six

Jack stood at his grandmother's side near the ballroom entrance, dutifully greeting guests as they arrived at the party. As it turned out, his grandmother's definition of *a small affair* was *his* definition of *a mad crush.*

Worse, his grandmother, who'd been in Town for only four days, had somehow managed to inform most of the ton that he was courting Eva. He needed to warn her as soon as possible.

"There's no need to fret, Jack," his grandmother whispered. "Miss Tiding shall be here shortly."

"I'm not certain about that," he said dryly. "When she sees the parade of carriages out front, she might turn around and run for the hills."

"She doesn't strike me as one who is easily intimidated."

"That's true," he said, feeling strangely proud. "She's no wallflower."

The words had barely left his mouth when she and her aunt entered the room and he realized the truth of what he'd said.

The sight of Eva hit him like a sucker punch to the belly. Her hair was piled high atop her head, save for a few thick curls artfully arranged over one shoulder. Her shimmering gold gown hugged her full breasts and skimmed her rounded hips; sparkling jewels dangled from her dainty ears and graced her kissable neck. *Holy hell.*

Pretending to be smitten with her would not be difficult in the least. No, the problem was—for reasons that were legitimate—Eva couldn't stand him.

But maybe he could make her forget that she hated him. Just for tonight.

She approached, her aunt at her side, and gave his grandmother a genuine smile. They were in the midst of exchanging a warm greeting when Jack saw another guest filing in—the last one he wished to see. Lady Rufflebum.

Good God. He couldn't have his grandmother asking the countess questions about how he and Eva met.

The moment Eva reached him, he offered his arm. "Would you mind if I whisked you away for just a minute?"

"My word, Jack," his grandmother chided, "Miss Tiding has barely stepped foot in the room and you're already scheming to separate her from Miss Bailey—her friend *and* chaperone."

"Guilty as charged." He shot Miss Bailey an apologetic smile as he led Eva away from the door. "I'll have her back in a trice."

"Are you daft?" Eva hissed under her breath. "You're creating a scene."

"Actually, I'm avoiding one." He guided her through the ballroom and out onto the terrace, even though it was so cold that finches could have ice-skated in the birdbath. Thankfully, no one else was braving the freezing temperature at the moment, so they stood near the house under a string of glowing lanterns. "Would you like my jacket?"

"No," she said through chattering teeth. "But let's keep this brief, shall we?"

"Lady Rufflebum was right behind you," he said.

Her eyebrows shot halfway up her forehead. "Gads."

"Right. When she and my grandmother talk, they'll both know we lied about her introducing us. How are we going to explain that?"

She nibbled her lip, and he made a valiant attempt not to stare at her mouth. Didn't succeed.

"Did you attend her ball last summer?" she asked.

"The one where Lord Sollingham drank too much, stumbled into the refreshment table, and broke a dozen crystal glasses?" Jack remembered it fondly.

"Precisely. We'll say we met there. That we don't recall the particulars because we could scarcely take our eyes off each other"—she wrinkled her nose—"but we credit Lady Rufflebum's ball for bringing us together."

"That's brilliant. It covers for our previous lie and makes us sound lovesick."

She shuddered at the very suggestion, then shivered, rubbing her gloved hands over her upper arms. "I'm glad you approve. Can we return to the ballroom now?"

"There's one other thing I wanted to discuss." He frowned at all her exposed skin, shrugged off his jacket, and thrust it at her. "Take it, please."

"Very well. Since it's apparently all that lies between me and a severe case of frostbite." She slung the jacket around her shoulders and sighed, snuggling into its warmth.

He couldn't help but be a little smug. The sight of her in his jacket made him . . . satisfied. Almost happy. "There. That wasn't so difficult, was it?"

"I suppose not. But we shouldn't stay out here much longer." Her gaze flicked longingly to the house behind him. "What's so pressing?"

He stuffed his hands in his pockets and contemplated the

best way to soften her prickliness. To make her forget he was her supposed nemesis. At least for a few hours.

"I just thought you should know," he began, "that you look breathtaking tonight."

She arched a brow, wary. "Thank you?"

"I already knew you were beautiful, of course. But I'm much more accustomed to seeing you bundled up in your winter coat."

"What I'd give to have my cloak now," she quipped, but there was no bite in her words.

"I wanted to thank you for coming and for letting people believe that you have tender feelings for me," he said, sincere. "I'll be the envy of every man here tonight."

She moved closer, searching his face as if she feared he was mocking her. "Do you mean that?"

"Hell yes." He gazed into her eyes, willing her to believe him. "And it's not just the gown or your hair or the way you look. There's something special about you, Eva."

She swallowed as though she was about to say something, but the next thing he knew, her hand was curled around his neck and her mouth was on his.

Sweet Jesus. Eva was *kissing* him. Not because he'd dared her or even suggested it. Not because she had anything to gain. Maybe, just maybe, she felt the same way he did— swept away by the moment. Bowled over by feelings he hadn't even realized he had.

Her warm, lush curves molded against his body. Her soft, sweet lips teased at the corner of his mouth. Her nearness was intoxicating—an invitation to lose himself in the heady rush of desire.

He cupped her cheeks in his palms. Slanted his mouth across hers. Deepened the kiss till her lips parted and their tongues tangled.

Everything he'd said before was true. Eva *was* special— and sure to attract plenty of attention at his grandmother's party. But right now it was just the two of them, all alone on a cold winter's night, generating more sparks than a black-smith's hammer.

The kiss in his apartment had been hot, too, but this one was different because Eva had started it. She wanted him.

The knowledge drove him half-mad—and made him harder than he'd thought possible.

She curled her fingers into his hair, caressed his nape, and moaned into his mouth. Everything she did chipped away at his control and pulled him further under her spell.

He tugged on her lower lip, alternately sucking and nip-ping. Trailed kisses down the side of her neck and back up again. Traced the shell of her ear with his tongue and smiled at her sharp intake of breath.

"Jack," she murmured. The sound of his name on her lips swirled in his chest and warmed his insides.

"Jack," she repeated, breathlessly. "It's all right. We can stop now."

The hairs on his arms stood on end, and he took a half step back. "What do you mean?"

"Your grandmother was watching us through the window over there." Eva smoothed her hair and pulled his jacket tightly around her. "She's gone now."

Shit. He should have known better than to think Eva was kissing him out of desire or affection. Should have known this was nothing but a game to her. A means to an end.

He was no better than his father—letting feelings for a woman get the better of him. Confusing fleeting attraction with something deeper. But Jack would never let himself be deceived by a woman like his father had. He'd been so wounded that he'd retreated from the entire world, abandoning everyone who counted on him—including his young, heartbroken son.

For the second time that night, Jack felt as though he'd been hit in the gut. Except this time, it hurt a hell of a lot more. A fact he'd sooner die than admit.

"Quick thinking on your part," he said. Like he was congratulating a friend for steering his curricle around a rut in the road.

"I didn't know what else to do," Eva explained. "What other logical reason could we have had for fleeing to the terrace?"

"Quite so," he said curtly. "If my grandmother harbored any doubts about our relationship, she certainly doesn't any longer."

"Jack," Eva said tentatively, "are you all right?"

"Never better," he said, avoiding her gaze. "We should go inside and mingle. Give people a chance to whisper about us."

"Very well."

She started toward the French doors of the ballroom, and he grunted, gesturing at his dark green evening jacket—the same rich green as her eyes. "You might want to leave that with me."

"Whoops." She blushed as she handed over his jacket. "Aren't you coming?"

"I'll let you go first and slip in later. We'll be less conspicuous that way." He forced a smile. "Good luck."

She took a few steps, stopped, and spun to face him again. "You're actually going to let me leave without calling me your 'vacuous vixen' or your 'simpering siren' or some other equally ridiculous name?"

He shrugged and wondered if she could see how hollow, how empty, he was inside. "There's no point really, is there?"

"No. I suppose not," she said, thoughtful and—if he wasn't mistaken—a bit disappointed. "I'll see you inside then."

Damn it all, he couldn't bear to let her leave looking so forlorn. Decided to bolster her with a parting shot. "If I *was* going to call you a ridiculous name, I can tell you mine would be one hundred times more original than the drivel you came up with."

Her face lit up. "Would it now?"

"No contest."

She arched a brow and raised her elfish chin. "It's good to know I inspire such creativity."

"You're my mercurial muse."

"Not bad, my lord," she said, pausing just outside the ballroom door. "But I think we both know it's far from your best work. I shall expect more inspired creations in the future."

As she slipped inside, Jack raised a sardonic brow, content to let her have the last word. For now.

He had bigger problems to grapple with—like figuring out how to squash the highly inconvenient and horrifyingly real feelings he'd developed for a woman who could barely tolerate his company.

Two hours later Laurel hooked her arm through Eva's. "Let's take a turn about the room," Laurel suggested, which meant she needed a respite from talking to other guests or wanted to exchange a bit of gossip. Possibly both.

Either way, Eva was grateful for her aunt's company. It seemed as though every set of eyes in the ballroom had been trained on her all evening, and it would be a relief to talk with someone who wasn't silently critiquing her or wondering what in the world Lord Frostbough—Jack—saw in her.

She and Laurel strolled along a row of massive potted palms and gazed at the sparkling chandeliers decorated with holly and ivy. Swags of red and ivory silk adorned the walls, lending a shimmering warmth to the large room. The duchess had procured an orchestra but had not arranged the room for dancing. Instead, several seating areas were set up, inviting guests to make themselves comfortable and settle in for cozy conversation.

"Beautiful, isn't it?" Laurel mused.

"Lovely," Eva replied. "Elegant and welcoming at the same time—much like the duchess herself."

"True." Laurel wore a simple but stunning apricot gown, the perfect complement to her golden tresses. And though she claimed she was firmly on the shelf, Eva held out hope that her aunt would fall in love. She simply needed the right gentleman to come along and sweep her off her feet.

"Have you ever stopped to think," Laurel continued, "that one day *you* might host a party in this very ballroom?"

Eva blinked, incredulous. "Me?"

"But of course," Laurel said smoothly. "I know you're not the mercenary sort, but Lord Frostbough *is* the heir to a dukedom. Surely you've considered what that might mean for your future?"

"No." Eva shook her head firmly. "That is, the earl and I are fond of each other, but he hasn't spoken of . . ." She couldn't bring herself to utter the word.

"Marriage?" Laurel offered.

Eva glanced around to make sure no one had overheard. "Most definitely not," she whispered. "We like each other, on occasion, but I'm not at all certain we'd suit."

"Why not?"

"He is impossibly stubborn," Eva said.

With an innocent roll of her eyes, Laurel said, "Like someone else I know?"

Eva felt her cheeks flush. "It's not just that. He can be rather infuriating."

"And yet . . ."

Eva swallowed. "He does seem to have a more vulnerable side." She was thinking about the hurt look on his face when she'd ended their kiss—and told him why she'd initiated it.

It was the truth, after all. She wouldn't have kissed him if his grandmother hadn't been watching them on the terrace. Even though he'd been saying the loveliest things and gazing at her with a heat that melted her insides like snowflakes landing on a tongue.

"I cannot believe you didn't tell me about him," Laurel scolded.

"I know. Forgive me," Eva replied. She detested keeping secrets from her friend, but the whole charade would be over soon. Jack would hand over the watch. His grandmother would leave Town. They'd end their fake courtship and have no reason to speak to each other ever again. The prospect left Eva feeling inexplicably . . . hollow.

"Don't look now," Laurel murmured, "but Lord Frostbough is headed this way. I'll give you a moment alone with him."

Eva was about to tell her aunt that she didn't need to leave but changed her mind when she saw the agitated expression on Jack's face. "Thank you, Laurel. I'll find you in a few minutes."

Jack inclined his head politely at Laurel and claimed his spot at Eva's side. Just like that, her pulse was off to the Ascot races.

After checking that no one else was near, he said, "There's been another development."

"That sounds rather dire. What is it?"

"We need to talk—privately. Do you think you could meet me in the library in a quarter of an hour?"

The duchess had pointed out the glorious library to Eva on her previous visit to Northcott House. "I suppose so. At least it will be warmer than the terrace," she teased.

He didn't crack a smile. "I'll be waiting for you."

As she watched him stride away, she shivered with apprehension—and anticipation.

Chapter Seven

Eva paused at the door of the library and looked up and down the hall to make sure no one had followed her. It felt like she was back in the Albany, standing outside Jack's apartment—except this time, thankfully, she didn't have to pick a lock.

She'd no sooner stepped inside the dimly lit room and shut the door when Jack took her hand in his and pulled her toward a reading nook nestled beneath mullioned windows that almost reached the ceiling. The rich velvet curtains had been opened wide, and moonlight illuminated the sharp angles of his handsome face as she sat beside him on the cushioned bench.

"Did you have any difficulty slipping away?" he asked, his forehead creased with concern.

Eva shook her head. "I told Laurel I was going to the ladies' retiring room. We mustn't stay away from the ballroom for too long, however. What was it you wished to discuss?"

"Lady Rufflebum is hosting a house party in two weeks. My grandmother has already informed her we'll be there." He raked a hand through his hair and groaned. "Grandmama is delighted at the prospect of a traditional country Christmas. I don't see how I can refuse."

"Nor do I," Eva said, thoughtful. "Would it be so terrible to endure? You'd have to miss the comforts of your apartment, the entertainments of Town, and the company of your . . ." She let her voice trail off suggestively.

He arched a brow. "Of my . . . ?"

She rolled her eyes. Figured she might as well say it. "Lovers."

"Lovers?" he repeated, incredulous.

"Never fear. I'm sure there will be plenty of beautiful, willing women at Lady Rufflebum's."

"I don't *have* a lover," he said slowly. "And I won't be looking for one at the countess's party. We're supposed to be courting, remember? Besides, the closest thing I have to a lover is *you*."

Eva ignored the happy flutter in her chest and kept her face impassive. "Then I'm not certain I understand your dilemma."

Jack scooted forward on the bench, so close that his very hard, very muscular thigh was almost touching her—a state of affairs that proved to be highly distracting. Eva forced herself to pick up the thread of conversation.

"Lady Rufflebum plans to invite you and Laurel also," he said. "My grandmother will almost certainly pressure you to attend. She can be very persuasive and will try to catch you in a weak moment. I had to warn you, so you'll be prepared with an excuse."

"I do owe you one more social engagement," Eva said.

Jack shook his head. "A week-long house party is too much to ask. And it's risky, besides."

"Yes, it would involve an awful lot of acting," she said, trying to act nonchalant as he stretched an arm across the silk cushion behind her, his large hand a mere breath away from her bare shoulder. It took a considerable amount of willpower to prevent herself from inching backward and sinking into him.

"We'll find another event that can serve as our third public appearance as a couple," he said definitively.

"It must be before Christmas," she added. "So I can give the watch to Papa."

"Understood." He slapped a hand against his leg. "I'm glad we have that settled."

"Yes," she concurred. Even though she felt anything but settled.

"There's one more thing I want to say." He looked into her eyes, his expression so earnest it raised goose bumps on her arms.

"Go on," she breathed.

"Earlier, when you kissed me . . ."

"Yes?"

"You don't have to do that again. That is, you shouldn't feel as though you need to kiss me just because someone's watching." He blew out a long breath. "That's not fair—to either of us."

Her heart pounded in her chest, and she had an inkling as to why.

She was on the brink of doing something impulsive and reckless and wonderful.

"What if I *want* to kiss you?" she said softly. "Not because someone's watching. Not because it's part of our deal. But simply because . . . I want to."

He sat perfectly still, frozen as an ice sculpture. "I suppose that would be a different story."

She leaned into him and brushed her lips against his. "This doesn't change anything about our relationship," she whispered.

"Right. We won't let it," her murmured against her mouth, and she could almost feel his muscles quivering with restraint.

She grabbed his jacket by the lapels and pulled him on top of her, savoring the weight of his hard body.

He braced his arms on either side of her head and touched his forehead to hers. "You're sure about this?"

"Yes." She'd never been surer. "This is the perfect setting for a tryst. 'Twould be a pity to waste it."

"I couldn't agree more," he said gruffly. "But I thought you wanted to hurry back to the ballroom."

"I must." She could feel his heart beating as fast as hers. "Do you have the watch with you?"

He frowned, pulled the watch from his pocket, and showed it to her. "Always."

"We can stay here for ten minutes," she said. "Do you think you can work within those parameters?"

"Leave it to me." His mouth curled into a rakish grin as he set the watch on the windowsill beside her. "You'd be surprised at the amount of wickedness I can accomplish in ten minutes, clothes or no."

Eva sucked in a breath as he traced a fingertip along the neckline of her gown, skimming the swells of her breasts. Beneath the thin gold silk of her ball gown, her nipples grew taut. Ached for his touch.

But his fingers trailed up the side of her neck and over her shoulder, leaving her skin tingling in his wake. His tongue plundered her mouth like he would never have enough of her, like he was on the edge of losing control—and his passion thrilled her.

She ran her hands over his chest, shoulders, and arms, frustrated by the layers between them. She could recall all too easily the sight of him shirtless in his apartment. "These clothes vex me," she said. "Almost as much as you do."

He shot her a smug, sultry smile. "I want to touch you, too."

With sure, deliberate strokes, he caressed the underside of her breast. Slowly, his fingers circled the mound, spiraling closer to the tip and coming tantalizingly close before drifting away, then back again.

"I think you mean to torture me."

He growled. "Would you have it any other way?"

When she arched her back in a silent demand, he tweaked the sensitive bud, then squeezed it. Pleasure flashed through her, and a little cry escaped her throat.

He skimmed a palm over her breast and lightly nipped at the pebbled peak. She speared her fingers through his hair and lifted her hips. Jack groaned as if he was tortured, too.

His hard length pressed against her core, making her dizzy with desire. She had the shocking urge to wrap her legs around his and writhe against him.

As if he knew, he reached down with one hand, lifted the hem of her gown, and circled her ankle with his fingers. He slowly slid his hand up her calf, his warm palm gliding over her silk stockings. He paused at the back of her knee to draw a few lazy circles and simultaneously turn her bones to jelly. Then his hand cruised upward.

He traced the edges of her garters, stroking the bare skin at the top of her thighs. Driving her quite mad.

"Eva," he rasped. His dark hair hung low over one brow, and his heavy-lidded gaze made her core pulse with longing. She'd do anything he asked. Strip off her gown. Take off his clothes. Lick his chest like he was a huge peppermint stick.

She looked up at him, utterly drunk with desire. "Yes, Jack?"

"Our time is up."

Blast. Ten minutes had never seemed so short—or so momentous. "Are you always this prompt?"

He lowered her gown and reached for her hand. "Let me help you up."

She took a moment to smooth her hair and compose herself—on the outside at least. She was going to need significantly more time to sort out her feelings. "Do I look as though I've been ravished?" she asked him.

"No. Do I?" Jack stuck the watch in his pocket, straightened his jacket, and grimaced as he adjusted himself inside his trousers.

"Perhaps you should wait here awhile," she said, congratulating herself for her diplomacy. "I'll return to the ballroom, collect Laurel, and prepare to leave."

"I'll join you shortly." He leaned forward as though he were going to kiss her, then hesitated. "Did you . . . enjoy yourself this evening?"

"Oddly enough, I did," she admitted.

Relief washed over his face. "I'll send word soon. About our third public event."

Eva nodded. She had to force herself to back away from him, turn, and head for the library door. Had to remind herself that she and Jack were just a pair of actors who got a bit carried away, confusing their onstage performance with behind-the-curtain shenanigans.

She hazarded one last look at him before slipping into the corridor. He stood in a swath of moonlight, watching her intently. Almost as if . . .

Impossible. The only thing that Jack—Lord Frostbough—felt for her was lust. And maybe that was all she felt for him. But maybe not, dash it all.

She hurried back to the ballroom and tried to make it seem like she'd been mingling. Laurel spotted her almost immediately and joined her, hooking an arm around her elbow.

"There you are." Laurel painted on a smile for the sake of

anyone watching. "You weren't in the ladies' retiring room, were you?"

"No." Eva winced, apologetic. "Is it that obvious?"

"It is to me," Laurel said. "But most of the other guests are probably too far into their cups to notice. The duchess and Lady Rufflebum were looking for you. Twice now I've told them that they just missed you."

"You're a true friend, Laurel," Eva said earnestly.

"I have about twenty questions I want to ask you, but I shall refrain—until tomorrow." Laurel gave her a sideways glance. "We should probably go before anyone has the chance to ask where you and Lord Frostbough have been."

"Agreed," Eva said. "And before Lady Rufflebum has a chance to invite us to her house party."

"The countess wants to invite us?" Laurel beamed. "How exciting!"

"I hate to disappoint, but we're not going."

"Oh dear." Laurel's face fell. "Have you and Lord Frostbough had a falling-out?"

"Not exactly," Eva said. "I'll explain later. Let's just retrieve our coats and be on our way."

She and Laurel were halfway to the ballroom door when the duchess intercepted them. "Miss Tiding and Miss Bailey," she said smoothly. "You're not leaving already, are you? The night is still young."

Eva flushed guiltily. "I'm afraid we were. Forgive me— I'm not very accustomed to the social whirl."

"We'll have to remedy that," the duchess said affectionately. "To that end, my dear friend Matilda has a proposition for you."

She waved an elegantly clad arm in the woman's direction, and Lady Rufflebum toddled over as though she'd been summoned from a genie's bottle. "Miss Tiding," said the countess.

She had two round spots of rouge on the apples of her cheeks, and with a bit more powder in her hair she could have passed for Marie Antoinette. "I understand that my ball last summer was instrumental in bringing you and Frostbough together."

"Yes," Eva said, hoping lightning didn't strike her dead right there in the ballroom. "We are in your debt."

"I never thought I'd see the day that the earl . . . That is, he's just so . . ." Lady Rufflebum let her voice trail off. "Well, that's neither here nor there, is it? My friend the duchess is delighted by this turn of events, as am I. And, in the spirit of the Season, I'd like to invite you and Miss Bailey to my Christmas house party in Bellehaven Bay."

"That's extremely gracious of you." Eva smiled apologetically. "However, my father needs me here, and we always look forward to spending Christmas together."

Lady Rufflebum clucked her tongue. "A shame."

"But not an insurmountable obstacle," the duchess interjected. "You must bring your father. Isn't that right, Matilda?"

"What? Oh, yes. Of course. Indeed."

Eva winced inwardly. "That's so kind. But you see, Papa avoids travel and prefers to stay at home this time of year."

"No matter," the duchess said brightly. "You and Miss Bailey can join us for most of the house party and simply return before Christmas Eve. We'll have such a grand time."

Eva knew attending the party would be ill advised. She was perilously close to crossing a line with Jack. The line separating a pretend courtship from real feelings. And yet she was tempted to walk that line. To see just how close she could get to it without falling off the cliff.

As if she'd conjured Jack with her thoughts, he strode across the ballroom toward their group, his broad shoulders parting the crush of guests like the Red Sea. The sight of him made her body tingle—as though his large, sure hands still caressed her skin.

He stood beside his grandmother and shot her a suspicious look. "Who'll have a grand time?"

"All of us," she said innocently. "At the countess's house party."

"Grandmama," he chided lightly. "You mustn't badger Miss Tiding into doing your bidding. It's my understanding that she already has plans." He gave Eva a conspiratorial smirk. "Isn't that right, Miss Tiding?"

Eva opened her mouth to agree with him, then hesitated. "No."

"You see?" Jack smiled smugly. "Unfortunately, she won't be able to join us."

"As it turns out, I *will*. I'd be delighted to accept your invitation, Lady Rufflebum."

Jack blinked as though he couldn't have possibly heard the conversation correctly. "You're coming?"

"Yes," Eva replied. "How could I refuse?"

"It's actually not that difficult," Jack muttered.

The duchess clapped her hands, wallowing in victory. "I can scarcely wait!"

And the truth was that Eva couldn't wait, either.

Not because she genuinely liked the duchess, though she did.

Not because she knew Laurel would enjoy herself, though she would.

Not even because she wanted to be done with her obligation to Jack.

She'd said yes to the party because tonight's ten-minute tryst hadn't been enough. She needed to understand him. To pick the locks of all the doors he kept shut. A week-long house party should provide enough time for her to get Jack out of her system.

And perhaps, before their charade was truly over, she'd let him teach her a bit more about passion—as a little Christmas gift to herself.

Chapter Eight

Jack checked his watch and continued pacing the length of Lady Rufflebum's immense drawing room at her estate in Bellehaven Bay. He and his grandmother had arrived at the breathtaking seaside resort hours ago. Guests had trickled in throughout the day, but now it was almost time for afternoon tea—and still there'd been no sign of Eva.

"I'm certain she'll arrive soon," his grandmother said from the settee where she perused the gossip pages.

"Who?" he asked, playing dumb.

"Miss Tiding, of course." She set down the newspaper and patted the seat cushion beside her. "Come, sit. There are a few matters we need to discuss, and since we have the room to ourselves, now is as good a time as any."

Alarm bells rang inside his head, but he strolled to the settee and joined her. "What's on your mind, Grandmama?"

"Your father," she said bluntly, "and your future."

The mention of his estranged father caused a familiar ache in Jack's chest. "I thought you said he was in good health. Has something happened?"

"No, my dear boy." She gave his arm an affectionate

squeeze. "You know how he is. Your father is as fit as can be—physically. He simply refuses to leave Northcott Manor. He says the house in Town holds too many bad memories, but he asks about you often. I read him the letters that you write to me, and he listens raptly—as though he's savoring every word."

"I'm relieved to hear he's well," Jack said truthfully. But a pang of resentment niggled at the back of his neck. He understood the depths of his father's pain, but he couldn't understand why he'd allowed those wounds to eclipse the bond between them. "Why are you concerned about him?"

His grandmother smiled wistfully, and with her bright blue eyes and sunny yellow dress she looked decades younger than her seventy years. "I worry that his limitations have impacted you. He hasn't been the father you deserve."

Jack stiffened. "He's done the best he can."

"I believe that's true," she said gently. "But sometimes our best isn't enough."

"You needn't worry about me, Grandmama. I've been on my own for most of my life and have managed just fine."

"You're different from him, you know," she said, thoughtful. "Made of stronger stuff. It's time for you to start a new chapter in our family's story. Turn the page and don't look back, Jack."

"I'm not sure I know what you mean," he said warily.

"You've been stuck—as surely as a carriage with a broken axle. But with a few repairs, you'll be set to rights and ready to roll onward. Good things lie ahead—happiness, laughter . . . even love."

"You're talking about Eva." He felt a niggle of guilt between his shoulder blades. "You like her?"

"Of course I do. And I can see the connection between you."

"You can?"

"Plain as day." His grandmother sounded so certain he almost believed it. "But she's not going to wait forever—especially if you insist on wearing a scowl all the time. You must tell her how you feel."

He dragged a hand through his hair. "I don't know how I feel."

"Balderdash," she scoffed. "You know what's in your heart. Propose to her before the end of the house party. Matilda is hosting a ball on Christmas Eve—it will be the perfect time to make an announcement."

Jack's palms turned clammy. "Even if I proposed and she accepted, she's planning to return home before the ball."

"Convince her to stay," his grandmother said with a shrug.

"I haven't spoken to her father yet," Jack said, clearly grasping at straws.

"Write to him," she said slowly, as though he were thick-headed. "Do what you must to move forward and embrace your future."

Damn it. He'd taken this farce too far. His grandmother truly believed he was going to propose, and the genuine hope on her face gutted him. He had to tell her the truth now—before she grew more attached to Eva.

"About Eva . . . ," he began.

"Oh, look!" she exclaimed, pointing out the window overlooking the front drive. "She and Miss Bailey have arrived at last. Let's go welcome them, shall we?"

Jack's confession withered on his tongue, lost in the flurry of greetings that ensued.

Lady Rufflebum met the newcomers in the main hall and instructed a footman to carry their bags upstairs to their room while Jack hung back, watching.

Eva's cheeks were pink with excitement. "Bellehaven Bay

is beautiful," she said, slipping off her fur-lined gloves. "The cliffs overlooking the ocean, the sandy white beaches . . . Even from the carriage, they took my breath away."

Jack studied her, looking past her shining green eyes and perfectly kissable lips. He searched for a clue that she was acting, dutifully playing the part of an enthused house party guest. But she seemed genuinely pleased. Happy even. He wanted to poke her in the ribs and remind her that this wasn't some sort of holiday. She was there to fulfill her end of the deal.

Unless . . . unless something had changed.

"This is my first visit to the seaside as well," said Laurel. "It must be quite a bustling place in the summer."

"Yes, indeed," Lady Rufflebum replied. "But the winter months have a special sort of charm, too. There's a sense of mystery and magic when you're on the beach all alone."

"I can imagine," Laurel breathed.

"And there are plenty of entertainments in Town as well," said his grandmother. "Lovely shops, lively taverns, and a darling tearoom."

"I can't wait to explore," Eva announced.

Jack cleared his throat, drawing all eyes. "Miss Tiding, perhaps you'll permit me to show you around the grounds once you've settled in."

Lady Rufflebum gasped. "She hasn't yet removed her cloak or had a proper cup of tea, Frostbough."

His grandmother chuckled. "I daresay little harm can come from a pre-dinner stroll—if Miss Tiding is so inclined."

"Of course." Eva turned to her aunt. "Laurel, will you join us?"

Miss Bailey's gaze flicked to his grandmother's face, then back to Eva's. "I think I'll stay here and unpack our things. Unless you'd rather I . . . ?"

"They'll be fine," his grandmother chimed in, her tone settling the matter once and for all.

A half hour later Jack met Eva met in the entrance hall. They slipped out the front door into the chilly, overcast afternoon and headed for Lady Rufflebum's garden.

He'd walked down the same path earlier that morning, but it seemed different now that he saw it through Eva's eyes. Tall green shrubs stood at attention on either side of a winding pebbled path, while a canopy of leafless tree branches formed a lattice overhead.

"I feel as though we've sneaked into one of Grimms' fairy tales." She shot him a sideways glance. "I do hope you're not planning to feed me to the wolves—or perhaps a cunning witch."

"No," he said blithely. "I need you, remember?"

"That's right—you do," she said smugly. "You needn't worry, though. I don't think your grandmother is the least bit suspicious. All has gone according to plan."

Jack grunted. Maybe all was going according to plan for Eva. She probably hadn't missed him over the last two weeks. Probably hadn't lain awake at night thinking about their encounter in the library.

"Speaking of our plan, I think it's time we devised an exit strategy," he said.

She slipped a hand into the crook of his arm and arched a brow at him, coy. "Is that how spies talk? I rather like the sound of it."

If it were any woman but Eva, he'd think she was flirting with him. "You've almost fulfilled your side of the bargain," he said. "We need to figure out how this fake relationship will end."

"I've only just arrived," she said. "Must we concern ourselves with staging a jilting already?"

"My grandmother is expecting us to announce our engagement on Christmas Eve," he admitted.

"Oh."

He waved a hand at a marble bench nestled between some bushes beside the path. "Shall we sit?"

She nodded and settled herself on the smooth seat, her expression thoughtful. "I must confess, I never dreamed our pretend relationship would become so . . ."

Jack held his breath, hoping she'd say *real*.

". . . involved."

Damn. "Nor did I. My grandmother likes you. I don't want to see her get hurt."

"I like her, too," Eva said. "Lying to her and my father has been the most difficult thing about this ruse. They're bound to be devastated when we break things off. How can we soften the blow?"

"Maybe we should give the impression that we've had a row. Act chilly and distant when we're around others. That way, when you leave Bellehaven and return home for Christmas no one will be surprised by the lack of an engagement."

"Yes, I can see how that would be best," she said, sounding oddly disappointed.

"Unless you have another suggestion?"

"No. Although I'd rather hoped that, as long as we were having a fake relationship, we might continue to . . . enjoy each other's company."

"In what way?" he asked warily.

"You're going to make me say it, aren't you?" She threw up her hands, frustrated. "Very well. I'd hoped we could continue to enjoy each other . . . physically."

"Physically," he repeated dumbly.

"As we did in the library alcove," she clarified.

Holy hell. It took every ounce of restraint he had not to haul her on top of him and plunder her mouth.

"However," she continued, "I can see how passionate kisses and late-night rendezvous might complicate matters. Perhaps it's best if we stick to your plan."

"No, no," he said quickly. "We'll do it your way—if you're sure."

"I've had some time to think about it. And I'm sure. This might be my only opportunity to feel the rush of passion, and, based on my limited experience, you and I seem to suit—at least in that respect." She glanced up at him from beneath a thick fringe of lashes. "Wouldn't you agree?"

Jack felt his jaw hanging open like a toy soldier's with a broken hinge. He quickly shut his mouth and did his best to collect his wits, which seemed to have scattered to the four corners of the earth. "Yes," he stammered. "I'd agree we are physically compatible." More than he'd ever been with anyone else. "But I disagree with what you said at the start—that this might be your only chance for passion. You're young and lovely, and you have your whole life ahead of you."

"Careful, my lord—that almost sounded like a compliment," she retorted. "You'll turn my head."

"That *was* a compliment, damn it." He frowned. "Why would you deprive yourself of pleasure? Unless you're planning to enter a convent?"

"No, but I don't intend to marry, and I wouldn't be comfortable making this sort of an arrangement with just anyone. I trust you. You're a known quantity, Jack." Her eyes grew dark and sultry. "I've seen what lies beneath your shirt . . . and I find myself wanting more."

Jesus. "Let me see if I understand this. You want us to have an affair for the duration of the house party?"

"Correct," she said firmly. "When we're in the company of others, we'll act a bit cool—as though we've had a disagreement. But behind closed doors, we may do . . . whatever we want to."

Damn, but there was a lot he wanted to do. "I have no objection to that," he choked out.

"Laurel and I will plan to return to Town no later than the morning of Christmas Eve. We'll let your grandmother down as gently as possible but also make it abundantly clear that you and I have discovered we are quite incompatible and will never marry."

"And that will be it?" he said, disbelieving.

"Yes," she said simply. As if it were all as straightforward as the dinner menu. "You'll give me the watch, and we'll go our separate ways."

"I've never done anything like this before," he said.

Eva leaned in and captured his mouth in a kiss that would have brought him to his knees if he weren't sitting. "Then it shall be an adventure for both of us," she murmured against his cheek.

"Come to my room tonight?"

"I will if I can." She sighed wistfully. "First, we must survive dinner with a houseful of guests. I haven't even met anyone yet."

"It won't be so terrible. I'll introduce you to my friend Will. He's a decent sort."

"You have a friend?" she quipped. "Does he have horns and cloven feet?"

Jack shook his head. "Shockingly, no. He's hopelessly good-natured. We've been friends since Eton."

"I look forward to meeting him," she said, sounding curious. "But mostly I look forward to our assignation, later."

"I'll be waiting, my ardent angel." He slid a hand into her cloak and caressed the sensitive spot at the base of her spine. "I'll be waiting."

Chapter Nine

Eva and Laurel had helped each other dress for dinner, since they hadn't brought maids with them, and they'd each picked a favorite gown to wear. Laurel looked like a perfect English rose in a cheery pink satin, and Eva had chosen a deep red silk that made her feel sophisticated and just a bit wanton—which seemed appropriate, given her plans for the evening.

They put the last touches on their hair—a strawberry ribbon threaded through Laurel's golden curls, and a string of tiny pearls woven in Eva's fair tresses—before leaving their guest bedchamber and heading to the drawing room for a glass of sherry.

"Do you think you'll be seated next to Lord Frostbough?" Laurel whispered on the way down the grand staircase.

"I don't know." Eva still hadn't confided in her aunt. Each time she tried, she found that she couldn't quite put her feelings for Jack into words. And she reasoned it was probably best not to pull her sweet, guileless friend into their madcap scheme anyway. "I might prefer it if I weren't."

"Truly?" Laurel asked. "Did something happen on your walk earlier? Have you had a falling-out?"

"Nothing so dramatic," Eva said. "But I'm not certain we're as well suited as I once thought." She congratulated herself on achieving a tone that was somewhere between wistful and resigned.

"What a shame." Laurel's forehead creased. "But you are right to listen to your instincts. Give yourself some time. You're bound to gain clarity over the next week."

"I hope so," Eva said sincerely. She paused outside the drawing room door and took a fortifying breath. "Ready?"

Laurel gave her an encouraging smile. "Ready."

They walked in, and Eva was pleased to find that the party wasn't so large after all. Lady Rufflebum and the duchess stood near the crackling fire, chatting animatedly to a pretty gray-haired woman with kind eyes. Jack stood on the opposite side of the room, his wavy, longish hair and dark beard stubble at odds with his tailored evening jacket and crisp white cravat—and yet the mere sight of him made her wish she'd brought her fan. He was speaking to a handsome fair-haired gentleman and a beautiful fiery-haired woman who seemed to share the same wide mouth and charming dimples.

Upon seeing Eva and Laurel, Jack hurried over, escorted them across the room, and poured them each a drink before introducing them to the unfamiliar man and woman. "Miss Tiding and Miss Bailey," he said smoothly, "this is Lady Beckham and her brother—my friend Will—known in most circles as the Marquess of Goulding."

Eva nearly choked on her sherry. "Lord Goulding?" she said dumbly.

Jack frowned slightly. "You've already met?"

"Not exactly." The marquess shot her a winsome smile. "But I've heard quite a bit about you from your father, Miss Tiding. And from Jack, as well."

Dear God. It *was* him—the marquess Papa wanted her

to marry. "It's a pleasure to meet you," she managed. "My father has told me much about you as well. He speaks highly of you."

"Isn't that grand," Jack said dryly.

"Don't mind him," Will said with a chuckle. "And the pleasure is all mine."

The five of them chatted amiably. Eva learned that Lady Beckham—who insisted they call her Eleanor—had, sadly, lost her husband to illness and was only recently out of mourning. She seemed to be about the same age as Laurel, and Eva could already see that the two women had similar temperaments; both were patient, loyal, and kind.

When Lady Rufflebum's austere butler proclaimed the time had come for everyone to go through to the dining room, Jack and Will first escorted the older ladies to their seats and then returned for Eleanor, Laurel, and Eva.

Jack approached Eva, and though she would have loved nothing more than to latch on to the hard, muscular forearm he offered, she kept her expression indifferent. "Why don't you escort Lady Beckham and Miss Bailey?" she said coolly. "And perhaps I can prevail upon Lord Goulding to indulge me."

The marquess arched a brow. "It would be my honor."

Jack bristled but took her suggestion, and, a scant few minutes later, they were all seated around the table. Eva found herself positioned between Lord Goulding and his sister, who proved to be diverting dinner companions. Jack sat across from Eva and scowled from the first course to the last.

She made a mental note to tell him later that, while she appreciated the need to lay the groundwork for a falling-out, he needn't pretend to be *quite* so cross with her.

Dinner was followed by tea and several rounds of charades in the drawing room. Jack declined to play, preferring to glare at the guests from the comfort of an armchair, while Lord

Goulding participated enthusiastically and was eventually declared the undisputed winner.

When Lady Rufflebum began to nod off, her guests took their cues and began to murmur that it was time for them to retire. Eva was relieved to bid everyone good night and head to her guest bedchamber, where she and Laurel helped each other undress, donned soft nightgowns, and crawled beneath the thick covers.

Before long, Laurel snored softly and Eva stared at the clock beside her bed.

The earliest she dared sneak down the hall to Jack's room was half past midnight, which was approximately one hour and twenty-seven minutes away.

She nestled into her pillow and passed the time by making a list of all the wicked things she and Jack might do together.

At half past twelve, when the house was quiet, Eva slipped out of bed, taking care not to wake her aunt. She scooped up her robe, tiptoed across the room to the door, and peeked into the hallway. All clear.

She held her breath as she closed the door behind her, stuffed her arms into her dressing gown, and crept down the corridor, counting the doors till she reached Jack's room. Once there, she smoothed her hair behind her ears and raised her hand to knock.

Before her fist made contact, the door swung open and Jack swiftly pulled her inside, then closed the door behind her. She drank in the sight of his thundercloud face and brawny physique, dismayed to find he still wore a shirt, trousers, and boots.

"You came." He sounded faintly surprised.

"I told you I would." She wandered farther into the dimly lit room, noting that the large bed was still made and the quilt wasn't even slightly rumpled. "What have you been doing for the past two hours?"

"Pacing. Waiting." His hair stood on end and his eyes had a wild look about them. "What took you so long?"

"I had to be certain the rest of the house was asleep." She made her way toward the toasty fireplace, rolling her eyes in case her irritation wasn't adequately conveyed through her tone. "Perhaps you've forgotten that if I was discovered sneaking into your room the consequences would be disastrous."

"Very true," he said sarcastically. "We wouldn't want to spoil the romance between you and my best friend. Or interfere with your plans to become his marchioness."

Eva faced him and blinked. "What in heaven's name are you talking about?"

"Will told me," he said, his words clipped and cool. "Your father wants you to marry him."

"That's true."

"You might have at least waited, Eva." He planted his hands on his hips and blew out a raspy breath. "Of course, you're free to wed whomever the hell you like—but would it have killed you to wait until after we finished our little act?"

She opened her mouth to reply, then stopped, mentally piecing all the clues together. "Lord Frostbough," she said coyly. "You're jealous."

"Don't be ridiculous," he scoffed. He sank into a large armchair and glared at the fire like it was his mortal enemy.

Warmth flooded her chest and her skin tingled with awareness. He *was* jealous. She glided toward him and perched on the arm of his chair. "I enjoyed meeting Will tonight."

Jack growled under his breath.

"But I had no desire to sneak into his room." She reached for the cloth tie at the end of her braid, slipped it off, and dropped it onto Jack's lap.

He stared at her hands as she loosened the plait and ran her fingers through her thick curls.

She leaned close to his ear. "I'm not sitting beside Will, am I?"

Jack swallowed. "Do you have to keep saying his name?"

With a soft chuckle, she stood, loosened the sash of her robe, and slipped it off her shoulders. Let it fall to the floor. "*You're* the one I'm with, Jack. You're the only one I want to be with right now."

He gripped the arms of his chair, his fingers dimpling the upholstered leather. "You're here tonight. But where will you be at the end of this? If you decide to marry Will"—he closed his eyes briefly as if the words pained him—"the two of you will have my blessing. But I can't do this if you're going to be his bride. It wouldn't be fair to any of us, and I . . . damn it, it would make it that much harder for me to say good-bye to you."

Eva's eyes stung and she blinked away tears before they could fall. Deliberately, she inched closer, settled herself on his lap, and curled an arm around his neck. "You never told me it would to be hard to say good-bye."

He heaved a sigh. "I don't think I realized it until tonight."

She wriggled closer to him and let her fingertips trail up the warm skin of his neck into the thick hair at his nape. "I think it will be difficult for me as well," she breathed. "I've grown rather accustomed to your grumpy face."

"What about Will?" he said tightly.

She looked deep into his eyes. Placed a hand over his thumping heart. "I've already told my father I won't marry him."

His grip on the chair eased; his body relaxed. Except for the evidence of his arousal, which, much to her delight, pressed hard against her bottom.

His gaze turned molten. "Then I suppose we can proceed as planned."

"Yes," she rasped, desperate to feel his lips against hers and his hands on her body.

In one smooth motion, he grasped her waist and lifted her so that she faced him, her thighs straddling his hips. He swept aside the curtain of her hair and sucked lightly on her neck as he showed her how to rock against him, stoking the sweet, insistent pulsing in her core.

"You looked beautiful at dinner tonight," he murmured. "From the moment I saw you in that red dress, all I wanted to do was tear it off you."

She ran her palms over his broad shoulders, nipped at his ear. "I hoped you would."

He moaned like she'd thrown gunpowder onto the blaze of their desire. "I like this nightgown, too." His big hands pushed the lacy straps off her shoulders, then slowly pulled the satiny fabric lower, exposing the swells of her breasts and taut rosy peaks to his scorching gaze.

"Eva," he moaned. "I'm going to kiss every inch of you."

"Do you think we could remove your shirt first?" she choked out.

He shot her a grin that made her belly flutter as he freed his shirttails.

She grabbed fistfuls of lawn, wrestled the garment over his head, and tossed it onto the bed. Greedily, she ran her hands over his torso, marveling at the smooth planes, hard ridges, and fuzzy softness.

He pulled her close so that the sensitive tips of her breasts brushed against the wall of his chest, and a little cry escaped her throat. She wanted more. More skin against skin. More of his wicked tongue. More of his sure touch.

She writhed against him as he caressed her bare back and

bottom. She arched as he suckled her breasts and stroked the insides of her thighs.

And when he reached between their bodies and touched the center of her pleasure, she whimpered, trembling with need. "Jack," she breathed.

"I know," he said, like he understood. "Let's go to bed."

Chapter Ten

Jack scooped Eva up like she weighed no more than a bag of oranges, carried her across the room, and set her on the bed. When he started to stretch out beside her, she pressed a palm to his chest.

"You're still wearing too many clothes." She frowned at his lower half. "I want to see all of you."

"Do you?" he drawled, arching a brow. "Lucky for you, I always aim to please."

"Lucky" was an understatement. She'd seen enough of him to realize the extent of her good fortune, and her whole body thrummed in anticipation. She scrambled to the head of the bed and leaned against the pillow as though she were taking a box seat at the Theatre Royal.

Jack casually bent over to remove his boots, and the exquisite muscles in his back put all the discus-throwing statues to shame. One boot thunked on the floor, followed by the next. When he straightened and slipped his thumbs inside his waistband, her mouth watered.

He met her gaze, a question in his eyes, and she nodded encouragingly. The trousers had to come off.

With a feral smile, he unbuttoned them. Shoved them down. Let them drop to the floor. His every move was easy, efficient, and unceremonious.

But trumpets played in her head.

Jack was just as magnificent as she'd imagined, and she'd imagined rather a lot. Narrow hips. A perfectly sculpted behind. Thighs that could make a Greek god green with envy. A long, hard shaft that jutted proudly from his body—and seemed to strain toward her.

She licked her lips and crawled to the edge of the mattress. Reached for the nightgown bunched around her waist and lifted it over her head. With deliberate slowness, she let the scrap of silk—the very last piece of clothing that separated them—slip from her fingertips.

And she'd never felt so free.

She knelt on the bed, trembling slightly with a potent combination of longing and need. Jack moved closer till he stood in front of her, the tip of his nose a scant inch from hers.

"Now what?" she whispered.

"That's up to you," he breathed. "But I'll tell you what I'd like to do. I'd like to kiss you. Here." He brushed a calloused fingertip over her lower lip. "Here." His finger trailed over her chin, down her neck, and around one pebbled nipple. "And here." He traced a meandering path down her belly and between her legs, caressing the folds at her entrance.

"Yes." She clutched at his shoulders and leaned into his hand, sighing with every expert, sensuous stroke.

"But more than anything," he growled into her ear, "I want to pretend, just for tonight, that you're mine." With that he slid his finger inside her, making her breath catch in her throat and sending shimmers of pleasure through her body. "Will you do that for me, Eva?"

She ran her hands down his chest and over his abdomen

and curled her fingers around his shaft, marveling at its smoothness. "Yes."

The word had barely left her mouth before he laid her back on the bed, making good on every promise—and then some. He kissed her eyelids and her ears. Nipped at her neck and shoulders. Licked the tips of her breasts and a path right down to her navel.

He moved lower, looking up at her as he settled himself between her thighs. "You don't know how much I've wanted to do this."

"I have an inkling," she choked out.

"I'm going to make you feel amazing." He nuzzled the inside of her thigh, and the light puff of his breath on her slick folds made her whimper. "So good that you'll never forget this night."

There was little chance of her forgetting. She speared her fingers through his hair as he touched his tongue to the center of her pleasure, sucking and stroking her until she was powerless to do anything but surrender.

Her fists clutched the sheets and her back arched. Her swollen breasts ached and her core throbbed. Her whole body was coiled tight, waiting for Jack to spring her free.

"Tell me," he murmured, sending delicious vibrations through her limbs. "Tell me you're mine." His wicked tongue teased, and his finger slid inside once more.

She moaned and writhed against his mouth. Thrilled in the knowledge that he wanted her after all. Wondered what it meant.

"I'm yours, Jack," she whispered.

He groaned, then rewarded her with the masterful swirl of his tongue, sending her perilously close to the edge.

"I'm yours," she repeated, panting. "All. Yours."

He lifted her bottom. Sucked and stroked till she was dizzy

with desire. Every nerve ending pulsed with need. Begged for release.

And then it came. Pleasure, pure and powerful, swept her into a spiral and slowly, exquisitely, unfurled. She shimmered from the inside out. From the roots of her hair to the tips of her toes.

As her body soared above the stars, she heard herself calling Jack's name. He reached for her hand and laced his fingers through hers, tethering her to the ground. Staying with her while the last sweet waves receded.

Dear God.

As she gradually floated down to earth, he stretched out beside her, a smug grin lighting his handsome face. "How was that?"

She rolled toward him, her body limp and sated. "I have no basis for comparison."

"But . . . ?" he prodded.

"But I suppose you've set the bar rather high."

He grinned, proud as a peacock. "Then I consider the night a success."

"Really?" She glanced down at his shaft, which looked impressive as ever. "Even though you haven't . . ."

His expression turned sober. "We have a few more days together, Eva. We don't have to squeeze everything into one night."

She leaned forward and planted a tender kiss on his mouth. "Maybe not. But as long as we're both naked, surely we can squeeze in a little more." She reached for his hard length and caressed him with her palm. "Like this?"

He groaned. "Yes. And like this." He showed her how to hold him. How to please him. How to make him shake with need. Before long, he was under her spell—just as she'd hoped. She wanted him to experience the same pleasure she had. To feel the way he'd made her feel. Glorious. Powerful. Free.

She stroked his shaft from the base to the slick top and back again, letting her fingers wander. She took her cues from the encouraging growling sounds in his throat—and kept going till he moaned in ecstasy.

"Eva." Just as he was about to climax, he covered his shaft with his shirt and spilled his seed into it. "Oh my God."

She waited until he rolled onto his back, then brushed the hair away from his face, gently smoothing away the creases in his forehead with her fingertips.

For a full minute, neither of them spoke. Then he gazed at her with a mixture of awe and confusion. "What are we going to do?"

She had a vague sense of what he was asking. The question itself was an acknowledgment that things had shifted; their relationship had changed. She sensed it, too.

"I'm not certain," she said truthfully. "I'd like to propose we take things day by day."

"I think I can do that." He stared at her like he was seeing straight into her soul. "But I have one request."

She rolled onto her belly and propped her chin in her hand. "And what might that be?"

He leaned close and touched his lips to her shoulder in a kiss as soft as the sweep of a feather. "That we leave ourselves open to the possibility, however remote, that the connection between us is more than physical."

Eva swallowed. "I confess, I've been wondering the same thing. I caught myself thinking about you while I was walking to the milliner's on Thursday. My maid inquired as to why I was smiling, and I didn't know what to say."

"I was counting the days till Lady Rufflebum's house party—and not because I was eager to play a mind-numbing game of charades," he said. "I couldn't wait to see you."

"An alarming state of affairs," she mused. "But here we are."

"Here we are," he repeated. "And, maybe this"—he waved a finger between the two of them—"was meant to be."

Eva's heart bounced in her chest. She closed her eyes and let herself imagine—just briefly—what a future with Jack might entail: Laughter, passion, and friendship. A true partnership. Perhaps a family. She could see it all.

But then she recalled the promise she'd made to Mama during the last horrible days of her illness. When disease had ravaged her body, leaving her weak and pale. *Take care of Papa when I'm gone*, she'd said. *He's going to need you.*

Even at the age of nine, Eva understood. She could scarcely conceive of a world where their cozy, loving family wasn't intact. It had always been the three of them. Mama couldn't stay, but Eva wouldn't leave her father alone. Ever.

Tears burned her eyes as she made a solemn vow. *I will, Mama. I'll look after him for you. I swear.*

Eva shook off the memory, sat up, and smoothed her curls behind her ears. "I can't make any promises, Jack." No matter how much she might want to.

"Then we'll do it your way. We'll take it day by day," he said soothingly. "I just want you to know that in spite of the rocky start we had . . . I like you."

Her belly fluttered, and she opened her mouth to tell him that she felt the same way. But that wouldn't be fair to him—not when a life together was impossible.

"I'd better head back to my room." She hopped off the bed, found her nightgown draped across a potted fern, and slipped it on.

Jack scooped up her robe and handed it to her, then hastily pulled on his trousers. "We'll talk more tomorrow?"

"Yes, of course," she said, perilously close to tears. "As long as we stick to our plan. We must remain distant in front of others—so they're not surprised when we eventually have a falling-out."

"*If* we have a falling-out." He reached for her hand and pressed a tender kiss to the back of it. "Maybe we don't have to."

"We've been fighting since the day we met, Jack."

"We're not fighting now."

Eva almost wished they were.

She gave him a sweet, lingering kiss that said everything she couldn't, and left him standing at the door of his bedchamber.

Chapter Eleven

When Eva awoke the next day, Laurel was already dressed and moving about their bedchamber.

"At last," Laurel teased. "You've missed breakfast, and I was wondering if I'd have to wake you for luncheon." She swept open the curtains with relish, and bright sunbeams assaulted Eva's sleepy eyes.

She groaned in protest and rolled over. "You are a cruel and unfeeling creature."

"Aren't I, though?" Laurel strode to the bed and poked Eva in the back. "I've been pacing this room for hours. It's a beautiful, unseasonably warm day, and I want to explore Bellehaven Bay."

"That does sound rather enjoyable," Eva admitted. She sat up and dragged her fingers through the tangles of her hair.

"What happened to your braid?" Laurel clucked her tongue. "No matter, I'll repair the damage and have you dressed within the half hour." She glided to the wardrobe and flung open the doors.

"Why the hurry?"

"I told Eleanor that we'd meet downstairs for luncheon and

walk to Town afterward." Laurel looked over her shoulder at Eva. "Unless you had other plans?"

"No." She hopped out of bed and hazarded a glance in the dressing table mirror, pleased to find no obvious signs of last night's wantonness. An afternoon outing with her girlfriends might be just the thing to give her some perspective where Jack was concerned. "I'd love to spend the day with you and Eleanor. We'd better find the brush immediately if we want to work the snarls out of my hair before dinnertime."

Eva, Laurel, and Eleanor had a grand time exploring Bellehaven Bay. They popped in and out of the shops, purchasing small gifts for their relatives and friends, then wandered into a cozy teashop where they could view the beach through a large picture window. They nibbled delicious cinnamon chip scones and sipped fragrant tea while they chatted about everything from gowns to politics to gossip.

Eva's initial assessment of Eleanor had been correct. The charming redheaded widow was kind and thoughtful, and she had a maturity about her that Eva found reassuring. To her surprise, neither Eleanor nor Laurel steered the conversation toward Jack, which Eva appreciated. It was almost as if her friends knew she needed the day to sort through her feelings where he was concerned—and they were both too considerate to pry.

"Would you ladies care for a fresh pot of tea?" asked a smiling, bespectacled waitress.

"We'd better not," Laurel said, apologetic. "Your shop is positively enchanting, but we've lingered far too long already."

"Yes," Eleanor agreed. "It will be dark in another half hour or so. We should begin walking back."

"I suppose you're right," Eva said. "I'd hoped we could go

for a walk on the beach, but we'll have to save that for another day."

Their trio reluctantly gathered up their parcels and bundled into their cloaks before heading outside onto the sandy, pebbled streets. The moment they left the teashop, the salty air swirled around them. The surf rumbled like the anxious murmurs of an audience before the curtain rose on a play.

Eva breathed it all in, utterly entranced. "It's hard to leave, isn't it?"

"We'll return soon," Laurel promised.

They'd begun walking up the main street of Town when Jack and Lord Goulding emerged from a somewhat suspect establishment called the Salty Mermaid. Jack's hair was wildly windblown, and his faded gray greatcoat and rough boots gave him the air of a huge, menacing Viking.

Which Eva found rather dashing.

"There you are!" Lord Goulding called. "We'd hoped to find you ladies."

"We shall have to do a better job of hiding next time," Eleanor teased.

"At least we'll have the pleasure of escorting you back to Lady Rufflebum's," said the marquess. He had more polish in his little finger than Jack did in his whole body, and yet *Jack* was the one Eva couldn't resist. She could scarcely take her eyes off his scruffy jaw and hulking shoulders.

He stared back at her. "I was wondering if Miss Tiding might like to walk on the beach for a bit."

"Would it be all right, Laurel?" Eva asked. "We'll return in plenty of time for dinner."

Laurel exchanged a look with Eleanor, then nodded. "Enjoy your stroll, and we'll see you back at the house." As an afterthought she added, "We'll all need time to change, so don't dally too long." She and Eleanor continued heading up the street with Lord Goulding, leaving Eva and Jack alone.

He gestured toward the dunes where long brown grass rustled invitingly. "Shall we?"

She nodded eagerly. "Let's go."

The sun had begun to sink in the peach-colored sky, and a brisk breeze whipped her skirts around her legs. She and Jack crossed the wide, deserted beach and headed straight to the water's edge, where the chilly spray tickled their faces and frothy waves lapped at the toes of their boots. Eva tugged off a glove and dipped her fingers in the icy cold water.

"There," she said, feeling rather accomplished. "I've touched the ocean."

"If you're thinking of going for a swim, I'll wait here," he quipped.

She arched a brow as she slipped her glove back on. "Coward."

They walked several yards along the shore, marveling at the vastness of the sea and the majesty of the rocky cliffs in the distance. And when the lights of Town had dimmed behind them, Jack took her hand. "We need to talk."

Her chest tightened. "I know."

He pointed to an area of the beach that was sheltered by the dunes on one side and a large rock on the other. "Let's sit for a while."

Eva nodded, and they made their way to the private spot, where the nip of the wind diminished and the roar of the ocean faded. He shrugged off his coat, spread it on the soft sand, and helped her sit before taking a seat beside her.

"I've been thinking today. About us," he began, and her heart tripped at the word "us."

"I have, too," she admitted. She'd realized they couldn't continue in this strange but wonderful purgatory where they were lovers and enemies. Where they glimpsed a future together but were destined to part.

He reached into his pocket, pulled out the watch, and

placed it in her hand. Even through her woolen gloves, the gold casing warmed her palm.

"It's yours now," he said. "From this point forward, nothing we do together is pretend or forced. As far as I'm concerned, our deal is over."

Eva blew out a shaky breath. "Over," she repeated.

"The *deal* is over," he clarified. "But we don't have to be."

Her belly tumbled like acrobats in a traveling band. "What are you saying?"

"That I care about you. And I think maybe you care about me, too."

She searched his face, and his soulful brown eyes had never looked more earnest—or more vulnerable.

"I do," she said slowly. "Care about you, that is."

He slid a hand around her nape and gave her a kiss so soft, so sensuous, that it took her breath away. With every thrust and parry of his tongue, he seemed to be telling her something important.

That his heart was hers for the taking.

"Lady Rufflebum was right." Eva murmured. "There *is* something magical about this beach."

He gazed out at the dusky horizon, where a few intrepid stars had begun to sparkle. "I have to agree. We'll overcome any obstacles in our way, Eva—as long as we face them together."

God help her, she was starting to believe him. She picked a pink shell out of the sand, idly dusted it off, and placed it on his coat between them. "A long time ago, when my mother was dying, I promised her I'd take care of my father."

Jack stiffened.

"I'm all he has left," she said. "I can't desert him."

His mouth stretched into a thin line. "I'd never ask you to."

Hope sprouted in her heart. "Truly? I had the impression you weren't fond of him."

"That's in the past," he said firmly—almost as if he was trying to convince himself.

"I've always secretly wished for a marriage like my parents had," she explained. "It's one reason this watch is so special." She flipped it over in her palm and brushed her thumb over the engraving. "They eloped, much to the dismay of their parents. But they were so in love that they couldn't bear to be apart. Mama sent Papa a note and asked him to meet her at a tavern on the way to Gretna Green. But Papa's coach got stuck in the mud, and he and the driver had to flag down another traveler to help them push the coach out of the muck. Papa arrived at the inn over an hour late and covered in filth. But he and Mama made it to Gretna Green the next day. They married and were blissfully happy for as long as she lived."

Jack shifted beside her as though all the talk of marriage and emotions made him distinctly ill at ease. "How nice for them."

"She gave him the watch on their first anniversary. The message she had inscribed—*So you'll never keep me waiting again*—made Papa smile each time he looked at it." Eva sighed. "It's so romantic, isn't it? Their love story didn't have an auspicious beginning, but it couldn't have had a happier ending."

"Sure, it was a happy ending for *them*," Jack grumbled.

She blinked at him. "What do you mean?"

"That perhaps they should have spared a thought for others—and considered the devastating consequences of their elopement."

A chill slithered down Eva's spine. "What are you talking about?"

Jack propped his elbows on his bent knees and stared out at the sea. "Your mother was engaged to my father."

"Mama never mentioned . . ."

"My father adored her," he said, his voice as cold as the December ocean. "Couldn't wait for the day when she'd be his wife. He'd been so sad after my mother died. But his beautiful young bride was supposed to fix everything. She was going to be my stepmother. And she was going to make my father happy again."

Oh God. That's why he'd wanted the watch. He had a vendetta against her father. "I'm sorry. I didn't know about any of that. But that doesn't have anything to do with us, does it? Surely it's in the past now."

He snorted. "Maybe it is for *you.* Some of us are still dealing with the damage. My father was so distraught over the betrayal that he went a little mad. He withdrew from society—and, worse, from me. He hasn't left his country house in years."

"Jack." She caressed his forearm. "That's awful."

"Right," he said bitterly. "So, forgive me if I don't share any idealistic notions about your parents' marriage. What seems romantic to you seems impulsive and selfish to me."

Eva's throat hurt like she'd swallowed a chestnut whole. "My mother may not have been perfect, but she was *not* selfish. She was kind and generous and full of passion. She was just the sort of person I hope to be one day. I won't sit here and allow you to disparage her."

She leaped up and strode down the beach, kicking up sand behind her. Tears stung her eyes and blurred her vision.

Everything made sense now.

Jack didn't care about her.

He didn't care about the watch or even his grandmother.

All he cared about was revenge.

He'd wanted to break her heart like his father's had been broken—and, damn it all, he'd succeeded.

"Eva. Wait." The low roar of the waves carried his words

out to sea, but she was vaguely aware of him following some distance behind her.

She didn't look back but kept walking as fast as she could. She wouldn't give him the satisfaction of seeing how badly he'd hurt her.

The future with Jack that she'd briefly imagined had been nothing more than a mirage over the sand, the sort of dreamy, enticing image one sees from a distance. But just when the fairy tale had seemed within reach, it vanished. Because it had never truly existed.

All the way back to Lady Rufflebum's, she held on to the watch like a talisman, squeezing it till her fingers went numb. At least she'd accomplished what she'd set out to do.

And she'd learned her lesson where Jack was concerned. She wouldn't make the same mistake twice.

Chapter Twelve

Eva was still in bed the next morning when Laurel returned from the dining room holding a tray laden with tea, eggs, ham, and toast.

"I know you're out of sorts," Laurel said, "but please humor me and eat something." She set the tray on the bed, and the delicious aromas tickled Eva's nose.

Eva sat up and shot her friend a grateful smile. "I'm starving, if you want to know the truth." She had pleaded a headache last night so she wouldn't have to face Jack at dinner, and she'd been too upset to eat from the tray that Lady Rufflebum had kindly sent up.

"I'm glad to hear that you're feeling better," Laurel said tentatively. "Because I've just received some news."

Eva bit the corner of her toast. "I didn't say that I felt *better*." She was still dead on the inside. Just the shell of a person who happened to be craving blackberry jam. "But I shall survive the day at least. If we weren't returning to London this afternoon, I'd insist on barricading myself in this room for the remainder of the house party."

Laurel winced. "Yes, about that . . ."

Eva set down her toast, wary. "You promised we could leave today."

"I know. But while I was downstairs just now, I received word that your father is on his way here."

"Papa's coming here?" Eva said, incredulous. "To Belle-haven Bay?"

Laurel worried her lip. "He should arrive by luncheon."

"I don't understand. Papa hates to travel. Why would he come?" Eva leaned against the headboard, aghast.

"Apparently, Lord Frostbough invited him a couple of days ago. I suppose your father felt he couldn't refuse." Laurel paced the length of the bedchamber. "I'm afraid we'll have to stay a few more days at least."

Eva gripped the edges of her tray, valiantly fighting the urge to fling her eggs at the wall in protest. "How dare he? The earl had no right to involve Papa in his twisted scheme."

Laurel's forehead creased. "What scheme?"

"It's beside the point now," Eva grumbled. "We'll stay one more night, and then I'll concoct an excuse so that we may all leave this horrid den of deception."

"I wouldn't call it *horrid*," Laurel ventured. "Our hostess and the duchess have been incredibly gracious. And Eleanor and her brother are a delight."

"Unfortunately, their good natures are overshadowed by one very large and exceedingly evil earl. The sooner we are gone, the better."

"Indeed," Laurel said soothingly. "But there's another bit of news I must relay."

Eva braced herself. "More news?"

Laurel wrung her hands. "It seems your father isn't the only other guest that Lady Rufflebum's expecting."

"Pray, don't keep me in suspense."

"The Duke of Northcott is also on his way. Expected to arrive later this evening."

Sweet Jesus. It shouldn't have surprised Eva that the reclusive duke, who never ventured away from his country estate would pick *this* occasion to make an appearance. "I presume the earl requested his presence as well?" Eva couldn't imagine what Jack hoped to accomplish by having both their fathers under the same roof. But, considering the hate he still harbored in his heart, his intentions in arranging a meeting couldn't be good.

Laurel shook her head. "It's my understanding that the duchess wrote to the duke and encouraged him to come. No one imagined he'd actually make the trip . . . but the speculation downstairs is that His Grace couldn't resist the chance to meet you."

"Well, the duke is destined for disappointment, isn't he?" Eva's voice dripped with sarcasm. "No hearts have been captured. Do you want to know why?"

Laurel cringed. "Yes?"

"It turns out that the earl doesn't *have* a heart." Eva waved her butter knife for emphasis, and Laurel took a prudent step back. "There's nothing but rubble inside his chest," she ranted. "Piles of stone, dirt, and charred wood. You could find enough ruins to rival the Acropolis in there."

"I see." Laurel approached carefully and gave Eva's shoulder a sympathetic pat. "Clearly, you and the earl have had a row. In the interest of avoiding further confrontation, I think you should remain here in our room until we're ready to leave for London. I'll say you're indisposed and must remain in bed."

"No." Eva set aside her breakfast tray, hopped out of bed, and marched to the wardrobe.

"No?" Laurel asked, clearly confused.

Eva yanked a green day gown off its hook and threw it on the bed, then knelt in front of her traveling trunk, searching for her corset. "I'll not leave Papa to face the wolves alone. I intend to be dressed and ready to greet him when he arrives."

"That's the spirit," Laurel said, half encouragement, half bewilderment. "Who, precisely, are the wolves?"

"It doesn't matter," Eva muttered. "As always, our best defenses are quick wits and confidence-enhancing gowns."

Laurel grinned. "Then we had better get you out of that nightgown."

Three hours later Eva and her father were strolling through Lady Rufflebum's greenhouse, their arms linked. Flanked by rows of carefully tended and immaculately pruned plants, they soaked in the earthy smells and colorful blossoms of summer.

And now that Papa was there, Eva realized just how much she'd missed him.

"I'm glad to finally have you to myself," she said. "I hope it hasn't been too trying, dealing with all the guests. I know you're unaccustomed to mingling with duchesses and countesses."

"I'll admit I'm a bit rusty. But I haven't completely forgotten how to comport myself in polite company," he said with a chuckle. "It helped that I received such a warm welcome from the duchess and Lady Rufflebum. Everyone has sought to put me at ease—especially you."

She gave his arm a squeeze, and they paused to admire half a dozen orchids boasting gorgeous petals of white, pink, and purple.

"It makes you think anything's possible, doesn't it?" Papa asked. "If these delicate plants can grow in the dead of winter, perhaps love can blossom, too."

Oh dear. "I know you had your heart set on me marrying Lord Goulding," she said. "And no one was more surprised than I was to find him here at the house party. He's a kind and decent gentleman, but there's no spark between us, Papa."

"I wasn't thinking about the marquess," he admitted.

Sensing he was about to steer the conversation toward Jack, Eva did a quick sidestep. "I believe the holiday has made you quite sentimental," she teased. "And speaking of the holiday, I want to give you your Christmas present. I know it's a bit early, but I can't wait."

She pulled the watch from her reticule, placed it in his hand, and kissed his cheek. "Merry Christmas, Papa."

He stared at the gold casing for several seconds, speechless.

"It's really my watch?" His hand trembled as he turned it over, and when he saw the familiar engraving tears filled his eyes. "Thank you, my dear. I don't deserve it, but I'm eternally grateful."

"Nonsense. Of course you deserve it. Lord Frostbough should never have swindled you out of it."

"No. I was too careless," Papa said. "And one should never be cavalier when it comes to matters of the heart."

"I won't allow you to blame yourself." Eva patted his shoulder. "Not when the earl is clearly the villain of this little tale."

"I'm not so sure about that. Frostbough pulled me aside earlier."

The hairs stood up on the back of Eva's arms. "He did?"

Papa nodded. "He apologized for taking the watch. Said he shouldn't have accepted something so personal in a wager."

Eva blinked, stunned. She hadn't thought Jack capable of an apology—or of seeing any viewpoint beside his own. "May I ask you something?" she ventured.

Papa beamed at her. "Of course."

"When you and Mama eloped, was she engaged to someone else?"

"Ah. I thought this might come up." He pointed to a bench nestled between two pear trees. "Let's sit, shall we?"

Eva sat beside him and nervously smoothed the skirt of her gown. She'd asked Papa the question, but she wasn't at all certain she wanted to hear the answer.

"It seems like a lifetime ago," he began. "But your grandfather wanted your mother to wed the Duke of Northcott—Frostbough's father—and decreed it would be so. Your mama and I were already madly in love, but her father wouldn't hear of her marrying a mere viscount when he could have a duke for a son-in-law." Papa sighed. "So, yes. Your mother was engaged when we eloped. But I don't think she had any regrets."

"Nor do I," Eva said firmly. She hesitated for a beat, then added, "The duke is arriving today as well. Will that be terribly awkward for you?"

"No," Papa replied, as if he was surprised by the question. "I'm not ashamed that I married your mother—just the opposite. And I assume that the years have healed any wounds that Northcott might have suffered at the time."

"One would think," Eva mused.

"Some days I still can't believe that she passed up the chance to be a duchess—just so she could be with me."

"You made her very happy, Papa."

"I tried," he said. "That's not to say I always succeeded. We fought sometimes, just like you and Frostbough."

"No, Lord Frostbough and I are nothing like you and Mama," Eva said.

"You can't deny that there's a spark."

"Oh, there's a spark," she countered. "The sort that's dangerous and difficult to control. The kind that could burn an entire village right down to the ground."

"Love is indeed a powerful force," he said sagely. "But it can be channeled in the right direction."

"Truly?" she asked, skeptical. "And how might one accomplish such a feat?"

Papa faced her and smiled. "You simply have to acknowledge that fiery spark for what it is—love. And that changes everything."

Eva didn't have the heart to tell him that she and Jack were a hopeless case, so she mustered a smile. "How did you become so wise?"

"I learn something with every mistake, and I've made plenty," he said with a laugh. "Such as trying to facilitate a match between you and Lord Goulding. I shouldn't have pressured you to marry anyone at all. I just don't want to be the reason you don't chase your own dreams and make your own mistakes."

If Papa only knew how many mistakes she'd made over the last few weeks. "I think I understand. I promise to keep an open mind."

"And heart," he added, kissing her on the forehead.

"And heart," she repeated. "But you must do the same."

"It's funny you should say that . . ."

If Eva didn't know better, she'd think her father was blushing. "Papa! Do you fancy someone?"

"No," he stammered. "Well, perhaps. What do you think of Lady Beckham?"

"Eleanor?" Eva struggled to make her tongue function properly. "Why, she's delightful."

"Good to know," Papa said gruffly. "That was my first impression, too. I shall look forward to furthering our acquaintance."

"Wear your blue waistcoat at dinner tonight," Eva advised. "It makes you look very dashing."

He gave a brusque wave. "That's enough of that. Shall we return to the drawing room?"

As they stood and started to leave the greenhouse, a

patter soft as a cat's footsteps sounded overhead. Eva looked up through the wide glass panels overhead where fat, fluffy white flakes fell from the sky. "Goodness. I hope this squall doesn't amount to much. I'm eager to return home."

"I had a feeling that a snowstorm was building," Papa said. "And my knees are telling me it's going to be a big one."

Chapter Thirteen

"Eva refuses to speak to me." Jack accepted a glass of brandy from Will and sank into a leather chair near the crackling fire in Lady Rufflebum's library. "She won't even look at me."

Will stood beside the mantel, swirling the amber liquid in his snifter. "I noticed the rift earlier. You must have made quite the egregious error."

Jack grunted. He'd insulted her late mother and called her father's honor into question. "You could say that."

"What happened?"

"A grudge I've been holding for the last twenty-four years spewed from my mouth like toxic volcanic ash. I thought I'd feel relief once I got the ugliness off my chest. Instead, I realized I have no legitimate reason for the hate I've been carrying around. And I let it poison what I had with Eva."

"You want my advice?" Will asked.

"Oddly enough, yes."

"Give her time to sort out her feelings. If and when she's willing to listen to you, apologize profusely—and tell her how you feel."

"I already told her how I feel. It was a disaster," Jack

grumbled. He'd had such high hopes last night on the beach. She'd admitted she liked him, too. And then everything had gone to hell.

Will leaned forward and narrowed his eyes. "Did you lay everything out, or did you dance around the edges, hinting at the truth without saying it?"

Jack snorted. Will knew him too well. "Damn you, Goulding. I don't have your silver tongue."

"What you lack in finesse you make up for with sheer determination. Don't give up."

"I don't intend to," Jack said firmly. "But now I'm also concerned with making sure my father survives his first social engagement in several years."

"He seemed well enough at dinner. Quiet, but I guess that's to be expected after being isolated for so long. I could be wrong, but it seemed to me as though he was . . . enjoying himself."

"I thought so, too." Jack supposed he should have been relieved, but instead he was hurt. And angry.

If it was that easy for his father to venture out into the world, why hadn't he done so earlier? It would have been useful to have him around years ago, when Jack was learning to ride a horse. Or when he'd struggled with his studies at Eton. Or when he was in London trying to figure out how the hell to run a dukedom that wasn't yet his.

"Shit," he muttered.

As if he understood that Jack needed a second to compose himself, Will stood and pretended to admire the holly decorating the mantel. "You have every right to be cross with him. Now's your chance to explain how he's let you down."

"What good would that do?"

"For one thing, you might stop directing your anger at everyone else," Will teased.

But Jack recognized a seed of truth in his friend's words.

He'd been blaming Eva's mother—a woman he'd never met—for his father's failings. And then he'd maligned her in front of Eva, which was truly reprehensible on his part. No wonder Eva wanted nothing to do with him.

He'd give anything just to talk with her again. He missed her sharp tongue and irrepressible spirit. But mostly he missed the hopefulness he'd felt around her—the belief that maybe he could trust another person with his heart.

"Forgive the interruption." Jack and Will turned toward the library door, where Jack's father stood. He may have been a few inches shorter than Jack and a bit gray around the ears, but he still cut an imposing figure, carrying himself with the unmistakable confidence and authority of a duke. "Son, I wondered if we might have a word."

Jack rose from his chair, and Will gave him a bolstering slap on the shoulder as he walked past. "I'll leave you to it."

The duke nodded at Will and joined Jack near the fireplace. "Please, sit," he said, taking a seat opposite him. "It's good to see you."

Jack bit his tongue. His father could have seen him at any point over the last decade. All he'd had to do was say the word.

"I suppose you're wondering what I'm doing here."

"The thought crossed my mind," Jack said dryly.

"Right." The duke leaned back casually and tapped one finger on the arm of his chair—like they were discussing something as trivial as horses or cigars. "Your grandmother wrote to me. Said you were courting a delightful young lady."

"I'm not anymore."

His father arched a graying brow. "Nevertheless, the news hit me like a punch to the gut. Made me realize all that's transpired during my absence. You've grown from a troubled lad into a fine man—and, to my everlasting shame, you've had to manage it on your own. I'm sorry."

Jack had expected his father to spout excuses or avoid the topic altogether, and the spontaneous apology stunned him into silence.

At last Jack said, "You play the hand you're dealt. And I've had advantages that many don't."

His father stared at him, his face impassive. "A very mature response. I don't suppose you'd consider shouting or cursing? Maybe smashing a vase against the wall? It would make me feel better."

"Believe me, I've had my share of outbursts," Jack admitted. "Being angry grows tiresome."

"So does isolation. At first it seemed the easiest course of action—avoiding everything. Pretending that none of it matters anyway. But it *does* matter, Jack. This life is precious. And I needed a kick in the arse to make me realize I've been wasting mine."

Jack met his father's earnest gaze. "Better late than never, I suppose."

"I'm sorry I've behaved so selfishly. I wish I could go back and undo the pain I inflicted. But all I can do is give you my word that I'm done hiding. I want to see you marry and have a family. I want to bounce my grandchildren on my knee." He paused and cleared his throat. "What I'm saying is, I'd like to be a part of your life—if you'll let me."

Jack leaned forward, resting his elbows on his knees. "You don't have to ask my permission. You don't have to wait for an invitation. All you have to do is be here . . . like you are right now."

His father nodded and swiped suspiciously at his eyes. "Thank you, Son."

"I'm glad you came to Bellehaven," Jack said gruffly. "But you should know that despite what Grandmama may have told you, Miss Tiding and I won't be getting engaged."

"No?" His forehead creased in concern.

"I thought that we might have a future together." Jack stood and braced his hands behind his neck. "We were on the brink of finding a way to make it work. But then I spoiled everything."

His father rose from his chair and stood beside Jack. "I don't know what you did—and that's obviously between you and Miss Tiding—but I will say this. If you can forgive me for what I've done, then God knows hope remains that she can forgive you."

He clasped Jack's shoulder, and, the next thing he knew, they were hugging.

It had been a long time, but Jack felt the same as he had when he'd been a lad of six. Protected. Understood. Loved.

The next morning, Eva awoke to find the landscape outside her bedchamber window transformed. Fluffy snow frosted every tree branch, and the pristine white lawn sparkled in the sunbeams that peeked through moody gray skies. Glittering icicles hung from the eaves outside, and a gorgeous winter paradise stretched for miles in every direction.

"This is disastrous." Eva whirled away from the window to face Laurel, who sat at the dressing table in her robe, sipping tea. "The roads must be impassable. We could be stuck here for days."

"I'm afraid so," Laurel said, and yet her expression was the picture of contentment.

"I don't think you understand," Eva said. "Every day that I must remain under the same roof as Lord Frostbough is torture." It was true. There was no avoiding the heat in his gaze when he sat across from her at dinner. No escaping the inexorable pull each time he was near.

But that night at the beach, he'd revealed himself to her,

and she couldn't unhear the bitterness in his voice when he'd spoken of her mother. She couldn't unsee the disgust in his eyes as he'd talked about her parents' marriage.

And she'd be twice the fool if she let him wriggle his way into her heart again.

"I know you'd hoped to return to London today, and I'm sorry it's so difficult for you to tolerate the earl's company," Laurel said. "But, at the risk of sounding unfeeling, I confess I'm glad that we'll be staying a bit longer."

"No one could possibly accuse you of being unfeeling." Eva sighed and flung herself on the bed. "There is a remote possibility, however, that I've been a bit wrapped up in my own problems." She rolled toward her friend. "You've been enjoying yourself, have you?"

Laurel's cheeks pinkened and she nodded. "I'm excited at the prospect of the Christmas Eve ball. Just think how beautiful the ballroom will look once the candles are lit and the greenery is hung," she said wistfully. "And now that your father is here, there's no need to rush home on his account."

"I suppose not." Noting the dreamy look in Laurel's eyes, Eva tilted her head, curious. "Is there someone in particular you're hoping to dance with?"

"I can assure you no one will be looking at me," Laurel demurred. "Especially while you're in the room."

Eva sat up, aghast. "That's nonsense—and you didn't answer my question."

"The duke was rather attentive at dinner last night."

"The *duke*? As in, Lord Frostbough's father?"

Laurel shrugged. "Beneath his imposing exterior, I've discovered he's quite human. I believe I even made him smile once."

"That *is* impressive," Eva said. "Are you certain you're not a sorceress?"

"I'm truly sorry you're so miserable. Perhaps if we concentrate on preparations for the ball, it will help take your mind off the earl."

"You're absolutely right, Laurel. We'll help Lady Rufflebum and the duchess with all the last-minute decorating and chores. I'll keep myself busy and steer clear of Lord Frostbough. The days will pass in the blink of an eye."

Laurel set her cup on her saucer, came to sit beside Eva, and wrapped a slender arm around her shoulders. "Exactly. Before we know it, it will be Christmas Eve, and we'll be walking into a ballroom resembling a winter fairyland."

Chapter Fourteen

By Christmas Eve morning, most of Bellehaven Bay's population had shoveled themselves out of their homes and were eager to enjoy a pint at the Salty Mermaid, purchase a last-minute gift at one of the shops, or exchange gossip in a neighbor's kitchen. Townspeople and visitors alike were making plans to attend Lady Rufflebum's ball, the biggest social event of the winter.

Indeed, it seemed everyone in Town looked forward to donning their finest clothes and joining in the merrymaking. Everyone but Eva.

For Laurel's sake, she went through all the motions. She sat dutifully while her friend pinned her hair at the crown and curled tendrils around her face. She wriggled into a silver silk gown with crystal beadwork on the sleeves and hem. She even pretended to be excited at the prospect of dancing and drinking champagne.

But all she really wanted to do was go home, nurse her broken heart, and, perhaps, make a rag doll resembling Jack to use as a pincushion.

"Oh, Eva." Laurel clasped her hands beneath her chin and

beamed. "You look like a princess. Lord Frostbough will be beside himself when he sees you."

Eva rolled her eyes. "He can swim out to sea, for all I care."

"Yes, I know." Laurel shot her a placating smile that drove Eva a bit mad.

Her dear aunt wasn't the only one who seemed to be wishing for a reconciliation. The duchess and Lady Rufflebum preferred to believe she and Jack were merely having a lovers' quarrel. Her own father had seemed slightly patronizing when she'd complained about having to endure Jack's company at breakfast.

But Eva knew it was over. She and Jack were like a fallen cake. Or a needlepoint project with a monstrous knot. They'd crossed a line that night on the beach, and there was no going back.

She caught Laurel's gaze in the dressing table mirror. Eva suspected that Jack's father was responsible for the wistful look in her eyes and the youthful glow on her cheeks. "You look beautiful," she said sincerely. "The duke will want to claim you for every dance."

"Do you suppose he'll ask me?"

"He'd be a fool not to."

"I've no doubt your dance card will be full as well," Laurel said with a wink.

Eva sighed. "I suppose we should go," she said, aware she sounded like they were off to attend a lecture on the mating habits of beetles rather than a delightfully festive Christmas ball.

When they arrived in the ballroom, it was already bustling with guests. Couples on the dance floor surged, swirled, and retreated like waves at high tide. The atmosphere bordered on raucous, while champagne—and plenty of other spirits— flowed abundantly.

"The decorations look magical in the candlelight," Laurel breathed.

"Mmm." Eva supposed that was true. They'd spent the last few days hanging Lady Rufflebum's large collection of seashells from swags of greenery above every window and door. The gold ribbon they'd used shimmered like a pirate's treasure, while the whimsical shells added pale pinks and purples to the room's palette. Decorating had been a tedious job but a welcome distraction for Eva.

Across the room, Lady Rufflebum toddled from one group of guests to the next, carrying a long, curved bough above their heads.

Eva leaned toward Laurel. "Dare I ask what the countess is up to?"

"Oh dear," Laurel said. "I believe there's mistletoe hanging from her branch."

Eva shuddered. "I'm sure she fancies herself a benevolent matchmaker, but I intend to stay far away from her and that diabolical fishing pole of hers."

"I'd agree that's for the best." Laurel gestured toward the refreshment table. "Look, there's your father—shall we join him?"

Eva nodded and followed Laurel across the room. She was weaving her way through the throng when she felt, rather than saw, Jack. Her fingers tingled and the air around her crackled like a thunderstorm approached.

In a way, it did.

She glanced up and found Jack's eyes on her. He wore a black jacket and an icy blue waistcoat that looked like it had been painted on his torso. His chiseled face was troubled—but that was no concern of hers.

"Miss Tiding." He sounded slightly breathless, as if he'd run across the room. "May I have a word?"

"I think not," she said coolly. She'd managed to avoid

speaking with him for the last few days. She wasn't about to let herself be ambushed at this ball—even if his evening clothes did make him resemble a dark, fallen angel.

"Eva," he choked out.

The anguish in his voice mirrored the pain in her heart. But she'd bandaged that wound tightly. Wrapped it in layers of anger and indifference so her emotions couldn't bleed out and expose the truth—that she'd loved Jack.

She didn't dare look into his deep brown eyes for fear of faltering. Instead, she pretended not to hear him and concentrated on following Laurel through the crowd toward Papa.

When they were still several yards away from the refreshment table, Laurel stopped and turned toward her. "Your father is speaking with Eleanor—and, unless I'm mistaken, Lady Rufflebum is headed in their direction."

Sure enough, the countess scurried toward the pair, brandishing her mistletoe bough like Cupid on a mission for the king. She sneaked behind Papa and Eleanor, holding the branch above them. "What's this?" Lady Rufflebum said slyly. "Lord Gladwood and Lady Beckham seem to have wandered beneath the mistletoe."

Papa and Eleanor blinked at the countess, clearly confused, then glanced up. As understanding dawned, their cheeks flushed.

Eleanor offered Papa her hand, and he gallantly leaned over it, lightly pressing a kiss to the back.

The small circle of guests around the couple signaled their approval with sighs and polite applause.

Lady Rufflebum narrowed her eyes. "I suppose that qualifies as a kiss even if it was not entirely in the spirit of the Season." Her shrewd eyes scanned the ballroom as if she was already looking for her next victims.

Laurel smiled at Eva. "Your father and Eleanor make a striking pair. Do you believe in second chances?"

"Of course." As long as the second chances were for other people—not her and Jack. "Papa deserves to be happy. So does Eleanor."

"I think we all do," Laurel said meaningfully. "Ah, we've dallied too long. It looks as though your father and Eleanor are heading toward the dance floor."

"Papa, dancing?" Eva watched with wonder as he and Eleanor joined the other couples swirling in time to the music. "I never thought I'd see him dance again."

"It's almost Christmas—the time of year when anything's possible," Laurel said. Her gaze flicked toward Jack's father, who approached, holding two glasses of champagne.

"Miss Bailey, Miss Tiding. You're looking especially lovely this evening." He handed them each a glass and stood stiffly at Laurel's side.

"Thank you, Your Grace," Laurel replied smoothly, while Eva tried to get over her shock. If a reserved duke could serve them champagne, maybe her aunt was right—perhaps anything *was* possible.

The duke commented on the weather, asked whether Laurel missed her beloved terrier, and inquired about their plans to return to London. But Eva sensed he was working up to asking Laurel to dance and wondered if she was inadvertently standing in the way.

She was about to make up an excuse to leave them when Lady Rufflebum came marching over, accidentally swatting the ostrich plume on one poor woman's headdress with her wildly swaying mistletoe.

"What have we here?" the countess said, sadistically dangling her poisonous berries over Laurel and the duke. "You mustn't flout age-old traditions!"

The duke looked up, clearly discomfited, then glanced to Laurel as if seeking guidance.

She smiled, leaned toward the duke, and planted a perfunctory-but-sweet kiss on his cheek.

"Well done, Miss Bailey!" the countess cried, and the guests all around them cheered in agreement.

The duke swallowed nervously and turned to Laurel. "Would you care to take a turn about the room?"

Laurel flicked her questioning gaze to Eva.

"Go on," Eva said, shooing her friend away. "I shall see if the duchess needs anything."

The duke shot her a grateful smile as he escorted Laurel away from the crowd, and Eva headed toward the ballroom entrance, where Jack's grandmother was chatting amiably with Lady Rufflebum's housekeeper.

The duchess's face split into a wide smile when she saw Eva. "Miss Tiding," she said warmly. "I'm not sure how you and Miss Bailey accomplished it, but you've transformed this ballroom into something special. The decorations are lovely."

Eva felt a pang of grief. She was going to miss the duchess when she left Bellehaven Bay, and it was highly unlikely their paths would cross once Eva returned to London. "Thank you. We couldn't have accomplished any of it without help from Mrs. Green"—she turned to the housekeeper—"and the rest of the staff."

"You're too modest," Mrs. Green said graciously. "If it had been left to us, there would be candles and a bit of greenery. Instead, we have . . ." She waved her hands at the hundreds of shells and ribbons, at a loss for words.

"Something resembling a mermaid's Christmas dream?" Eva said with a chuckle. Turning to the duchess, she asked, "May I fetch you anything? A glass of champagne or lemonade perhaps?"

"No, thank you, my dear. I'm quite content." She frowned

slightly. "But if you should happen to see my grandson, do let him know I wish to speak with him."

"Of course," Eva said tightly. She raised her champagne glass to her lips, tipped it back, and drained it.

"I haven't seen you out there yet." The duchess inclined her head toward the dance floor. "I know Jack isn't terribly fond of dancing, but you mustn't allow him to shirk his duties. He should be more attentive."

Eva's cheeks heated. "We're not . . . That is, I don't expect him to . . ."

The duchess looked over Eva's shoulder and beamed. "Speak of the devil."

The devil indeed. Eva steeled herself and prepared to face temptation incarnate.

"Grandmother," Jack said, pressing a kiss to her cheek. "Looking beautiful, as usual."

"Don't waste your compliments on me," she scoffed, rolling her eyes in Eva's direction.

Jack winced. "I'm not certain Miss Tiding wants compliments from me."

"Nonsense," replied the duchess. "You've had a spat, as couples do. You'll overcome this temporary setback. All you must do is listen to each other."

Jack looked at Eva, his expression imploring.

"I can't." Her voice cracked, and her throat ached.

"It's all right," he rasped, but his face was full of pain and regret.

"Aha!" Lady Rufflebum tottered over and thrust her mistletoe bough above them like a knight preparing to joust. "I've been waiting all night for this opportunity. No couple should quarrel on Christmas Eve. You lovebirds must reconcile immediately, and the first step is to kiss."

The empty champagne glass Eva was holding slipped from her fingertips, hit the floor, and shattered—drawing all eyes.

The orchestra set down their bows.

Couples on the dance floor stopped midtwirl.

Every guest in the ballroom turned expectantly toward her and Jack, where they stood frozen—beneath Lady Rufflebum's dastardly mistletoe.

Chapter Fifteen

Eva blinked at the curious faces staring at her: the duchess, Lady Rufflebum, Laurel, Papa, and others.

Four weeks of compounded lies, stolen kisses, and dashed hopes swirled inside her like a dark and dangerous funnel cloud, picking up speed and growing in size till there was no place left for it to go—except out.

She cleared her throat and addressed the crowd. "I have an announcement to make."

Lady Rufflebum tittered. "How exciting! In my day, the announcements were left to the gentleman, but we shan't stand on ceremony. Do share your good news."

Eva barely resisted the unladylike impulse to swat at the mistletoe dangling over her head. "It's not good news," she began. "But it's the truth."

"Eva," Jack said softly.

She met his gaze. "We need to tell them."

He hesitated, then nodded, giving her the floor.

"Lord Frostbough and I are *not* a couple. Moreover, we were *never* a couple. The whole thing was a farce."

The crowd erupted in a collective gasp.

"We met a month ago, and we've been fighting ever since. But we made a deal to pretend to like each other. We each had our own reasons. Mostly we thought it would make our families and friends happy to know we were courting. But we shouldn't have lied to you—and I'm sorry for that."

Murmurs traveled through the throng of guests like a crack spreading through a sheet of ice.

"We didn't mean to disappoint you, but surely you must see that we aren't well matched. Some things simply aren't meant to go together, like ball gowns and muddy boots, or ice cream and pickled fish. That's the way it is with Jack— er, Lord Frostbough—and me." Eva swallowed the huge knot in her throat. "We simply don't work."

The duchess sighed.

Lady Rufflebum frowned. "Then there's not to be an engagement? Or even a *kiss*?"

Sweet Jesus. Eva opened her mouth to reply, but Jack spoke first.

"I also have an announcement to make," he called out. His deep voice echoed off the high ceilings and vibrated over her skin.

"Miss Tiding is right about a few things."

She rolled her eyes, incredulous. "A few things?" she muttered.

Jack shot her a smug half smile. To the crowd, he said, "We did make a deal. And we were pretending—at first."

Eva blinked at him, wary.

"But shortly after we met, I stopped pretending. I didn't have to pretend anymore—because I had real feelings. Feelings that were fierce and unexpected and highly inconvenient." He swallowed and looked deep into her eyes. "I fell in love with you."

Eva's hand fluttered to her chest. "You did?" she whispered.

"I did. I love the awful way you sing Christmas carols and your abominable handwriting. I love that you would do anything for your family and friends and that your face shows every little thing you're feeling inside. Right now it's showing me that you're torn between wanting to throttle me and kiss me."

"Jack . . ."

"I know we've had a tumultuous relationship, but it's more real to me than the ground I'm standing on. Besides, I don't think we've been fighting so much as . . . flirting."

"Flirting?" she repeated, disbelieving.

"Some people give flowers and write poetry. Some pay compliments and sing ballads. We bait each other and throw barbs. It's how we show we care."

"Then we must care an awful lot."

He held out his palm, and she slipped her hand in his. Her whole body tingled with awareness—and with the rightness of it.

"I'm sorry I hurt you that night on the beach. I said things I didn't mean. Things I don't even believe."

Eva searched his handsome face. "I don't understand."

He hesitated, then said, "For years I've been walking around in a tempest of anger and distrust. But when I met you, the clouds lifted—and I realized all I'd been missing before. I wasn't even really living."

"I'm not certain I was, either," she admitted.

"Maybe we *are* like ice cream and pickled fish," he said with a shrug. "But the combination could be better than you think. At least it's not boring."

That coaxed a smile out of her. "Never boring."

"Miss Eva Tiding," he said slowly. "If these last few days have taught me anything, it's that I never want to be without you again. You mean a thousand times more to me than any watch, game, or grudge. Marry me and let me spend every day making up ridiculous names for you, baiting you, and making you smile. Let's promise we'll always spar with each other and love each other—the way only we can."

Her eyes welled and her throat ached and her heart pounded.

The room was so silent that she could almost hear the snowflakes falling outside. Papa stood on the edge of the dance floor, smiling proudly. Laurel's kind eyes shone with encouragement. The duchess pressed her lips together as though she was holding back her own tears.

Eva squeezed Jack's hand and let the rest of the ballroom melt away.

"Yes," she breathed.

Jack cocked an ear like he couldn't quite believe what he'd heard. "Yes?"

"Yes!" she cried. And the next thing she knew, his lips were on hers in a kiss that was tender but sure. Brief but true. A kiss that felt like a promise.

"Hurrah!" Lady Rufflebum shouted in an uncharacteristically gauche display. "Mistletoe never disappoints."

The room exploded in a cacophony of cheers, exclamations, and applause.

Eva held tight to Jack's hand, but in the next minute they were swept up in a flurry of kisses, embraces, and well-wishes. When Jack's friends dragged him away for a celebratory glass of brandy, she met his gaze and saw a heat that matched her own.

She resolved to do her best to enjoy the rest of the ball.

But she was already counting the minutes till she could go to him.

In the wee hours of the morning, long after the ballroom had emptied and the guests had gone, Jack paced the corridor outside the bedchamber that Eva shared with her aunt.

He stared at their door, willing it to open. He knew Eva would come to him if she could. But he worried that Laurel might never fall asleep or that Eva was so exhausted that she'd dozed off herself.

God, he'd missed her. He missed her reluctant smile when he teased her and the warning look she gave him when he went too far. He missed her fiery kisses and the way she stared at his chest when he wasn't wearing a shirt.

She was everything he never knew he needed, and—miraculously—she'd agreed to marry him. But it wouldn't feel real until he could hold her again—and hear her say the words.

He'd been waiting for half an hour when the doorknob finally turned and Eva tiptoed out of her room. Her golden hair floated around her shoulders, and her lacy nightgown clung to every curve.

She shot him a smile that warmed his chest, then traveled due south.

"Been waiting long?" she whispered.

"Just a lifetime."

He laced his fingers through hers and led her back to his bedchamber. Locked the door behind them.

Eva melted into him, her body molding to his. He pressed her back to the wall and lifted her by the thighs, savoring the feel of her skin against his palms. She squeezed her legs around his hips, rocking against him and kissing his neck, his face, his mouth.

"I thought I'd never touch you again." He cupped her bottom. Nipped at her bare shoulder. "And I couldn't bear it."

"I missed you, too." She grabbed his shirt in her fists and ripped it down the front. Ran her hands over his chest like she was staking her claim.

"I love you, Eva, and I'll prove it to you every day—with every breath I have left."

"I love you." Her thumb cruised over his lower lip and caressed his face. "No more pretending. I'm yours, and you're mine, forever . . . starting now."

They collided in a kiss that was hot, wild, and primal. Stumbled their way to the bed, leaving a trail of clothes on the floor. And when he laid her back on the mattress, nothing separated them. No secrets, no lies . . . not a stitch of clothing.

In the soft light of the lamp, her skin seemed to glow, and shadows kissed the lush curves of her body. Her sultry green eyes were half-closed; her plump pink lips were half-open. And when he lay down beside her, she tangled her legs with his.

She reached between them and took his length in her hand, stroking him till he was one second away from losing control. "I want you, Jack."

He growled and laid her head back onto the pillow. "No need to rush, love. We have all night."

With deliberate slowness, he kissed and caressed her body, lingering on her neck, the undersides of her breasts, and the small of her back. When he teased the slick folds between her legs, she moaned and grasped at his shoulders.

And he couldn't wait any longer.

He positioned himself at her entrance and touched his forehead to hers. "Tell me if you're hurting," he said. "I'll go slowly."

He began to ease himself in—and groaned from the sheer pleasure of it.

"I've waited so long for this," Eva said breathlessly. She arched her back and thrust her hips toward him. "I don't think I want to go slowly."

She writhed against him, pulling him deeper and setting his blood on fire.

"Yes," she panted. "This is what I've wanted."

Jesus. It's what he'd wanted, too. To be this close to her. To hear her sigh with bliss. To make her his.

Each time he thrust, he heard her whimper, saw her reaching for her release. And he redoubled his efforts.

"Come for me, Eva." He teased the pebbled tips of her breasts and moved his hips faster.

"Like that," she said. Her eyes fluttered shut. "Just. Like. Th—"

Before she could finish the word, her head fell back and she moaned, climaxing around him. He came next, pleasure pounding through his veins, potent and powerful. She clung tight to him while he spent himself inside her, kissing her neck and murmuring her name.

"Eva." His Eva.

When Eva stirred a couple of hours later, Jack was lying next to her, lightly running his fingers through her hair and smiling at her like she was the center of his world. "Merry Christmas, my mistletoe maven."

"Odious plant," she said groggily. "A tradition best left in medieval times."

"It worked for us," Jack countered.

She drank in the knee-weakening sight of his bare chest and muscular arms. "I suppose it did."

He reached into the drawer of his bedside table and produced a small but heavy package wrapped in gold paper. "For you."

Eva tucked the bedsheet under her arms and sat up against her pillow. "What's this?"

"Take a look."

She carefully peeled away the paper, revealing an exquisite box with a hinged lid, painted in ocean-like shades of green and blue. "Oh, Jack. It's lovely."

He sat up beside her, and the bed coverings slid down around his hips, making her belly flutter and distracting her from the task at hand.

"Open it," he urged.

"Right." She tipped back the lid and peered at the objects nestled in the cream-colored velvet lining, then reached in and picked up a pink shell.

"From our walk on the beach," he explained.

"And this?" She held up a nondescript piece of ribbon.

"The hair tie you dropped in my lap on the first night you visited me here."

She arched a brow. "Very sentimental of you, Lord Frost-bough."

He scoffed at that, then conceded, "Maybe a little, but only for you. There's something else inside."

"My silver hairpin," she said with a smile. "I used this to pick the lock of your apartment."

"You left it at the scene of the crime." He trailed his fingertips down her bare arm, making her sigh with pleasure. "I kept it as evidence."

"Thank you," she said sincerely. "Thank you for never giving up on us."

She set the box on her lap and kissed his shoulder, intent on making the most of their time alone.

"Not yet," he drawled. "There's one more surprise." He picked up the box, turned it over, and wound a small knob at the back. Then he pressed a switch—and music began to play.

She cocked an ear toward the box and smiled when she recognized the song. "'God Rest Ye Merry Gentlemen.' I had no idea you were so fond of my singing. Perhaps you'd like a repeat performance?"

"Once was enough," he said quickly.

She let her sheet fall away and circled her arms around his neck. "Are you certain? It seems like you're ready for an encore."

His hungry gaze roved over her body, and her skin tingled with anticipation. "You know," he said gruffly. "I believe I *am* ready for an encore."

He hauled her close and kissed her so that singing was nigh impossible.

But her *heart* sang with happiness.

And that was the best present of all.